DR. SPILSBURY
AND
THE CAMDEN
TOWN KILLER

D. L. Douglas has been fascinated by true crime ever since she came face to face with Dr Crippen in the Chamber of Horrors at Madame Tussaud's. So it's fitting that her new series features Sir Bernard Spilsbury, the forensic pathologist who helped send him to the gallows.

A Londoner born and bred, D. L. Douglas now lives in York with her husband and family.

DR. SPILSBURY
 AND
THE CAMDEN
TOWN KILLER

D. L. DOUGLAS

ORION

First published in Great Britain in 2023 by Orion Fiction,
an imprint of The Orion Publishing Group Ltd.,
Carmelite House, 50 Victoria Embankment
London EC4Y 0DZ

An Hachette UK Company

1 3 5 7 9 10 8 6 4 2

A CIP catalogue record for this book is
available from the British Library.

ISBN (Mass Market Paperback) 978 1 4091 9207 7
ISBN (eBook) 978 1 4091 9208 4

Typeset by Born Group
Printed and bound in Great Britain by Clays Ltd, Elcograf S.p.A.

www.orionbooks.co.uk

To my wonderful family – Ken, Harriet, Lewis, Sebastian and Marjorie

Chapter 1

The mourners were already gathered inside St John's Wood Church when Dr Bernard Spilsbury arrived. He did his best to be discreet, but at well over six feet tall, even without his black silk top hat, it was difficult to be unobtrusive.

A tide of whispers followed him as he made his way down the aisle.

'Is it really him? I can't see without my glasses.'

'I'm telling you, it's him. I've seen his picture in the *Daily Mirror*.'

'I expect he and Dr Franklin were friends.'

'He's not as handsome as he looks in the paper, is he?'

With relief, Spilsbury quickly slid into the empty place beside William Willcox, who was seated at the end of a row of the great and the good from St Mary's Hospital.

'Making an entrance as usual, I see?' Willcox muttered, shuffling to make room for Spilsbury. The other doctors shifted reluctantly amid much tutting and rustling of prayer books.

'Don't.' Spilsbury stared ahead of him rigidly, aware of all the curious stares boring into his shoulder blades. 'My train was late.'

'Where were you this time?'

'Ipswich. Someone found a leg at the bus station.'

'I hope they handed it in to Lost Property?'

'It was in a bin.'

'At least they were tidy. What about the rest of him?'

'I left the local constabulary searching.'

Spilsbury flicked through the tissue-thin pages of the Book of Common Prayer that had been thrust into his hands at the door, squinting at the small print in the dim light of the flickering candles. The church was sharply cold, and the air smelt of melted wax, dust and old, musty wood.

'And do they know who they're looking for?' Willcox asked.

'Male, early twenties, around five feet six inches tall with a slight build and a limp.'

'A limp, eh? Hardly surprising, if his leg's missing.'

An eminent physician cleared his throat and sent them a warning frown from the far end of the row. Spilsbury ignored him.

'There were fragments of shrapnel buried in the thigh,' he said to Willcox.

'A soldier, then?' Willcox sent him a sideways look. 'I'm surprised you didn't offer to stay and help them. I know you can't resist a mystery.'

'I have far too much to do here.' January was always the peak time for dying. The cold, damp weather, thick fogs and long dark nights caused many a poor soul clinging precariously to life to give up the struggle.

As he sat in the draughty church listening to the mournful drone of the church organ, Spilsbury mentally ran through the list of post-mortems that waited for him in the hospital mortuary. Two fatal cases of bronchitis and a pneumonia, a war widow who had gassed herself – whether accidentally or not had yet to be determined – and a soldier who had survived two years in Mesopotamia, only to be knocked down by an electric tram while cycling home from a night shift in Kensal Green.

And then there was the man in the casket before them. As consultant physician and Professor of Anatomy and Physiology, Sir James Franklin might have enjoyed a god-like status at St Mary's, but his all too human frailty had caused him to succumb to the perils of winter at the age of forty-eight.

Spilsbury hardly knew him. Their paths had crossed occasionally, when Sir James came down to Pathology seeking out slides for his lectures, but they had barely exchanged more than a few polite words.

It was Willcox who had insisted Spilsbury should come to pay his respects; it would never have occurred to him otherwise. Why should he spend his time mourning a stranger when he had so many more pressing matters at hand? It made no sense to him. Besides, he very much doubted that Sir James, were he to be looking down on them all, would notice his absence.

But Willcox said there were social niceties to be observed. 'People will expect it,' he had said.

By people, Spilsbury presumed he meant the consultant physicians, surgeons and professors who filled the row beside them. As if he cared what they thought of him.

He took a sideways glance at the row of solemn faces. He had seen the way they clawed and fought amongst themselves. Even as they sat there grieving for the deceased, they were probably already calculating how they could worm their way into his role.

At least Spilsbury was honest in his indifference. He made no effort to pretend he felt any kind of affection for Sir James or anyone else. Willcox always liked to joke that the reason Spilsbury had become a pathologist was so he didn't have to engage with anyone with a pulse, and he was partly right.

Although why Willcox had chosen the field was a mystery to him. He genuinely seemed to care about his fellow man. His interest in people, and his compassion for them, left Spilsbury frankly astonished at times.

He was doing it now, leaning over to exchange pleasantries with the cardio-thoracic specialist on his other side. He not only knew everyone, he also knew their families, their dogs, even their servants. While Spilsbury walked everywhere very fast, his head down and his eyes averted, forbidding anything but the briefest civilities, Willcox was forever allowing himself to be waylaid in the hospital corridors.

And from the number of mourners who crowded into the church, Spilsbury surmised Sir James must have been rather more like Willcox than himself.

The vicar mounted the pulpit and began to speak at last.

'Heavenly Father,' he intoned solemnly, 'you promised eternal life to those who believe. Remember for good this your servant *James*, as we also remember *him*. Bring all who rest in Christ into the fullness of your kingdom where sins have been forgiven and death is no more . . .'

Spilsbury looked at the coffin under its pall of white silk, adorned with a simple arrangement of lilies. Given his experience, it was hard to believe in the concept of eternal life. Their souls notwithstanding, the people he encountered on his mortuary table were far too dead to ever return to any form of life, eternal or otherwise.

And the unfortunate Sir James was no exception. Spilsbury had looked up the cause of his death. Congestive cardiopulmonary failure, according to his notes. He had suffered from mitral stenosis for three years following an attack of rheumatic fever while serving with the Royal Army Medical Corps in France.

Spilsbury could almost picture the enlarged upper chambers of his heart, and the blood and fluid that had filled his lungs. Was it wrong, he wondered, that he could bring to mind the man's damaged and failing organs more clearly than he could the man's face?

One of the consultants was now standing behind an ornate brass lectern, delivering the eulogy. His stentorian tones rose into the vaulted ceiling as he declared what a wonderful man Sir James was, loved by all who knew him.

'One only has to look around to see how beloved he was,' he made a sweeping gesture around the crowded church. 'Not only his friends and family, but colleagues, students and grateful past patients have all come to offer their respect and thanks.'

Willcox nudged him. 'You wouldn't have many grateful past patients at your funeral. Eh, old boy?'

Not many friends and family, either. Who would come to mourn him? he wondered. Certainly none of the eminent men who were seated down the row from him now. They all loathed him, although they hardly dared show it.

At least the press would probably be there to see him off. They were always there, dogging his steps. He had nearly missed his train at Ipswich, running the gauntlet of them at the station. Even after ten years, he had yet to get used to all those flashbulbs popping in his face.

He glanced over his shoulder and instantly met a row of avid, gawking gazes. He turned back sharply.

Now a young man had stepped up to the lectern to give a reading from Corinthians. He was in his twenties, tall and slim, his fair hair slicked back from an almost girlish face, with wide-spaced grey eyes, high cheekbones and a pointed chin. He spoke well, in a light, almost amused voice, which seemed to jar with the solemnity of their surroundings.

5

'Sir James's son,' Willcox whispered in his ear.

Spilsbury's gaze drifted to the two women sitting in the front row. From the similarity of their delicate fair colouring, the younger one must have been the young man's sister, Sir James's daughter. Her grief was plain for all to see as she wept into a lace-trimmed handkerchief.

Beside her sat a much older woman, poker-straight in her old-fashioned black coat. Spilsbury could just make out a gaunt, expressionless face behind her thick veil.

Their mother? He doubted it. If she was, she certainly wasn't a loving one. She made no effort to comfort the weeping girl beside her; if anything, she looked impatient at her loss of dignity. But there was still a resemblance in their height and their bone structure . . .

More likely an aunt, he thought.

The reading ended, and more prayers began. Spilsbury eased his watch from his waistcoat pocket and cast a surreptitious glance down at it. It would be another late night at the mortuary if he was going to get through all those cases.

Willcox was always telling him he should take on an assistant, but Spilsbury would not hear of it. Apart from anything else, he could not bear the thought of having someone in his laboratory day after day. Sooner or later he would have to make conversation with them, and the idea of small talk horrified him.

He caught a movement in the corner of his eye and looked up to find himself being observed. At the far end of the front pew a small boy, no more than three years old, had twisted round in his seat to stare at him. Spilsbury looked away, but he could feel the child's gaze still on him. Every time he glanced back, the solemn green eyes were fixed on him over the edge of the pew.

He glanced at Willcox to see if he had noticed the boy, but his friend had his head bowed in prayer. Spilsbury tried to do the same, but the weight of the child's stare was beginning to make him feel absurdly uncomfortable.

The prayers ended and he lifted his head. The boy was still watching him. Spilsbury glared back. Really, this was too much. Why was the child's mother not paying attention?

Just at that moment, the young woman beside him did finally notice what was going on. She turned round in her seat and stared straight at Spilsbury. He waited for the familiar look of recognition to light up her eyes, but it did not come. She turned away abruptly, her arm going protectively around the boy's shoulders.

Spilsbury stared at the back of her fashionable cloche hat. Even he couldn't fail to notice he had been well and truly snubbed.

'Come In, O Come! The door stands open now . . .'

No sooner had they sung the words than the doors at the back of the church suddenly crashed open and a figure strode in, amid a blast of icy January air.

'Hello, what's this?' Willcox whispered.

Confusion quickly descended over the congregation and everyone turned to look at the stocky, dark-haired young man who stood there, brushing a light dusting of snow off his black suit.

Two of the pallbearers hurried forward and there was some muffled conversation at the back of the church.

'But I have a right to be here!' The young man's voice rose. 'I haven't come to cause trouble. I just want to pay my respects, the same as everyone else.'

He made to move forward down the aisle, but the men closed in on him, barring his way.

'Let me past! Lydia!' he called out, craning his neck to see past the men's shoulders. 'For pity's sake, tell them who I am!'

Spilsbury looked at the fair-haired girl in the front row. The handkerchief pressed to her face could not hide the deep blush in her cheeks. She stared fixedly down at her feet.

Her brother stood up and went to speak to the young man. More hushed words were exchanged, but whatever he said did nothing to ease the unwanted guest's agitation.

'But I want to see Lydia.' His voice came out as a wail of despair.

'She doesn't want to see you. Now go home, Robert, before you make an even bigger fool of yourself.'

The young man stopped for a moment and looked around him. He seemed bewildered, as if he had just woken up from a dream and found himself standing there.

The next moment the pallbearers had closed in on him. As he was bundled out of the church, Spilsbury noticed the fair-haired girl steal a quick backward glance before dragging her eyes back to her prayer book.

Chapter 2

The funeral didn't quite manage to regain its solemnity after that, despite the best efforts of the vicar. It was a relief when the service was finally over and they spilled out of the church into the cold January air. Even though it was barely two o'clock, the sky was already leaden, and light flurries of snow swirled about them, settling on the shoulders of Spilsbury's morning coat and the brim of his top hat.

'Well, I never!' Willcox rubbed his hands together. 'That was some unexpected excitement, wasn't it?'

'It was a distraction I daresay we could have all done without.' Spilsbury consulted his watch again.

'I'm guessing that was Miss Franklin's would-be suitor?'

'More like would-be husband.'

Willcox looked at him questioningly. 'Oh?'

'I noticed Miss Franklin looked down at her left hand as she was putting on her gloves, as if she was rather taken aback not to see a ring there. Their engagement ended quite recently, I would imagine.'

'He clearly wasn't the one to call it off.'

'I'm not sure she was, either.'

'You're wrong there, old boy. Didn't you see the way she kept her head down? She couldn't bring herself to look at him. After that disgraceful performance, she was probably thinking what a lucky escape she'd had!'

'Or she was trying to hide her true feelings.' Spilsbury thought about that last sorrowful glance at the doors as they had closed on the young man. 'I'm inclined to believe she had been forced into the parting.'

'Her father didn't approve? I'm hardly surprised. The chap seemed positively unhinged.'

Spilsbury shook his head. 'I believe it's more likely her aunt who disapproves. The girl was very guarded around her, I noticed.'

Willcox stared at him. 'You know, it never ceases to amaze me how someone who dislikes the company of other people as much as you do could understand and interpret so much about them.'

'I simply observe,' Spilsbury said. 'Most people are too busy trying to fit in and be liked to notice anything.'

'But you don't care about being liked?'

Spilsbury was silent. Willcox already knew the answer to that one.

'I must say, I'm rather looking forward to seeing what the rest of the afternoon has in store,' Willcox went on. 'I wonder if the spurned fiancé will turn up at the burial?'

'If he does, I won't be there to see it,' Spilsbury said, pulling on his gloves.

'You're not coming?'

'I don't have time.'

'But we should pay our respects.'

'Isn't it enough that we came here?'

'You can spare an hour, surely?'

'Hardly. I shall be at the mortuary until midnight as it is.'

'You work too hard,' Willcox said.

Spilsbury sighed. 'Not another lecture, please.'

'I mean it. I'm worried about you, old man. You're forever running up and down the country, working into the early hours. God knows when you find time to eat or sleep. You'll send yourself to an early grave if you're not careful.' He nodded towards the coffin, which was being loaded on to a horse-drawn carriage. 'You don't want to end up like that poor devil, do you?'

Spilsbury looked at his friend. Fifty-year-old William Willcox was seven years his senior and the sharpest mind he had ever known. But for all his extensive expertise in the field of medico-legal chemistry, he sometimes displayed the medical acuity of an old wife.

'It wasn't overwork that killed James Franklin, it was a failing heart. And frankly, given the state of him, he was lucky to live as long as he did.'

Willcox cleared his throat noisily. It took Spilsbury a moment to realise that he was trying to draw his attention to someone standing behind him.

He turned to find himself facing the woman from the church, still clutching the small boy's hand.

'What a comfort you are, Dr Spilsbury,' she said in a tight, cutting voice. Her rough accent was a startling contrast to the expensive sable fur she wore. 'If that's your idea of a bedside manner, it's a good thing your patients are not in a fit state to hear it.'

Spilsbury stared at her, baffled and astonished as she walked away.

'Well, well,' Willcox chuckled. 'It looks like you've had a bite from the Black Widow.'

'Who?'

'Franklin's wife, Violet. That's what they call her, the Black Widow.'

'And why on earth would they call her that?'

'I suppose because everyone thinks it was a rather dubious match.' He gazed after her. 'I must say, she's rather formidable, isn't she? They say she has quite a past, for all that she was twenty years younger than him.'

Spilsbury watched her making her way across the church-yard towards the waiting car. Willcox was right, there was something formidable about her. While the other mourners gathered around Sir James's sister and his children, he noticed that no one tried to approach her.

Not that she seemed to care, since all her attention was fixed on the small boy at her side.

Something about her resonated with him. The proud tilt of her head, the look of studied indifference on her face. It was a mask he understood all too well.

Reject them before they reject you.

'And how do you know all this?' he asked.

'It was the talk of the hospital a couple of years ago. I'm surprised you didn't hear about it.'

'I make a point of never listening to gossip.'

'Apparently the family were appalled when he returned home from the war with a new bride and a baby in tow. They immediately thought she must be after his money.'

Spilsbury looked at the older woman, flanked by her niece and nephew, stiffly receiving condolences from the other mourners. From the downturned lines of her mouth he could make out under her veil, he imagined she would find most things appalling.

'Did he have any money?'

'He had a title. Some minor baronetcy up in Yorkshire, so I understand. I daresay there must have been some kind of family fortune somewhere.' He took off his hat to brush snow from the brim. 'I suppose they might have had cause to be concerned. I mean, why else would a young woman marry a sickly middle-aged widower, if not for his money?'

'Why indeed?' Spilsbury looked from the aunt on one side of the churchyard to the widow on the other. Hardly a family united in grief, he thought. 'I take it they don't get on?'

'That's an understatement, old boy. They loathe each other. And the worst of it is they've all been living under the same roof since they came home from France. Can you imagine? No wonder poor Franklin's heart gave out, having to keep the peace between those two.' He smiled impishly. 'I daresay the wake will be a lively affair. I can't wait to see it!'

'Then I hope you enjoy it.' Spilsbury consulted his watch again.

'Are you sure you don't want to come?'

'I've already wasted too much time.'

'But aren't you curious to see what happens?'

'I'm curious as to who would leave a leg in a bin at Ipswich railway station. I'm curious about whether a mother of three children deliberately failed to ignite the pilot light on her heater before she turned on the gas. But unlike you, I have absolutely no curiosity about Sir James Franklin or his family.' His tucked his watch back into his waistcoat pocket. 'I'm going back to the hospital,' he said. 'I'll leave you to your gossip-mongering.'

'Sorry, old boy, but I don't think you're going to St Mary's today.'

Spilsbury followed his friend's gaze to the gate, where a policeman stood huddled against the cold. He caught Spilsbury's eye and nodded to him.

'Perhaps they've found the rest of your missing soldier?' Willcox said.

But there was something in the policeman's keen expression that told a different story.

'Or found another,' Spilsbury sighed.

Chapter 3

St Pancras Public Mortuary was buried deep in the basement under the old South Infirmary of St Pancras Hospital. The ante-room was long, narrow and oddly proportioned, as if it had been turned on its side, the green-tiled walls stretching high upwards to a sloping ceiling of thick grimy glass that did nothing to ease the oppressive atmosphere.

It was also as cold as a tomb, which was quite appropriate considering the half-dozen bodies in tin boxes lined up on trolleys against the far wall.

PC Charlie Abbott blew on his hands to warm them, his breath curling in the frigid air. He had long since ceased to be able to feel his feet, as the cold seeped up through the stone-flagged floor, penetrating the thick soles of his police-issue boots.

It wouldn't be long before he was as stiff as the room's other occupants, he thought gloomily.

He wasn't sure he should even still be there. He had been told the coroner's officer would be taking over from him, but he had been standing there for nearly half an hour and no one had arrived.

The door to the post-mortem room was ajar, and through it Charlie could see a marble table with lights arranged over it, and a long wooden bench lined up with instruments, from delicate forceps to a rather brutal-looking saw. But there was no sign of the mortuary keeper, nor anyone else.

Except all those bodies.

He whistled tunelessly to break the silence, but gave up after a couple of bars. It seemed disrespectful, somehow. He was sure his mother had once told him it was unlucky to whistle in front of the dead. Or was that at sea? He could hardly keep up with Elsie Abbott's long list of superstitions.

Outside in the passage the floorboards creaked and Charlie swung round to face the door, but no one entered.

Perhaps he should leave? He'd done his part and delivered the body to the mortuary. It was all labelled, with a sheaf of notes from the police surgeon. There was nothing more for him to do.

And yet it didn't seem right to leave her on her own.

Charlie was no stranger to dead bodies. Two years in the trenches had seen to that. But there was something about seeing the woman lying face down on the cobbled towpath beside the Regent's Canal that had made him feel strangely protective of her.

It was no way for a lady to end up, down there in the murky water among the rusting prams and bicycles and all the other old rubbish. She seemed so ordinary, in spite of her blueish pallor and the tarry black mud that caked her blond hair. The skin on her hands was thick, white and wrinkled like a pair of ill-fitting gloves. It was hard to make out her age, but Charlie would have guessed she was at least ten years older than him, in her thirties or possibly her forties.

She lay there on the path where the bargeman had dumped her after pulling her out of the water. Her shoes and stockings were missing and her skirt was rucked up around her hips, exposing her drawers and naked thighs the colour of mouldy pastry. Without thinking, Charlie had adjusted her clothes to make her decent. He wouldn't want anyone to see his wife or his mum in such a state of disarray, dead or not.

God forbid they should ever end up like her.

Numbness crept up his legs, stiffening his calves. Charlie shifted his weight from one foot to the other to ease the cramp. It was late afternoon, and what little light managed to permeate the filthy glass above him was fading fast. Soon it would be completely gone, and he would be left here alone in the dark, with no one but the dead for company . . .

'Boo!'

Charlie nearly shot out of his skin. He turned round to see Detective Sergeant George Stevens grinning at him from the doorway.

'All right, Beanpole? Give you a scare, did I?' he said, grinning.

'No.'

'Don't give me that. You were shaking like a leaf!'

'So you would be, if you'd been standing in the freezing cold for the past half an hour.'

George Stevens took out a packet of Woodbines and lit one up. He was a head shorter than Charlie, his skinny frame swamped by a cheap brown suit. But he thought he was Douglas Fairbanks, with his dark hair slicked carefully back from his narrow, weaselly face.

'What are you doing here, anyway?' George asked. 'Why aren't you out directing traffic and looking for lost cats?'

Charlie gritted his teeth. Typical George, never missed a chance to get a jab in. The pair had belonged to the same boxing club when they were kids. They had met in the ring a few times, but even though Charlie was taller and stronger, somehow he always came off worst because George was sneaky and partial to a low blow.

'She turned up on my beat.' He looked longingly at George's cigarette, but he knew he would never offer him one. 'What about you?'

'Inspector Mount sent me.'

Charlie's heart quickened. 'So you think it might be murder, then?'

George smirked knowingly. 'Don't get too excited, mate. If it is murder we'll be taking it straight back to Scotland Yard. This is as close as you'll ever get to detective work.'

That's what you think. Charlie had been in uniform for two years, and he was already counting the weeks until he could put in his application for Scotland Yard. It was all he had ever wanted, right from being a kid.

He might have been there now, if the war hadn't got in the way.

But it hadn't stood in George's way. The only reason he was already a detective was because he'd slithered out of serving his country. While Charlie had been up to his neck in mud and blood in the trenches, George had been wheedling his way up the ranks.

But Charlie was determined to follow him soon enough.

George took a long drag on his cigarette. 'Anyway, we won't know for sure till Spilsbury's given her the once-over,' he said.

'Dr Spilsbury's coming here?'

'Dr Spilsbury has already arrived.'

Charlie turned round to see a tall figure in a black morning suit and top hat standing behind him, carrying a battered leather Gladstone bag.

It was really him. The famous Dr Spilsbury. A man almost as famous as King George himself.

It was hard not to be overwhelmed. Ten years earlier, his mother had been in the public gallery at the Old Bailey when Bernard Spilsbury gave evidence at the trial of the murderous Dr Crippen and his mistress Ethel Le Neve. She had been so enthralled, she had queued up several times since to watch the Honorary Pathologist to the Home

Office give another performance. And when she couldn't go to see him in person, she would cut clippings of his cases out of the newspapers.

'It's the way he talks,' she would say to Charlie. 'You can tell he's a clever man the minute he opens his mouth. Honest to God, it's better than anything you'd see at the picture house.'

Charlie could see now why his mother was so impressed. Spilsbury commanded the room the moment he strode into it.

'Put that out,' he ordered tersely, with a nod at the cigarette dangling from George's lips. 'I can't smell anything through the smoke.'

'Yes, sir.' George fumbled it in his haste, nearly setting fire to his own cuff. Charlie stared down at his boots to stop himself laughing.

Spilsbury disappeared into the post-mortem room, only to reappear a moment later, minus his morning coat and hat.

'Where is the body?' he enquired.

'She's there, sir.' Charlie pointed to the far left of the tin boxes.

Spilsbury appraised the row in silence, then said, 'And where is Mr Blake?'

Charlie looked along the line of coffins, nonplussed. 'I– I'm not sure which one he might be, sir . . .'

'He's the mortuary keeper, constable.'

'Oh!' Colour scalded his face. 'I don't know, sir.'

'He isn't here?'

'No, sir.'

'Are you the Coroner's Officer?'

'He's just a beat constable, sir,' George put in before Charlie could answer him. 'I'm Detective Sergeant—'

'So the body has not been prepared for post-mortem?' Spilsbury cut him off.

'Not that I know of, sir.'

Spilsbury sighed. 'Very well, I suppose I'll have to take a quick look at her now and do the full post-mortem later.' He turned to George. 'Go upstairs and try to find Mr Blake or the Coroner's Officer, will you?'

George looked at Charlie. 'You heard Dr Spilsbury, constable.'

Charlie was about to leave when Spilsbury said, 'Oh no, constable, you must stay. I assume you're the one who found the body?'

'I was called to the scene, sir. It was a bargeman who found her first.'

'Then I will need to speak to you.' He looked back at George. 'Don't just stand there gawping, man. Go and fetch the mortuary keeper, or we shall be here all day.'

George stared at Dr Spilsbury, and Charlie could see him trying to muster the courage to argue. But in the end he slunk away, slamming the door behind him.

Spilsbury hardly seemed to notice. 'And where was she found?' he asked Charlie.

'Camden Lock, sir, near Dead Dog Hole. The bargeman had to stop at the interchange, which is when he noticed her floating face down in the water.'

'What time was she found?'

Charlie fumbled for his notebook in his top pocket and flicked hurriedly through the pages. 'It was twenty-three minutes to two when we pulled her out, sir.'

Spilsbury was silent for a moment as he examined the body. Charlie held his breath, not daring to make a sound in case he disturbed some great musing.

The pathologist looked at the body for a moment or two longer, then straightened up and reached for the notes that the police surgeon had sent.

'And you've no idea who she is?' he asked.

'No, sir. There was nothing left at the scene.'

'That's hardly surprising, since she probably floated some distance. I would have to look at a map of the canal layout to know for sure.'

'I don't think she would have come too far from the east, sir, otherwise the locks would have stopped her,' Charlie said without thinking. Then he caught Spilsbury's sharp look and he realised he'd spoken out of turn.

But to his relief, the pathologist said, 'That is a very good point, constable. I bow to your superior knowledge of the area.'

Just at that moment George burst back into the room. 'The Coroner's Officer has been delayed, sir,' he said.

'And Mr Blake?'

'He's indisposed, sir. They're sending for someone else now. They might have been here already if Constable Abbott here had thought to let them know what was going on.' He glared at Charlie.

'Yes, well, never mind that now.' Spilsbury picked up the woman's notes and consulted them in silence for a moment.

'The police surgeon seems to think she didn't drown, sir?' George ventured.

'And judging from what he says in his notes, I would say he was quite right,' Spilsbury said.

'So it's murder, then?'

'As to that, Sergeant, I could not say until I've had a proper look at her myself. But from the police surgeon's observations as to the state of her lungs and the absence of fluid in her airways, I would suspect that she was already dead when she went into the water.' He set the notes aside, then turned to Charlie. 'And you're certain she could not have come from the east?'

'I don't believe so, sir.'

'Very well. Then I suggest you find out if anyone has been reported missing from the Camden Town area. You might even search as far as Little Venice, although I don't believe she could have come very far.' He glanced back over his shoulder at the coffin. 'The very least we can do for the poor woman is give her a name,' he said.

Chapter 4

'Well, this is a rum way to spend the day you bury your husband!'

Mickey Malone grinned at Violet as an elephant lumbered past, laden down with people. There were at least a dozen of them perched atop the animal's back, shrieking with laughter as they clutched each other and tried not to fall off. An unperturbed zookeeper led the way, steadying the elephant with one hand while he swept a path between the onlookers who crowded on either side.

'Thomas loves it here.' Violet looked down at her son fondly. The three-year-old was staring up at the towering beast with eyes full of wonder and amazement. 'It's been such an awful day, I thought he deserved a treat.'

It was a mercy that he was too young to properly understand what was going on. Even this afternoon, after the funeral, he had asked her when Daddy would be coming home.

'Shouldn't you be at the house, hosting the wake?' Mickey asked.

Violet shuddered. 'I couldn't face it. Anyway, Elizabeth can manage it a lot better than I can.'

'I can just imagine her holding court. I'll bet she's loving every minute.'

'I don't care.'

For once, Violet was happy to let her sister-in-law do as she pleased. She felt out of her depth with James's friends.

They might have been nice to her face, especially while James was alive, but she knew what they all called her behind her back.

The Black Widow. A ruthless spider that devoured its mate when it had got what it wanted from them.

Mickey put his arm around her. Violet leaned in to him, grateful for his solid, protective bulk. This was her real family, Mickey and her son. The Franklins could go to hell.

'Can I ride on the elephant, Mama?' Thomas tugged at her skirt, his little face turned up towards her, full of appeal.

'I don't know, love. It might be too dangerous.'

'Tell you what, I'll give you a ride instead.' Mickey grabbed the boy and swung him up onto his broad shoulders. 'But what's this? I've broken free of the keeper and now I'm charging around the zoo!'

He set off running, bellowing loudly and scattering the crowds before him while Thomas bounced and squealed on his shoulders. Not many people would stand in Mickey's way, even if he wasn't pretending to be a rampaging elephant. His powerful height and size made him intimidating, especially with his battered-looking Bull Terrier, Pistol, bounding along beside him.

Violet laughed to see them, then immediately felt guilty. What would people say if they saw her now, grinning away on the day of James's funeral? They would say they were right about her, of course. That she was a heartless hussy dancing on her husband's grave.

But the last few days since his death had been so awful and oppressive, she desperately needed to release some of the tension she felt.

Elizabeth had taken charge of the funeral arrangements. She had just assumed she could run everything, as usual, and Violet had been too numb with grief and shock to do anything about it.

She still couldn't believe he was gone.

She had known how ill he was. She had helped nurse him when he caught rheumatic fever in France. He had even warned her when he proposed that they wouldn't have long together.

'My darling, are you sure you want to tie yourself to an old sick man?' he had asked, with that rueful smile of his.

Of course, she had said yes. She was already pregnant with Thomas by then, and even if she hadn't been, she loved James so much she could not even consider living without him.

But now their time had run out, and she had to learn to navigate the world without him. She was nearly twenty-five when she and James had married, and hardly a blushing flower. In fact, she had probably been through more in her life than most people would ever want to experience. But her marriage had plunged her into a new and unfamiliar world, and she felt lost in it without his protection.

She caught up with Mickey and her son by the lions' enclosure.

'The zoo will be closing soon,' she called out to them. 'We should be getting back.'

'But Thomas wants to feed the monkeys first!' Mickey protested, pulling a face.

'Are you sure it's Thomas who wants to feed them and not you, you big kid?' Violet smiled reluctantly. 'All right, five more minutes. Then we've really got to go.'

In truth, she was in no hurry to return to the house. She could almost feel it lurking just beyond the trees on the fringe of the park, its blank windows watching her, resenting her very existence. She had never liked the place, but now she felt a tug of dread whenever she thought about it.

They found the monkeys, and Mickey went off to buy some food for them.

'I'll get it.' Violet immediately reached for her bag, but her brother stopped her.

'I know I'm on my uppers, but even I can afford to buy a bag of nuts!' he said, smiling.

Violet watched them feeding the animals. Mickey held Thomas up so he could reach the monkeys' leathery hands, outstretched through the bars. Pistol sat at their feet, alert and watchful as ever. Thomas had the Malones' green eyes and curly black hair, but his features were as fine and delicate as his father's. When he smiled, she saw James and it nearly broke her heart.

It was so sad that he would never know his father. James had adored him. He was the child he had never expected to have, and he had lavished attention on him that he had never given to his older children.

He had been a much younger man when Lydia and Matthew were born, putting all his energy into building his medical career. And then his first wife had died and for years he had been too consumed with his own loss to attend to his grieving children. Violet knew it was one of the biggest regrets of her husband's life that he had not been a better father to Lydia and Matthew.

Violet often felt guilty that she and Thomas had benefitted from so much of his time and attention. She had tried her best to make up for it by being a loving mother to the two older children, even though there were only a few years between them in age. But while Lydia had loved her fiercely in return, Matthew did not even try to hide his contempt for her.

He was his aunt's creature, all right.

'Penny for them?'

25

She turned to see Mickey looking questioningly at her. 'You don't want to know,' she sighed.

'I bet I can guess.' Mickey shook his head. 'Honest to God, Vi, why do you put up with her? It ain't like you to be backward in coming forward.'

'I promised James.'

He had told her all about Elizabeth while they were still in France. His spinster older sister who had shared the family's home ever since he married his first wife.

'I know it's a lot to ask,' he had said. 'But I owe her so much, and she has nowhere else to go. You wouldn't mind if she went on living with us, would you?'

Of course Violet hadn't minded. Coming from the back streets of South London, she was used to large families all being in crammed together, sleeping several to a room. And the grand house at Gloucester Gate was hardly a tiny terrace.

'Of course not. The more the merrier,' she had said.

If only she'd known. But foolishly, she had assumed that they would all be able to live happily together. She even thought Elizabeth might become the sister she'd never had.

But instead Elizabeth had gone out of her way to make her feel unwelcome. She treated her like an unwanted guest, and encouraged James's children to do the same. Violet often caught her and Matthew exchanging looks, or laughing about some error in etiquette she had unwittingly made.

She had tried to talk to James about it, but he had simply shrugged and said, 'You have to understand the situation from Elizabeth's point of view. It's bound to be difficult for her, having another woman coming in after all this time.'

And what about how difficult it is for me? Violet had wondered. But by then James was ailing, and she did not want to add to his worries.

'At least you won't have to put up with it for much longer,' Mickey laughed. 'Soon it'll all be yours.'

'Don't,' Violet said.

'Why not? It's true. You're his wife, you'll inherit everything.'

'I didn't marry him for his bloody house!'

'I didn't say you did.'

'That's what everyone thinks though, ain't it?'

The irony of it was that finding a husband had been the last thing on her mind when she had signed up as part of the Voluntary Aid Detachment to France. She was looking for a way to make a new start, to escape from the mistakes she had made in her life. But she never dreamed she would end up falling in love and becoming the wife of a baronet.

Lady Violet Franklin. She never used the title, it was too ridiculous. Especially given who she was and where she had come from.

In an area already full of thieves and criminals, Violet's family had carved themselves out quite a reputation. Everyone south of the river from Borough down to Lambeth had heard of the Malones. They were quick-tempered, violent thugs and hard-drinking thieves who never backed away from a fight. And it had cost them dear, too. Her father and older brother had both been killed in street brawls, while another brother was rotting in prison for armed robbery.

No wonder Elizabeth Franklin's hair had nearly turned white when her brother had brought home his new bride. In her place, Violet would have felt just the same. But Elizabeth did not even give her a chance to prove herself. She had dismissed her right from the very start.

And Violet *was* different. Yes, she had made some mistakes. But inside she knew herself to be a decent person, trying to do her best in the harsh world into which she had been born. She wondered if Elizabeth Franklin would have fared any differently if she had been born in a Southwark slum, instead of a grand house in Regent's Park.

'Come on,' Mickey said, taking her arm. 'I'll walk back with you.'

They talked as they walked down the leafy avenue towards Gloucester Gate.

'Are you working?' she asked.

'Here and there.' He shrugged. 'You know what it's like.'

She knew only too well. She had seen the old soldiers lined up outside the Labour Exchange on Borough High Street. And she had seen them shivering in shop doorways and outside pubs, begging for pennies so they could get a bed for the night.

A land fit for heroes, they had been promised. But all Mickey had got was a new suit, and a bullet injury to his right hand that put paid to any hopes of resuming his boxing career. He had been about to turn professional when he was called up.

She sent her brother a sideways look. It would have been so easy for Mickey to go down the same road as their father and brothers, and she wouldn't blame him for it. Violet knew from her own experience how difficult it was not to get drawn into that kind of life. There was easy money to be made for a bright boy like Mickey who was good with his fists.

'You're staying out of trouble, I hope?' she said.

He held up his hands. 'You know me, sis. Pure as the driven snow.'

As if on cue, Pistol started to growl at a squirrel sheltering high in the bare branches of a chestnut tree.

Violet laughed. 'Even your dog knows when you're lying!'

'Now then, boy, don't you go giving away my secrets!' Pistol was instantly alert to the sound of his master's voice, his stumpy tail wagging furiously. Just after he had been demobbed, Mickey had rescued him from a gang of dog fighters. The poor old dog had fought his last fight and was about to be put out of his misery, but Mickey tenderly nursed him back to health and found himself a friend for life.

Pistol and her brother were similar in many ways. They were both wary and distrustful of strangers, but fiercely loyal to those they loved. And they both had a vicious streak deep inside them.

All Violet had to do was to keep Mickey out of trouble, and make sure that streak never had cause to surface.

They approached the tall wrought-iron gates that led from the park. As the trees thinned, Violet caught sight of the terrace of elegant Georgian houses, their cream stucco facades bright against the fading afternoon light, and a feeling of dread washed over her.

Instantly Mickey's hand closed over hers. 'It won't be forever, sis,' he whispered. 'Once that house is yours, you can get rid of her.'

She shook her head. 'James wouldn't want me to do that.'

'James is dead, Vi. It's your house now. You can do as you please.'

She paused, letting his words sink in.

It's your house now.

She forced herself to look back at the terrace. If only he knew how little she wanted it. She had always hated the place, even when James was alive. It was more like a museum than a home, cold and forbidding and full of antiques. She had done her best to fill it with warmth and love and laughter, but it was as if the house itself rejected her.

She wanted nothing to do with it. There were even times when she longed to be back on the battlefields of France. Strange as it seemed, it was where she had been happiest, just her and James with the baby.

29

Her doubt and despair must have shown on her face because Mickey said, 'Like it or not, you've got to make a home for you and Tommy, Vi. You owe it to him. And it's what James would have wanted.'

'He wouldn't have wanted me to fall out with his sister.'

'You didn't start this, Vi. But I've never known you to back down from a fight.'

He was right, Violet thought. It wasn't like her to back down. She had bitten her tongue for too long to keep the peace, for James's sake. But not anymore.

Elizabeth Franklin might have started it, but Violet was damn well going to finish it. It was time her sister-in-law found out what it was really like to take on one of the Malones.

Chapter 5

'Thank God that's over,' Matthew said, when the last guest had finally gone.

He helped himself to a drink from the decanter, then flopped into the wing armchair by the fireside, carelessly slopping whisky onto the polished leather. He had already had far too much, Elizabeth thought. She had not said anything in front of the guests but now she watched her nephew with distaste.

'Must you?' she said.

Matthew looked up at her blankly. 'What?'

'That was your father's favourite armchair.'

'Yes, well, he won't be needing it any more, will he? Nor these, come to think of it.' He took a cigar out of James's carved wooden box.

'Matthew!' Lydia said in a shocked voice. 'Don't you have any respect?'

'Respect?' Matthew smirked at his sister. 'You're a fine one to talk. It wasn't my fiancé who turned our father's funeral into a sideshow!'

'I didn't ask Robert to come,' Lydia said quietly. 'I didn't want him there.'

'You obviously didn't tell him that.'

'I did!'

Matthew lit his cigar and aimed a careless smoke ring towards the ceiling. 'If you ask me, I'm not even sure you've called it off with him,' he said.

'Of course I have!'

'He certainly doesn't seem to think so.' He yanked off his tie and ran his finger around the inside of the collar. A stud came loose and bounced across the parquet floor. 'In fact, I wouldn't be surprised if you two weren't still having secret lovers' trysts. What do you say, Aunt?'

'Don't be ridiculous!' Colour rose in Lydia's cheeks.

'I'm sure she knows better than that. Don't you, Lydia?' Elizabeth said.

'Yes, Aunt.' Lydia lowered her gaze demurely. But not before Elizabeth caught the guilty look on her face.

Lydia might be twenty years old, but she was still very much a child. She needed to be protected from herself, or she was apt to land herself in all sorts of unsuitable entanglements.

Like this wretched engagement.

Elizabeth had known there was something unsuitable about Robert Dillon the moment she set eyes on him. He might have fooled everyone else, but she had sensed from the start he was not all he seemed.

She had tried to warn James, but he wouldn't listen.

'He seems like a nice enough young man to me,' he had said. 'And Lydia loves him. So that's all that matters, isn't it?'

So typical of her brother! As if love really was all that mattered. How could Elizabeth ever expect him to understand, when he himself had lost his head so completely over that common little tart?

She might not have been able to save her brother from making a colossal mistake, but at least she had made sure right thinking prevailed where Lydia was concerned. Of course her niece had been heartbroken, but she had done the sensible thing in the end.

Although looking at Lydia's furtive expression now, she wondered if Matthew was right. She wouldn't put it past Robert to try to worm his way back into her niece's affections. He was certainly tenacious enough. And he had no shame, either, if his performance at the church earlier was anything to go by.

Young Dr Dillon might be determined, but he had met his match in Elizabeth Franklin. He would not find a place in the family. Not while she was there to prevent it.

But Elizabeth was certain Robert wouldn't be the last man to try to take advantage of her niece. Lydia was a beauty, with her father's height and her mother's delicate, doll-like features, wide grey eyes and soft blond curls. She might think she knew her own mind, but she understood little of the world. She needed to be shielded from her worst impulses.

Matthew got up and poured himself another drink from the decanter.

'Must you drink so much?' Lydia pleaded.

'Why not? I might as well enjoy it while I can. There'll be nothing left for us once our beloved stepmother gets her hands on everything. Where is the delightful Violet, anyway?' Matthew looked around the drawing room. 'I thought she'd be here, bundling up the silverware ready to take down to the pawn shop.'

'She's taken Thomas to the zoo.'

'The zoo! Shows how much she cared about our father, doesn't it? What do you say to that, Aunt?'

'I expected nothing less of her,' Elizabeth said tautly.

'I think she wanted to take Thomas's mind off the funeral,' Lydia said. 'It's been such a sad day for him.'

'It's been a sad day for us all,' Matthew said. 'But we're not all going off for a jolly day out, are we?'

'I suppose we all have to find our own way of drowning our sorrows.' Lydia eyed the glass in her brother's hand.

'Matthew is right,' Elizabeth said. 'Your stepmother should have been here. Several people asked where she was.'

'And what did you tell them?'

'I said she was indisposed and had taken to her room.'

'I wish she was indisposed,' Matthew muttered into his glass. 'Preferably something fatal.'

'Oh Matthew, you don't mean that!' Lydia cried.

'Don't I? You do know what will happen now Father's dead? She'll inherit everything. We'll be lucky if we're left with the clothes we stand up in—'

He stopped speaking abruptly. Elizabeth scarcely needed to turn her head to know that Violet was standing in the doorway.

'Where have you been?' Elizabeth asked, even though she already knew the answer.

'I took Thomas out.'

'Until this time? It's past seven.'

'I didn't realise I had to answer to you.'

They stared at each other in hostile silence. Elizabeth was the first to lower her gaze.

'It is not done to miss one's husband's funeral,' she said.

'I was at the funeral. Or didn't you notice?'

Her rough accent grated across Elizabeth's nerves, making her wince.

'You should have been here for the wake.'

'I'm sure you all managed all right without me.'

'Of course we did,' Elizabeth snapped. 'But that's hardly the point. You should have been here.'

Violet gave her a weary look, as if she could scarcely be bothered to argue. 'I'm going to put Thomas to bed,' she said.

'You should let Mary do it.'

'Why?'

'Because that's what servants are for. Anyway, it's high time that child had a nanny.'

'He's got me.'

Elizabeth gave a pained sigh. 'I'm only trying to guide you,' she said. 'I know children are probably brought up differently wherever it is you come from . . .'

'I'll say,' Matthew muttered. 'I daresay the boy would be picking pockets on London Bridge by now.'

Violet ignored him, her unblinking gaze still fixed on Elizabeth. It was supposed to be unnerving, she imagined, but she was made of sterner stuff.

'It's customary for children of our class to be brought up by a nanny,' Elizabeth went on. 'I discussed the matter with James, and he saw the sense in it—'

'When?' Violet interrupted her. 'When did you discuss it?'

'A few days before he died. He said he was going to talk to you about it, but then he was taken ill.'

'I'm sorry he didn't speak to me, because I would have told him what I'm telling you. My son is not going to be brought up by the maid, or a nanny, or anyone else but me.'

Once again their eyes met across the length of the drawing room.

'You're tired and overwrought,' Elizabeth said. 'We will speak about it again in the morning.'

'No, we won't. We won't speak about it again. I've already said my piece.'

'But James—'

'James is dead.' Violet's green eyes glittered. 'I'm in charge now, and I'll do as I please in my own house.'

The words hung in the air between them, the challenge thrown down. Even Matthew had fallen silent. He gawped at them over the rim of his glass, looking from one to the other and back again.

'Now if you don't mind, I'm going to put my son to bed.'

Without waiting for an answer, Violet turned on her heel and left the room.

Elizabeth stood rigid for a moment, staring at the door that had just closed so abruptly in her face.

'Well,' Matthew said. 'I suppose that's told you. Eh, Aunt?'

Elizabeth ignored her nephew's taunting comment. It scarcely bothered her what Matthew said. But it was the look in Lydia's soft grey eyes that really stung her.

It was a look of pity.

Chapter 6

Mary the maid was in the bedroom, drawing the curtains. She started guiltily when Elizabeth walked in, as if she had been caught doing something she shouldn't.

'I'm sorry, miss, I wasn't expecting you to be retiring so early.'

'It's been a trying day, and I'm rather tired.' Elizabeth sank down at her dressing table.

'Would you like me to help you prepare for bed?'

'No, I can manage. Carry on with what you were doing. And mind you don't use too much coal when you make up the fire.' She nodded to the bucket standing ready by the empty grate.

Not that it should trouble her any more, since she wouldn't be balancing the household accounts for much longer.

'No, miss.'

Mary sank to her knees in front of the fire. Elizabeth watched her out of the corner of her eye. There was something about the maid that always grated on her nerves, but she didn't know why. Mary was in her forties, so at least there was no girlish silliness about her. And for such a tall woman, she was unobtrusive almost to a fault. Elizabeth was often caught unawares by her silent presence, lurking in a corner of the room. She seemed to be everywhere, and even though she carried out her duties in sullen silence, Elizabeth had the feeling those beady eyes of hers missed nothing.

She pulled the pins out of her hair, scarcely bothering to look at her reflection in the mirror. Why bother, when the same face had stared back at her for more than fifty years? Besides, she was under no illusions. She had never been blessed with the kind of beauty that would turn a man's head. And at her age, the chances of finding a husband had long since gone. She was a woman on her own, with no means of her own, destined to be reliant on the charity of others.

And never had she felt that more keenly than this moment. All the peace of mind Elizabeth had ever known was gone, dead and buried in the ground with her brother.

She had been mistress of the house in Gloucester Gate for as long as she could remember. It had always been her home, since her father the eleventh baronet Franklin gave up the family seat in the West Riding of Yorkshire and took up permanent residence in London with his family.

As a child, Elizabeth had learned from her mother about managing household accounts and dealing with servants. The elegant four-storey Georgian house, with its tall windows and beautifully proportioned rooms overlooking Regent's Park, had been her home and her sanctuary, and she loved it more passionately than she had ever loved anyone or anything in her life.

If she had been a man, the house would have been hers when their father died. Her younger brother James had no interest in it. He had his books and his medical career to think about. Elizabeth knew he would happily have handed everything over to her.

But that was not the way their world worked. James had inherited his father's title and the house. He had moved there with his new wife Frances, and Elizabeth had prepared herself to leave the home she loved.

But Frannie was a frail little thing, hardly up to the task of running the house. She had been only too grateful for Elizabeth to stay on and help her, especially after the babies arrived. Frances might have been the nominal mistress of the house, but the servants all knew who was really in charge.

Then, when Frances had died, Elizabeth had seamlessly resumed the role of mistress of the house, leaving her brother to his all-consuming grief.

And so it had gone on, until three years ago, when James returned from the war with his new wife and baby son.

Violet. Elizabeth shuddered at the thought of her. Ever since that wretched creature had come into their lives, things had gone wrong. Even James's health had suffered since he married her.

What had possessed him? Some madness borne of the battlefield, Elizabeth assumed. She could only imagine what horrors he must have witnessed in those field hospitals. Perhaps it had turned his mind, or perhaps he had sought some kind of comfort from all the blood and filth and death that surrounded him. Whatever it was, it had driven him right into the arms of Violet Malone.

She must have been unable to believe her luck, Elizabeth thought bitterly. A vulgar, ill-educated creature, born in the gutter and brought up in a den of thieves. What hope would she ever have to prosper?

And then along came Sir James Franklin. Wealthy, titled, with a distinguished career as a physician, still scarred by the death of his beloved wife. He must have seemed like easy pickings to someone as cunning as Violet.

James might not have been able to see through her wiles, but Elizabeth had been wise to her right from the start. And she was determined Violet would never become mistress of the house. She was simply not worthy of it.

Of course, she hadn't really had much choice in the matter. Violet might easily have turned her out of the house. But Elizabeth made sure she appealed to James first, reminding him how selflessly she had helped him over the years, how she had sacrificed her own prospects for him. He owed her.

Of course, he had agreed. Her brother had a distaste for conflict, and tried to avoid it at all costs.

But Violet was another matter. Elizabeth had expected more resistance from her. But for some reason Violet seemed to acquiesce. Perhaps she did it for James's sake, knowing he was ailing? Or perhaps she tacitly accepted that she was out of her depth when it came to running a household such as theirs?

Or perhaps she simply knew when she was beaten?

Until now. Elizabeth remembered the triumph in her sister-in-law's eyes as they had faced each other across the drawing room. She gasped in pain, her hand to her stomach as she if she suffered a physical blow.

'Are you all right, miss?' The maid hovered beside her, concern written all over her face.

'Yes. Yes, I'm quite all right.' Elizabeth quickly regained her composure, determined not to allow her mask to slip in front of the servant.

Violet would probably run the house into the ground within a month, she thought. Elizabeth had already made up her mind she would not stay to see it. Not that her sister-in-law would give her much choice in the matter, she was certain.

But where could she go? She stared bleakly at her reflection in the mirror. There were very few options open for an old woman with no husband to take care of her.

And she could hardly rely on her niece and nephew. Matthew was far too selfish to think of anyone but himself. And as for poor, stupid Lydia . . .

The sound of scrunching paper caught her attention. Elizabeth turned her head to see the maid still kneeling in front of the fire, a stack of old newspapers beside her.

'Where did you get those?'

Mary looked up, clearly surprised by the sharp note in her voice. 'I found them in the basket, over there.' She pointed. 'I thought I could use them—'

'Put them back,' Elizabeth ordered.

'But they're weeks old . . .'

'I said put them back!' Elizabeth's voice rose. 'You're not to touch those newspapers, do you understand?'

'Yes, miss,' Mary mumbled.

She finished making up the fire then got to her feet, carefully brushing down her apron. She made a great show of carefully stacking up the newspapers and replacing them where she had found them.

'Will that be all?' she asked stiffly.

Elizabeth nodded. 'For now.'

Mary lingered for a moment in the doorway. Elizabeth noticed her reflected in the mirror behind her, like a creeping shadow. 'Was there something else?' she asked impatiently.

'A letter arrived for you, miss, in the afternoon post. I left it by your bedside.' And then she was gone, closing the door behind her softly. Elizabeth listened for her footsteps on the landing, but there was only silence.

She turned to look at the envelope on the bedside table. Even from across the room she recognised the familiar scrawl on the envelope.

It was a while since he had written to her, and Elizabeth had almost given up on him. She smiled to herself. Perhaps things might not be so bleak after all?

Chapter 7

Lydia looked towards the drawing-room door, her expression anxious. 'Do you think I should go up and make sure she's all right?'

'God, no! She won't thank you for it.' Matthew set down his empty glass. 'Best leave her to unruffle her feathers.'

'Poor Aunt Elizabeth,' Lydia sighed.

'Indeed.' He leaned back in his father's chair, tapping the polished leather with his fingertips. He itched to reach for the crystal decanter again, but he knew Lydia would pass comment.

'If only she'd made more of an effort with Violet, I'm sure she wouldn't be in this position.'

'Like you, you mean. Talk about hedging your bets. It was very clever of you to keep in with both of them.'

'I just try to be nice to everyone, that's all. You should try it.'

'Me? Be nice to her? I can barely tolerate her.'

The urge finally overcame him and he crossed the room to refill his glass. He could feel Lydia's eyes fixed on his back as he poured the whisky.

'Do you have to drink so much?' she said. 'You know Aunt Elizabeth doesn't like it.'

'Have you forgotten, Aunt Elizabeth doesn't rule the roost anymore?' Matthew turned to face her, waving the glass defiantly. 'Anyway, I'm sure she'd approve, if it stops our stepmother getting her hands on it—' He downed his drink and reached for another.

Lydia crossed to the window and gazed out at the wintry evening.

'I wish it didn't have to be so awful,' she sighed. 'We shouldn't be arguing, not at a time like this. Father's death should have brought us all together. I wish we could all just forgive and forget.'

Matthew laughed. 'You really are a naïve little duck, aren't you? There's as much chance of Tsar Nicholas ruling Russia again as there is of us uniting in grief.'

'I suppose you're right,' Lydia turned away from the window. 'I'm just worried about what will happen to Aunt E. She so loves this house.' She paused for a moment, then said, 'I wonder, if I talked to Violet, she might let her stay . . .'

'Go begging to her, you mean? Aunt Elizabeth would love that.' Matthew shook his head. 'I truly believe she would rather sleep under a bench in Regent's Park than rely on our stepmother's charity. Besides, there probably won't be room for any of us once she's filled the place with her ghastly, loutish family.'

'There's only one brother, I think,' Lydia said quietly.

'One is more than enough.' Matthew nodded towards the painting of the eighth baronet over the marble mantelpiece. 'You mark my words, half of this will probably be in the pawn shop within a month.'

'It won't be the first time, will it?' Lydia murmured.

'Ouch.' Matthew sent her a reproachful look. 'So much for forgiving and forgetting.'

Lydia pouted but said nothing. She knew she had spoken out of turn. Aunt Elizabeth had decreed they should not talk about his past mistakes.

But then she did not know the half of his present transgressions. And with any luck it would stay that way.

'You know your trouble, Matthew?'

'No, but I'm sure you're going to tell me.'

'You're a ghastly snob. You and Aunt E both think you're above everyone else, just because you live in this big house. But that means nothing any more. People don't have to stay in the gutter just because they were born there. Things are different now. Society is starting to change.'

Her pretty doll-like face was so earnest, Matthew couldn't help laughing. 'Have you been reading *The New Statesman* again?'

'I mean it. Things can't stay the way they've always been. It's too unfair.'

'And what would you know about it?'

'I talk to people.'

'Don't we all?'

'I mean different people, Matthew. From all walks of life.'

'You mean those letters you used to write? All those lonely soldiers who used to pour their hearts out to you from the trenches?'

'They had some very interesting things to say.'

'I'm sure they did,' Matthew leered. 'I hope you didn't send them your photograph?'

'Don't be disgusting!'

'I assure you I'm not. I was there, remember? I know how those soldiers used to slaver over those *billets doux* from pretty young girls like you.' He saw how Lydia's cheeks flamed. She really was an unbearable little priss, with her letters and her charity work.

'Make fun all you like, Matthew,' she said. 'But things have to change. If you'd met some of those poor men at Rowton House . . .'

Matthew rolled his eyes. 'Oh God, not this again! You go to that rat-infested hostel once a week to stack books in the library and you think you're George Bernard Shaw! You know nothing about real life, Lydia, so don't lecture me about it. You might like to make yourself feel better with your good deeds, but the truth is you're every bit as snobbish and overprivileged as I am.'

'That's not true!'

They were interrupted by a soft knock on the door. A moment later Mary entered, carrying a small package, wrapped in crumpled brown paper and tied with string.

'Pardon me, sir, but this just came for you.' She spoke in a hushed voice, her head down, eyes averted. Their aunt always insisted that servants should be neither seen nor heard until they were required.

'For me?' Matthew took the package. There was no address on it, just his name scrawled in large red letters. 'Where did it come from?'

'I found it on the doorstep just now, sir.'

'How odd,' Lydia said. 'Open it, Matthew. There might be a note inside.'

'I'm trying to, but there's a blasted knot in the string – ah!' He tugged at it, wrenching the string apart, then gave up and tore open the paper.

'What is it?' Lydia craned forward to see.

'It looks like a handkerchief.'

'But who would be sending you a single – oh!' Lydia jumped back, her hand over her mouth, as Matthew unfolded the cloth. 'Oh, how horrible!'

Matthew stared down at the blood-stained handkerchief. There was a charred hole through the centre that looked very much like—

'Is that – a bullet hole?' Lydia asked in a tremulous voice.

'It looks like it,' he said grimly.

'But what on earth does it mean, Matthew?'

'I don't know. Some kind of prank, I expect.'

'A prank?'

'One of my old soldier pals playing a joke. We used to do it all the time.'

'But how is this supposed to be funny? And on the day of our father's funeral, too.' His sister reached out with trembling fingers to touch the handkerchief. 'I wonder if we should tell the police?'

'And say what? Someone sent me a handkerchief smeared with pig's blood?' Matthew shook his head. 'No, I expect the culprit will reveal himself at the regimental dinner next month.'

Lydia looked at it fearfully. 'Well, you can tell them from me I don't think it's very funny.'

Matthew looked at the blood-soaked rag in his hands. It was all he could do to stop them trembling.

'I agree,' he said quietly. 'It's not funny at all.'

Chapter 8

By midday the following day, Spilsbury knew almost everything about the woman in the canal. Except her name.

The water had been very cold and, thankfully, she had not been immersed in it for long enough for any serious damage or decomposition to have taken place. He could tell she was in her late thirties, five feet four inches tall, well nourished to the point of plumpness. She had never given birth, nor had any intimate relations with a man. From the state of her liver it was clear she was no drinker. Her only vice might have been a fondness for sweets, judging by the extensive decay in her teeth and two missing back molars.

She liked to look nice, he thought. Her fingernails were painted pink, and from the tell-tale mousey roots close to her shaven skull, she was in the habit of enhancing her blond hair with peroxide.

'Strychnine,' he declared. 'My colleague Dr Willcox found traces in her liver, kidneys, bowel, stomach and blood.'

Inspector Alec Mount let out a low whistle. 'Someone definitely meant to kill her, then?'

'Judging by the amount Willcox found in her system, it would be difficult to assume she ingested it by accident.'

Inspector Mount nodded, taking in the information. He was in his late forties, a quietly spoken man with a long, narrow face and disconcertingly pale grey eyes. Thinning brown hair sprang from a high, domed forehead. Despite his unpromising appearance, he was known to be one of the shrewdest detectives at the Yard.

'So she definitely didn't drown?'

Spilsbury stared at the young man at Mount's side. No one could ever have accused Detective Sergeant Stevens of being shrewd.

'Definitely not,' he said firmly.

'And what makes you so certain?'

Spilsbury was not given to emotional judgements, but he had taken rather a dislike to George Stevens from the first moment he met him. There was something too cocky about him. His slicked dark hair, cheap suit and thin pencil moustache made him look more like a dubious gigolo than a police officer.

'There was no sign of pulmonary oedema or emphysema aquosum, nor is there any debris in her stomach that would suggest drowning,' he explained patiently. 'Also, as I said, she had taken enough strychnine to kill a horse. Several horses, in fact.'

Spilsbury caught Inspector Mount's apologetic look. He was used to such dogged questioning from defence barristers intent on proving their client's innocence. But he did not expect it from a junior detective.

'Of course, you're welcome to read through my notes if you require further clarification?' He proffered a handful of small index cards. Sergeant Stevens looked warily at them, as well he might. Spilsbury prided himself on being the only one able to decipher his own untidy scrawl.

'I'm sure that won't be necessary, doctor,' Mount said hastily. 'But who would want to kill her, I wonder?'

'As to that, I do not know. I daresay it would help if you knew who she was.' Then he saw the look they exchanged. 'But you do know, don't you?' he said.

Once again, the two officers looked at each other. Then Mount said, 'Possibly. We've had a report of a missing woman in Camden. A Miss Jean Hodges. Her friend reported her missing when she didn't turn up for work on Monday morning.'

'And where does she work?'

'Selfridges on Oxford Street. She sold ladies' fashions, apparently.'

That would fit with her well-kept appearance, Spilsbury thought. 'What sort of woman was she?'

'We haven't begun our inquiries yet. We have to make sure we've got the right woman first. But from what we can gather so far, she was very pleasant and quiet. Lived with her sister, kept herself to herself.'

'So how did she end up dead in the Regent's Canal, I wonder?'

This was where Spilsbury differed from many of his colleagues in the medico-legal world. It was rarely considered useful for pathologists to concern themselves with how a person had lived. It mattered little whether they had been lively and outgoing, whether they had been loved or despised. Their task was to work with what was left behind after death, to try to gain answers that might help find out why or how they had died, to ascertain if a crime had been committed and who might be responsible.

But Spilsbury could not help but be intrigued by the dead. Every post-mortem built up a picture for him, not just of a person's death but of the life they had lived. His knife and scalpel uncovered all kinds of secrets about them, as if they were telling their story from beyond the grave.

As Willcox never tired of pointing out, the dead fascinated him far more than the living.

But he was jumping to conclusions with Jean Hodges, he realised. Perhaps appearances were deceptive, and she wasn't such an ordinary woman after all? Perhaps she was unpleasant, vicious, someone who made enemies. She must have upset someone enough for them to want her dead.

'Perhaps she did it herself?' Once again, George Stevens piped up with another asinine observation.

Spilsbury stared at him. 'I beg your pardon?'

'You know what women are like. They're always having fits of this and that, getting nervy and depressed. She might have gone hysterical over something and decided to do away with herself.' He looked from Spilsbury to the inspector and back again. 'We shouldn't rule it out,' Stevens said.

Once again, Spilsbury caught Mount's apologetic look.

'Indeed we can rule it out,' Spilsbury said. 'Unless you're also suggesting that somehow post-mortem she managed to transport herself down to the canal and throw herself in?'

Sergeant Stevens looked sullen. 'She might have gone down to the canal to take it?' he muttered.

'And then got someone to push her body into the water?'

'Or rolled in?'

'It was a freezing cold night and she was not wearing a coat. Or shoes.'

'I imagine that would be the least of her worries if she planned to do herself in. Or she might not have noticed if she was having a fit of nerves?'

Spilsbury glared at him. 'Indeed,' he said through gritted teeth. 'It might well be worth asking if any witness saw a half-naked woman wandering the streets of Camden Town the night before last.'

Sergeant Stevens seemed satisfied as he scribbled down a reminder in his notebook.

'What about the time of death?' Inspector Mount asked, breaking the tension.

'Obviously, one can't be completely precise,' Spilsbury said, returning to his notes. 'But given the temperature of the body compared to the water, and assuming a loss of perhaps four degrees an hour, plus the fact that rigor mortis was no longer present when the body was found, I would expect death to have occurred sometime on Sunday afternoon or evening.'

'You can't be more precise than that?'

'I'm afraid not. I can tell you she was probably in the water for around twelve to fourteen hours by the time she was found, which would have meant she went in around midnight. But I can't say with absolute certainty how long she had been dead beforehand. The absence of liver mortis may be some indication,' he conceded. 'It becomes fixed after around eight hours, which means the body had been moved before that.'

'So death occurred up to eight hours before midnight?' Mount pursed his lips. 'Any time from four o'clock onwards?'

'I'm sorry I can't be more accurate.'

Inspector Mount scribbled in his notebook. 'Well, thank you for your help, doctor,' he said. 'I daresay we'll be back in touch when we've carried out a formal identification.'

His words sparked the question that had been tickling at the back of Spilsbury's mind. 'She lives her with sister, you say?'

'That's right.' He consulted his notes. 'Hilda Hodges. She runs a grocer's on Camden High Street.'

'And yet it was a work colleague who reported her missing? I wonder why her sister didn't come forward?'

'I was wondering the same thing myself, Doctor.' Inspector Mount closed his notebook with a smile. 'I reckon it's time we asked her, don't you?'

Chapter 9

'I'll tell you why I didn't report her missing. Because I didn't know, that's why!'

Hilda Hodges was in her late forties but looked much older. She was short, sturdy and eminently sensible, from her curled mousey hair to her tweed skirt and twinset. She perched on the settee in her tidy little front room, clutching a handkerchief in her fist. The room was silent but for the slow, ponderous ticking of the clock on the mantelpiece and the shouting and squeaking of wheels outside as the costermongers slowly pushed their heavy barrows down the High Street.

As the local beat bobby, Charlie had been given the job of breaking the news of Jean Hodges' death to her sister. But since he was only a lowly constable in uniform, the task of questioning her had been left to George.

It was teatime, and Hilda had been putting up the shutters on the windows of the grocer's shop when they arrived. She had not looked in the slightest bit dismayed to see a uniformed policeman on her doorstep. If anything, she had seemed rather put out at the news that her sister was dead.

'I assumed she'd gone off up to Yorkshire,' she said. 'That was where she said she was going the last time we spoke.'

'And when was that?' George asked.

'Last Friday. I know it was then because I was just about to go off and stay with my friend Joyce in Hammersmith.'

George scribbled down the name in his notebook. 'And when you came back she was gone?'

Hilda nodded. 'Her wardrobe and drawers were all empty. I just thought she'd packed up and gone.'

Charlie looked around him, breathing in the overwhelming smell of violets and beeswax polish. The room was tidy but deathly bland, with sickly green wallpaper, a dull brown moquette couch and a faded rug. There wasn't a single adornment – no paintings, ornaments, not even a lace-trimmed doily to liven the unrelenting dullness.

'You say she was heading up to Yorkshire?' George said. 'Was that for a holiday?'

Hilda's lips tightened. 'She was going to be with him.'

'Who?'

'Her fancy man.'

'Her fancy man?' George leaned forward in his seat, his pencil stub poised. 'Who was that, then?'

'I don't know. She met him through the newspaper. You know, one of those advertisements?'

'You mean the Lonely Hearts column?' Charlie put in, earning himself a quick glare from George.

'That's it.' Hilda's mouth folded even tighter. 'Lonely Hearts, indeed! I ask you, what sort of respectable woman answers an advertisement from a strange man? I told her she'd end up in trouble, and look what happened!'

Charlie stared at her. Hilda Hodges seemed more concerned with being proved right than with the fact that her sister had ended up dead in the canal.

'So how long had she known this man?' George asked.

'A few months, I think. Not that she ever told me anything about him. She was always very secretive, scuttling off to meet him, lying to me about where she was going. As if I didn't know what she was up to! She thought she was so clever, but I could read her like a book.'

'What was he like?'

'How should I know? I told you, she was secretive about him.'

'She must have told you his name, at least? Or shown you a photograph?'

Hilda Hodges shook her head. 'I knew nothing about him.'

'Then how did you know he existed?' Charlie put in.

'Because she was giving him money.'

Charlie glanced sideways at George. 'She gave him money?'

'I noticed it going missing from our account a few weeks ago. Just small amounts, here and there, made out to cash. She said she was taking it out for herself, but then she admitted she was sending it to him.'

'And what did you think about that?'

'I wasn't best pleased, I can tell you!' Her pale blue eyes were frosty. 'It's not as if it was her money. Our father left it to us to share. What right did she have to start dipping into it and sending it to a stranger? I told her, that money was meant for both of us, it wasn't just hers to give away as she pleased.'

The room fell silent, except for the sound of George's pencil scratching away on his notepad.

'And what did she say to that?' he asked.

'She said she needed it because she and this man were planning to get married, and they wanted a place to live. Thank the lord that Father had the good sense to arrange his will so she couldn't take it all without my say-so. He knew as well as I did what she was like.'

'And what was she like?' Charlie asked.

'Gullible,' Hilda said firmly. 'Honestly, she had no common sense. And she was stubborn with it. Once she'd made up her mind about something, she wouldn't listen to reason. If only she'd seen things my way, none of this would have happened.' She stopped, her words catching in her throat. It was the first time Charlie had heard any real emotion in her voice. Perhaps it was all just starting to sink in, he thought.

'So you talked to her about this man?' he prompted gently.

'I tried.'

'And what did she say?'

'We had words. It all got very nasty, and that was when she announced that she was going to pack her bags and move up to Yorkshire to be with him. I told her she could do as she pleased as long as she didn't touch our money, and then I left to go and visit my friend Joyce. I thought a couple of days away would be what we both needed to calm down. But when I got home, she was gone.'

'When was this?' George spoke up.

'I came home on Sunday morning.'

'And it didn't occur to you to report her missing?' Charlie said.

'Why should I? She'd already told me she was leaving. And all her clothes were gone.' She stared at him blankly. 'I hope you're not saying I'm to blame for what happened to her?'

'Of course not, Miss Hodges,' George put in quickly. 'But you're sure there's nothing more you can tell us about him?'

Hilda shook her head, her hard gaze still fixed on Charlie. 'I don't know anything.'

'In that case . . .' George closed his notebook with a snap. 'I think we've got everything we need for now. You will tell us if you do remember anything, won't you?'

'Of course.'

As they rose to leave, a thought suddenly occurred to Charlie.

'Do you have any photographs of your sister, Miss Hodges?' he asked.

Hilda frowned. 'Why?'

'It might be useful to the investigation.'

'Wait there,' she muttered, then she disappeared off into the hall.

'What do you think you're playing at?' George hissed, as soon as she had gone. 'Why do you want a photograph?'

'I thought it might help.'

'You're not part of this investigation. You shouldn't even be here. You were only meant to tell her—'

They were interrupted by Hilda bustling back in, carrying a photograph. 'Will this do?' she asked, handing it to him.

Charlie looked down at the faded photograph. Jean and Hilda were on a picnic, sitting arm in arm. Jean was wearing a flowery dress, while Hilda was shrouded in a dowdy skirt and cardigan very similar to the one she wore now.

In life, Jean Hodges was just as he had imagined. No one would have called her pretty, but she had made the most of herself. Her kind face lit up when she smiled.

Charlie studied her plump features, glad to be able to put a face to the ghastly remains that he had seen lying on the canal towpath. He hadn't wanted to admit it to George, but the real reason he wanted to see a photograph was so he could shake the gruesome image from his mind.

They were more or less shoved out of the shop into the cold January evening. A freezing mist had begun to descend, shrouding the empty shops of Camden High Street. Charlie immediately turned left, heading back towards Mornington

Crescent, but George said, 'Let's go down to the canal while we're here. I want to see where she was pulled out of the water.'

'But it's pitch-dark!' Charlie protested.

George leered at him. 'What's the matter, Beanpole? You frightened?'

'No, but you needn't think I'm going to dive in and save you when you slip arse over tit on the cobbles and end up in the drink.'

Jean Hodges had been found just west of the lock, close to the interchange that the bargemen called Dead Dog Hole. But rather than leading George straight down Camden High Street, Charlie crossed the road to Park Street and then turned right down Arlington Road. Given what Dr Spilsbury had said about her body floating some distance, Charlie thought it might be worth searching from where the railway line crossed the canal. If he was going to dump a body then this was where he would do it.

'Don't you think there was something odd about her?' Charlie asked George as they headed down Arlington Road.

'In what way?'

'She just seemed a bit, I dunno – cold. You'd have thought she'd be more upset about her sister dying like that.'

'Shock,' George said confidently. 'I see it all the time. They can't take it in. Once they see the body, that's when it really hits them. You mark my words, Beanpole, she'll be hysterical by the time she gets out of that mortuary.'

'You might be right.' But Charlie could hardly imagine Hilda Hodges being roused to any kind of emotion, let alone hysterics.

'I'm always right.'

They passed the junction with Wellington Street, and George started to look a little more nervous as they left the hustle and bustle of the High Street behind them and the gas lamps barely pierced the icy gloom.

'Is it much further?' he asked through chattering teeth.

'What's the matter? You frightened?' Charlie parroted his words back to him.

'No, I just – hang on a minute. What's that?'

He turned towards the enormous building around six storeys high, topped off with pointed Gothic pinnacles. Its redbrick facade ran almost the length of the road between Wellington and James Street.

Fifty or so men stood in a snaking line outside the impressive front doors in the centre of the building. Some were huddled in blankets, while others stamped their feet and blew on their hands to keep warm. Many had a desperate, hungry look about them.

'That's Rowton House,' Charlie explained. 'It doesn't open till seven o'clock – those men are waiting for a bed for the night.'

'It's a workhouse?'

'A hostel,' Charlie corrected him. 'It's a good, clean place, not like some of the doss houses they used to have around here. You can get a bed and a bath for sixpence a night.'

George curled his lip. 'That sounds like a workhouse to me.'

'It's mostly for working men,' Charlie said. 'Labourers and market porters and the like. You get all sorts staying there, sometimes for weeks or months at a time. It's a good way of getting cheap lodgings.'

'I'll bet it's got its fair share of ne'er-do-wells and villains, too,' George said.

Charlie bristled. 'If there are, I ain't heard of them,' he said. 'We never get any trouble from Rowton House.'

'We'll see about that.' George started across the road towards it.

'Where are you going?' Charlie asked, falling into step beside him. 'I thought you wanted to see the canal?'

'I want to take a look in here first.' George tapped the side of his nose. 'I've got a sense for these things, Beanpole. And if there was ever a place a killer might hide, I reckon it would be here.'

Chapter 10

There was some hostile grumbling from the men waiting outside as George strode past them to the front of the line. Others just shrank back, eyeing them warily. George ignored them all as he hammered on the front door with his fist.

'You know the rules,' a voice bellowed from inside. 'Doors open at a quarter past seven.'

'It's the police,' George shouted back. 'Open up!'

Bolts groaned as they were drawn back, and a key turned in the lock. A moment later the door opened a crack and a man's face appeared.

'What do you want?'

'We're making enquiries about a murder,' George said. 'We need to ask you some questions.'

The door closed again briefly, then creaked open again.

'You'd best come in,' the man said. 'The rest of you can wait,' he shouted to the men as they surged forward eagerly. 'Another ten minutes and the first lot can come in.'

As they entered the entrance hall, a tall, burly man with a red face and mutton-chop whiskers appeared from a door to their left. Charlie instantly recognised him as ex-military – most likely a sergeant major from his bearing and his no-nonsense, brisk manner.

'I'm Mr Frazer, the superintendent,' he introduced himself gruffly. 'What's all this about a murder?'

'A woman was found dead in the canal two days ago,' George said.

'And what's that got to do with us? We don't have women staying here.'

'We need to know who was staying here on the night of Sunday the eighteenth of January.'

The superintendent rolled his eyes. 'You do know we have room here for nearly a thousand men?'

'You keep records, don't you?'

'Of course. But I don't know how much good it will do you to know their names. If one of them did murder your woman they would have certainly moved on by now. And I daresay they would have given a false name.'

He had a point, Charlie thought. But George looked stubborn.

'All the same, we'd like to see your records,' he insisted.

The superintendent looked as if he might argue, then gave in.

'Wait in the reading room.' He indicated a set of doors going off to the right. 'I might be a while,' he added, with a sour look at George.

He went off, slamming the office door behind him.

'Did you hear that?' George muttered. 'I reckon he's got something to hide.'

'I just don't think he was keen on all that extra work.'

'It's what he's paid for.' George crossed to a door at the far end of the entrance hall. 'What's in here, I wonder?'

'He told us to wait in the reading room . . .' Charlie pointed to the doors the superintendent had indicated.

'Yes, but I want to have a poke about first. Honestly, Beanpole, how do you ever hope to become a detective if you only look at what people want you to see?' He stuck his head through the door, then closed it again quickly.

61

'Well?' Charlie said. 'What was it?'

'A broom cupboard.' George was tight-lipped as he threw open another door. 'Ah, now this one leads somewhere . . .'

He stepped inside and the door closed behind him. Charlie hesitated for a moment, then followed him.

His feet disappeared from under him and he tumbled headlong down a short flight of steps. He had just picked himself up when the light flicked on to reveal George's smirking face.

'Watch it, Beanpole.' He grinned. 'There are some stairs there.'

Charlie said nothing as he dusted down his trousers. George was already making his way through another door that led to a long corridor. It ran the length of the building, so far that the dim electric light barely penetrated the far end.

'What have we here?' George walked down the passageway, looking left and right. 'It looks like some kind of dormitory.'

On either side was a row of doors, all open to reveal cubicles, separated from each other by wooden partitions. Each cubicle was furnished with a narrow single bed with a chair beside it. There was a small window above each bed, with a shelf and three iron hooks for the men to hang their clothes.

'Look at this place,' George shook his head. 'Imagine ending up here.'

Charlie could imagine it only too well. Many of his old comrades from France had found themselves in such places or worse.

'Not exactly a home from home, is it?' George tested the bed with his hand. 'Mind you, I bet they steal everything that isn't nailed down.'

'Not everyone who falls on hard times is a criminal,' Charlie said.

'What would you call them, then?'

From beyond the door came the sound of shuffling foot-steps. They must be letting them in, Charlie thought. He could hear the doorman barking out directions as he checked their tickets.

'Unlucky,' he said.

George sneered. 'You make your own luck, Beanpole. Take it from me, most of the men who end up here are either drunks or thieves, or too lazy to find work.'

Charlie fought to keep his temper. 'It ain't easy to find work when no one will take you on.'

'I'm sure there's work for those that want it.'

George stretched out on the bed, his boots on the blanket. Charlie stared at him with loathing. But before he could reply, the doors flew open and the men started to stream in. A couple of them stopped briefly at the sight of a police officer standing in front of them, then shuffled awkwardly past.

'We'd best be going back upstairs . . .' Charlie said, but no sooner had the words left his lips than there was a commotion in the walkway, and a moment later a young man appeared in the doorway to the cubicle where they stood, trapping them inside.

He stopped dead, staring at them both with wild eyes for a moment. Then, without any warning, he started screaming.

'What the—?' George shot to his feet. 'What's happened? Has he gone mad?'

Charlie did not move. He recognised the desperate terror on the man's face, a look he had seen so many times before in the trenches.

The other men had obviously seen it too. They paid the young man no heed as they shuffled past to claim their cubicles.

Suddenly the man let out a cry, lurched forward and threw himself at George, knocking him off his feet and pinning him to the ground.

'Don't just stand there, man – hit him with your truncheon!' George's voice emerged as a strangled cry as he tried to fight the man off.

'That won't be necessary.'

Out of nowhere, another man shouldered his way past Charlie and pulled the young man off George and back on to his feet.

'All clear, corporal,' he said in a firm voice. 'You can stand down.'

For a moment it did not seem as if the young man had heard him, as his cries of terror still rang the length of the room. But the older man turned him by the shoulders to face him, staring into his eyes until his screams gradually subsided to a whimper. He trembled like a sapling, tears running down his face.

'It was a direct hit, captain,' he whispered.

'I know,' the older man said. 'Lucky we all lived through it. Now let's go and find you a smoke, shall we?'

He led him away without a word or a look in their direction. George struggled to his feet.

'Why didn't you hit him?' he demanded. 'He could have killed me.'

'He was trying to save you,' Charlie said. 'He thought we were under attack.' He followed the two men with his eyes. The older man held the door open and ushered his young friend through it as tenderly as if he were his own son. 'Shell shock,' he explained to George. 'Poor bloke should really be in hospital.'

'He should be locked up somewhere, that's for sure.' George smoothed back his hair. 'Now do you see why I wanted to come here? That's exactly the sort who'd murder a woman.'

'He's more likely to do harm to himself than anyone else.' He turned to face George. 'Does he look to you like the sort who could woo Jean Hodges, let alone work out how to poison her?'

Before George could reply, the superintendent appeared. 'There you are,' he growled. 'I thought I told you to wait in the reading room? As if I've got time to chase around, looking for you two.' He eyed them both with dislike. 'I've got those records in my office, if you want to see them?'

'We do,' George said firmly. As they followed the superintendent up the stairs back to the entrance hall, he leaned over and whispered to Charlie, 'I've got a feeling about this, Beanpole. Even if that madman didn't kill Jean Hodges, I reckon someone here might know something about it.'

Chapter 11

'You should have heard the way he spoke to the superintendent,' Charlie said. 'Talk about showing us up! Honest to God, I wished the ground would open up and swallow me.'

'That sounds about right,' his wife Annie said grimly. Like Charlie, she had known George Stevens since they were kids. 'He always was above himself.'

'Above himself, my arse,' Charlie's mother Elsie said with feeling. 'Just because his family came into money and moved to Blackheath. They forget we all remember them when they didn't have a pot to piss in. I remember when his mother used to send the kids round the market, begging for specked apples.'

It was nearly eleven o'clock by the time Charlie had got home to Southwark. George had insisted they copy down every single name from the superintendent's records. The children had long since gone to bed, but Annie had kept him some bread and dripping for his supper. Charlie wolfed it down gratefully as he sat by the fire, watched by his wife and his mother.

They should have been in bed a long time ago, he thought. They had to be in Borough Market at the crack of dawn. But bless them, they had both wanted to see him home safe. Or more likely, to hear the latest instalment in the Jean Hodges case. After two years of having nothing more exciting than a pub brawl or the occasional burglary to tell them about, Charlie finally had something interesting to report.

'Anyway, it sounds like a complete waste of time to me,' Elsie said. 'Even if the killer was staying there, I daresay he would have made himself scarce by now.'

'Try telling that to George Stevens,' Charlie sighed. 'He kept reminding me he was the detective and I was just a constable.'

'Big-headed sod!' Annie said. 'You're twice the detective he'll ever be.'

'You'd be where he is now if you hadn't been fighting for your country,' his mother chimed in.

Charlie looked from his wife to his mother and back again. *They've changed their tune*, he thought. There was a time when they never wanted him to join the police force.

It had been his dream for as long as he could remember. But as his father made clear, people where they came from did not join the police force. Not if they wanted their neighbours to go on speaking to them, at any rate.

Southwark was a close-knit community, lurking in the shadow of London Bridge. Ever since Shakespeare's time, the area had had a certain reputation. Back in the old days, the toffs from the City left their respectable lives behind to cross the river and enjoy all kinds of dark, forbidden thrills, from bear baiting and bull fighting to gambling and brothels, and everything in between.

The dark streets and narrow alleyways, hemmed in by looming wharves and warehouses at the river's edge, still echoed with the illicit secrets of its past. It was home to gangs, thieves and swindlers and pickpockets, men and women who would rob you blind and think nothing of it. Even his own wife Annie came from a long line of petty criminals. But everyone was in the same boat, so they were all rough and ready together.

His father had been right. To join the police would have set him apart, made him and his family outcasts, people not to be trusted. And it would have lost him the only woman he had ever loved, his childhood sweetheart Annie. Her family would never have allowed her to get involved with a traitor like him.

Not only that, his father was growing older, and struggling with the hard life of a costermonger. Charlie was his only son, and so it was his duty to take over the family business.

For all those reasons, he had put his dreams aside and buckled down to a life of early morning trips to the wholesalers, hefting sacks of potatoes and selling his wares. Until the war came along.

Along with thousands of others, Charlie left his wife and babies behind, and went off to do his duty.

He almost did not come home. He was caught in enemy crossfire at Passchendaele, took a bullet to the chest and spent months in hospital, his life hanging in the balance.

Nearly losing him must have changed his family's attitude. When Charlie finally returned home, they urged him to follow his dream.

'Life's too bloody short, mate,' his father had said, fighting back tears. A week later, Charlie had gone off to enlist yet again, this time with the Metropolitan Police.

Annie refilled their cups with cocoa from the pot on the stove and they talked about the case.

'I keep thinking about that poor woman,' Elsie sighed. 'She must have been so happy, thinking she'd found herself a boyfriend at last. And then he killed her.'

'You don't know it was her boyfriend,' Annie pointed out.

'Who else would it be?' Elsie slurped her cocoa. 'I daresay he was one of them gigolos, preying on daft women.'

'That's not a very nice thing to say.' Annie looked reproachful.

'It's what her sister thought, too,' Charlie said.

'You see?' Elsie said. 'She sounds like a sensible woman to me.'

'Bitter and jealous, more like,' Annie muttered. She thoughtfully sipped her cocoa. 'Anyway, why would he murder her, if he was after her money? Surely it would make more sense to keep her alive? He ain't going to get his hands on it after she's dead, is he?'

'Unless they were married?' Elsie said. 'Here, you don't think they wed in secret, do you?' she asked Charlie. 'He could make a claim on that inheritance of hers then. Or he might have taken out an insurance policy on her life. Like that other bloke – you know, the brides in the bath?'

'George Joseph Smith,' Charlie said.

'That's the one. Murdered three of them before he was caught, he did. Mind, Dr Spilsbury soon put a stop to him!' Elsie's eyes gleamed with pride. She had not been able to contain herself since Charlie told her he had actually spoken to the great man.

'It's a thought,' Charlie conceded. 'I suppose it might be a good idea to see if anyone comes forward with a claim.'

'Well, he'd be daft if he did,' Annie said. 'You'd know straight away it was him, wouldn't you?'

'Perhaps it was the other way round?' Elsie said. 'Perhaps she wanted to get married and he didn't?'

'He could have just said no,' Charlie pointed out. 'He didn't have to do her in.'

'Yes, but what if he was already married? What if she was threatening to tell his wife? He might do something desperate if he had a lot to lose. You never know what people will do when they're pushed into a corner, do you?'

Annie shook her head. 'No, I reckon you've got it wrong, Ma. If he did kill her it was probably because she wouldn't let him have any more money. You never know, she might have taken her sister's words to heart. She thought she'd test him out by seeing what he'd do if she stopped paying.'

Charlie looked from one to the other with a grin. 'Listen to you two! You're both wasted on that stall. You should be at Scotland Yard.'

'We'll leave that to you, love,' Annie said.

'Oh no, I won't be involved. That's a job for the detectives. I'm only a humble bobby, as George Stevens never gets tired of reminding me!'

'Then you'll just have to prove him wrong, won't you?' Annie pointed her finger at him, fire flaring in her eyes. 'You listen to me, Charlie Abbott. This is your big chance to show what you're made of. You deserve to be a detective, and I want you to show them that!'

'She's right, Charlie.' Elsie nodded. 'I don't always say that, but for once it's true.'

Charlie looked from one to the other. They were both so strong, how the hell they hadn't killed each other by now he had no idea. Especially now his mother was widowed and they all lived under the same roof. The atmosphere in the little terraced house in Thrale Street could be tetchy at times, to say the least.

But the one thing they had in common was their love for him. And he knew that his career had come at a cost for both of them. Annie had become estranged from some of her family over it. And Charlie would always feel guilty that overwork might have contributed to his own father's death at the age of fifty. God knows how long he might have gone on if he hadn't had to carry the burden of the stall alone. Now his mother was doing the same, getting up before dawn and standing out in all weathers.

But that only made him even more determined to succeed. Whatever it took, one day he would become a detective and make his family proud. He owed them that.

And he would start by finding out who killed Jean Hodges.

Chapter 12

February 1920

It was the day Elizabeth Franklin had been dreading, but she did everything she could to hide her anxiety as she sat with her niece and nephew in the book-lined office of James's solicitor, Frederick Marchmont. If this was the day she was to lose everything, then she was determined to do so with dignity.

She had already made her preparations. Her belongings were all packed up in a trunk, ready to leave. She had booked a room in a boarding house in St John's Wood. Elizabeth had made discreet enquiries and found one she was satisfied had an impeccable reputation. The landlady had assured her that she only took in respectable ladies, no fast types and certainly no gentlemen.

'Ladies such as yourself, who find themselves in altered circumstances.' She had looked Elizabeth up and down when she had said it, clearly trying to place whether she was a war widow, a heartbroken bride-to-be, or one of the thousands of spinsters whose marriage prospects had died on the fields of France.

Elizabeth did not care to find herself keeping company with such women. She did not want to be the subject of anyone's pity or scorn. And yet this was the situation in which she now found herself, no longer mistress of a grand house, but instead living out her days with the other desperate, forgotten women.

She felt a light pressure on her hand and looked up to find Lydia watching her, her grey eyes filled with tenderness. Elizabeth checked her irritation. She knew her niece meant well, but her sentimentality irked her. She moved her hand away and turned instead to the solicitor on the other side of the mahogany desk.

'How much longer is this going to take?' she said.

'We can't begin until Mrs Franklin gets here.'

Elizabeth stared at him with dislike. She had never met Frederick Marchmont before. Up until recently, all her family's dealings had been with his father, Ernest. But he had retired three months earlier and his son had taken over. The junior Mr Marchmont was in his forties, a rather finicky-looking little man with a beard trimmed into a neat point. A purple silk handkerchief sprouted from his top pocket, matching his cravat. He was altogether too flamboyant for Elizabeth's liking.

'I do hope a terrible accident hasn't befallen her?' Matthew murmured under his breath.

'Matthew!' Lydia hissed. 'That's an awful thing to say.'

Elizabeth looked down at her hands and tried not to smile. Really, her nephew could be incorrigible at times. She knew she shouldn't encourage him, but it was hard not to laugh at some of the outrageous things he came out with.

Although Frederick Marchmont did not seem to agree, judging by the stern look he sent him across the desk. Matthew had already told her what a stickler he was. He had come in like a new broom, determined to make his mark on his ailing father's practice. Matthew was finding the new, disciplined regime very tiresome indeed.

72

Poor Matthew, he did not have the temperament for office life at all. Elizabeth had said as much to his father, but James was determined that his son should find a suitable career.

'God knows, it's about time he did something useful,' he had said.

Had it been anyone else but Matthew, Elizabeth would have agreed. But in spite of all his terrible shortcomings, she had a soft spot for her nephew.

She had tried to plead his case. Was it any surprise Matthew hadn't been able to settle at anything since he came home from the war? He must have seen some terrible things while he was away. Surely James could give him more time to discover what he really wanted to do?

'You don't have to tell me how hard the war was,' was her brother's growling response. 'I know you're blind to my son's faults, Elizabeth. But you know as well as I do that, given the choice, Matthew will not settle to anything except frequenting the gaming dens of St James's Street.'

He had a point, but it still wrenched at her to see the poor boy so confined. Matthew was a clever young man. He was made for much greater things than drawing up contracts and filing paperwork.

She jerked upright, every muscle in her body tensing at the sound of a knock on the door. A moment later Violet entered in a flurry, looking breathless, her cheeks flushed.

'I'm sorry I'm late, Mr Marchmont,' she addressed herself to the solicitor, ignoring Elizabeth and the others. 'The maid was supposed to be watching my son but she went out, so I had to take him to my brother's in Southwark.'

Elizabeth could feel her sister-in-law glaring at her as she said it. She had to admit, sending Mary out on a last-minute errand was a petty act, hardly worthy of her. But she was still glad she had done it.

It served her right for not taking Elizabeth's advice about a nanny.

They all waited in tense silence as Violet took her seat on Lydia's other side, at the far end of the row. Her sister-in-law's expression was carefully neutral, Elizabeth noticed. At least she had the good grace not to gloat.

But then, she could afford to be magnanimous. By the end of today, Violet would have everything and she would have nothing.

Once again, Lydia reached for her hand and this time Elizabeth did not pull away. At least she would not be alone in her misery. Lydia had agreed to move to the boarding house with her. Elizabeth was relieved. She did not want to imagine the perils that might befall her, left to her stepmother's care.

And then there was poor Matthew. Elizabeth glanced across at her nephew. She had been pressing him for some time to make arrangements for when Violet took over the house. But typical Matthew, he had done nothing about it.

'I'm sure something will come up,' was all he said.

Now he lounged in his chair, his face surprisingly calm. Only his fingers, relentlessly picking away at his cuticles, gave away his inner strain.

The solicitor picked up the thick brown envelope containing her brother's last will and testament. The document that would damn them all.

'Shall we begin?' he said.

Chapter 13

'No!'

The word filled Elizabeth's mind, but it did not come from her lips. It was Lydia who uttered the cry.

'No, it can't be. There must be some mistake!'

'There is no mistake, I assure you,' Frederick Marchmont said. 'The will was witnessed and signed by my own father.'

'Then – then it must be an old will, surely? Those aren't Daddy's wishes. He would never do such a thing!'

'Oh, do be quiet, Lydia!' Matthew snapped. 'You heard what Mr Marchmont said. Everything is in order.'

'Quite.' The solicitor looked pained. 'According to the date on this document, Dr Franklin changed his will on the twentieth of June last year.'

'But I don't understand . . .' Lydia retreated into silence, tears rising in her grey eyes. 'Daddy wouldn't . . . He couldn't . . . It's too cruel.'

Elizabeth was scarcely aware of her niece beside her as she sat numbly staring at Frederick Marchmont. All she could hear were the solicitor's words, replaying in her head over and over again.

'To my sister Elizabeth, I give, devise and bequeath all the rest, residue and remainder of my estate, whether real or personal, and wheresoever situated . . .'

It was hers. The house, his fortune, everything. It all seemed so bizarre, she could scarcely take it in.

And neither, it seemed, could her sister-in-law. Violet said nothing as she sat rigid, the colour gone from her face, her hands knotted tightly in her lap.

Ten pounds. That was all James had left his wife and her son. It was not a paltry sum, but it was certainly no fortune either. Nothing like anyone of them had been expecting.

And certainly nothing like Violet had been expecting, judging by the stricken look on her face.

'Well, I suppose that's that, then.' Matthew rose to his feet.

'Matthew!' Lydia whispered.

'What? Surely there's nothing more to be said?' He looked at the solicitor. 'What's done is done. Isn't that right, Mr Marchmont?'

'That is correct. Unless anyone wishes to contest the will?' His gaze shifted expectantly to Violet.

'I shouldn't think that will be likely,' Matthew interrupted. 'Our stepmother has always maintained she didn't marry our father for his money. Isn't that right, Violet?'

Violet stared back at Matthew, her dark eyes so full of hatred they sent a chill over Elizabeth's skin. It was as if someone had opened a window, letting in the cold February air.

What a clever little beast her nephew was, she thought. He had cornered Violet like an animal, forcing her to either reveal her true nature or remain silent forever.

Elizabeth eyed her sister-in-law. Cornered animals had a tendency to come out with their teeth and claws bared, ready to fight for their life.

But when she finally spoke, her voice was calm, almost resigned.

'Your brother's right, Lydia. If those are your father's wishes, then we should abide by them.'

She rose to her feet, and for a moment Elizabeth almost admired her for the dignity she managed to muster. She handled it almost like a lady.

'I'll go back to the house and pack our belongings,' she said stiffly. 'I'll be gone by this evening.'

'No!' Lydia gave a muffled sob.

Elizabeth kept her gaze fixed on Violet. She could afford to be magnanimous now her own future was secure.

'There is no hurry,' she said. 'Of course you may stay until you find somewhere else to live.'

'I'd never stay where I wasn't wanted.'

'And yet you've lived under our roof for the past five years,' Matthew muttered.

'That's enough, Matthew,' Elizabeth warned.

Violet shot him a cold look, then turned back to Elizabeth. 'You've got what you wanted,' she said. 'Enjoy it while it lasts, won't you?'

And then she was gone.

Lydia was still whimpering as the three of them left the solicitor's office some time later. There had been paperwork to do, and documents to be signed. But finally they stood together in the frosty February afternoon.

'I still think Violet should contest the will,' Lydia said. She put a hand up to hold onto her hat as a sudden gust of wind tried to tear it from her head. 'Thomas is our brother. It's only right that Daddy should have provided for him.'

'He did provide for him,' Matthew said. 'Or weren't you listening?'

'Ten pounds is hardly enough to bring up a child!'

'Violet will manage. I'm sure she can be very – resourceful.' Matthew smirked. 'Anyway, why are you so concerned about our beloved stepmother, when it's Aunt Elizabeth you should be thinking about?' He turned to smile at her.

77

'This is wonderful news, don't you think? And I for one think she deserves it. Father knew how much she loved the house. He obviously wanted it to stay in our family.'

It took a moment for it to sink in. The house was hers. For the first time in her life, she was no longer the begrudged house guest, the unfortunate spinster dependent on the charity of others. She was a woman of property, of substance and standing.

Enjoy it while it lasts, won't you?

Her sister-in-law's parting shot came back to her. Was it just the bitterness of a woman who had gambled and lost, Elizabeth wondered, or was there a threat behind her words?

She pushed away the thought. Violet could not hurt her now.

No one could.

Chapter 14

Queen's Buildings had been built fifty years earlier on the site of the former Queen's Bench Prison in Bermondsey, to house the poor of South London. It was supposed to be an improvement on the squalid slums they had previously inhabited, but the grim, five-storey slabs of whitish brick still had the oppressive air of the prison about them. More than three thousand people crammed into six hundred dwellings, divided between blocks that joined at right angles, overlooking closed-in yards where children played and washing hung from limp lines that never saw the sunlight.

Violet hauled her heavy bag up the stairs to the third floor. The leather strap of the bag cut into her fingers and she shifted its weight, then turned to head up the next flight of stairs. She had made the same journey so many times, she knew the feel of each worn stone step before her foot touched it.

She paused on the second-floor landing and breathed in the familiar smell of stale cooking, unwashed bodies and the acrid tang of factory smoke.

Above her, silhouetted in a small patch of fading daylight, three young men lounged on the landing, smoking and laughing. As Violet went to move past them, she could feel them sizing up her fur-trimmed coat and the bag she carried.

'You lost, love?' one of them called after her.

'No.'

Violet kept on climbing. The young men fell into step behind her.

'Can I carry that bag for you?' one of them offered. 'It looks heavy.'

The other men sniggered. Without turning round, Violet said, 'I'm all right, thanks.'

'It's not right to let a lady struggle. Here—'

As the young man made a grab for the bag, Violet ducked, made a quick swipe at her boot, then turned on him.

'I said no!' she spat out. 'And I'd take that for an answer, if I were you.'

'S'all right, love.' The young man backed off sharply, his hands held up, eyes fixed on the flashing blade Violet now wielded. 'We was only trying to be helpful.'

Violet watched them ambling down the stairs. It was a long time since she'd had cause to use the blade she always kept in her boot, but thankfully old habits died hard.

She reached the third floor, made her way to the far end of the walkway, and pushed open the door.

'Mickey?' As she opened the door, she heard Pistol's frenzied barking and the scrabbling of his paws on the oilcloth floor. A moment later he came charging up the passageway, ears flattened and teeth bared, only to skid to a halt when he saw her.

'All right, boy?' Violet put out a hand to greet him. There was some movement further down the passageway and the next moment Mickey appeared from the gloom in his vest and braces.

'All right, Vi? Come to collect your boy, have you? He's been as good as gold – here, what's wrong, love? You look like you've seen a ghost.'

Violet did not reply. She picked up her bag and walked past him into the hall.

The passageway was narrow, with a room on either side and a WC at the far end. Violet turned left into the room that served as a living room and kitchen. A thin green curtain was strung from the ceiling, hiding the stove, the copper and the sink.

A fleeting image of the bathroom at Gloucester Gate came into her mind, with its deep tub and soft, thick towels, but she pushed it away. She could not let herself think about that, not now.

Thomas sat on the rug in front of the hissing gas heater, playing with his bricks. Violet bent down, gathered him in her arms and hugged him fiercely until he wriggled out of her arms.

Mickey watched them. Even Pistol had picked up on the mood and started to whimper.

'Vi, what's happened?'

Violet crossed to the kitchen area. She snatched up the kettle and filled it, leaning over the pile of unwashed dishes on the scrubbed wooden draining board. For once, she was too weary to take her brother to task over his poor housekeeping.

'He's left everything to Elizabeth,' she said, her words nearly lost over the sound of running water.

There was a long silence. Violet could tell Mickey was struggling to make sense of her words. She didn't blame him; she was still trying to understand it herself.

'No,' he said finally. 'It can't be. There must be some mistake?'

'There's no mistake, believe me.'

'But what about you and Tommy? Don't you get anything?'

'Ten pounds.'

'What?'

81

'That's how much he left us.'

Once again Mickey was silent as he struggled to take in what she was saying. Violet turned back to watch the kettle as it bubbled on the hob.

It had been buried among other paltry bequests to distant relatives and charitable organisations. Even Mary the maid had been mentioned before her. She had also received ten pounds.

Mr Marchmont had looked almost embarrassed as he read out the bequest.

It wasn't the amount, it really wasn't. It was the thought, the fear that somehow, even for a moment, James might have doubted her love for him.

Had he listened to the gossips? He always brushed off the comments people made about the difference in their ages, their situations, the haste with which they had wed. But perhaps those barbs had hit their mark after all.

And what about Thomas? Her gaze strayed to her son, perched on the edge of the grubby couch, still intent on his bricks. Surely he deserved better treatment than this from his own father?

Unless James suspected he wasn't his son? If he allowed himself to believe that Violet was after his money, what other dark thoughts might he have conjured? Especially with Elizabeth whispering in his ear, spreading her poison as Violet knew she did.

That was what truly hurt. That after all the time they had spent together, all the love they had given each other, her husband must have still doubted her feelings for him.

The kettle boiled and she went to pick it up from the hob, but Mickey gently took it from her.

'Sit down,' he said. 'I'll do it.'

Violet sat down at the kitchen table. A moment later Mickey set a glass down in front of her.

Violet stared at it. 'What's this?'

'Brandy, for the shock. You look as if you could do with it.'

Violet took the glass reluctantly, wincing as the amber liquid blazed a fiery trail down her throat. She had a feeling if she started to drink, she might never stop.

Mickey sat down opposite her. 'You can fight this,' he said.

She shook her head. 'I can't.'

'But I'm sure you'd have a good case to appeal . . .'

'And prove I'm the gold digger everyone thinks I am?'

Violet took another gulp of her drink, gripping the glass to stop her hand shaking.

Our stepmother has always maintained she didn't marry our father for his money. Isn't that right, Violet?

'It ain't about that, Vi. It's about standing up for what's right. Do it for the little lad, if not for yourself.'

He nodded towards Thomas, still playing with his bricks while Pistol watched over him.

'I can look after him,' she said. 'I don't need them, or their money.'

'Yes, but it ain't fair, is it? The boy's lost his home and his inheritance. You can't just stand by and let that happen.'

'I said I'll look after him!'

She knew her brother was right, and that she was letting Thomas down. He had lost his father and now he had lost the only home he had ever known, too. But her pride would not let her go begging to the courts, to have other people standing in judgement of her.

'So what will you do now?' Mickey said.

'What I've always done, I suppose. Carry on somehow. Get a job and find a place to live.' Life had taught her to be a survivor. And no matter how much she hurt, she knew she had to get back on her feet and start fighting back as quickly as she could. 'I wondered if Thomas and I could stay here for a bit?'

'You don't even have to ask, girl. You and Tommy can have the bedroom, and I'll sleep on the couch.'

'Thanks, Mickey. It won't be for long, just till I get back on my feet.'

'Stay as long as you like. You've done enough for me over the years, it's about time I did something for you in return.'

Tears of gratitude sprang to her eyes and she dashed them away impatiently. There would be a time for weeping when she was alone. For now she had to pick herself up and get on, for Thomas's sake, if not for herself.

That she might prove the gossips wrong.

Oh, she'd prove them wrong, all right. It was what she had been doing all her life.

Chapter 15

'But I've already talked to the police.'

'I know that, Miss Patterson. I've just been sent to get some background information.'

Charlie could not meet the young woman's eye as he said it. In spite of his uniform, he felt like an absolute fraud.

It was a wonder he had made it to the West End. He had nearly got off the underground train at King's Cross. Then he had spent another ten minutes walking up and down Oxford Street, dodging the busy Saturday morning shoppers, until he'd finally found the courage to walk into the grand, baroque building that housed Selfridges department store.

It had all seemed like a good idea when he talked to Annie about it at home. Where would be the harm in speaking to Jean Hodges' friend again, to see if there was anything that might have been missed? It was hardly interfering in the investigation to ask a few more questions, was it?

And besides, it wasn't as if the police were getting anywhere with it. Nearly a month had passed since Jean Hodges' death, and they seemed no nearer to catching the killer.

But every moment he expected to be found out. He was surprised the manager of the ladies' fashions department had not noticed his knees knocking when Charlie first approached her. He was risking his badge, and he knew it. If anyone were to find out . . .

It was too late now, he thought, as he sat in the manager's office across the desk from Dolly Patterson.

Her name suited her, with her fluffy blond curls and wide china-doll eyes. She was in her late twenties, the same age as Charlie.

'What do you want to know?' she asked.

'What was Miss Hodges like?'

She looked relieved, as if this was an easy question to answer. 'Oh, she was lovely. Very kind-hearted, she'd do anything for anyone. She really took me under her wing when I started working here. And so much fun, too. We had a right laugh sometimes. Although don't tell Mr Trevis that, will you?' She put her hand over her mouth to stifle a giggle.

'Did she have many friends?'

'Of course, everyone liked Jeannie.'

'What about admirers?'

Dolly's smile slipped a fraction. 'What do you mean?'

'Did she have many men friends?'

'I don't know what you're insinuating, but Jeannie wasn't like that at all,' Dolly bristled. 'She was a decent woman.'

'I'm not saying she wasn't,' Charlie assured her hastily. 'I just wondered if she had said anything to you about a man she'd been courting.'

'Jeannie? Courting?' Dolly looked blank. 'That's the first I've heard about it.'

'She didn't mention him to you? Someone she met through the Lonely Hearts column of the newspaper?'

'Not once. The only man she ever spoke about was her fiancé.'

'She was engaged?' Charlie scribbled a quick note.

Dolly nodded. 'He was killed at Neuve Chappelle. Poor Jeannie, she was heartbroken. She used to say she'd never get another chance at love.' She looked down at her engagement ring and then back up at Charlie. 'And she met him through the newspaper, you say? I wonder why she didn't say anything to me.'

'She was quite secretive about him, according to her sister.'

Dolly screwed up her nose. 'Yes, well, I'm not surprised about that. She was probably frightened Hilda would scare him off.'

'What makes you say that?'

'She was always bossing her about, she never wanted her to have any life. She would have had her working in that grocer's shop all the time if she'd had her way. Poor Jeannie, I reckon she actually used to look forward to coming to work to get away from her!'

'They didn't get on, then?'

'I told you, Jeannie got on with everyone. She wouldn't hear a bad word said against Hilda. She reckoned she owed her a lot. But it wouldn't have done for me, being cooped up together in that cramped little flat. It must have got her down sometimes, don't you think?'

'I really couldn't say.'

'Well, I think so. And if she found herself a man, then good luck to her. She deserved to find someone to make her happy.'

Even if it could have got her killed? Charlie thought.

As he was taking his leave, Dolly said, 'So how did it happen?'

'I beg your pardon?'

'Did she drown? I asked the detective, but he couldn't say.'

Charlie wasn't sure he could say, either. But the words were out before he could stop them.

'We believe Miss Hodges was poisoned.'

'Poisoned!' Dolly Patterson looked shocked. 'How awful. Poor Jeannie. Who on earth would do such a thing to her?'

Something tickled at the back of Charlie's brain, too fleeting and unformed to be called a memory. He tried to turn his attention towards it, but it was already gone.

'That's what we're trying to find out, Miss Patterson,' he said.

Hilda Hodges was at the back of the shop slicing bacon for a customer when Charlie arrived just before lunchtime.

'You'll have to wait,' she said tersely as she bustled past, a brown-paper package in her hand.

He hesitated for a moment by the door, then meekly joined the queue of customers lining up to be served. He could feel everyone watching him from the corners of their eyes, whispering amongst themselves.

Finally, it was his turn.

'Does it have to be now?' Hilda said. 'Saturday's our busy day.'

'I'm sorry, Miss Hodges. I just wanted to ask you a couple more questions, if that's all right?'

She sighed heavily. 'I suppose it will have to be, won't it? But you'll have to be quick or I'll have a riot on my hands.'

There were groans from the rest of the people in the queue as she ushered them out of the shop.

'My father would turn in his grave if he saw me turning away custom,' Hilda muttered as she closed the door. 'If they all end up going to the Co-op, I shall know who to blame.' She put up the closed sign and turned to face him. 'Well?' she said.

Charlie fumbled in his pocket for his notebook and pencil. 'I was just wondering if you'd managed to remember any more about your sister's mystery man?'

Hilda sighed. 'Is that it? I would have told you by now if I had.'

'Yes. Yes, of course. Only I went to Selfridges and spoke to her friend just now, and she knew nothing about him.'

'Would that be Dolly Patterson?' Hilda's mouth curled. 'Well, I'm not really surprised. My sister wasn't that close to her.'

'Really? Miss Patterson gave me the impression they were good friends.'

'She would, wouldn't she? She's that type. Likes to think she's in the centre of everything. But to be honest, she got on Jean's nerves.'

'So did she have any other friends she might have confided in?'

'Not that I know of.' Hilda went back behind the counter, closing the wooden flap behind her. 'She kept herself to herself. We both did. Father didn't like anyone knowing all our business.'

Charlie flicked back through his notes. 'Your father died last year, is that right?' Hilda nodded. 'And he ran the shop before you took over?'

'That's right.' Her chin lifted slightly. 'Jean and I grew up here, living upstairs. Our parents ran it together until our mother died ten years ago. Then I took over helping my father until he retired and handed it over to me.'

'But not your sister?'

Hilda allowed herself a small smile. 'I told you before, he didn't trust her. He knew she didn't have a proper head for business. I was the only one allowed to deal with the finances.'

Charlie watched as she picked up a cloth and swiped it over the polished wood counter. She was wearing a flowery dress and pink cardigan, which somehow did not seem to suit her as much as her dour twinset and tweed.

'What about your sister's fiancé?' he asked.

Hilda looked up at him sharply. 'What?'

'You didn't mention she'd been engaged before.'

She hesitated for a moment, then went back to her dusting. 'I didn't think it was important. He died years ago.'

'He was killed in the war?'

'Dolly Patterson had a lot to say for herself, I see?' Hilda raised an eyebrow.

'That must have been terrible for your sister, losing the man she loved?'

'Oh, she was heartbroken. Cried and cried, she did. Father and I thought she'd never get over it. But I told her, it's better to have loved and lost than never to have loved at all.'

'Very comforting, I'm sure,' Charlie murmured. Hilda sent him a sharp look.

'It's true,' she said. 'There are lots of women who'll never get the chance, thanks to this wretched war—' She stopped suddenly, pressing her lips together.

'What?' Charlie said.

'I've suddenly thought of something.'

Charlie leaned forward, across the counter. 'Yes?'

'Do you mind? You're getting fingermarks all over my fresh polish.' Hilda shooed him off. 'I'm sure I remember her telling me he'd fought in the war.'

Charlie's heart sank slightly. Him and millions of others, he thought. 'Anything else? Did she mention a regiment, or a particular battle?'

'She might have said he'd won a medal.'

'I thought she didn't tell you anything about him?'

'It wasn't like we sat down and had a cosy chat about it!' Hilda snapped. 'It just came out, the last time we spoke. I was asking her why she thought she could trust him, and she told me he was some sort of war hero.' She snorted. 'A likely story, I reckon. Just like all the others he was spinning her.'

'What kind of medal?'

'Eh?'

'You said he'd won a medal. What sort of medal was it?'

'I don't know, do I? How many medals are there?' Hilda glared back at him. 'Anyway, we were arguing at the time, so I didn't bother to stop and ask her about it. I just recall her saying he'd been given this medal, and it was the same one as her Leslie had been given just after he died.'

'And what medal was that?'

'I already told you, I don't know! To be honest with you, I never listened half the time when Jean was prattling on. Anyway, for some reason she seemed to think that meant she could trust this man.' She shook her head. 'That was my sister all over. She'd believe anything anyone told her. But if you ask me, there was no medal in the first place. He was probably one of those cowards who never even went to war!'

The bell over the door jingled as it opened and a cheery-looking man in a brown overall came in.

'Why have you shut up shop, Hil— oh!' He stopped when he saw Charlie. 'Sorry, I didn't realise you had company.' He looked from one to the other and back again. 'Is everything all right?'

'Everything's fine, Bill. You wait there, the constable was just leaving.'

'Are you sure? I could come and collect the deliveries later if it's not convenient?'

'No, you won't. I've got them out the back, waiting for you. Besides, he's already disrupted my business enough for one day.' She sent Charlie a hard look.

'It's all right, I've got everything I came for.' Charlie closed his notebook and put it into his pocket. 'Thank you for your help, Miss Hodges.'

'Well, I don't know how much help I could have been,' Hilda muttered.

'We'll have to see, won't we?' Charlie said.

Chapter 16

The case of Harold Ferris at Chelmsford Crown Court had been a trial in more ways than one.

It should have been very straightforward. A husband had poisoned his wife so he could run off with his secretary. It had echoes of Spilsbury's first case, the infamous Hawley Harvey Crippen. But unlike the mild-mannered little American, rather than burying her dismembered remains in the cellar, in this case the murderer had obligingly left his wife's body in bed. A body which was found to contain a more than reasonable amount of arsenic.

But still Mr Ferris protested his innocence, claiming that his wife had been ailing for some months and was taking a number of proprietary medical remedies of which he had no knowledge. If anyone should be in the dock, he argued, it should have been the chemist who supplied her with the aforementioned remedies.

The fact that he had purchased a large amount of rat poison only a couple of weeks earlier, and even had a receipt for it in his pocket, was neither here nor there, according to his barrister.

It was a tiresome case, and Spilsbury was feeling rather short-tempered by the time he returned to St Mary's.

He walked into the basement mortuary just as Alf Bennett, the hospital's mortuary keeper, was closing the door on the cold store.

'Another one?' Spilsbury asked

'Just come in, sir. From the men's medical ward. That makes three waiting for you.'

Spilsbury consulted the notes that had arrived with each patient. Besides the fellow who had just died, there was a woman who had collapsed at a bus stop that morning, and a butcher from Smithfield Market, who had been crushed when half a cow fell on him.

'Thank you, Mr Bennett. I'll look at the butcher first, if you please. It sounds the most straightforward.'

'Right you are, sir.' As the mortuary keeper headed back to the cold store, Spilsbury went to the office to divest himself of his coat and hat. There was an almighty rumble overhead on the Great Western Line, shaking the floor under his feet. Being so close to Paddington Station could be a blessing, but he often had to poise his scalpel during a post-mortem to wait for a train to pass.

The office was little more than a glorified cupboard at the far end of the passageway, with barely room for a desk and a chair. Spilsbury rarely used it, preferring to write up his notes as he conducted his post-mortems. The only pieces of furniture he ever used were the battered green filing cabinet where he kept his notes, and the bentwood stand on which he hung his hat and coat.

As the rumbling of the train subsided, another sound rose to take its place. A strange, irregular clacking sound was coming from beyond the closed office door.

No sooner had he heard it than it stopped again. Spilsbury thought it must be his imagination but suddenly there it was again, halting at first, but slowly gathering pace.

He strode into the office, and was shocked to see a woman sitting at the desk with her back to him, pecking away at the typewriter.

'When was the last time this was used?' she asked. 'The keys are all jammed with dust.' She looked over her shoulder and caught sight of him. 'Oh, I beg your pardon, I thought you were Dr Willcox.' She rose to her feet and held out her hand. 'Good afternoon, Dr Spilsbury. I'm—'

'I know who you are.' He cut her off, too shocked to be civil.

He recognised her immediately. She wore a dark green dress in a fashionable style that barely skimmed her ankles. Her black curls were pinned up in a businesslike bun at the nape of her neck. But that slightly mocking glint in her eye was just the same.

'Of course. We met briefly at my husband's funeral.' Her accent was unpolished, at odds with her elegant appearance.

'What are you doing here?' Spilsbury looked around him. The answer was plain, of course; she was seated at the desk, and her coat and hat occupied his space on the bentwood stand. But for once he could not believe the evidence of his own eyes.

Now it was Violet Franklin's turn to frown. 'I thought Dr Willcox would have told you?'

'Told me what?' He took another look around the office. It was all very disconcerting. Everything had been carefully polished, and the hatstand had been moved into another corner.

Then he noticed something else. Or rather, the absence of it.

'Where are my slides?' he demanded.

She looked nonplussed for a moment. 'Oh, you mean that old cardboard box that was gathering dust on top of the cabinet? I took them back to the Pathology Museum.'

'You did what?' he turned on her. 'You had no right to do that. They were my property.'

'As I understand it, they belong to the hospital. That's why they should be in the Pathology Museum, to keep them all in one place so everyone can use them.'

'But I made them.'

'And you'll be able to use them whenever you want. As will everyone else.' She spoke calmly, like a mother soothing a fractious child. Spilsbury did not like her tone.

'This is too bad! Where is Willcox? He needs to explain himself.' He turned to leave the office just as Willcox was coming down the passage towards him.

'Ah, Spilsbury. You're back. I was just coming to see you.' He nodded towards the office. 'I take it you've already met Mrs Franklin?'

'We were just getting to know each other,' Violet said. The maddening glint was back in her green eyes.

'Splendid, splendid. And everything is going all right, is it? You don't need anything?'

'I'm having a bit of trouble with the typewriter, I'm afraid.'

'Ah yes, I'm sure. It hasn't been used in a long time.'

'Never mind. I'm sure it will be as good as new once I've given it a good old clean.'

Spilsbury looked from one to the other in amazement. Had the world gone completely mad? He felt as if he had stepped into another universe.

'May I have a word in private?' he said to Willcox.

'Of course.'

Willcox followed him outside.

'Good trip, old man? How was Chelmsford?'

'Never mind Chelmsford! Would you care to tell me what's going on?'

'You mean Mrs Franklin?'

'Of course I mean Mrs Franklin! Why is she here?'

'I've taken her on as our new secretary.'

'Why?'

'Because we needed one.'

'The devil we do!' Spilsbury glanced over his shoulder at the closed office door, aware that Violet Franklin was probably listening on the other side of it. 'We've managed perfectly well without one for years.'

'But we haven't, have we? The office was a mess. No one could ever find a blasted thing.'

'I could.'

'You were the only one. We don't all have time to work out your idiosyncratic system, old boy. Anyway, Mrs Franklin is a marvel. She's only been here two days and she's already got everything shipshape.'

Spilsbury thought about his precious slides. He did not dare even look in the filing cabinets. He dreaded to think what she would have done with his notes.

'You should have consulted me,' he said sulkily.

'You would have said no.'

'Precisely. Now you've landed me with a secretary I don't want.'

Willcox glanced back at the office door, then ushered him further down the passageway. 'There is another reason why I engaged her services,' he said in a low voice. 'You've heard what happened to her, I take it?'

Spilsbury glared at him. 'Of course I haven't – what do you take me for?'

Willcox sighed. 'I forget you never look up from your microscope long enough to pay attention to anything. It seems Sir James left her next to nothing in his will. He gave it all to his sister instead.'

So much for the Black Widow, Spilsbury thought. 'And what does that have to do with us?'

'She has a child to support and no one to help her. She needed to find employment, so she wrote to me.'

'Why you, may I ask?'

'Because I said I'd help her. When we spoke briefly at the funeral, I told her if she ever needed assistance, she should let me know.'

Spilsbury sighed. How typical of Willcox to concern himself with the plight of someone he barely knew.

Which was all very well, except he wasn't the only one who had to deal with the consequences.

'Is there nowhere else she could work?' he asked.

'Have some pity, man! Do you know how hard it is for a woman to find work? There are scarcely enough jobs to go around as it is. Think of it from her point of view,' he urged. 'Her life has been turned upside down, first by the death of her husband and then by this. It must have taken a great deal for her to swallow her pride and come cap in hand to us. I couldn't very well turn her down, could I?'

'I would.'

'I'm aware of that.'

Spilsbury glanced back at the office door. From beyond came the sound of more hesitant pecking, interspersed with muttered curses.

'Is she qualified?' he asked.

'She is proficient in typing and shorthand. And she has some experience of nursing too. She served as part of the Voluntary Aid Detachment during the war.'

'Making beds and scrubbing bedpans will hardly help her here.'

'There was rather more to it than that. As you'd know if you'd been there.'

It was a low blow, and it hurt. During the war, Willcox had served as a consultant to the armies in Mesopotamia. He had been given the rank of colonel and had been mentioned in despatches several times for his work.

Spilsbury had also offered his services, but he had been turned down as it was considered he was of more value to his country in his present role. It felt like a stain on his character.

'So what do you say?' Willcox interrupted his thoughts. 'Shall we give her a chance?'

Beyond the door, the clacking of the keys had recommenced, gathering pace.

'It's a bit late to ask me now, don't you think?' Spilsbury said bitterly.

'Let's just see how she gets on, shall we?' Willcox urged. 'You never know, you two might really hit it off.'

Spilsbury looked back towards the office.

'I very much doubt it,' he said.

Chapter 17

'How do I look?'

Matthew strutted in front of the mirror in his formal suit, turning this way and that to admire his reflection. As he moved, the row of medals on his chest glinted in the lamplight.

So they should, Mary thought. She had been polishing them all afternoon.

'Very smart, Mr Matthew, I'm sure,' she murmured, reaching up to give the shoulders of his jacket a final brush.

'Of course, I used to have a batman to do this for me when I was in France. But I suppose you did a decent enough job,' he conceded.

'Thank you, sir. I did my best.'

Matthew reluctantly dragged his gaze away from his reflection and consulted his pocket watch. 'Lord, is that the time? I promised I'd meet Bunter and the others at the club in ten minutes. Won't do to keep them waiting, eh?' He straightened his tie and smoothed down his fair hair.

'No, sir.'

'Don't lock up tonight, will you? I daresay I won't be home until the early hours. These regimental dinners can really drag on. Once all us old soldiers get together, there's no stopping us.'

'I can well imagine, sir.'

Matthew cast a quick glance towards the ceiling. 'Is my aunt having supper in her room again?'

'Yes, sir.'

'Say goodnight to her for me, will you?'

Why don't you say it yourself? But Mary already knew the answer to that one. For all his medals, Matthew was too scared to face his aunt. He had been doing his best to avoid her since their argument.

Mary had no idea what had caused it. All she had heard were raised voices coming from the drawing room, followed by three days of prolonged and frosty silence.

Mary had never known anything like it. She had witnessed Miss Franklin's exasperation with her nephew before, especially when he had 'misbehaved', as he liked to call it. But he was usually able to charm his way back into her good books within a few hours.

But this — well, this was something quite different. It seemed Miss Franklin did not even want to give him the opportunity to win her over. If he walked into a room, then she walked straight out. She spent most of her time closeted in her bedroom or writing letters in the small library that Mr Franklin had used as his study. She had only ventured out of the house once. Mary had had no idea where she had gone, but when she returned she was in an even worse mood than when she had left.

Whoever said money didn't bring happiness had it right, Mary thought. Elizabeth Franklin certainly wasn't behaving like a woman who had just inherited a fortune. She looked more like someone who carried the weight of the world on her shoulders.

Whatever it was, it had put her in a foul mood. No wonder poor Miss Lydia had sought refuge in her charity work to get away from the miserable atmosphere that prevailed in the house.

Which left Mary to bear the brunt of her mistress's temper. But not tonight, thank God. It was her evening off, and she intended to make the most of it.

She prepared some bread, cheese and cold meats, being careful to cut the bread into the paper-thin slices that Miss Franklin preferred. Then she brewed a pot of tea in her favourite china pot, arranged it all neatly on a tray and took it to her study.

The door was half open, and Mary stood for a moment, observing her mistress. She was seated at her desk, writing yet another letter. Who did she find to write to? Mary wondered. It wasn't as if she had many friends to keep up a correspondence with.

Perhaps she was making charitable endowments, giving her fortune away to various good causes. Mary smiled at the thought – Elizabeth Franklin wouldn't give anyone the time of day, let alone a farthing of her money.

'Yes? Did you want something?' Mary started guiltily at the sound of that imperious voice, like a blade slicing through her.

'I just brought you some supper, miss.'

'Then bring it in. Don't just stand there in the doorway, letting the draught in.' Elizabeth gestured to her with a wave of her hand. The dim light from the gas mantle threw shadows onto the harsh planes of her face, making her look even more austere.

As Mary entered the room, she noticed Elizabeth slip a letter into the top drawer of her bureau and close it. As if she imagined she could hide anything from her! She was the maid of all work. She moved like a shadow through every room in the house, ignored and largely unnoticed. She had access to every drawer and cupboard. Even those the family kept locked up were only a twist of a hatpin away, if she chose to seek them out.

Perhaps the Franklins might treat her with more respect if they knew how many of their secrets she kept?

'Has Lydia returned home yet?' Elizabeth asked.

'No, miss. She said she would be home by ten o'clock.'

'Her charity work keeps her very busy.'

'Indeed, miss.' She set the tray down. 'Shall I pour the tea for you?'

'What? Oh, no. Just leave it.' Elizabeth waved a weary hand. 'By the way, I'm expecting a visitor this evening. Show them straight in here when they arrive, will you?'

Mary hesitated for a moment. 'But it's my night off, miss.'

She crossed her fingers in the folds of her apron, praying that tonight of all nights she would not decide to be difficult and ruin her plans. But to her relief, Elizabeth sighed and said, 'So it is. Well, perhaps it's for the best if you're not here when they arrive. It's hardly a social call, after all.' Her face took on a hard, distant look.

'Will that be all, then, miss?' Mary asked.

'Yes. Yes, I think so. No, wait!' She had almost reached the door when Elizabeth called her back. 'I have a letter here that needs posting. Perhaps you could put it in the box on your way out?'

'Yes, miss.' Mary started towards her, her hand out, but as she reached her, Elizabeth suddenly snatched the envelope back and said, 'On second thoughts, I'll post it myself tomorrow. I need a few more hours to sleep on it.'

'As you wish, miss.'

As Mary left the room, she glanced back over her shoulder. Elizabeth was staring down at the letter in her hands. She had tried to hide it, but Mary had noticed the solicitor's address on the envelope.

She had an expression of such sorrow on her face, for a moment Mary almost felt pity for her.

But then she remembered, and the moment quickly passed. Mary slipped out of the library, leaving the old woman to her letters and her secrets.

Chapter 18

'You did what?'

Charlie cringed. It had taken him over a week to summon up the courage to confess to what he had done. At the time, it had seemed like a good idea, but now he was here, standing before Inspector Mount in his office, suddenly he began to see the folly in his plan.

And just in case he couldn't see it himself, it was written all over Alec Mount's severe face as he sat on the other side of the desk.

'I went to see Hilda Hodges again,' he repeated quietly.

'And why would you do that, constable?' Inspector Mount's voice was menacing in its softness.

Charlie opened his mouth but no sound came out. What could he say? That he didn't feel Inspector Mount and his team were doing their job properly? Because that was what it amounted to, wasn't it?

But he had set himself on this calamitous course, and now he had no choice but to see it through. Tell the truth and shame the devil, as his mother would say.

He just wished George Stevens was not there to witness his humiliation.

'I thought she might have remembered something else after this time,' he said.

George gasped in outrage. 'You had no right to interfere with our investigation! You do realise—'

Mount held up his hand to silence the sergeant, his gaze still fixed on Charlie. 'And what did she tell you?' he asked.

'She recalled her sister's mystery man was a soldier, sir.'

George laughed. 'Oh well, that's a big help, isn't it? That only narrows it down to every man under fifty in the country!'

'It lets you out,' Charlie said.

George's mouth shut like a trap and colour rose in his face.

'Go on, constable,' Inspector Mount said.

'She said he'd been awarded a medal, and that he was one of the first to receive it.' He cleared his throat nervously. 'The Military Cross was first awarded a year after the war started, so I thought it might be that.'

'And how many of these medals were given out?'

'Thousands, sir. But only seventy were awarded that first year. And the names are all listed in the *London Gazette*.' He cleared his throat again. 'And since this mystery man came from Yorkshire, I thought we might be able to narrow it down even more.'

'It sounds like a complete waste of time to me,' George Stevens muttered.

'It's better than anything we've come up with so far.' Inspector Mount looked thoughtful. 'Why don't you follow it up, constable?'

'Me, sir?'

'Why not? It was your idea.'

Charlie stared at him. It was more than he could ever have hoped for. He had come in fully expecting to receive a carpeting, and instead he had practically been promoted.

Of course, George had to stick his oar in.

'Are you sure, Inspector?' he said. 'Abbott's not even CID. Don't you reckon we'd be better off using one of our own?'

'But it was PC Abbott who came up with it. And as you've said yourself, Sergeant, it might be a complete waste of time. Surely it's better not to lose a valuable detective to such a task?'

George glared at Charlie. 'I just want the job done properly, sir,' he grumbled.

'Speaking of which, how are you getting on looking into those Lonely Hearts advertisements?' Inspector Mount asked.

It was an innocent enough question, but the timing could not have been more barbed. George's colour deepened.

'I'm doing my best, sir, but it would help if I knew where to start looking. All the newspapers have them. And there are whole magazines, too, full of Lonely Hearts advertisements. Quite honestly, it's like looking for a needle in a haystack.'

'I'm aware of that, Sergeant. But Jean Hodges must have found her mystery man somewhere. So you'd best get searching.'

Chapter 19

'And that, gentlemen, concludes my lecture.'

Spilsbury looked up from his notes at the rows of glazed faces staring back at him. Lecturing students was not something he often did, but unfortunately his tenure at the hospital required it.

He wasn't sure who enjoyed it least, himself or the students.

They certainly seemed to be in a great hurry to get out. The banked rows of the lecture theatre were half empty before he had finished packing up his notes.

'Another stellar performance?' He looked up to see Willcox standing on the steps above him, his eyes twinkling with their usual mirth. 'What was the subject?'

'*At what point does death occur?*'

'Looking at your students, I would have said shortly after you started speaking.'

'Very amusing, I'm sure.' Spilsbury shoved a handful of notes into his leather bag. 'If they want entertainment, they can go to the music hall.'

Willcox looked around at the dejected-looking young men shuffling past him up the steps. 'No wonder they're disappointed. They come here, expecting to see the great Dr Spilsbury, showman of the high court, a man who can have a jury eating out of his palm just by adjusting his carnation. And what do they get? Some dull old stick.'

'Jurors don't have the same level of technical expertise one expects from medical students. Therefore, my presentation is different. In either case, I certainly don't set out to entertain.'

'As most of these poor souls will testify.'

'If you can think of a way of turning medical jurisprudence into a comedy turn, please tell me. Better yet, tell the Dean and then perhaps you can give these lectures instead of me.' Spilsbury fastened the buckle on his bag. 'Now, if you'll excuse me, I have to return these slides to the Pathology Museum.'

'She's got you well trained, I see,' Willcox smirked.

'I beg your pardon?'

'Mrs Franklin. She's been here less than a week, and you're already tidying up after yourself and returning items to their proper place. Mind you, I wouldn't want to get on the wrong side of her either,' he said.

'Nonsense,' Spilsbury retorted. 'It's nothing to do with getting on the wrong side of anyone. I can simply see the advantages of keeping an orderly system.'

'I'm sure Mrs Franklin will be pleased to hear it.'

Spilsbury ignored him and started for the door, but Willcox followed him back down the passageway, heading for the stairs that led down to Pathology. 'It's a shame she's not here to appreciate your efforts,' he said.

Spilsbury turned at the top of the stairs to look back at him. 'Why? Where is she?'

'She didn't come to work this morning. I presume she must be indisposed.'

'Well, I must say that's too bad.' Spilsbury stared down at the box of slides in his hand. 'What is the point of her being here if she doesn't intend to keep regular hours?'

'I'm sure there must be an explanation.'

'Nevertheless, it's most inconvenient,' Spilsbury said as he descended the stairs. 'How on earth are we supposed to rely on her if she's never here?'

'Oh, so you rely on her now?' Willcox raised his brows.

'It was a figure of speech.' Spilsbury reached the foot of the stairs and was almost relieved to see a uniformed police constable waiting outside the office at the far end. He immediately recognised PC Wargrave, the Coronor's Officer for St Pancras.

'What now?' Willcox sighed under his breath.

'Dr Spilsbury.' The policeman started up the passage towards him. 'You're needed down at St Pancras Mortuary. They've pulled another dead woman out of Regent's Canal!'

Chapter 20

Spilsbury was rarely startled by the sight of a dead body. But he had felt a momentary jolt when he'd came face to face with the woman lying on the porcelain table, her head supported by two wooden blocks.

Death often softened and blurred the features, lending them an expression of peace and contentment. But somehow Elizabeth Franklin still managed to look harsh and disapproving.

'You know her?' Inspector Mount asked when he and Stevens came to the mortuary later that day to hear the results of the post-mortem.

'Her name was Elizabeth Franklin. Her brother was a physician at this hospital. I encountered her at his funeral recently.'

'Little did she know her own was just around the corner!' Sergeant Stevens said.

Spilsbury stared at him. He was pleased to note that as usual, his first instincts had been wholly correct. George Stevens really was as crass and obnoxious and he had first appeared.

'At least we don't have to go to the trouble of identifying her,' Inspector Mount said. 'What else can you tell us?'

'Thankfully the body was not in the water long enough for any real damage to be done. Rigor mortis was still present, and livor mortis was fixed, which meant death must have occurred more than twelve hours ago. Given the temperature of the body compared to the water, and allowing for it to have retarded the cooling somewhat, I would say that Miss Franklin died some time yesterday evening between eight and midnight.'

'Drowned?'

'There is no sign of pulmonary oedema, nor is there any debris in her stomach that would suggest drowning.'

He was aware he had said those same words before, not so many weeks earlier. And Inspector Mount was aware of it, too. He could see it in his keen expression.

'Jean Hodges,' he murmured.

'It's too much of a coincidence, surely?' Sergeant Stevens joined in. 'Two women, pulled out of the canal in Camden Town—'

'Actually, this one was further west, closer to the park,' Spilsbury pointed out.

'But not too far from where Miss Hodges was found. I don't suppose you know if she'd been poisoned?' The inspector looked hopeful.

'I've sent some samples of her organs to be analysed,' Spilsbury said. 'I would not like to say until I see the results. But I'll admit there are certainly superficial similarities between the two cases,' he added cautiously.

'If this one's been poisoned then I'd say they were pretty much identical. Two old desperate spinsters looking for love,' Sergeant Stevens mused. 'Easy pickings, I'd say.'

Then you did not know Elizabeth Franklin. From his brief encounter with her, Spilsbury did not imagine she would be easy pickings for anyone.

'I found something else,' he said. 'Perhaps you would care to look?'

He crossed the post-mortem room to where his microscope was set up on a bench in the corner, and motioned for the officers to join him. He positioned a slide in place, adjusted the focus and stepped aside for Inspector Mount to look.

The inspector peered into it. 'What am I looking at?' he asked.

'Greenish brown fibres. I found them on Miss Franklin's clothing.'

'Where are they from, do you know?'

'I've seen something like it before. They come from blankets, such as those issued by the military.'

'Someone wrapped her in an old army blanket?' Sergeant Stevens spoke up again.

Spilsbury nodded. 'Presumably to help with the disposal of the body.'

'There were no such fibres on Miss Hodges' body, were there?'

'Not that I could find.'

George snorted. 'Even so, there can't be two killers preying on lonely old biddies, surely?'

Spilsbury stared at the young man and thought again how much he disliked him. 'At this point, you can't be sure there's even one,' he snapped.

'Dr Spilsbury's right – we shouldn't jump to conclusions,' Inspector Mount said. 'But I think it's time we found out a little more about Miss Franklin, don't you?'

Chapter 21

'I'm very sorry.'

Charlie stared at the young woman sobbing in front of him. He was astonished that anyone could cry as much as Lydia Franklin. But then women didn't have that kind of sensibility where he came from. They were more likely to scream abuse or stick a boot up someone's backside than to weep.

He looked around the room, not quite sure what to do or say.

It was a large room, high-ceilinged with tall Georgian windows that overlooked the rolling expanse of Regent's Park. He was quite sure that the whole ground floor of his tiny terraced house could fit into this single room. Although he shuddered to think of his kids let loose around all those valuable-looking antiques and polished parquet floors.

And yet for all the space, it still seemed oppressive.

'Where – did you find her?' Matthew Franklin sat beside his sister, his arm around her shoulders. He was a lot more subdued than he was when he'd stomped down the stairs half an hour earlier, barefoot and still in his dressing gown even though it was nearly noon.

'Why the devil did you wake me up, Mary? I told you I didn't want—' He'd stopped short when he saw Charlie standing there in the tiled hall, his helmet tucked under his arm. He was dressed now, but he still looked a wreck, his bloodshot eyes ringed with purple shadows.

It must have been quite a night, Charlie thought. He could smell the stale alcohol coming off him from across the room.

'As I understand it, she was pulled out of the canal, sir.'

'Good God!' What little colour there was drained from his face. 'Was it suicide?'

'I'm afraid I can't tell you that.'

'Aunt E would never do something like that,' Lydia spoke at last, her voice choked with tears. 'Someone did this to her, I know they did.' She slumped against her brother, sobbing again.

Charlie cleared his throat and dragged his gaze back to Matthew. 'Mr Franklin, I'll have to ask you to come and formally identify your aunt's body.'

'Oh God!' Matthew ran his hand over his face. 'Well, I suppose I'll have to, won't I? There's no one else to do it.' He shot a quick look at his sister, still weeping on his shoulder. 'Should we go now?'

'It might be better to wait until the detectives have spoken to you, sir.'

'The police?' Matthew's voice was sharp. 'Why would they want to speak to us? We had nothing to do with this.'

'I know, sir. But if they want to find out who did, they're going to need to talk to you about your aunt.'

'What about her?'

Charlie stared at the young man. He supposed grief took people in different ways, but Matthew Franklin seemed positively belligerent.

'They'll want to build up a picture of her last movements. Before she . . .' He shot a worried glance at Lydia Franklin. Her violent weeping had thankfully subsided into gentle, hiccupping sobs.

'I see. Right. Well, I don't suppose I'll be much help, since I was out at a regimental dinner last night.'

'Nevertheless, sir, I'm sure they'll want to speak to you.' Charlie rose to his feet. If he was a real detective, he would be the one questioning them, talking to them about their aunt, her habits and who might have wanted her dead. But looking at them now, for once he was grateful it wasn't his job, what with her howling and him still bleary-eyed from the night before. Charlie doubted if Sherlock Holmes himself could get any sense out of either of them.

There was no sign of the maid who had let him in, so Charlie let himself out. It was a grey, rainy morning, and the leafless trees beyond the railings opposite shivered in the bitter chill.

Charlie stood at the top of the stone steps and took a measure of his surroundings. Gloucester Gate was an elegant curve of around a dozen four-storey Georgian houses. This was where the truly well-to-do lived – the surgeons, the lawyers, the families with generations of old money behind them. It was a million miles from the turbulence of his own home in Thrale Street, with its dirt and noise.

At the far end of the terrace, a delivery cart was parked, the old brown carthorse nodding patiently. Two doors down, a harassed-looking nanny was struggling to get a pram down the short flight of steps.

Charlie was just heading down the stairs to help her when a voice called out, 'I say! You there!'

Charlie looked over his shoulder to see an elderly man, leaning heavily on a stick.

He was the oldest man Charlie had ever seen; he had a wrinkled neck, beady eyes and a toothless mouth like a tortoise emerging from its shell. Rain flattened what was left of his hair to his age-spotted scalp.

'It's about time you showed up,' he croaked. 'I've been complaining for weeks, and no one's done anything about it.'

'About what, sir?'

'That man, of course. Hanging about here all hours of the night.'

Charlie promptly forgot all about the struggling nanny. 'You've seen a man loitering around here?'

'I said so, didn't I?' The old man fixed him with a glare, his yellowing eyes filled with anger. 'This used to be a respectable area, and now we've got all sorts hanging about. I told my daughter she should report it, but of course she didn't pay any attention.'

'Perhaps I'd better take some notes . . .' Charlie fished his notebook and pencil from the inside pocket of his uniform, and opened it to an empty page. 'Now, could you tell me your name, sir?'

'My name? What do you want my name for? I'm not the one loitering with intent, am I?'

'Well, no, but—' Charlie took one look at the old man's stubborn expression and gave up. 'Could you tell me when you saw this man?'

'Last night. My room is up there.' Charlie ducked out of the way as he swung his walking stick around to point at an upper window of the house next door. 'So I see everything that goes on. I like to keep an eye on everything. And it's just as well I do, since we never seem to see a policeman around here from one month to the next.'

'And what time was this, sir?' Charlie asked patiently.

'Let me think . . .' The old man considered for a moment. 'It was after I'd had my cocoa and my pills, so it must have been past seven o'clock. My daughter likes me to go to bed early,' he said. 'Utter nonsense, of course, but at least it means I can get some peace and quiet from her and that dreadful bore of a husband—'

'So you saw this man at around seven?' Charlie interrupted as politely as he could.

'No! Are you listening?' The old man tutted. 'I said I had my cocoa at seven o'clock. This was long after. I couldn't sleep. Marjorie was playing the piano again.' His lugubrious face took on a look of distaste. 'How anyone is supposed to sleep through that dreadful noise I can't imagine. I've told her, she has no talent for it.' He shook his head. 'Now, where was I?'

'The time you saw this man, sir?' Charlie prompted him gently.

'Oh yes. Well, I couldn't say. I suppose the long case clock must have struck nine. Or was it ten?' His wrinkled face folded into a frown. 'No, it can't have been ten, even Marjorie couldn't endure her own playing for that long. Or perhaps it was eight?' he mused, his rheumy eyes turning heavenwards. 'Goodness, it's so hard to remember, isn't it? Anyway, I looked out of my window and there he was.' The old man swung his walking stick round to point at the railings that separated the terrace from the park beyond, narrowly missing the end of Charlie's nose.

'And what exactly was this man doing?'

'He was watching, of course. That's what he always does. He stands there and watches the house. Riff-raff!' His lungs wheezed like ancient bellows as he fought for breath.

'Father?' A woman came running from the house, a mackintosh thrown around her shoulders. Her anxious expression relaxed into a look of relief when she spotted the old man. 'There you are!' She threaded her arm through his. 'What have I told you about wandering off into the street without telling me?'

'I'm not a child, Marjorie!' the old man retorted. 'Even though you insist on treating me like one.'

The woman gave Charlie a flustered smile. 'Is this about Father's phantom watcher?'

'I told you, I saw him!'

'You also saw Archduke Ferdinand sitting on a bench in the park the other day, didn't you?'

'I'd know the blighter anywhere,' the old man grumbled.

'Of course you would.' She patted his arm affectionately. 'You must forgive him, constable,' she said to Charlie. 'His mind wanders.'

'I know what I saw,' the old man insisted. 'I see everything from my window.'

'If you remember to put your spectacles on!' The woman rolled her eyes. She gave Charlie another quick, harassed smile and then started to lead her father away, back up the garden path.

Charlie watched them go. Their progress was painfully slow as the old man would not allow his daughter to help him.

He looked back up at the window, and then at the square. Then, with a sigh, he stuffed what was left of his soggy notebook back in his pocket, just as a motor car pulled up at the kerb and Inspector Mount got out, followed by a now-familiar tall figure in a top hat.

Chapter 22

Spilsbury recognised the young PC straight away. He remembered the red hair and the freckles and his lanky awkwardness as he stood in the ante-room of the mortuary, staring at the coffins as if he was seconds away from vomiting.

Sergeant Stevens seemed particularly put out to see him.

'What are you doing here, PC Abbott?' he demanded.

'I was told to inform the family about Miss Franklin,' he said.

'And have you done that?'

'Yes, Sergeant.'

'Right, then. You can sling your hook, can't you?'

The young policeman caught Spilsbury's eye, embarrassed colour flooding his face. He made a move to go, but Inspector Mount called out to him.

'Who was that you were speaking to, constable?'

'A neighbour, sir. Reckons he saw a man hanging about outside the house last night.'

'And what time was this?'

'He's not sure, sir. Some time between seven and ten, I think. But I'm not certain he's a very reliable witness.'

'We're the detectives,' Sergeant Stevens said. 'We decide who's a reliable witness and who isn't.'

Spilsbury looked from one to the other with interest. There was definitely some bad blood between them, he thought. They spoke to each other with the familiarity of old acquaintances, if not friends.

'Feel free to go and question him, then.' PC Abbott shrugged. 'But I'm warning you, he ain't the full shilling. Not according to his daughter, anyway.'

'Shall we go in?' Spilsbury interrupted. Without waiting for an answer, he strode up the steps to the house, leaving the others to follow behind.

The house was typically Georgian in style, with high ceilings and elegant plaster mouldings. The black and white tiled hall had two doors leading off to the left and an elegant staircase in front of him. To the left of it, the hall narrowed into a passageway with a door at the end – leading, Spilsbury guessed, down to the kitchen in the basement. A long case clock ticked ponderously, breaking the silence. The smell of beeswax polish could hardly mask the dusty smell of age. All the furnishings were old and heavy, as if they had been in the family for generations.

'This place is like a museum,' Sergeant Stevens commented, looking around.

'Indeed.' It was not a home, it was a living testament to the generations who had come before. The place was so stuffed with the dead, their belongings and their images on the walls, that there was hardly space for the living.

'Where are the family?' Inspector Mount asked the young PC.

'Upstairs, sir. In the parlour.'

'You mean the drawing room?' Sergeant Stevens smirked.

'I'll go up and speak to them. Dr Spilsbury?' The inspector turned to him expectantly.

'In a moment. I want to take a look around first.'

Spilsbury waited until the policemen had trooped upstairs to the drawing room, then he went to investigate the ground floor. He found a cloakroom full of coats, a dining room with tall windows that overlooked the park and, as he had expected, a short flight of steep stairs that led down to the kitchen.

There was a second room on the ground floor, tucked in behind the dining room towards the back of the house. Spilsbury pushed it open, starting briefly at the presence of a tall, angular woman in a black dress standing over the fire, her austere profile outlined by the flickering light as she stared unsmiling into the flames.

For a moment he thought he was seeing a ghost. Then she moved to throw something else onto the fire and he caught a glimpse of the white maid's cap perched on top of her head.

'What are you doing?' he asked.

She swung round with a gasp. 'Oh, sir, you gave me a start.' She had the trace of a northern accent. Yorkshire or Lancashire, he couldn't quite tell. 'I was just making up the fire.'

Spilsbury looked around the book-lined study, taking in the heavy, leather-bound volumes on the shelves, the wing chair and the solid mahogany desk. 'Who uses this room?'

'It used to be Mr Franklin's study, but lately Miss Franklin has been using it herself. She likes the peace and quiet.'

She had made no effort to change the masculine lines of the room, Spilsbury thought. Perhaps she had not had time? Or perhaps she liked it the way it was. Elizabeth Franklin had not struck Spilsbury as the sort of woman to bother with feminine fripperies.

'So it's unlikely anyone else would use it?'

'No, sir.'

'And yet you're making up the fire?'

The maid stared at him, then at the fireplace. 'Force of habit, I suppose, sir.'

Definitely Yorkshire, he thought. There was a brusque, clipped note to her voice.

Spilsbury stared into the flames, and fancied he could see the curled and blackened edges of a letter being consumed. 'What exactly were you burning?'

'Just some kindling, sir.'

'It looks like some sort of correspondence to me.'

'Oh no, sir. It's just kindling, I assure you.'

He set down his bag and took his time taking out his various bags and boxes and laying them out. Then he took off his jacket and hung it over the back of a chair.

'Has anything been disturbed in here?' he asked.

'Not that I can tell, sir.'

'Open the curtains, please. I need light to look around.'

The maid crossed to the window and carefully drew back the heavy velvet curtains. The window was smaller than those at the front, with a view over a small, cheerless back garden. The dismal square of greyish light did little to pierce the gloom.

'You'd best light the lamps, too.'

She hesitated. 'Will you be in here long, sir? Only Miss Franklin didn't go to the trouble of lighting the lamps unless they were going to be used for a while . . .'

'Yes, well, Miss Franklin isn't here, is she?' Spilsbury snapped, his impatience getting the better of him. 'And if we want to find out why, I'm going to need some light. So if you please?'

'Yes, sir.'

Spilsbury watched as she set about taking the shade off the lamp and lighting the mantle. She was every bit as belligerent as her mistress, he thought.

'Have you worked here long?' he asked.

'Four years, sir.'

'So you arrived – what? Halfway through the war?'

'That's right, sir.' The maid lit the mantle with a pop and carefully replaced the shade. She turned the light down as far as she dared, Spilsbury noticed.

'Would you say you and Miss Franklin were close?'

'She was my employer, sir. I don't hold with servants getting too familiar, and neither did she.'

'But did you like her?'

The maid paused. 'I don't like to speak ill of the dead, sir.'

'I'll take that as a no, shall I?' Spilsbury looked around the room, his nose wrinkling, seeking out the various smells like a bloodhound.

All the while, he sensed the maid watching him with beady, bird-like eyes. Those eyes missed nothing, he thought. She probably knew more than she thought, certainly more than she was going to let on.

There was a Turkey rug on the polished parquet floor. Spilsbury sank to his knees and peered at it closely.

'Were you here last night?' he asked.

'No, sir. It was my night off.'

'What time did you leave?'

'Just after seven o'clock, sir. I took Miss Franklin her supper and then I left.'

'And how did she seem to you?'

'I beg your pardon, sir?'

'What sort of mood was she in? Elated? Depressed? Bored?'

'Much the same as usual, sir. A bit put out, I think, because she'd forgotten it was my night off.'

Spilsbury crouched lower, pressing his face to the wooden floor, and peered across the polished wood surface.

'And how about this morning?' he said.

'I didn't see her, sir. I took her tea up to her room at seven o'clock but she wasn't there, and her bed hadn't been slept in.'

'And you didn't mention it to anyone?'

'I didn't think it was my place.' The maid's mouth tightened. 'Besides, who could I tell? Miss Lydia and Master Matthew were both still in bed, and they don't like to be disturbed.'

'You could have gone to the police?'

'As I said, I didn't think it was my place. Anyway, I told Miss Lydia when she came downstairs, and she said it was nothing to worry about.'

'She wasn't perturbed?'

'Not particularly, sir. She seemed to think her aunt had just gone out for a walk, or on some errand or another.'

He looked at her keenly. 'But you didn't think so?'

'I've never known Miss Franklin to make her own bed, sir.'

Before Spilsbury could reply, his attention caught on something that chased all other thoughts from his mind.

'Pass me some forceps from my bag, would you?' He reached out a hand for them, his gaze still fixed on the floor as if he did not dare take his eyes off it. 'No, not those,' he said, as she pressed some into his palm. 'The smallest ones.'

He carefully plucked the tiny fibres from the crack in between the floorboards, placed them in a test tube, which he sealed and labelled.

'Surely you don't think she died in this room?' The maid's question came out of nowhere.

'I think it's entirely possible. Probable, in fact.' Especially given what he had just discovered. 'Now, I'll need to take some photographs. If I could trouble you to turn up those lamps . . .' He turned to look at the maid. 'Good heavens, what is it? You look as if you've seen a ghost.'

'She had a visitor.'

'What?'

'Miss Elizabeth. The night she . . .' She swallowed hard. The night she died,' she said.

'How do you know?'

'She told me she was expecting someone, sir.'

'Did she say who it was?'

She shook her head. 'I offered to stay and let them in, but she said she could manage.'

'And was that usual?'

'Oh no, sir. Miss Franklin always said a lady never answered the door in her own house.'

'And yet she decided to make an exception this time?'

'Yes, sir.'

'How very curious.'

'Yes, sir.'

His gaze shifted around the room, trying to picture the scene. Elizabeth Franklin entertaining a caller on the evening everyone in the house happened to be out. Had she deliberately planned it because she knew they would be alone?

And then his gaze found the stack of old newspapers wedged under the bureau.

'What are those doing there?' He crossed the room to take a closer look.

The maid sighed. 'I really couldn't say, sir. I tried to put them on the fire, but Miss Elizabeth wouldn't let me touch them. I'm not sure why, since she usually couldn't abide clutter . . .'

But Spilsbury wasn't listening. He was flicking through the stack of newspapers. *The Times*, going back some six months, to the previous summer. The most recent was dated the day before yesterday.

The day before she died.

And they were all carefully folded open at the same page.

'I'll take these, if I may?' he said.

'Of course, sir. I don't suppose Miss Franklin will be needing them anymore, will she?'

Spilsbury looked at her. Was that genuine sorrow in her voice? It was difficult to tell.

Chapter 23

A moment later, the lanky police constable appeared in the doorway to request Spilsbury's presence in the drawing room.

He tucked the newspapers into his leather bag and followed him upstairs, with a last glance over his shoulder at the maid. Her face gave nothing away. At least nothing deliberate. But it was surprising how much people revealed without meaning to, if one knew what to look for.

Inspector Mount was in one of the brocade armchairs, facing the sofa where Matthew and Lydia Franklin sat side by side. Matthew was clutching his sister's hand. Lydia sat upright, her gaze fixed firmly ahead of her. She looked as if she had made up her mind to be stoical, but her swollen, red-rimmed eyes and trembling lower lip betrayed her.

'Ah, Dr Spilsbury,' the inspector greeted him. 'I was just talking to Mr and Miss Franklin about their whereabouts last night.'

'Don't let me stop you. You don't mind if I look around while you talk, do you?'

Spilsbury prowled the room, taking in his surroundings. Once again, it reminded him of a museum, stuffed full of expensive but rather soulless antiques that must have been in the family for generations.

Inspector Mount turned back to Lydia. 'I'm sorry, Miss Franklin. You say you were doing some kind of charity work?'

'That's right. Rowton House in Camden Town. I help out in the reading room twice a week.'

'Rowton House?' Inspector Mount queried.

'It's a men's hostel, Inspector,' Sergeant Stevens said. 'I know the place. It's in Camden Town, near where Jean Hodges' body was found.' Spilsbury noticed the glance he shot at the constable as he said it.

'You see?' Matthew turned on his sister. 'You see the kind of people you're mixing with? I hope you haven't brought this trouble to our door.'

'That's a horrible thing to say,' Lydia snapped back. 'The men at Rowton House are quite harmless. They're just down on their luck, that's all.'

'Aunt Elizabeth didn't approve of you mixing with those people.'

'She didn't approve of some of the people you mix with, either.'

They both fell silent. Spilsbury noticed the colour rising in Matthew Franklin's face, and wondered if the inspector had spotted it too.

But if he had, he gave no sign of it. 'What time did you come home last night, Miss Franklin?' he asked.

'Just after ten o'clock, I think.'

'And did you see your aunt?'

'No, she was already in bed.'

'Did you see her?'

'I knocked on her door, but there was no answer.'

'No doubt she was dead and halfway to the Regent's Canal by then,' Spilsbury said.

He'd meant it as nothing more than a statement of fact. But Lydia gulped back a sob, her grey eyes filling with tears.

'Mary Jeevons said she informed you that Miss Franklin's bed had not been slept in last night,' Spilsbury said.

'Yes, but I didn't think there was anything suspicious about it.' Lydia looked at her brother. 'I just assumed she must have gone out or something.'

'Gone out wandering the streets all night?'

Lydia stared at him for a moment, then promptly burst into tears. Inspector Mount stepped in quickly.

'We'll need someone to confirm both your whereabouts last night,' he said.

'Yes. Yes, of course.' Matthew braced himself as his sister sobbed beside him. 'I can tell you I was at a regimental dinner.'

'And where was this dinner being held, Mr Franklin?'

'The Café Royal.'

'Which regiment did you serve with?'

'I was with General Headquarters. The Adjutant-General's branch.'

Spilsbury noticed the inspector's face tighten a fraction. 'When did this gathering finish?'

'It didn't!' Matthew grinned. 'It all got rather riotous, as I recall. I think it was still going on when I left just before dawn. You know what these kinds of reunions are like!'

'I'm afraid I don't.' There was a chilly note in the inspector's voice. 'Very few of my old regiment returned from the war, as I recall.'

'Oh.' Matthew sobered quickly, his chumminess disappearing like mist. 'Yes, well, it was a bad show all round,' he mumbled. 'Lots of good men were lost.'

'Quite. And you were there all night, you say?'

'Yes, I was.'

'We'll need names of people who could vouch for you.'

'Of course. Although I can't imagine many of them will remember where they were themselves, let alone me!'

Spilsbury stood at the window and ran his finger along

the frame. It had been freshly dusted that morning. Mary was very industrious, he thought.

'Do either of you know anything about your aunt's visitor?' he asked.

Inspector Mount turned to stare at him, while Matthew looked blank. Even Lydia managed to stop her incessant weeping for a moment.

'A visitor?' Matthew asked.

'According to the maid, your aunt was expecting a visitor last night.'

They looked at each other, and their bewilderment seemed utterly genuine.

'This is the first I've heard of it,' Matthew said.

'Me too,' Lydia added.

'And me.' Inspector Mount sent Spilsbury a hard look.

'Who could it have been, I wonder?' Lydia mused.

'A friend, perhaps?' Spilsbury suggested.

Lydia shook her head. 'Aunt Elizabeth didn't have any friends.'

'How about an admirer?'

They both stared at him for a moment, identical nonplussed expressions on their fine-featured faces. Then Matthew laughed.

'An admirer! Now I've heard everything.'

'Matthew, please!' Lydia said quietly. 'Show some respect.'

'But it's utterly absurd!' He shook his head, still chuckling.

'It might be possible.' Lydia cut across her brother's laughter.

'Come on, Lyd! This is Aunt E we're talking about. Can you imagine it?'

'No, I can't,' she admitted. 'But I can't imagine her having a late-night visitor to the house, either. So how do we know she didn't have a secret life?'

Chapter 24

'So Miss Franklin had a visitor?' Inspector Mount said, when they were in the car travelling back to Scotland Yard together. 'I don't think we need to look much further for our murderer, do you?'

They all fell silent. It was crowded in the car, with the inspector and Sergeant Stevens wedged in beside Spilsbury in the back, and young PC Abbott riding in the front next to the driver. The police car smelt of worn leather and stale cigarette smoke, which he found most unpleasant.

Spilsbury would have preferred the solitude of his own car back to St Mary's. But Inspector Mount had made it clear that he wanted to discuss the case further.

'We know Elizabeth Franklin died in the house, thanks to those blanket fibres Dr Spilsbury found on the rug in the study,' he said, starting to count up the points on his fingers.

'They were certainly similar, but I couldn't say they perfectly matched those found on Miss Franklin's body,' Spilsbury corrected him.

'We also know she was expecting someone that evening. She had invited them at a time when she knew there would be no one else in the house.'

'Not necessarily,' Spilsbury butted in again. 'The maid seemed to think Miss Franklin had forgotten it was her night off.'

Inspector Mount ignored him. 'He arrived, and she let him in. And then what?'

'He killed her,' Sergeant Stevens said.

'He must have planned it. Poison is hardly a spur-of-the-moment way to kill someone.'

'We don't know for sure yet that it was poison that killed her,' Spilsbury pointed out. 'Not until we receive the toxicology results.'

'Can you think of anything else it might have been?'

Spilsbury considered it for a moment. The post-mortem had not revealed any other possible cause of death. Elizabeth Franklin had not apparently died of any natural causes he could find. She had not been stabbed or beaten, there was no bruising, and no damage to the hyoid bone that might suggest strangulation. Her mildly inflamed oesophagus might indicate poisoning, but could equally well have been caused by heartburn or a dozen other reasons.

'Not at the moment,' he conceded.

'He also brought the blanket with him,' Sergeant Stevens said. 'So he must have intended to do away with her body.'

'He might not have brought it with him. Perhaps he found one in the house? Mr Franklin was in the army. Perhaps he kept an old blanket from those days.'

'Really, Spilsbury!' Inspector Mount turned on him in exasperation. 'We're trying to build a case here. You might do something to help us!'

'Very well.'

Spilsbury opened his battered leather case and took out the sheaf of newspapers. 'I found these in the study.'

'*The Times*?' The inspector studied the newspaper, and Spilsbury watched as his frown shifted to a smile. 'Well, I'll be—'

'The Personal columns,' Spilsbury said. 'And some of them are even circled.'

'"My darling Soldier Boy",' Inspector Mount read out. '"Meet me next Friday at seven o'clock where we shared our first kiss. I'll be waiting".'

Sergeant Stevens wrinkled his nose. 'Soldier boy?'

'And then there's this one. "Dearest, I waited for you on Saturday but you didn't come. When can I see you again?" Is there a reply, I wonder?' He checked the date at the top of the page, then leafed through the rest of the newspapers. 'Let's see . . . Ah, here it is. "Darling Soldier Boy, I will try to get away tomorrow. Three o'clock, by the fountain. Your Sweetheart."'

He set the newspaper down and looked up. 'They used the newspaper to arrange their meetings. Why, I wonder?'

'Perhaps she thought it was romantic?' Spilsbury said.

'Pathetic, more like.' Sergeant Stevens looked disgusted. 'Soldier Boy, indeed! A woman her age should know better than to carry on like that. Turns my stomach, it does.'

'You know what they say. Love knows no bounds,' Inspector Mount said.

'More like there's no fool like an old fool.' Sergeant Stevens picked up another of the newspapers. 'I suppose this mystery man thought no one would find him amongst this lot. Little did he know Elizabeth Franklin would want them as a keepsake. Sentimental old soul!'

'From what I can tell, Miss Franklin was not the least bit sentimental. Nor was she a fool, old or otherwise,' Spilsbury said shortly.

'I think this proves there's a connection with the Hodges case, wouldn't you agree?' Inspector Mount said. 'Two unmarried women, living within a mile or two of each other, both of whom had been in contact with a man through the Personal column in *The Times*.'

'How do you know it was *The Times* in the case of Jean Hodges?' Spilsbury asked. 'It might have been any one of a dozen publications.'

'Don't I know it?' Sergeant Stevens muttered under his breath.

'Both turn up dead within a few weeks of each other, most likely poisoned and then tossed into the same canal,' Inspector Mount went on. 'It's more than a coincidence, wouldn't you say?'

'I can see how you might come to that conclusion,' Spilsbury conceded. 'If, as you say, Elizabeth Franklin was indeed poisoned. But I believe it would be a mistake to exclude any other possibilities at this point.'

'Such as?'

'Such as the fact that the maid served Elizabeth Franklin her supper before she left for the evening. If anyone had the opportunity to poison her, then it would be Mary Jeevons.'

'And why would she suddenly decide to murder her, after four years of devoted service?'

Spilsbury pictured Mary's unsmiling countenance. She hardly struck him as devoted. But neither did she seem particularly passionate in her dislike, either. Indifference was seldom a motive for murder.

'But you're quite right, Doctor,' Inspector Mount was saying. 'We mustn't allow ourselves to get carried away at this stage. We'll confirm everyone's alibis, and question Mary again. But at the same time, we need to find out the identity of the mystery visitor, and the person who placed those advertisements. Because I have a feeling they might be one and the same person.'

Chapter 25

'I just thought you ought to know. I didn't want you to find out from the newspapers.'

Violet looked at her stepdaughter, perched on the edge of the couch. Lydia looked tense and shaken, clutching the teacup in her hand like a lifeline.

'It was good of you to come to let me know.' Violet looked down at her tea, cooling untouched in the cup. She still couldn't quite take in what she had been told.

Elizabeth Franklin was dead. Her old enemy, the woman who had made her life a misery for the past three years, was no more. It seemed impossible to believe that such an indomitable force could be snuffed out so quickly and completely.

'They think she was poisoned, and then thrown into the canal.' Lydia's voice trembled. 'Who would ever do such a thing?'

Violet glanced over her shoulder at Mickey, who was cleaning his boots at the sink. Pistol lay at his feet, his tail thumping rhythmically.

It was early evening, and Thomas was in bed. A pan of mutton stew bubbled on the hob for their supper.

'When did it happen?' she asked quietly.

'Last night, so the police said. That's what Dr Spilsbury thinks, anyway.'

'Spilsbury?' Violet looked up sharply.

'He did the post-mortem. And he came to the house earlier. He's a rather odd man,' she said. 'The police were all so kind, but he was very – distant.'

That's one way of describing him, Violet thought. After nearly a week of working in the Pathology department, she could think of others. Fortunately, their paths did not cross too often.

Her cup rattled in its saucer and she put it down quickly. She had not been to work at St Mary's that day, having woken up with one of her blinding headaches. Otherwise she might have found out about Elizabeth sooner.

She might even have come face to face with her. Panic rose in her chest, but she quelled it quickly. Even if Elizabeth had been brought to St Mary's, which was unlikely, Violet had never been near the mortuary, or the post-mortem room. That was very much Dr Spilsbury's domain.

A sudden outburst of crying from Lydia distracted her from her own unsettled emotions.

'Oh, Lydia!' Violet moved to the couch beside her and wrapped her arm around the girl's slender shoulders. Lydia collapsed against her like a rag doll.

'I'm so afraid!' she sobbed. 'It's all so horrible, it doesn't seem real. I've lost everyone. First Father and Robert, then you and Thomas, and now Aunt Elizabeth. I can't bear it!'

'There, don't take on.' Violet hugged her closer. 'You've still got me.'

'Have I?' Lydia pulled away to look at her, her grey eyes brimming with tears. 'I so wish you and Thomas were still living at Gloucester Gate. I'd feel much better if you were with me.'

'Your tea's gone cold. Here, let me get you a fresh one.' Violet gently took the cup from her and went over to the sink. As she refilled the cup from the big brown china pot, she looked across at Mickey and read the unspoken message on his scowling face.

Get rid of her, his look said.

She shrugged helplessly back. *How can I?*

She looked back at her stepdaughter. Lydia looked so out of place, like a delicate flower that had somehow found itself transplanted into a field of stinging nettles. Seeing her there made Violet painfully conscious of her humble surroundings – the rumpled blankets on the couch where Mickey slept, the damp stains creeping up the walls, the smell of cooked mutton and old boots. Violet did her best, but no amount of scrubbing and polishing could make a silk purse out of a sow's ear.

She was aware of her own appearance, too. Her curls were pinned up hastily, her skirt and blouse concealed by a stained apron. What must Lydia think of her, she wondered.

Violet shook herself, annoyed by her own embarrassment. What did she care what anyone thought? She had nothing to feel ashamed of – this was her home now, the place that had welcomed her with open arms when she had nowhere else to go.

She handed the cup to Lydia. 'Here, drink it while it's hot. It will make you feel better.'

'Thank you.' Lydia sipped it delicately. Violet saw her wince as the tea touched her lips. The brew was strong, just how she and Mickey liked it, nothing like the pale greyish liquid in delicate bone china that they served in the fine houses. But Lydia was far too polite and well bred to say anything as she set her cup carefully aside.

'All I've done today is drink tea,' she said with an apologetic little smile. 'Mary's been making it all day. I don't think she knew what else to do with herself, poor dear. She's as lost as the rest of us.'

Violet had never really had much to do with the maid. She did not feel comfortable giving orders to servants, and besides, Mary was very much Elizabeth's creature. On the few occasions Violet had asked her to do something, her request had been overruled by Elizabeth or else quietly ignored. Violet knew Mary spied on her and reported back to Elizabeth. She had even taken to locking away her belongings in case Mary went through them.

And yet strangely, the maid had a soft spot for Thomas. Even though she would never do Violet any favours, Mary never minded looking after him. He was fond of her, too. Violet sometimes caught them playing games, or Mary would teach him a rhyme or a song. It was the only time she saw any softness under that hard exterior.

'How's Matthew?' she asked.

'He's very upset, of course.' Lydia had hesitated just a fraction too long before replying. 'You know how close he was to Aunt E. He was her favourite.'

She said it without rancour. It was just a fact, after all. Violet knew it too. While Lydia tried hard to please her aunt, Matthew pleased only himself. But no matter how appallingly he behaved and how many scrapes he got into, Elizabeth would always defend him. He could do no wrong in her eyes.

Violet could recall several exasperated arguments between James and his sister, as he tried to impose some kind of discipline on his wayward son, and Elizabeth resisted him all the way. While she was good at spotting faults in everyone else, when it came to Matthew she saw none.

'The police think Aunt Elizabeth had a secret admirer.'

Lydia's comment was so unexpected, Violet almost choked on her tea.

'An admirer? Elizabeth?'

'It sounds absurd, doesn't it? But apparently another woman was pulled out of the canal a couple of weeks ago, and it turned out she had met a man through one of those Lonely Hearts columns in the newspaper. They found copies of *The Times* in the study with the same sort of advertisements marked.'

'And do they know who placed these advertisements?'

'That's what the police are trying to find out. And there's something else,' she went on. 'Aunt E had a visitor on the night she—' She broke off, unable to say the word.

'A visitor? Who?'

'No one knows, but Aunt Elizabeth told Mary she was expecting someone.'

Pistol's claws scrabbled on the oilcloth as he got to his feet. Violet looked round to see her brother pulling on his newly cleaned boots.

'Are you going out?'

'Looks like it,' he grunted.

'What about your supper?'

'I'll have it later.'

He shot Lydia a sideways glance as he reached for his coat from the peg on the back of the door. *When she's gone*, his look said.

Violet turned back to Lydia. She was looking at Mickey, wide-eyed with dismay. Her brother had that effect on people, with his burly build, snarling expression and wild mane of black curls.

They sat quietly until they heard the door slam.

'He doesn't like me, does he?' Lydia said.

'Take no notice of him. He's just wary around strangers, that's all.'

'All the same, I'd better go home.' She glanced anxiously towards the door where Mickey had disappeared. 'I don't think I should be here when he comes back.'

'His bark's a lot worse than his bite. Unlike his dog!' But even Pistol had been unusually subdued that evening, as if he had sensed the leaden atmosphere.

'I wouldn't blame him for hating me, after the wretched way my family has treated you. Oh, Violet, I so wish you would come home,' she blurted out. 'I can't bear it with just Matthew and me in that house. I want us to be a family again.'

We were never that. Violet looked pityingly at her stepdaughter.

'This is our home now,' she said.

'But surely now Aunt E—'

'Don't,' Violet cut her off. 'It doesn't feel right to talk like that.'

'I suppose not.' Lydia fished in her bag for a handkerchief. 'Take no notice of me, I'm being silly and selfish. Of course you and Thomas are settled and happy here now.' She sniffed back her tears and dabbed her eyes. 'You are happy, aren't you? Please tell me you are, because you deserve it.'

Violet did not reply. She had put in so much effort since they returned to South London, making the flat tidy and respectable, looking for work and trying to make things right for her son, she had not had time to consider her own feelings.

And perhaps that was just as well, she thought. Because if she stopped to consider everything that had happened, and the way her beloved husband had betrayed her . . .

'We're doing all right,' she said.

'Are you?' Lydia sent her a searching look. 'Are you sure? Because if there's anything you need . . .' She reached for her bag. 'Perhaps I could give you some money?'

'Put your purse away, I don't need it.'

'But surely I could help?'

'I said I don't need your money!'

She hadn't meant to raise her voice, and regretted it when she saw Lydia flinch. 'Of course. I'm sorry. I didn't mean to offend you,' Lydia said in a faltering voice.

'I know. I'm sorry, I shouldn't have snapped like that.'

Poor Lydia. None of this was her fault. Out of all of them, she was the one who had welcomed Violet into the family. Probably because she had been so starved of affection, she thought.

Lydia insisted on walking to the cab rank on Tooley Street, much to Violet's dismay.

'You don't know what it's like here at night,' she warned. A well-dressed young woman like Lydia would be too easy a target for the ne'er-do-wells who inhabited the narrow warren of streets after dark. 'I could fetch our neighbour Nan to watch Thomas while I walk you up to the Bridge?'

'I'll be fine, honestly. I can look after myself.'

Her brave, hopeful face gave Violet a pang of sorrow. The Gloucester Gate house was cheerless at the best of times. But now it wore the heavy mantle of a murder scene, too.

'Isn't there someone you could stay with? A friend, perhaps?' she asked.

'I'm better off at home. Someone has to keep an eye on Matthew.' Lydia gave a small, wry smile.

'He should be the one looking after you.'

'Not all brothers are as protective as yours, I'm afraid.' She reached her hand out to grasp Violet's. 'You will take care of yourself, won't you?'

'And you.' Violet held both her hands, suddenly unwilling to let go.

She stood at the doorway and watched until Lydia had reached the staircase at the end of the walkway. Even then she listened to the clack of her heels as they descended, growing fainter and fainter.

I shouldn't have let her go, she thought. *I should be there to protect her.*

She wrapped her arms around herself to keep out the sudden gust of cold.

Chapter 26

'Well, this is interesting,' Inspector Mount said.

Charlie looked up from the copy of the *London Gazette* he had been poring over. 'What's that, sir?'

'We've just managed to get our hands on Elizabeth Franklin's bank records. And guess who she was making payments to?'

'Her mystery man?' Charlie perked up. 'Has he got a name?' It would save him a lot of eye strain ploughing through yet more copies of the *London Gazette* if he did.

'No mystery man, I'm afraid. But she was writing cheques to her nephew.' He consulted the sheaf of documents in his hand. 'Almost every month, according to her statements. And an extra payment the week before she died.'

He passed the documents to Charlie, who scanned through them. As the inspector had said, there was at least one payment a month. Not huge amounts, but they certainly added up. 'I wonder what that was about?'

'There's only one way to find out, isn't there?' Inspector Mount took the documents back. 'We'd better speak to Mr Franklin.'

We, he said. Charlie beamed at the word. Inspector Mount had said it so casually, but Charlie almost had to pinch himself that it was really happening. His life had become like one long dream ever since his temporary transfer to Scotland Yard.

It had been nearly two weeks now, and he was still filled with trepidation every time he walked through the doors of the banded white and red brick building on Victoria Embankment, certain that at any moment he would feel a hand on his collar steering him back out again.

And yet here he was. And even though he had done very little but sit at a desk ploughing through old copies of the *London Gazette*, it was still more exciting than pounding the beat around the streets of Camden Town, especially in such atrocious weather.

'But we've checked his alibi, sir,' Charlie pointed out. 'There are at least half a dozen men at the regimental reunion who swear he was still drinking with them hours after his aunt was murdered.'

'Of course, the reunion.' Inspector Mount's mouth curled. 'I can't say it would do for me, talking over old times with my old army pals.'

'Nor me, sir. But I daresay it was all different for that lot at GHQ.'

GHQ, or General Headquarters, were the people who commanded the expeditionary force in a particular area. There were three main sections: the General Staff, who planned the various military operations, the Quartermaster's Branch, which handled supplies, and the Adjutant-General's Branch, which managed discipline, medical and sanitary services.

No doubt being the son of a prominent army physician had helped Matthew Franklin secure his coveted job in the latter. It was a safe place from which to observe the messy business of war, without actually getting his hands dirty.

'Where did you serve?' the inspector asked.

'Second Battalion, Rifle Brigade, sir.'

'You saw a lot of action, then?'

'I'll say we did, sir.'

'Injured?'

'A bullet to the chest at Passchendaele, sir. Might have killed me if it hadn't been for the tobacco tin in my pocket.'

'I was a rifleman, too. Part of the British Expeditionary Force in Mesopotamia.' Inspector Mount took out a packet of cigarettes and offered one to Charlie. After a moment's hesitation he took it, then dipped into his pocket for his matches and lit them both.

'How are you getting on looking for our old soldier?' The inspector nodded at the stack of copies of the *London Gazette* on Charlie's desk.

'I've been all the way through 1915, and noted down all the officers and warrant officers who were awarded the Military Cross.' Charlie showed him the list he had scrawled down.

'That's a long list.'

'Yes, but if you only include officers from Yorkshire regiments, it cuts out at least half.' Charlie showed him another list. 'That's less than thirty names. It shouldn't take me long to go through them all.'

'And how do you plan to do that? Write to them and ask them if they've murdered any women lately?'

'Not exactly, sir. I was hoping that George – Sergeant Stevens – will come back from the newspaper office with a list of names so I can cross-reference this lot against them.'

'I hope so too.' Inspector Mount took a long, thoughtful drag on his cigarette. 'Of course, we don't even know if our man really is from Yorkshire. Or even if he's received a medal. He's hardly likely to reveal his true identity if he's planning to murder them, is he?'

'True, sir. But we've got to start somewhere.'

'I suppose so.'

They were both silent for a moment, smoking. Inspector Mount looked lost in thought, while Charlie was desperately trying to muster up the courage to say what was on his mind.

In the end, he decided to take the plunge. 'I've been thinking, sir,' he began.

'Yes?'

Charlie stared at the glowing tip of his cigarette. 'It might be a good idea if we went to Miss Franklin's funeral this Friday. Just in case . . .'

'Just in case our killer decided to turn up, you mean? It's not unheard of, I suppose. Although I must say, Abbott, you seem to be placing a great deal of faith in this man's integrity. First you assume he's telling the truth about who he is and where he comes from, and then you expect him to mourn the woman he murdered.'

'It was just a thought, sir,' Charlie mumbled. 'Like you said, it ain't unheard of, to return to the scene of the crime.'

'True,' Inspector Mount agreed. 'At any rate, it wouldn't do any harm to keep an eye on the family. It might be a good chance to speak to Mr Franklin too, ask him about those payments from his aunt's account.' He took another drag on his cigarette. 'Let's hope Stevens comes up with something,' he said. 'Although I must admit, the more we look into Elizabeth Franklin's life, the more I find myself doubting that she even had a mystery man.'

'I know what you mean, sir.' Charlie tipped his ash into the tray. They had spent several days trying to piece together what kind of woman Elizabeth Franklin really was – the life she led, her friends and interests – and they had come to the conclusion that she had neither. According to those who knew her, she was a very prickly character. 'Forthright', 'intolerant' and 'outspoken' were a few of the kinder adjectives Charlie had scribbled in his notebook. There were a few more he hadn't liked to write down. But it had been enough to build up a picture of a woman with a strong moral character and impossibly high standards, who did not suffer fools gladly. She had few friends, sat on no charitable committees and rarely went out. She had never shown the slightest interest in romance, even as a young girl.

She hardly seemed the sort of woman to take up with a fancy man on a whim.

'But if it wasn't a secret admirer, then who might it be?' Charlie asked. 'One of the family?'

'I'm not ruling anyone out,' Inspector Mount said. 'We haven't spoken to the widow yet, have we? By all accounts there was no love lost between her and Elizabeth Franklin. Especially since she inherited everything.'

'She might have had a motive, sir, but would she have had the means or the opportunity? The maid says she hasn't been near the house since the day she left.'

'Ah yes, the maid. Another one we need to keep an eye on. If we're talking about means and opportunity, then she certainly had both. She was the last one to see Elizabeth alive. She could easily have slipped some strychnine into her supper.'

'If that's how she died,' Charlie reminded him. 'Dr Spilsbury still hasn't confirmed Miss Franklin was poisoned.'

'I daresay he'll tell us in his own good time.' The inspector's mouth twisted. 'And once he's confirmed it, we'll question Mary again.' He tipped the ash from the tip of his cigarette. 'That just leaves Lydia Franklin, the niece.'

'I spoke to the superintendent at Rowton House, sir.' Charlie consulted his notes. 'He confirms she was there that night, helping out in the library.'

Inspector Mount frowned. 'Don't you think it's a strange thing for her to do?' he said. 'A men's hostel is hardly the place for a young lady.'

145

'I get the impression Miss Franklin holds strong views, sir.'

'Well yes, I understand that. And I sympathise. But I'm not sure I'd like one of my daughters spending her evenings there. Why wouldn't she help out through her local church or something?'

'In my experience, women are a great deal tougher than they look, sir.'

Inspector Mount smiled wryly. 'There speaks a married man!'

'With a wife and a mother under the same roof,' Charlie said.

'God Lord! And there was me thinking I had it bad with three daughters.'

'I've got three girls too, sir.'

They were still laughing when George Stevens arrived, rain dripping off the brim of his bowler hat.

'Care to share the joke?' he said, looking at them sourly.

'Are you married, Sergeant?' Inspector Mount asked.

'No, sir.'

'Then you probably wouldn't understand.' The inspector tapped his cigarette. 'How did you get on at *The Times*?'

'I didn't, sir.' George removed his hat and shook the rain off the brim.

Inspector Mount frowned. 'What do you mean?'

'Apparently someone broke into the office last month and stole all the files from their advertising department.'

Inspector Mount and Charlie looked at each other. 'All of them?' Mount asked.

George nodded. 'Everything from the last six months, sir. There are no records left at all.'

'Forget what I just said. It looks like our secret admirer theory might be right after all.' Inspector Mount ground out his cigarette in the ashtray, his expression grim. 'And if it is, he's one step ahead of us.'

Chapter 27

'So it was definitely poisoning?'

'No question of it, old man. There were traces in the liver, stomach and bowel.'

'Traces?' Spilsbury pounced on the word. 'So not as much as you found in the Hodges woman?'

'I'd have to consult my notes to be certain,' Willcox said. 'But from what I recall, I would say not nearly as much. I seem to remember Miss Hodges had been given an enormous amount.'

'That's interesting.' Spilsbury mused over the report his friend had handed to him. 'If it was the same killer, why would they administer less this time?'

'Perhaps he didn't have access to the same amount?' Willcox suggested. 'Or perhaps he felt he could risk giving less. Miss Franklin was, after all, considerably older than Miss Hodges. Some twenty years, I believe. It had the same effect, at any rate.' He paused. 'You say she consumed a meal shortly before she died?'

'The maid said she served her bread and cheese for supper. Why?'

'I found no trace of any food in her stomach. Only a cup of cocoa.'

'How curious.'

'I'll tell you something even more curious. I also found traces of chloral hydrate in her blood.'

'Sleeping tablets?' Spilsbury frowned. 'But why would she take a sleeping draught if she was expecting a visitor?'

'Why indeed?'

On the face of it, the case of Elizabeth Franklin seemed to be open and shut. The police seemed to think so, at any rate. They were putting all their energies into tracking down the mysterious admirer – The Lonely Hearts Killer, as the press had dubbed him – who had been preying on lonely spinsters.

Spilsbury didn't blame them. On the face of it at least, the evidence was too compelling to ignore. Two women, living within barely a mile of each other, both found dead in the same canal, both poisoned with strychnine. And both of them had been found to be corresponding with a mystery man via the Personal column of *The Times*.

Not only that, Spilsbury had just learned from Inspector Mount that the files giving details of who had placed the advertisements had been stolen from the newspaper office.

No wonder the police were so convinced.

But in spite of the overwhelming evidence, Spilsbury still had his doubts. The two women's deaths might have been similar, but their lives had been completely different. Was it really possible that they had both fallen prey to the same man?

He thought back to those poor women who had fallen prey to George Joseph Smith. The press had a name for them too: the Brides in the Bath, after the unique way they had perished, just days after their marriage.

Their names had been lost to history, but Spilsbury remembered them all. Alice Burnham, Margaret Lofty, Bessie Mundy. They had all been different in their own way, too. Bessie was an heiress, while poor Margaret had little to her name. Alice was a worldly-wise nurse, while

Margaret, several years older, lived a sheltered life as a lady's companion.

And yet they had all fallen under Smith's spell. So perhaps it wasn't outside the bounds of possibility that a thirty-seven-year-old shop assistant and a fifty-eight-year-old heiress might do the same?

And yet . . .

Something troubled him. He couldn't help feeling that in his haste to crack the case, Inspector Mount had been too keen to close the door on other possibilities.

'Good morning, gentlemen.'

Spilsbury turned round as Violet entered the office.

'Good morning, Mrs Franklin. Delightful day,' Willcox greeted her.

'Yes, it is. I do believe spring might be on its way at last.'

Spilsbury watched as she took off her coat and hat and hung them on the stand, then carefully smoothed down her skirt. It had been scarcely a week since Elizabeth Franklin's death, but one would never know it from Violet's calm, unflappable demeanour.

She had arrived in the office the day after her sister-in-law's body had been found, apologising for her absence the day before. She had had a headache, she said. Then she had just carried on with her work as if nothing had happened. Since then, she had made no reference to Elizabeth's death, or to the drama that was unfolding around her former family.

Even Willcox seemed aware of it. He snatched up his report from the desk just as Violet sat down. Spilsbury felt sure she must have noticed, but she made no comment as she rolled a fresh sheet of paper into her typewriter and began her work.

'I'd best be on my way,' Willcox said. 'I'm giving evidence at the Old Bailey at ten o'clock.'

'I'll walk with you,' Spilsbury said.

Outside the office, Willcox started towards the stairs that led up to the ground floor, but Spilsbury waylaid him.

'What are you doing? I told you, I'm due at the—'

'I need to speak to you.' He ushered him further down the passage, towards the post-mortem room. 'This can't go on,' he said in a hushed whisper.

'What are you talking about, old boy?'

'Her.' He nodded towards the office door.

Willcox sighed. 'Oh lord, what's she done now? Don't tell me she moved your coat to the wrong hook again?'

'I'm being serious, Willcox. Do you really think she should be here under the circumstances?'

'The circumstances?' Willcox's frown cleared. 'Oh, I see what you mean. I don't think there's anything to concern yourself with, old boy. I must admit I was worried about it myself, her being here while all this business with her sister-in-law was going on. But she seems to be all right, don't you think?' He shook his head. 'She must be made of jolly stern stuff, that's all I can say.'

'I'm not talking about that! Do you think she should be working here when she's a suspect in a murder enquiry?'

Willcox stared at him. 'A suspect? But I thought the police had their man?'

'Until they've identified and arrested someone, we have to assume anyone could have carried out the murder.'

'But not Mrs Franklin, surely?'

'Why not? You told me yourself there was animosity between her and the dead woman, even before she cheated her out of her fortune. Who knows what she could have done?'

'Yes, but—'

'I'm telling you, Willcox, I don't think it's wise to have her working here. Apart from anything else, we might find ourselves accused of having our evidence compromised . . .'

'Dr Spilsbury's right.'

They looked behind them. Violet stood in the doorway to the office. How long had she been eavesdropping? Spilsbury wondered. Long enough, by the stony expression on her face.

Willcox was immediately all bluster. 'Mrs Franklin, my dear lady, I hope you don't think—'

'I know exactly what you think. You've made yourself very clear.' She was looking at Spilsbury as she said it. 'And I can see your point. I don't wish to cause you any further embarrassment, so I'll hand in my notice.'

'There's really no need—' Willcox started to say, but Spilsbury cut him off.

'I think that would be a good idea,' he said.

For a moment he thought he saw her falter. But then she stiffened her shoulders and said, 'Very well. I'll work out my notice and leave at the end of the week. If that's all right with you?'

Spilsbury was about to say that it would be better if she left that day, but this time Willcox got in first.

'If that's what you really want, Mrs Franklin,' he said.

Once again, her hard gaze found Spilsbury. 'It doesn't look as if I've got much choice,' she said.

They watched as she stalked back to the office, closing the door behind her so hard the pane of glass rattled.

'Well,' Spilsbury said. 'That's all worked out very satisfactorily.'

'Oh, you think so, do you?'

'Don't you?'

But Willcox only walked away from him, shaking his head as he went.

Chapter 28

The following afternoon, Spilsbury returned to Gloucester Gate with Inspector Mount. But they were not the only visitors.

'Miss Lydia has company.' Mary greeted them at the door in her usual surly way. 'If you'd like to come back another time?'

'That would not suit us at all.' Spilsbury strode past her into the house, leaving the inspector to explain, 'The doctor would like to look at Miss Franklin's bedroom, if that's possible?'

'Her bedroom?' Mary looked put out. 'I'm not sure that would be right. Miss Elizabeth liked to keep things private . . .'

'I suppose it's up here, is it?' Spilsbury ignored her, mounting the stairs. 'Second floor?'

As he reached the first landing, the door to the drawing room opened and Lydia appeared.

'Dr Spilsbury!' She blinked at him. 'And Inspector Mount. What are you doing here?'

'I beg your pardon for the intrusion, Miss Franklin, but we have further enquiries we need to make.'

'Do you wish to speak to me?'

'That won't be necessary. We would like to take a look at your aunt's room, if that's all right with you?'

'Well, yes, of course. If you think it would help.' She pointed up the staircase. 'It's on the next floor, the second door on the right.'

'Thank you, Miss Franklin. We'll try not to disturb you too much. Spilsbury?'

Inspector Mount turned to look at him, but Spilsbury did not follow. He had become distracted by the dark-headed young man he glimpsed through the half-open door to the drawing room.

As if he knew he was being observed, the man rose to his feet and came to the door. He was stockily built, in a suit that was expensive but not made to measure. It did not fit his proportions; the seams of the sleeves strained over his upper arms and the shoulders finished too short. Second-hand, Spilsbury thought. Or a cancelled customer order he'd bought off the peg from a Savile Row shop.

'Is everything all right, Lydia?' he asked. His dark eyes were watchful, flicking from her to Inspector Mount warily.

'Yes, everything's fine. These gentlemen have just come to look at Aunt Elizabeth's room.'

'And you are?' Inspector Mount asked, although Spilsbury already knew the answer.

'This is Dr Dillon. He's – a friend of mine.' She chose her words carefully. 'Robert, this is Inspector Mount and Dr—'

'Oh, I know who you are!' The young man seized Spilsbury's hand and pumped it enthusiastically. 'It's a great honour to meet you, Dr Spilsbury. I'm a former St Mary's man myself.'

'Indeed?'

'I'm a physician at Bart's now. Moved there six months ago.'

Probably about the same time as his engagement to Lydia Franklin ended. He imagined it might have been rather awkward for him, working in the same department as the father of the girl who'd jilted him.

Although he and Lydia were clearly back on good terms now. He glanced past them to the drawing room. They had been sitting side by side on the couch, two teacups in front of them.

'I even attended several of your lectures while I was at St Mary's, but I daresay you don't remember me?'

'I do remember you,' Spilsbury said. 'But not from St Mary's.'

'Oh?'

'The last time I saw you, you were being forcibly ejected from a funeral.'

A deep blush flooded Dr Dillon's face. 'That was a misunderstanding,' he mumbled.

'Apparently so.' Spilsbury looked at Lydia Franklin's guilty face. 'But at least it seems to have been cleared up now.'

'Indeed.'

'We'll leave you to get on with your investigations,' Lydia said swiftly. 'Come on, Robert.'

'Poor Elizabeth,' Dr Dillon shook his head in sorrow. 'Such a tragedy. Who could have done such a terrible thing, I wonder?'

'That's what we're here to discover,' Inspector Mount said.

Spilsbury turned to head for the stairs, but the young man's voice followed him.

'Of course, I have my own suspicions.'

Inspector Mount stopped. 'Would you care to enlighten us?'

'Robert!' Lydia hissed, but he paid her no attention.

'The Black Widow, of course. She and Elizabeth loathed each other. And she's definitely got a grudge against this family.'

'That's not true,' Lydia protested. 'Violet didn't care about the money.'

'It was everything to her! Why else do you think she married your father?' Robert turned back to Inspector Mount. 'That's who you should be questioning, Inspector.'

'Thank you for your advice, Dr Dillon,' Inspector Mount said quietly.

Chapter 29

Elizabeth Franklin's room was exactly as Spilsbury would have expected: functional, no-nonsense, and devoid of any kind of feminine frippery. There was no lace at the windows, no frills on the high wooden bed. The only adornments were a faded silk coverlet of an indeterminate pinkish grey shade, and a pair of heavy silver candlesticks on the mantelpiece. The dark antique furniture had clearly been passed down through several generations. An ivory-backed hairbrush and mirror sat on the dressing table, perfectly aligned, next to a simple ebony jewellery box.

Mary the maid watched them from the doorway, a silent presence observing their every move as they donned their gloves and began to search.

'Has anything been touched since Miss Franklin died?' Inspector Mount asked.

'Not that I know of, sir. If it has, I certainly haven't done it. And I've kept the key with me all the time.' She showed it to them, still clutched in her fist.

'Why did you lock the door?' Inspector Mount asked.

'I don't know, sir. It just seemed like the right thing to do.'

There was something she wasn't saying, Spilsbury thought. Her eyes moved to the jewellery box as she spoke, as if satisfying herself it was still there.

He threw open the wardrobe door, releasing a gust of mothballs. The clothes inside were similarly plain and functional, although good quality. Spilsbury was no student of women's clothing, but even he could see they were stiff and old-fashioned.

'Miss Franklin did not go in for the latest fashions, I see?' he commented.

'She didn't approve of such things, sir,' Mary said. 'And she didn't hold with waste, either. She reckoned there were years of life left in what she'd got.'

No spending sprees for her, then, Spilsbury thought. He wondered what happiness her new-found fortune had brought her.

It might even have hastened her death, one way or another. Either through this mysterious admirer as the police believed, or someone closer to home.

A picture of Violet Franklin came into his mind. Dr Dillon certainly seemed sure she'd had something to do with her sister-in-law's death, and Spilsbury could not rule it out either.

He knew it was only right that she had left the office while she was still under suspicion. But it was rather peculiar not to hear the sound of her muttering curses over the clacking typewriter keys.

'Dr Spilsbury?'

He turned around to see Inspector Mount peering into an open bedside drawer.

'Come and have a look at this,' he said.

Inside the drawer was a carefully folded lace handkerchief, a pair of reading spectacles, a Bible, and a small clear glass bottle with a white label. Printed on the label in curled script were the name of a chemist in Camden High Street, and the words, 'Easton's Syrup'.

'Well, well,' he said. He took the bottle from the drawer. 'How long has Miss Franklin been taking this?'

'Not long, sir.' Mary sounded defensive. 'She sent me to fetch a bottle just after her brother died. For her nerves.'

'What is it, Doctor?' Inspector Mount asked.

'Easton's Syrup is a tonic of iron phosphate, laced with quinine and strychnine.'

'Strychnine!'

'Yes, but not enough to be fatal. For a child, perhaps, but an adult would have to take a great deal of it.' He held the bottle up to the fading light. 'How long did you say she had been taking it?'

'Since Sir James died, sir. But she didn't take it every night. Hardly at all, I'd say. Last time I looked, it was nearly full.'

'Well, it's practically empty now.'

'I don't know how that could be, sir.'

'Unless someone gave her the whole bottle?' Inspector Mount said.

'I think she would probably notice,' Spilsbury said. 'Easton's Syrup has a very bitter taste.'

'They could have put it in her food?'

'I hope you're not looking at me?' Mary burst out. 'I had no reason to kill her!'

'You did serve her supper on the night she died?' Inspector Mount pointed out.

'Yes, but she didn't eat it! I found her plate and the pot of tea untouched the next morning when I went into the study.'

'What did you do with it?'

'I threw it away, of course.'

'Pity,' Spilsbury murmured.

'I'm telling you, I didn't have anything to do with it,' Mary insisted. 'Why would I want to kill her?'

'Why indeed?'

'You say it was your night off, but you haven't told us where you were?' Inspector pointed out.

'That's my business.'

'It might help if you told us?'

'I don't see how, since I'm supposed to have poisoned her before I left!' Mary looked truculent for a moment. Then she said, 'Very well. If you must know, I went for a walk.'

'Until midnight?'

'There's no law against that, is there? I like the peace and quiet.'

'Where did you go?'

'Just around the edge of the park.'

'Were you alone?'

'I told you, I like the peace and quiet. I prefer being by myself, after being at other people's beck and call all day.'

'I seem to remember the weather was rather inclement that night?' he said.

'Was it? I can't say I noticed.' She looked from one to the other. 'I'm telling you, I had nothing to do with Miss Franklin's death. If you're going to start pointing fingers, then you're pointing them at the wrong person!'

'And who should we be pointing them at?' Inspector Mount asked.

Mary tightened her lips, weighing her words. Then she spoke.

'I don't like to speak out of turn,' she said.

'If you have something that might help our enquiry, you need to tell us,' the inspector urged.

Mary paused again. Then she turned to Spilsbury. 'You asked me how Miss Franklin seemed, the night she—' She broke off. 'The truth is, she'd been out of sorts for a while. Ever since she and Mister Matthew had their falling-out.'

'They'd argued? When was this?'

'A few days earlier, sir.'

'And what was the argument about?' Inspector Mount asked.

Mary looked at him sharply. 'I'm sure I don't know, sir. I'm not the sort to go around listening at doors, if that's what you're thinking. Although if I was to guess . . .' She glanced around the bedroom, as if to satisfy herself no one was listening. 'I'd say it was about money.'

'Money?'

'Yes, sir. If they fell out about anything, it was usually money.'

'What about it?'

'I couldn't say for sure. But I know Miss Franklin often had to help him out of a tight spot with his finances. I think she was getting a bit fed up with it.'

Once again, her gaze strayed to the ebony jewellery box.

'And that's what they argued about?'

'I don't know. All I heard was raised voices coming from the study, and the next moment Mister Matthew flew out of the room as white as a sheet. Nearly knocked me off my feet, he did. They barely spoke to each other after that.'

'So they weren't speaking when Miss Franklin was killed?'

'Oh no, sir. I believe Mister Matthew would have liked to make it up with her, but Miss Franklin couldn't even bear to be in the same room as him.'

'And was it usual for an argument to go on this long?' Inspector Mount asked.

Mary shook her head. 'He usually managed to get round her within a day or two. He was her favourite, you see. She put up with a lot more from him than she would from anyone else, I'll tell you that. When I think of some of the things he did . . .'

This time her gaze shifted to the candlesticks on the mantelpiece, and suddenly Spilsbury clicked.

'He stole from the family?' he said.

Mary stared at him in dismay. 'How do you know that? I swear I never said a word!'

'You didn't need to. You keep looking at Miss Franklin's belongings as if to satisfy yourself they're still there. I imagine there have been times when they weren't? What did he do? Pawn them?'

Mary's face reddened. 'No one was allowed to say anything,' she muttered. 'I used to be sent down to the shop with the ticket and some money to get them back. And then they'd all just carry on, as if nothing had happened. Until the next time.'

'Why didn't you tell us this before?' Inspector Mount asked.

'I didn't think it was important.' Mary shrugged. 'Besides, Miss Lydia said you already know who'd done it. Some mystery admirer or other?'

'Do you think she had an admirer, Mary?' Inspector Mount asked.

'I couldn't say, sir. I make a point of staying out of other people's business.'

'But you would have surely known if she had a gentleman caller? Or did she go out to meet someone?'

'Not that I know of, sir.'

'What about the letters?' Spilsbury asked.

'What letters, sir?'

'The ones you were burning the morning after she disappeared.' He turned to face her. 'Were they from a mystery admirer, perhaps?'

'I don't know what you're talking about, sir. I was burning some old receipts, that's all.'

They stared at each other across the room. Either Mary was an accomplished liar or she was telling the truth.

They finished searching the room, but there was nothing more of interest to be found. Spilsbury wrapped the near-empty bottle of Easton's Syrup carefully in brown paper to take with them, but he knew any fingerprints they found would be useless.

As the maid was showing them out, another thought occurred to him.

'We didn't find her sleeping pills,' he said.

'I beg your pardon, sir?'

'Chloral hydrate? There were traces in her system. But there were no pills in her bedside cupboard. Might she have kept them somewhere else?'

Mary shook her head. 'Miss Franklin never took them, sir.'

'Are you sure?'

'Not as far as I know, sir. Miss Franklin never had any trouble sleeping.'

'And she never consulted a doctor about her insomnia?'

'No, sir.'

'I see.'

But he didn't. He was still puzzling over the matter as he and Inspector Mount descended the steps.

'Well?' the inspector said. 'What did you make of that, Doctor?'

'I don't think the maid was responsible, if that's what you mean. There was no evidence of food in Miss Franklin's stomach, so it's quite likely she did not touch the supper Mary had left for her. And she distinctly said she made her a cup of tea, yet Willcox found traces of cocoa.'

'She might be lying?'

'I think if she was creating an alibi for herself, she would have been rather more careful about it.'

'I agree,' Inspector Mount said. 'So we're back to the idea of the mysterious late-night visitor?'

'Or someone closer to home?' Spilsbury said.

Chapter 30

'Now let's get one thing straight. You're not to say anything, all right? Just keep quiet and let me do the talking.'

'Whatever you say.'

George sent Charlie a sideways look. 'I mean it, Beanpole. I daresay the inspector only let you come because these are your sort of people.'

'And what sort of people would that be?' Charlie enquired innocently.

'You know.'

Common people. Labourers and dock workers, coster-mongers and thieves, the kind who inhabited the dank streets of South London, with its warehouses and wharves, factories and sweatshops.

Charlie certainly knew Queen's Buildings well. He had worked on his parents' stall in Waterloo for years. Some of Annie's relations still lived in Queen's Buildings. They had done a lot of their courting on the stone staircases, shrouded in shadow.

'It's a fool's errand anyway, if you ask me,' George grumbled. 'It's obvious to anyone those two old biddies were killed by the same man.'

'All the same, Inspector Mount says we've got to question everyone who might have a connection to Elizabeth Franklin.'

'You don't have to tell me that!' George snapped. 'I'm the detective, remember?'

'Here we are,' Charlie said, as they turned the corner into Scovell Road. 'Queen's Buildings.'

The tall slabs of grey brick looked even less appealing under the darkening sky. George looked up at them, his mouth curling.

'Jesus,' he murmured. 'How do people live like this?'

Charlie sent him a sidelong look. George might like to distance himself from his past now his family had moved out to the suburbs, but he had once lived on these same streets.

'It's better than the slums that used to be here.'

'Yes, but they're still living on top of each other. It can't be sanitary.'

Charlie kept quiet. He didn't want to repeat some of the stories his parents told, how they had lived a dozen to a room and taken turns to sleep in the bed.

Footsteps fled before them as they made their way into the building, disappearing down alleyways and up staircases, like cockroaches scuttling into the cracks in a wall.

'They don't like the law around here, do they?' George sneered.

'They're scared.'

'They'd have nothing to fear if they haven't done anything wrong.'

Charlie looked sideways at him. Had he forgotten so quickly? He wasn't in leafy Blackheath now, where the local bobby smiled and waved and did not come hammering on the door at midnight with his truncheon raised.

Violet Franklin took her time getting to the door, and George had just lifted his fist to pound on the peeling woodwork again when it suddenly flew open.

She was about his age, less than thirty at any rate. Charlie's first thought was how tired she looked. Shadows stood out like bruises on her pale, translucent skin. Her dark hair was drawn back in a loose knot, revealing a strong face and high cheekbones. She wasn't beautiful, but there was a vibrancy about her that was compelling. She wore an apron over her clothes, the sleeves of her white blouse rolled up to reveal slender forearms.

She did not seem at all surprised to see them. She looked from one to the other, a look of weary resignation in her tired green eyes.

'I thought you lot would turn up sooner or later,' she said in a dull, flat voice. 'You'd best come in.'

She ushered them inside, looking up and down the concrete walkway, then closed the door quickly, plunging them into shadowy darkness.

'How the mighty are fallen, eh?' George whispered, as Violet showed them into the house.

Charlie cringed, afraid she would hear. But if she did, she gave no sign of it as she led the way into the main room of the house, a living room with a stove, sink and kitchen table at one end. She walked upright, with a proud, almost queenly bearing that belied her humble surroundings.

The flat might have been cramped, but it was clean and tidy, smelling of lavender and beeswax. Violet had obviously been hard at work before they arrived, judging by the wet floor and the mop and bucket propped in the corner.

A small boy sat at the table, his legs swinging, playing with a wooden car. He was a clean, well-dressed little lad, not like the urchins who ran wild in the courtyards down below. He looked up at Charlie, who greeted him with a wink.

'Been cleaning?' George said, looking around.

'No wonder you're a detective. Nothing gets past you, does it?' Her accent was working class and very familiar to Charlie's ears. She reminded him of his wife, insolent to the point where it would get her into trouble.

'I wonder that you waste your time,' George snapped. 'I daresay this place is crawling with lice and bugs.'

An angry flush rose in Violet's pale face, and Charlie could see her battling with her anger.

'You don't mind if I carry on, do you?' Without waiting for an answer, she picked up the bucket and set it down in the middle of the floor with a clatter.

George sat down without being invited. 'A cup of tea would be nice,' he said.

'There's a café on the corner.'

They watched as she went on cleaning, swishing the mop back and forth across the worn oilcloth.

'I daresay you know why we've come?' George said. 'It's about your sister-in-law.' Violet said nothing as she went on with her work. 'I wonder you haven't come forward before.'

'Why should I?'

'To tell the police what you know.'

'I don't know anything.' Violet plunged her mop into the bucket and swilled it round. She kept glancing towards the door, Charlie noticed, as if she expected someone to appear at any moment.

George went back to his notebook. 'When was the last time you saw her?'

'The day I left the house.'

'When the will was read? The day you realised you weren't going to inherit a fortune?' Violet said nothing. 'That must have hurt, eh? All those years wasted on a sick old man, and nothing to show for it?'

Charlie opened his mouth to speak, but before he could say anything the small boy suddenly piped up, 'Mama?'

He must have picked up on his mother's agitation, Charlie thought. Kids understood more than adults gave them credit for.

'It's all right, Thomas.' Violet Franklin's face lost its hard lines, her voice softening. She bent to his level, tenderly putting her arms around him. 'Why don't you go in the bedroom and play?'

Thomas did not move. He stared at Charlie and George, his large eyes wary.

'Thomas, is it?' Charlie said. 'How old are you, Thomas? Three? Four?'

'Three.' The word came out reluctantly. 'Nearly four.'

'My little boy's four, too. And do you know what his favourite thing in the world is?' Thomas shook his head, his little face solemn. 'Humbugs.' Charlie reached into the pocket of his uniform and drew out a twist of brown paper. 'It just so happens I called in at the sweet shop this morning. Would you like to try one?'

The little boy turned to his mother, who smiled and nodded.

'It's all right,' she said. 'You can have one.'

Charlie held the paper towards him. Thomas hesitated for a moment, then darted forward and took a sweet and stuffed it into his mouth.

'Remember your manners?' Violet said.

'Thank you,' Thomas mumbled, the sweet lodged firmly in his cheek.

'That's for being such a good boy,' Charlie said. 'Now why don't you take your toy into the other room while we finish talking to your mother? We won't keep her long, I promise.'

He winked at him. Thomas snatched up his wooden car and disappeared into the other room.

'He's a lovely lad,' Charlie remarked.

'Yes, he is.' Violet looked after her son, still smiling.

'I'm sure it hasn't been easy, since your husband died?'

She whipped round to face him. All the softness disappeared from her face, the hard mask back in place.

'We're managing,' she said.

Charlie backed off and held his hands up. 'I was only making conversation, Mrs Franklin.'

'Bit touchy, aren't you?' George taunted. 'Got something to hide?'

'If I did, I'd hardly tell you, would I?'

'So you didn't see Miss Franklin or go back to the house after you left?'

'No.'

'I bet you were glad to hear she was dead, eh?'

Violet turned to him. 'Is that what you think?' she said in a cold, flat voice.

'Did you get on with her?' Charlie asked. Violet turned to look at him.

'I'm sure you already know the answer to that,' she said.

'I'd like to hear you tell us.'

She inhaled slowly. 'No,' she said. 'We didn't get on.'

'And why was that?'

'Because she thought I was after her brother's money.'

'And were you?'

'It didn't work if I was, did it?'

'That must have been hard to take,' George cut in, his face triumphant. 'Elizabeth Franklin made your life a misery for years, and then at the end of it she got everything and you ended up with nothing. That must have made you angry, surely? Angry enough to kill her, perhaps?'

'And what would I have to gain by that?' Violet's voice was lethally calm.

'But you must have felt you were owed?' George persisted.

'I wasn't owed anything. I came into the marriage with nothing, and I left with nothing.'

'Oh, come on! No need to play the innocent. There was a reason why you married that old man, wasn't there? You're seriously telling me you didn't expect something out of it?'

A prickle spread up the back of Charlie's neck. George was goading her deliberately, he thought. He stared at Violet, willing her not to rise. He had a feeling all hell would break loose if she did.

Before she could reply, the front door creaked open and a voice called out, 'Vi? Vi, are you there?'

There was a sudden volley of ferocious barking and the next moment the most vicious-looking dog Charlie had ever seen exploded into the room and threw itself at them. They both shot to their feet, ready to defend themselves, but Violet got there first, seizing the creature by its thick leather collar and dragging it back.

'Pistol? What the hell—' A burly young man appeared in the doorway. His face fell when he saw them. 'What's all this, then?'

Charlie recognised him straight away. That shock of black hair, the belligerent green eyes – once seen, never forgotten. He looked from him to Violet and back again. Why hadn't he seen the resemblance before?

'They're police,' Violet said, still holding back the snarling dog with all her strength.

'I ain't blind, Vi.' The man stared at the helmet Charlie nursed in his hands. 'What are they doing here?'

'We've come to speak to Mrs Franklin about her sister-in-law,' Charlie said, keeping his voice deliberately level. The young man exuded even more menace than his dog.

Unfortunately, George seemed oblivious to it. 'And who are you?' he demanded.

'I'm her brother.' The man squared up to George, his hands balling into fists at his sides.

George opened his mouth to speak, but Charlie got in first. 'I think we've already taken up enough of your time,' he said hurriedly, one eye still on the dog's slavering jaws.

Violet gave him a curt nod, her eyes barely meeting his. Her gaze was fixed on her brother. She looked as wary as Charlie felt.

'But I haven't finished my questions yet,' George protested.

'Then we can come back another time.' Charlie was ready to haul him to his feet but thankfully George moved to put on his bowler hat.

'I daresay we'll be back,' he muttered.

'And I'll be waiting for you,' the young man growled in response.

Chapter 31

'What was all that about?' George hissed, as soon as the door had closed on them.

'Not here.' Charlie took his sleeve and dragged him along the walkway towards the staircase. He made his way down the stairs, George following.

'You had no right to interfere with my investigation,' he whined. 'I told you I was in charge, didn't I? I warned you to keep out of it . . .'

'If I'd done that I would have been scraping what was left of you off these cobbles!' Charlie reached the ground floor and turned to face him. 'Don't you know who that was?'

'Who?'

'Mickey Malone.'

George looked blank for a moment, then realisation dawned. 'The boxer?'

'London amateur middleweight champion. I wouldn't fancy your chances against him.'

George pulled himself to his full height. 'I'm not scared of him,' he said. 'He wouldn't dare strike a policeman.'

'Mickey Malone would strike down the King of England if they spoke to his sister the way you just did. Just thank the lord he didn't hear you, that's all I can say. Why did you have to be so hard on her, anyway?'

'She's a suspect.'

'So are the rest of the Franklin family, but I didn't hear you talking to them in that way.'

'Yes, well, they're different.'

'Because they've got posh accents and live in a big house?'

George was silent for a moment. 'I daresay she's been treated worse. Anyway, you've got no right to lecture me about how to question suspects. I'm the detective here, remember?'

'Then start acting like one,' Charlie muttered as he followed his cocky, strutting figure down Scovell Road.

He had saved George from a beating, and now he was beginning to wish he hadn't bothered.

'You shouldn't have let them in,' Mickey said.

'What was I supposed to do, leave them on the doorstep so all the neighbours could gawp and listen to our business?' The tension Violet had been holding in finally exploded. She released her grip on Pistol's collar and he immediately ran to his master's side.

'I just don't like coppers in my house, that's all. I don't trust 'em.' He put his hand down to calm the dog, who was still growling under his breath.

'Yes, well, they've gone now.'

Violet picked up the bucket and carried it to the front door.

'Why did they want to talk to you, anyway?'

'I'll give you three guesses.'

'But it's nothing to do with you. You weren't even living there.'

'They're still bound to ask, Mickey.'

'And what did you tell them?'

'What do you think?'

Violet opened the front door and emptied the dirty water out, watching it run in muddy rivulets down the walkway.

'They've got no right, coming round here snooping.'

'Like I said, they've gone now.'

'But they'll come back, you can be sure of that. Once they've got a name in their heads, that's it.'

Violet looked at her brother, bent low over his dog. Poor Mickey. He had been in trouble with the police just like the rest of the family. He knew more than anyone what it was like to find himself in their sights.

And he was right. That smarmy little detective in the brown suit would be back asking more questions before long.

The other one, the tall one in uniform, seemed decent, at any rate. Although Violet wondered if his kindness with Thomas had all been part of an act to trick her into lowering her guard.

If it was, he'd have to try a lot harder than a humbug.

'Yes, well, we'll cross that bridge when we come to it.' She reached behind her to tighten the strings on her apron. 'I'll make a start on supper, shall I?'

'Not for me. I'm going out tonight.'

'Again? That's the third night in a row you've been out.'

'I didn't know you were keeping tabs on me?' Mickey was smiling when he said it, but his green eyes were deadly serious.

'I'm allowed to ask, ain't I?' she said.

'If you must know, I'm working.'

'At night?'

'I've been doing a few shifts as a watchman down at the docks. Here . . .' He reached into his pocket and pulled out a pound note, which he set down on the table.

Violet stared at it. 'What's that?'

'What does it look like? It's for the nipper. You're going to need it now you're out of work.'

His words stung. Violet's pride would never have allowed her to stay anywhere she was not wanted, but she had enjoyed her job at the hospital, and the wound of losing it was still raw.

He proffered the money again, but still Violet would not take it. 'Where did it come from?' she asked.

'I told you, I earned it. Ask Jack Morrow, if you don't believe me. He was the one who put me onto the job.'

Violet stared down at it, as if she was afraid it might bite her.

'All right, if you don't want it I'll have it back.'

He went to take the note back but Violet snatched it from him. 'I'll keep it,' she said. 'You'll only spend it down the pub, anyway.'

Mickey grinned. 'That's right, girl. You stop me getting into trouble.' He reached out and ruffled her hair.

If only I could, Violet thought as she watched him at the sink. After so many years, she knew when her brother was lying to her.

And Mickey had been quick, but not quick enough for her to miss the state of his hands, smeared with dried blood. God only knows how he'd got into that state, but she was damn sure it wasn't watching over a warehouse.

Chapter 32

That evening, Charlie met Annie outside the Albert Arms. One of her many relatives owned the pub on Gladstone Street, and Annie sometimes helped him out with a shift behind the bar if he was short-handed.

His wife always insisted she could make her own way home, no matter how late it was.

'I can take care of myself,' she said, and Charlie knew that was true. The streets of South London had been Annie's playground ever since she was a nipper. If anything, he felt sorry for anyone who might make the mistake of taking her on.

But he always insisted on walking her home anyway. And tonight he was even more keen because he couldn't wait to tell her what he had discovered. So he had left the children in bed and his mother Elsie snoring in front of the fire and walked up Southwark Bridge Road to meet his wife.

'Can you imagine? Mickey Malone! You could have knocked me down with a feather when I saw him standing there.'

Back in his schoolboy boxing days, everyone knew of Mickey. Even as a kid, he'd been knocking out opponents several years older and a lot more experienced than himself.

He and Charlie had fortunately never met in the ring – Mickey was in a different class to him in more ways than one. If it hadn't been for the war, he might have turned professional and ended up being the next Bandsman Blake. But like so many other young men, the war had put paid to his ambitions.

'So this woman you went to question – she's Violet Malone?' Annie said.

'That's right. Why? Do you know her?'

It was a daft question. Annie knew nearly everyone from Lambeth to London Bridge.

'Oh, I know her, all right. Or at least, I know of her. She was a good friend of my cousin Ethel. You remember Ethel?'

'The one who did time in Holloway?'

'That's the one.'

It took a moment for the penny to drop. 'You don't mean to tell me Violet—'

'They were in Alice Diamond's gang together. They got sent to prison at the same time.'

Alice Diamond ran the biggest crew of female hoisters and thieves south of the river. There was a vast network of girls working together, mothers and daughters, sisters, aunts and cousins. They called themselves the Forty Elephants because of the voluminous skirts where they hid stolen goods when they went hoisting up west. They were every bit as ruthless and greedy as their male counterparts, and just as violent too, judging by the amount of fights they got into.

Annie had been in the gang for a while too, with her aunt, her two sisters and several of her cousins. But she had walked away from that life when she and Charlie got engaged.

Charlie's picture of Violet Franklin shifted in his mind. That queenly demeanour was all put on, he realised. He imagined it would come in very useful when it came to mingling with the upper-class shoppers in Selfridges and the like.

Annie laughed at his dumbfounded expression. 'She proper took you in, didn't she?' She squeezed his arm. 'Don't worry, love, you ain't the first to fall for it. Violet was one of Alice's best girls. She could fool anyone.'

'And that's supposed to make me feel better, is it?' Charlie said gloomily. 'Some detective I'm going to make!'

'You would have worked it out in the end, I'm sure.'

'I doubt it.' He could have kicked himself for not making the connection. But now he knew what sort of family she came from, he had a completely different view of her.

'Their father's dead, ain't he?' he said.

Annie nodded. 'And one of the brothers. The other one's still in jail for armed robbery. Beat a man nearly senseless, he did. It's a miracle he ain't been hanged for murder.'

'They sound like a lovely bunch.'

'Oh, they are. There ain't many round here who'd mess with the Malones.' She paused. 'Of course, you know she was married before?'

Charlie stared at her in shock. 'No!'

'It's true. A gangster, Harry Baines. You must have heard of him? He was in charge of the Elephant Boys?'

'He was a bad 'un, then?'

'I'll say. Rich, too. He ran most of the racetracks between here and the south coast.'

'What happened to him?'

'He died. Left Violet a wealthy widow, by all accounts. Although it didn't last long. She spent it all and was back living in Queen's Buildings with her brother before the year was out. That was just before war was declared.'

Her words were not lost on Charlie as they crossed Southwark Street in silence.

Perhaps Elizabeth Franklin had been right: when one rich husband died, Violet wasted no time in finding another.

But it was one thing to marry for money, but quite another to murder for it.

And besides, what did she have to gain from her sister-in-law's death? It wasn't as if the fortune would somehow end up with her.

But then, Violet was a Malone. And they were a law unto themselves.

'How did he die?' he asked.

'Come again?'

'Harry Baines. How did he die?'

Annie sent him a long look, as if she had known all along he was going to ask that question.

'They pulled him out of the river,' she said.

Chapter 33

'You shouldn't go. You won't be welcome.'

'There's nothing new in that.'

Violet put on her heavy sable coat. She didn't know why it hadn't gone to the pawn shop with the other things, but James had given it to her as a gift, and she could not bear to part with it.

'They won't want you there. *She* certainly wouldn't want you there.'

She allowed herself the smallest of smiles in the mirror as she adjusted her hat. Elizabeth Franklin would probably spin in her grave if she knew Violet was going to attend her funeral.

'I told you, I promised Lydia,' she said.

'But everyone will be whispering, pointing fingers.'

'All the more reason I should be there, to show them I ain't got nothing to hide. Besides, someone's got to look after Lydia. I don't want her to face this on her own.'

'And who's going to be looking after you?'

'I'm a big girl, Mick. I can take care of myself.' She tilted her head, tipping the brim of her hat so her eyes were in shadow. The less her face gave away, the better.

'I'm sure Miss Lydia Franklin can take care of herself, too,' Mickey muttered.

'I wouldn't bet on it.' Violet stepped back to scrutinise her reflection. In spite of what she had said to Mickey, she felt as if she was donning armour ready for a battle.

Her confidence began to fail her when she saw the reporters gathered around the church in St John's Wood.

'It's the widow,' one of them cried, and the next moment there was a clamour around her, with cameras clicking and voices shouting over each other.

'What do you have to say about your sister-in-law's death?'

'Is it true you hated each other?'

'Are you sorry she's dead?'

'Who do you think killed her?'

'Do you know anything about her mystery lover?'

Violet kept her head held high as she swept past them.

'Was it you who killed her?'

She swung round, stung by the question. But then one of the reporters thrust a camera in her face, and the pop of the flashbulb released her, shocking her back to her senses. She turned on her heel and hurried up the path towards the church.

Two men in suits and bowler hats flanked the doors, one ginger and lanky, the other wiry with slicked-back hair and a pencil moustache. The tall one caught her eye as she hurried past and Violet recognised them instantly as the policemen who had called to see her two days earlier.

The church was depressingly empty. Violet chose a pew at the back, two rows behind Mary the maid. Lydia and Matthew sat side by side at the front, with a few aged relatives Violet recognised from James's funeral scattered in between.

Had it really been only a few weeks since they had said goodbye to him in this very church? It felt like an eternity. There had been no empty seats that day, as friends, family and colleagues all crowded to pay their last respects.

But then, her husband had been loved and respected, while Elizabeth was only despised and feared.

Her sister-in-law had got the funeral she deserved, Violet thought bitterly.

There was another young man on the front row beside Lydia. Violet stared at the back of the dark head. Surely it couldn't be?

As if he knew she was watching, he turned his head slightly and their eyes met.

Robert Dillon.

A shudder of revulsion ran through her. The one thing she and her sister-in-law had agreed on was that Robert Dillon was bad news.

She watched as he leaned across and whispered to Matthew. Her stepson swung round to look at her, his face pinched with anger. Violet stared back, not in the slightest bit intimidated. She had faced down far worse men than Matthew Franklin in her time.

No sooner had the church organ swelled into life than the doors at the back creaked open. Out of the corner of her eye, Violet noticed a tall figure in a top hat, morning coat and spats enter the church and seat himself at the far end of her row.

She stole a quick glance and found herself looking at the imperious profile of Dr Bernard Spilsbury.

Her gaze dropped to her prayer book. Oh God, what was he doing here?

Thankfully, the vicar mounted the pulpit and began to speak.

The atmosphere in the church was oppressive. In spite of the cold, Violet sweltered inside her black dress, the fabric thick and itchy against her skin.

Mickey was right, she thought – she shouldn't have come. Funerals were for people who genuinely mourned the passing of a loved one. It was almost as if God himself could see the guilt in her soul.

It was a relief when the service finally ended. Violet had planned to slip away as quickly as she could. But Matthew caught up with her outside.

'What the hell are you playing at?' he snarled. 'You have no right to be here.'

'I've come to pay my respects, like everyone else.'

'Your respects?' His lip curled. 'Is that supposed to be some kind of joke?'

'Stop it, Matthew.' Lydia appeared behind him. 'You're making a scene and everyone is watching.'

Violet glanced at the two policemen. The tall, red-haired one had started towards them, but the shorter man held him back.

'Yes, but she shouldn't be here!'

'I asked her to come.'

'You did what?'

'I wanted her here,' Lydia said. 'She's still family, after all.'

'She's no family of mine!' Matthew snapped. 'Nor my aunt's.'

'He's right.' Robert Dillon joined in. 'Elizabeth would be most upset if she knew she was here.'

'I'm sure she wouldn't be too happy to see you, either,' Violet retorted.

'I'm here for Lydia's sake.'

'As am I. So that's all right, ain't it?'

They stared at each other in mutual dislike, until Matthew broke in. 'Lydia's right, this is neither the time nor the place for an argument.' He turned to Violet, lowering his voice. 'Just know you are not welcome.'

'Oh, I'm well aware of that, don't you worry. You've spent years making it abundantly clear. But I ain't staying. I want nothing from this family.'

Unlike some. She shot Robert a look of dislike.

She started to walk away, but Lydia caught up with her. 'Take no notice of Matthew,' she whispered. 'I'm glad you came.'

'I wanted to make sure you were all right. But it looks like I needn't have bothered.' She glared back at Robert, who stood a few feet away, watching them intently. 'I see it didn't take him long to worm his way back in?'

'It isn't like that,' Lydia said. 'He's been very kind. He wrote to me as soon as he found out about poor Aunt Elizabeth.'

'I bet he did.' She was probably scarcely cold before he saw his chance.

'He's been very kind,' Lydia said.

'All the same, you want to watch him.'

'It's nothing like that, honestly. He just wants to be a friend to me, that's all. And I really need someone, Violet. You understand that, don't you?' She pleaded for understanding.

'Of course, love.' Violet reached for her stepdaughter's hand. Poor Lydia, she was so alone and vulnerable, easy prey for the likes of Robert Dillon.

She just hoped she wouldn't fall for him a second time.

Chapter 34

Charlie watched the altercation from across the churchyard.

'What do you think's going on there?' he asked.

'God knows.' George Stevens lounged against the doorway and lit up a cigarette. As usual, he did not offer one to Charlie. 'All I know is it's starting to rain and I'm going to get soaked.'

'We'll have to go to the cemetery after this,' Charlie reminded him. 'Just in case.'

'Talk about a bloody wild goose chase!' George groaned. 'Why the inspector agreed to this I don't know.'

'He thought it was a good idea.'

Charlie kept his gaze fixed on the scene a few yards away. Violet was walking away now. He watched her long strides as she headed off back towards the gates, sweeping aside the press men who crowded around her. There was pride in the way she walked. This was not someone who would allow herself to be chased away by anyone, least of all the likes of Matthew Franklin.

He was seeing her in a new light after what Annie had told him. She no longer had his sympathy, that was for sure.

He had looked up Harry Baines in the police files. His criminal record had run to several fat folders that took up half a drawer in the cabinet. Armed robbery, assault and battery, suspected murder – he was a nasty piece of work, all right. Violent, ruthless and cold-blooded to the core, he had wreaked havoc over South London for most of his short career.

He could only imagine what kind of woman would have married a man like that. Not a blushing flower, that was for sure.

'So you know what the inspector's thinking now, do you?'

Charlie looked round at George, who was blowing plumes of smoke into the air. 'Come again?'

'You think you're well in with us, just because Mount's using you as the errand boy.' He pointed his cigarette at Charlie. 'But let me tell you, it won't last forever. I'll still be there long after you've been packed off back to uniform, looking for missing cats. And don't you forget that.'

'I won't.' Charlie frowned at him. What had brought this on? he wondered.

As if he'd made his point, the next moment George Stevens was all smiles again. 'Right, so the inspector wants us to talk to Matthew Franklin first so you'd best go over and collar him.'

'Shouldn't we wait a couple of minutes? They've just come out of the church.' Charlie scanned the rest of the churchyard.

'Still hoping the Lonely Hearts Killer will show up with a wreath?' George grinned.

'You never know.'

'I do. He's probably wining and dining his next victim by now, planning when he's going to do away with them. I daresay we'll be pulling another one out of the canal next month.' He tipped his ash carelessly on to the ground. 'What a way to make a living, eh? Getting desperate old women to fall in love with you. Catch me doing it!'

'Surely no woman would be that desperate,' Charlie muttered.

George bristled. 'For your information, I could have any woman I wanted.'

'And yet you're still single?'

'I'm choosy, mate. And careful.'

Now it was Charlie's turn to bristle. 'What's that supposed to mean?'

'It means I'm not mug enough to get a girl in the family way and then have to marry her.'

Charlie's hand balled into a fist at his side. He toyed with the idea of planting it in George's smug little face, but then he decided against it. He didn't want to have to explain to Inspector Mount how George Stevens ended up with a busted lip.

'It's a wonder he ain't been caught though, don't you think?' he said instead.

'Eh?'

'What you just said about wining and dining. Don't you reckon it's strange no one ever saw him out and about with Jean Hodges or Elizabeth Franklin? I mean, he must have taken them out, surely?'

'Perhaps he was embarrassed to be seen with them. Perhaps they do all their courting indoors, if you know what I mean?' George smirked.

Charlie turned back to watch the mourners. 'I wonder why he killed them?' he said. 'I mean, he didn't stand to gain anything, did he? It wasn't as if they were married, or he'd taken out any insurance policies on their lives.' They had checked thoroughly and nothing had come up against either Jean Hodges or Elizabeth Franklin's names. 'They might have been giving him money while they were alive, but all that would have stopped when they died. It makes no sense to kill them, does it?'

'Perhaps they just got on his nerves?' George shrugged.

Charlie considered it. 'You might be right,' he said. 'Hilda Hodges said her sister was planning to move in with this mystery man. Perhaps she was pushing it and wouldn't take no for an answer? He must have been courting her and Elizabeth Franklin at the same time. He probably decided Elizabeth was the better bet.'

'So Jean Hodges had to go?'

'Something like that.'

'Then why kill Elizabeth?'

'Maybe she turned him down?' Charlie suggested.

'Don't be daft! An old biddy like her? She'd jump at any chance.'

Charlie shook his head. 'I get the impression Miss Franklin was a difficult character. No pushover, that's for sure, and not daft, either. Perhaps she started to see him for what he really was, and tried to call it off—'

'Thank Christ, they're heading for the gate,' George interrupted him. He tossed his cigarette onto the grave and ground it out with his heel. 'Let's get hold of Franklin before he has time to leave.'

Charlie followed him across the grass to where the funeral party was starting to disperse.

'Mr Franklin?'

Matthew Franklin swung round, a look of dismay on his face. 'Yes? What do you want?'

'We wondered if we could have a word with you, sir?'

'What, here? Now? It's my aunt's funeral.'

'I know, sir, but—'

'Is everything all right, Franklin?'

A man approached them. He was in his late thirties, with close-cropped fair curls, a ruddy complexion and piercing blue eyes. His stocky build was a contrast to Matthew's slender height.

'Everything's fine,' Matthew Franklin said in a clipped voice.

'It doesn't seem fine to me.' The man turned to George. 'Who are you?' he demanded.

'We're police officers, sir. And you are?'

'Never mind who I am. You've got a damn cheek, harassing poor Franklin at a time like this. Does your superior officer know you're here?'

George drew himself up to his full height. 'As a matter of fact, sir, he was the one who sent us.'

'Then he should be thoroughly ashamed of himself.'

'Keep your voice down, Warriner!' Matthew Franklin shot a sideways look at the other mourners.

'I hope you're not trying to implicate him in all this?' the man said, still glaring at George. 'He had nothing to do with any of it. I can vouch for that. I was with him at the regimental dinner the whole evening.'

'It's nothing to do with that,' Charlie stepped in placatingly. 'We just wanted to ask him a few questions.'

'What sort of questions?'

'Warriner, please . . .' Matthew gave a weary sigh. 'Look, I can't talk to you here,' he said to George. 'Come to the house tomorrow.'

They watched the pair of them walking away down the avenue.

'What did you make of that?' Charlie asked.

'Obnoxious fool,' George muttered. 'I wish I could have arrested him, just to wipe that smirk off his face.'

'He did seem very keen to stop Franklin talking to us. Why, I wonder?' Charlie followed the two men with his gaze. The man sauntered with his hands in his pockets while Matthew walked with his head down, like a man with the weight of the world on his shoulders. 'What was his name again?'

'I think Franklin called him Warriner.'

Charlie thought about it for a moment. 'I'm sure I've heard that name before. But I can't remember where.'

His face was familiar, too. It hovered on the edge of Charlie's mind, fleeting as a ghost.

'I can't see as it would be important anyway.' George shrugged. 'Come on, let's get to the cemetery before the Lonely Hearts Killer gives us the slip!'

Chapter 35

As Spilsbury left the church in his car, he caught sight of a figure walking through the rain ahead of him in a drenched black sable coat.

His first instinct was to carry on past. But as the car drew level, on impulse he leaned forward and instructed the driver to slow down the car.

'Mrs Franklin?' he called out, as they drew level. She carried on walking, her head down, sodden collar pulled up. 'Mrs Franklin, may I offer you a lift?'

'No, thank you.'

'But it's raining?'

'I don't mind the weather.'

The car crawled along beside her for a moment. People were turning to stare at them, and Spilsbury began to feel rather foolish. 'Do let me give you a lift,' he offered again.

'I'm going in the opposite direction to you.'

This made sound sense to him, and he was about to wind up the window and continue on his way. But then he said,

'Get in the car, Mrs Franklin. I want to talk to you about something.'

A moment's hesitation, and then she was climbing in beside him, filling the back of the car with drenched fur, like an enormous wet dog. Spilsbury cringed back in his seat and began to regret his decision.

'Well? What did you want to speak to me about?'

He admired her directness. He never cared to waste time on pleasantries either.

'I saw what happened after the funeral. The way Mr Franklin and that other young man spoke to you.'

'What of it?'

'They were very ungentlemanly towards you.'

'It's not the first time it's happened.'

She sent him a hard look. The meaning was not lost on him. Spilsbury opened his mouth to protest, then closed it again.

'I seem to remember Dr Dillon receiving a similar welcome at your husband's funeral?'

'So he did.' Violet allowed herself a small smile at the memory.

'You took exception to him being there?'

'Dr Spilsbury, I was burying the man I loved. Do you really think I cared who was there? Jack the Ripper could have walked in with a bloody knife and I would have scarcely noticed him.' Her gaze dropped to her hands, laced in her lap. 'It was Elizabeth who took exception, not me.'

'Why was that?'

'She disliked him.'

'Why?'

'From what I could gather, she didn't think he was good enough for Lydia.'

'Is that why she forced her to call off the engagement?'

'It was Lydia's decision to call it off in the end. But I daresay she did it to please her aunt. She was always so desperate to please, much good it did her.'

'What do you mean by that?'

She raised her gaze to meet his. 'Haven't you realised it yet, Doctor? No one ever won my sister-in-law's approval. She found fault with everyone.'

'And what fault did she find in Dr Dillon?'

Once again, Violet smiled. 'I take it you've never met him?'

'Indeed I have. He was at the house with Miss Franklin when I called with the inspector a few days ago. He struck me as a very personable young man.'

'Oh, I'm sure he was. I daresay he was most eager to make your acquaintance. Robert likes to mix with the rich and well connected. And woe betide anyone who stands in his way,' she murmured.

The irony of her words was not lost on him. 'You're saying he was a fortune hunter?'

Violet's mouth twisted. 'What are you thinking, Doctor? That it takes one to know one?' She shook her head. 'It was Elizabeth who called him that, not me.'

'And what did you think of him?'

She shifted her gaze to look out of the car window, even though the view was blurred by rain. 'I thought he was one of the nastiest, most underhanded men I'd ever met. And believe me, I've met more than my fair share!'

'Would you care to explain why?'

Violet paused. He could feel her weighing him up, wondering how much to tell him.

'I first met him in France,' she said at last. 'He was working with James in the Medical Corps. And of course they'd known each other at St Mary's. James was a consultant physician while Robert was a student there. James was very impressed with him, as I recall. He thought he was bright, hard-working, and very good with the patients.'

'And what did you think?'

'Oh, he was bright, there's no doubt about that. And hard-working, too. But he made sure his efforts didn't go unnoticed, if you know what I mean?'

'He was trying to make a good impression on your husband?'

'Like I said, Robert likes to mix with the rich and well connected. You might not believe it, but he was even charming to me back in those days. I suppose he saw the way the wind was blowing and decided it was worth his while to get on my good side.'

One look at her shrewd expression told him the young man's plan had not worked.

'You didn't like him?'

'I could see right through him, when even James couldn't. Robert Dillon only bothers with people he thinks might be useful to him. Once he's finished with them, he casts them aside.'

Violet took off her hat and carelessly shook the rain from its brim. Spilsbury fastidiously shifted his legs to avoid the drips landing on his spats.

'He told us his family were wealthy landowners up in the north, but that his parents were dead,' she went on. 'James took him under his wing. After we were married and had returned to England, Robert came to stay with us while he was on leave. That was when he met Lydia.' She shook her head. 'Poor little Lyd. She'd led such a sheltered life under Elizabeth's care. She hadn't even been sent to school. The only time she left the house was to go to church or a walk round the park with her aunt. It's hardly surprising Robert was able to sweep her off her feet,' she said bitterly. 'Before anyone knew what was happening, they were engaged.'

'It was love at first sight?'

'For her, perhaps. I'm sure Robert had already calculated the advantages of such a match well before they even met.'

'So you're saying he *was* a fortune hunter?' Spilsbury said.

'Put it this way: it didn't hurt that Lydia was so sweet and beautiful. But I reckon he would have married Elizabeth if it meant getting what he wanted.'

'And what did he want?'

'James had a private practice on Harley Street. He promised that once the war was over and Robert and Lydia were married, he would take him on as a partner.'

'Quite a step for a newly qualified doctor, to have his own brass plate in Harley Street?' Spilsbury commented.

'Robert's a very ambitious man.'

'There's nothing wrong with being ambitious.'

'It depends how you treat people along the way, doesn't it?'

The bitterness in her voice made him turn to face her. 'You saw another side to Dr Dillon?'

Once again, she turned to look out of the window.

'There was a girl in the village, close to where we were stationed,' she said. 'Her father was the mayor, and he owned a lot of land in the area. So of course, Robert made a beeline for him – or rather, his daughter.' She smiled at the memory. 'She was such a sweet girl, like Lydia in a way. Beautiful, but very naïve. She truly believed Robert when he told her he wanted to marry her. He even gave her a ring. I remember how she used to show it off to everyone.'

'But then he met Lydia Franklin?'

'I think the idea of being in private practice in London appealed to him more than being master of a chateau, although I can't say I blame him for that. None of us ever wanted to go back to France after what we'd been through.' She closed her eyes briefly at the memory.

'I'm sure that was very distressing for the young girl,' Spilsbury said. 'But surely he was allowed to change his mind. Engagements end every day—'

'You don't understand,' Violet interrupted him. 'It wasn't the way the engagement ended. It was what happened afterwards.'

'And what did happen?'

'Madeleine died. They found her body two days after Robert returned to England.'

He sat up straight. 'She'd been murdered?'

'As good as. She died as a result of sepsis after a ham-fisted abortion.'

Spilsbury was silent for a moment, taking it in. He had seen more than his fair share of young women who had died in the same horrific way, after putting themselves in the hands of backstreet butchers.

'Are you saying Dillon was the one who—'

'I don't know,' she admitted. 'But I do know Madeleine put her trust in him, and he betrayed her. Perhaps it wasn't him who did it to her, although I can well imagine him going to any lengths to rid himself of what he saw as an obstacle.' Her face was bitter. 'Or perhaps she went to someone else? The poor girl probably felt she had no choice once her fiancé had abandoned her. All I do know is that within a month he was engaged to Lydia. And he's never looked back.' She raised her gaze to meet his. 'Now do you see why I don't like him, Doctor? A young girl died a brutal, horrible death, and he doesn't even have it on his conscience.'

'I take it Elizabeth found out about this?' Spilsbury said.

Violet shook her head. 'That's not why she took against him. He committed a far more heinous crime in her eyes.'

'What's that?'

'He was poor.' Violet's mouth twisted. 'Elizabeth somehow found out that he had lied about his background. His father wasn't a wealthy landowner, he was just a poor tenant farmer.

Robert's education was funded by scholarships. Can you imagine?' She feigned horror.

'And that made a difference to her?'

She looked at him pityingly. 'It made a world of difference. Status and breeding were everything to Elizabeth. Which is why she hated me so much. But at least I've never been ashamed of where I came from. I didn't lie about my family, or polish my accent, or buy second-hand suits from Savile Row and try to pass them off as tailor-made. You know what you're getting with me.'

Their eyes met and held, and Spilsbury read the meaning in her clear, green gaze.

'Mrs Franklin, I—'

'Stop the car.' Violet cut across him, leaning forward to speak to the driver.

Spilsbury peered out through the blurred windows at the shape of St Paul's looming over them. 'But we haven't reached the bridge yet . . .'

'It's all right, I can walk from here.' She was already opening the door as the car slowed to a halt at the kerb. 'Thank you for the lift, Doctor Spilsbury. I hope you find your murderer soon.'

'I hope so too, Mrs Franklin. And perhaps when this is all settled, we can consider the matter of your position at the hospital.'

She stared at him, her eyes turning to chips of ice.

'I wouldn't come back if you begged me,' she said.

And then she was gone, walking fast through the rain, her dark shape disappearing quickly into the crowds of city commuters heading for the station.

Spilsbury was startled, but he had put Mrs Franklin out of his mind by the time he returned to St Mary's in Paddington. It was early evening, but as he descended the stairs, he could hear the ever-faithful mortuary keeper Alf Bennett still plodding away as he always did. He seemed to go home even more rarely than Spilsbury.

He entered the cold store, already tearing off his jacket.

'How many today, Mr Bennett?'

'Just one from this morning, sir. Got run over by a milk lorry and died on the operating table. But Inspector Mount arrived ten minutes ago.'

'Good lord. Alive, I hope?'

'Oh yes, sir. Very much so.' Alf Bennett chortled, which quickly turned into one of his wheezing coughs. 'I asked him to wait in the office. I hope that was all right?'

'Thank you, Mr Bennett.'

Inspector Mount sprang from his seat like a jack in the box when Spilsbury entered the office. He noticed the policeman's uneasy expression and a thought struck him.

'You haven't found another body?'

'No,' Inspector Mount said. 'But we've found a witness.'

'Alive?'

'Very much so.'

'Well, that's good news, isn't it?'

'That depends, Doctor.' The inspector cleared his throat. 'You see, this particular witness claims Elizabeth Franklin was alive and well two hours after you say she was lying dead at home.'

Chapter 36

'Impossible,' Spilsbury said.

Inspector Mount looked almost apologetic. 'I've got a witness who says different,' he insisted.

'Then your witness is lying.'

The inspector looked taken aback. 'And why would she do that?'

'I don't know. Perhaps she's merely mistaken?'

'Or perhaps you might be?'

Spilsbury was still staring at the inspector when Willcox stuck his head around the door.

'Just to remind you we've got to be on that train to Bedford at half past – oh, hello.' He looked at Inspector Mount. 'Sorry, old man, I didn't know you had company. Good to see you, Inspector.'

'And you, Dr Willcox.'

Willcox looked nervously at Spilsbury. 'Is everything all right?'

'No,' Spilsbury replied, tight-lipped, still glaring at the inspector.

'Whatever is the matter?'

'I was just explaining to Dr Spilsbury that a witness has come forward who claims to have spent time with Elizabeth Franklin on the night she was murdered.' Once again, Inspector Mount looked almost apologetic.

'I see. Well, that's a good thing, isn't it?'

'No,' Spilsbury snapped. 'It isn't.'

'Dr Spilsbury estimates that death occurred some time between eight and eleven o'clock in the evening. But this witness has stated that at around eleven Miss Franklin was drinking with a man in a nightclub.'

'It's utterly preposterous,' Spilsbury muttered. 'And it's not an estimate,' he added. 'That was precisely the time she was murdered.'

'It might have been a couple of hours either way?' Willcox reasoned. 'Surely it's harder to tell if a body has been immersed—'

Spilsbury turned on him. 'Do you think I haven't taken that into account?'

'I'm just telling you the facts, Dr Spilsbury,' Inspector Mount muttered.

'And I'm telling you the facts, too! There is no possibility that Elizabeth Franklin was anywhere but submerged in the Regent's Canal at midnight.'

'Nevertheless . . .'

'Which nightclub was it?'

They both looked round at Willcox, their argument momentarily forgotten.

'What does that have to do with anything?' Spilsbury asked.

'Nothing, old man. I was just interested.'

Inspector Mount consulted his notes. 'The Blue Angel, in Ham Yard.'

'Soho, eh?' Willcox raised his eyebrows. 'Miss Franklin was a game old girl, wasn't she?'

'Actually, she wasn't,' Spilsbury snapped. 'Which is another reason why I find this whole idea so absurd.' He turned to Inspector Mount. 'Honestly, can you imagine Elizabeth Franklin frequenting a nightclub?'

A flicker of doubt crossed the inspector's face. 'I must say I can't,' he admitted. 'But I can't rule anything out at this stage of the inquiry.'

'Then there's nothing else for it,' Willcox declared. 'We must go to the Blue Angel and talk to this mysterious witness.'

'Indeed,' Spilsbury said. 'I'd very much like to hear what this person has to say for herself.'

'I've actually arranged to meet her at the nightclub the day after tomorrow,' he said. 'She's the proprietor of the establishment, and she's been out of the country for the past three weeks, which is why she hasn't come forward before. You're most welcome to come with me, Dr Spilsbury.'

'Excellent.' Willcox rubbed his hands together. 'We'll look forward to it. Won't we, old boy?'

Spilsbury turned to him. 'We?' he said.

'You don't think I'd let you step into such a den of iniquity without me, do you?'

'The police will be there. I'm sure I shall be quite safe.'

'Yes, but even so . . .' Willcox looked amused. 'You? In a nightclub? I wouldn't miss this for the world!'

Chapter 37

'I really don't see what any of this has got to do with you.'

Matthew Franklin shifted uncomfortably on the brocade sofa in the drawing room of Gloucester Gate. He reminded Charlie of a sulky child on the receiving end of a reprimand.

'But you admit your aunt was making payments to you?' George said.

'Of course I admit it!' Angry colour rose in Matthew's face. 'I wouldn't be stupid enough to deny it, would I? Not when it's all there in black and white.' He glared at the sheaf of bank statements in George's hand.

'Why didn't you tell us about this before?'

'I saw no reason to bring it up. It was a private matter between my aunt and me. And it certainly didn't have anything to do with her death. Why are you here, anyway?' he changed the subject abruptly. 'Why aren't you out there, trying to find the man who came calling the night she was murdered?'

'We're making every effort to find him, Mr Franklin,' George said patiently. 'We're following up every possible lead—'

'And yet here you are, wasting your time with me! May I remind you, I wasn't even there the night she was killed? As my friends have already told you, I was—'

'Why did she give you the money?' Charlie cut across his bluster.

Matthew deflated like a balloon, shrinking back into himself. 'That's personal,' he muttered.

'You need to answer our questions, sir,' George pressed him.

'You won't mind answering if you have nothing to hide, will you?' Charlie added.

Matthew hesitated for a long time. 'I had debts,' he revealed reluctantly.

'What kind of debts?'

Matthew sent him a dark look. Then he said, 'I had a run of bad luck.'

'So they were gambling debts?'

'It wasn't a problem,' Matthew jumped in quickly. 'I'm actually a very skilled card player. But I'd just—'

'Had a run of bad luck?' Charlie finished for him.

Matthew glared at him but said nothing.

'It was quite a long run, wasn't it?' George consulted the bank statements. 'These payments go back several months. I wonder you didn't give it up as a bad job?'

'I would have won it back eventually,' Matthew muttered. 'Anyway, it wasn't all to pay off my debts. Aunt E was kind enough to give me an allowance, too.'

'For what?'

'My expenses.' Matthew looked from one to the other. 'I couldn't possibly live on the pittance they pay me at Marchmont, Marchmont & Fincham. The salary was a positive insult.' His mouth curled. 'I'm the son of a baronet, for God's sake. I do have a certain standard to keep up. Aunt Elizabeth appreciated that, even if no one else did.'

He plucked at the cuffs of his shirt. It must have come from one of those expensive shops on Jermyn Street, Charlie thought. And those polished leather shoes were definitely handmade.

Perhaps he should try keeping a wife and four kids on a PC's salary. Then he might have something to complain about.

Matthew must have caught the look of disgust in his eyes because he dropped his gaze. 'Anyway, I don't know how any of this is relevant,' he said. 'If anything, it surely proves my innocence. My aunt was paying my bills. Why on earth would I want to kill her?'

'Because she stopped paying?' Charlie suggested.

'She would never do that.'

'Isn't that what you were arguing about?'

Matthew looked at him sharply, his face giving him away before he had a chance to control his features.

'I don't know what you're talking about,' he said flatly.

'The maid says she heard you and your aunt arguing on –' he consulted his notebook, flipping back several pages – 'the seventeenth of January. That was a week before she died, wasn't it?'

'The maid shouldn't go around telling tales!' Matthew's cheeks were a deep crimson. 'I've a good mind to sack her for snooping.'

'But there was an argument?' Charlie said.

For a moment it seemed as if he wouldn't answer. Then he said, 'It was nothing to do with my debts.'

'Then what was it about?'

'It was personal.'

'We need to know, Mr Franklin,' George said.

Matthew sighed. 'Very well. It was to do with work.' He paused for a moment. 'My aunt knew how much I'd always loathed working at that wretched solicitors' office, but my father insisted I should settle to doing something useful after I came out of the army. As if serving my country wasn't use enough!' There was anger in his eyes. 'I had no desire to follow a career in law. I found the work utterly tedious, and I thought Aunt Elizabeth understood that. She always seemed very sympathetic to my plight, at any rate.'

His plight, Charlie thought in disgust. Anyone would think he was working as a Victorian chimney sweep's boy.

'Anyway, as soon as my father died, I thought I might resign and look for some other work. But Aunt E said I had to honour my father's wishes.'

'And that was what you argued about?'

'Yes.'

'How old are you, Mr Franklin?' Charlie asked.

'I'm twenty-four.'

'Then surely you didn't need your aunt's permission to do anything?'

Matthew's smile was bitter. 'My father, in his infinite wisdom, decided Lydia and I weren't fit to have any money of our own until we turned twenty-five. He left everything in trust to my aunt. She held onto the purse strings. That was how she controlled us.'

'She controlled you?'

'What else would you call it?' Anger spilled out into Matthew's words. 'I'm a grown man, for Christ's sake. I've been through a war. I should be able to make up my own mind what I do with my life.'

'And that's why you argued?' He nodded. 'And then what happened?'

'Aunt E got her way, as usual. She always had to have the last word. But that doesn't mean I killed her,' he said quickly, glancing up at them with panic in his eyes.

Charlie and George looked at each other. 'No one is saying you did, Mr Franklin,' Charlie said.

But he had just given them the perfect reason why he might.

Chapter 38

The Blue Angel was one of several clubs situated in Ham Yard, just off Great Windmill Street, in Soho. Spilsbury imagined the area might look rather glamorous at night, with all the bright lights and streets thronged with smart young people. But in the daylight it just seemed tired and tawdry, with only a lonely street cleaner sweeping between the dustbins, clearing up the detritus from the previous night's revelry.

The club was accessed via a nondescript wooden door with only a small brass plaque on the wall beside it. Inside it was dark and dusty and reeked of stale alcohol and perfume. The room was set out with a small stage at one end, with a dozen or so tables and chairs set out in front of it. A bar ran along the length of one wall. The barman eyed them with suspicion as he polished glasses, holding them up to the dim light to inspect each one for marks before placing it on the shelf above him.

'Can I help you, gentlemen?' he asked finally.

'We have an appointment with Miss Rogers.' Inspector Mount showed him his badge. The barman eyed it with dismay.

'Police? We're not in any trouble, are we?'

'Not as far as I know.'

The man's gaze flicked to Spilsbury, standing with Willcox a few feet away. 'I know you, don't I? Have you been in here before?'

Spilsbury ignored Willcox's snort of laughter. 'I most certainly have not!'

'But your face is familiar. I'm sure I—'

'Could you tell Miss Rogers we're here?' Thankfully, Inspector Mount interrupted before Spilsbury had to go through the tedious routine of being recognised.

The barman put down his polishing cloth and disappeared up a narrow flight of stairs at the back of the club.

'Well, this is all rather fun, isn't it?' Willcox chuckled.

'If you say so.' Spilsbury looked around him. At the far end of the room, a sleepy-eyed woman drifted onto the stage in what appeared to be a silk dressing gown, a cigarette in one hand and a glass in the other. She draped herself at the piano but made no effort to play.

From another room came the sound of voices raised in an argument. Inspector Mount swung round, instantly alert.

'Take no notice, it's only the socialists.' The woman's lazy drawl was husky from too many cigarettes and alcohol. 'They always get very heated when they get together.'

She caught Spilsbury's eye and winked. He looked away sharply.

'She seems to like you, old boy,' Willcox whispered. 'Are you sure you haven't been in here before?'

'Don't be absurd.' He was beginning to realise why Willcox had been so keen to accompany them. He was enjoying every moment of Spilsbury's discomfort.

Spilsbury had faced down murderers and witnessed crime scenes so grisly they had reduced experienced policemen to tears. But he would rather deal with a hundred dismembered and decomposed body parts than spend an evening making small talk in a nightclub – or worse yet, dancing. An occasional evening at the music hall was as far as his limited social life went.

And frankly, he could not imagine Elizabeth Franklin frequenting such a place, either.

'Gentlemen?'

They all turned to see a diminutive, dark-haired woman approaching them. In spite of her small stature, there was an air of quiet authority about her.

'Welcome to the Blue Angel,' she said, with a gentle Irish lilt. 'I'm Josephine Rogers.'

'How do you do?' Inspector Mount introduced himself, then Willcox and Spilsbury.

'Oh, I know Dr Spilsbury.' Josephine Rogers smiled in delight. 'Imagine, a celebrity in our humble establishment!'

'Careful, madam. You'll make him blush,' Willcox said.

'Hardly,' Spilsbury snapped. Out the corner of his eye, he could see the waif-like creature in the dressing gown still draped over the piano, watching him with those sleepy, hooded eyes of hers.

There was another shout from the next room.

'I'm sorry about the noise,' Miss Rogers said. 'It can get rather rowdy in here when there are meetings on.'

'Meetings?'

'We let out the club during the day for meetings and talks. We have quite a lot of eminent thinkers coming in, actually. Artists, writers, philosophers—'

'Socialists,' Spilsbury murmured, as another shout rang out.

Josephine Rogers smiled. She was in her forties, her dark hair shingled fashionably around her heart-shaped face. 'Why don't we go up to my office? It's a bit quieter up there.'

She led them back up the narrow staircase to a small room with a window that looked down over the club.

'My eyrie,' Miss Rogers said. 'Where I can watch everything.'

'I can imagine you must see some sights?' Willcox remarked.

'Oh, I do!' Josephine smiled. 'But I'm very discreet.'

'How long have you managed this place?' Inspector Mount asked.

'Oh no, I'm not the manager, Inspector. I own the club.' She laughed. 'You seem surprised?'

'Well, I . . .' It was rare that Spilsbury saw the inspector lost for words, but he seemed rather flustered now. 'It just seems rather . . . unusual.'

'It wasn't my intention, I assure you. But when my husband left me with four children to bring up, I had to find some way to keep us. So I put all the money I had into buying a partnership in this place. By the time my partner decided to move on, I had enough to buy him out.'

'Very impressive.'

'For a woman?' Josephine Rogers' brows rose. 'You'd be amazed what we can do when we're pushed into it, Inspector.'

She seemed like such a warm, intelligent woman, Spilsbury had to remind himself the reason they were there was because she had approached the police with an idiotic notion.

'Why did you leave it so long to come forward?' he asked bluntly.

Josephine looked taken aback, but answered him calmly. 'As I explained to the inspector, I was in Ireland visiting family. I only returned the day before yesterday, so I had no idea what had happened to poor Elizabeth.' She shook her head. 'I still can't quite believe it,' she said.

Neither can I, Spilsbury thought.

'How well did you know Miss Franklin?' Inspector Mount asked.

'She was a regular at the club.'

'How regular?'

'She came in at least once a week.'

'Ridiculous,' Spilsbury muttered.

Josephine frowned. 'I beg your pardon, Dr Spilsbury?'

'It's utterly absurd. The very idea that Elizabeth Franklin would come to a place like this.' He looked around him. 'You clearly did not know her at all.'

'On the contrary, I knew her very well.' The woman's voice was steady, but there was fire in her eyes. 'How well did *you* know her, Doctor?'

Behind him, Willcox stifled a laugh. 'Did she have a particular evening every week?' Inspector Mount asked, breaking the tension.

'It was generally a Thursday, I think.'

'You think?' Spilsbury said.

'It was a Thursday,' Josephine Rogers said firmly. 'She was usually with her friend, but the last time I saw her she was alone.'

'A friend?' Inspector Mount said. 'Male or female?'

'Male. They used to meet here every week, but on that particular night he didn't turn up. That's how I remember that she was here. We had a conversation about it. She said he must have been called away. She seemed rather disappointed, as I recall.'

'Do you have a name for this man?'

'I believe his name might have been Eddie. He was rather handsome, I remember that. Fair-haired. I noticed that particularly, because I've always liked a man with lighter colouring myself.' Her gaze travelled slowly up to Spilsbury's face. He didn't have to look round to know that Willcox was probably beside himself with mirth.

'But she didn't go home when he failed to turn up?' Inspector Mount said.

'Oh no, she stayed. We had a rather good band on that night, and I think she was enjoying the music. She got talking to a couple of other people, anyway. It's a very friendly club.'

'I'm sure it is,' Spilsbury murmured.

'Come to think of it, she was with another man later in the evening,' Josephine Rogers said. 'He came over to join her. They talked for a while, and then they both left.'

'Together?'

'I'm not sure. Possibly.' Josephine hesitated. 'I don't think I saw them leave. I seem to remember a couple of the dancers got into a catfight backstage, and I had to go and sort it out. By the time I'd got back upstairs, Elizabeth's table was empty.'

'And what time was that?'

'It would have been around midnight. Elizabeth always left just before midnight. I used to joke about it with her. I called her Cinderella because she had to get back home before her clothes turned back into rags. She always found that very amusing.' She smiled at the memory.

'What did the man look like?'

'He was dark, well built. Square-jawed – rather handsome, as I recall.'

'But you don't know if they left together?' Inspector Mount said.

'I really couldn't say. As I told you, I was trying to break up a fight at the time. Dancers can be very highly strung,' she explained apologetically.

'And what did Elizabeth Franklin look like?' Spilsbury asked.

Miss Rogers smiled archly. 'Are you trying to trick me, Dr Spilsbury?'

'Not at all. I'm just trying to make sure we are talking about the same woman.'

She paused, thinking. 'She was tall – taller than average, I'd say. But she never hunched like some tall girls do. She stood poker-straight, with very good bearing. She had grey eyes, and brown hair, greying a bit, which she always wore up and off her face, like this . . .' She demonstrated with her hands, pulling her face taut. 'Well?' she asked. 'Did I pass your test, doctor?'

'It sounds like her,' Spilsbury admitted grudgingly.

'I never forget a face.'

The inspector asked a few more questions and then they took their leave.

'I'll have to ask you to come down to the station and make a statement,' the inspector said, as they were heading down the stairs.

'Of course, I'd be glad to. Anything to help catch whoever did this. Poor Elizabeth, I still can't quite believe she's gone – oh!' She stopped dead on the stairs, her hands to her face. 'Oh my lord, I almost forgot.'

'Forgot what, Miss Rogers?'

'Wait there.'

She left them standing at the foot of the stairs and disappeared through a doorway behind the bar. She returned a few minutes later with her arms full of black fur.

'Elizabeth left this behind that night,' she said.

'Her coat?' Spilsbury took it from her. It was a full-length, black astrakhan fur.

'I can't imagine why she would have gone off without it,' Josephine Rogers said. 'It's a very valuable coat, isn't it? And it was so cold that night. You'd be surprised what people leave behind here, but I can't imagine anyone forgetting their coat when it was freezing outside.'

'Unless they left in a hurry?' Willcox said.

'Or they were taken against their will,' the inspector murmured. 'May we take this with us?' he asked Josephine.

'Yes, please do.'

'Well, this is all rather bizarre, isn't it?' Willcox spoke up as they left the club. 'I must say, I'm rather inclined to believe her story, aren't you?'

'It seems plausible,' Inspector Mount said. 'But at the same time, it makes no sense. How can a woman be murdered in her own home, then alive and well at midnight?'

'Unless you've made a mistake?' Willcox turned to look at Spilsbury.

Spilsbury ignored him. 'May I look at that?' he asked, gesturing to the coat.

'Of course.' The inspector placed it in his arms. The black astrakhan fur was heavy and smelt faintly of mothballs, mingling with another scent. He pressed his face into the fur and breathed in deeply. It was not a light, feminine perfume, but an eminently practical, almost soapy smell. He remembered the same scent hanging in the air in Elizabeth Franklin's study, and her bedroom.

He absently stroked the tightly curled fur. There was something about it, something that didn't quite ring true.

'Perhaps this mystery man she met at the nightclub took her home and then murdered her?' Inspector Mount suggested.

'But that doesn't fit in with the time of death, surely?' Willcox said.

'Unless . . .' Inspector Mount let the word hang in the air.

'Unless Spilsbury has miscalculated,' Willcox finished for him.

'I assure you I have not miscalculated.'

'Don't take it personally, old man. No one could blame you for not being entirely accurate. Especially given that the body was immersed in water—'

'I am not wrong,' Spilsbury cut him off sharply. 'Even if Elizabeth Franklin was still alive after midnight, how on earth could she have been murdered in the house when Lydia and the maid were both at home by then? Surely they would have noticed—' He stopped abruptly as he plunged his hand into the pocket of the coat and his fingers closed around a piece of screwed-up paper.

'What is it?' The inspector leaned forward to see. 'What have you found?'

Spilsbury smoothed out the scrap of paper and smiled. 'Something that I believe proves Elizabeth Franklin was not in the Blue Angel on the night she was murdered,' he said.

Chapter 39

'*Captain Tobias Warriner. For conspicuous gallantry and devotion to duty in rushing to a dug-out in which men had been buried by shell fire and attempting to dig out the men, aided by two other officers. He himself was in a state of collapse, but insisted on helping to carry the wounded to a dressing station under shell fire.*'

Charlie put down the *London Gazette* and looked up at Inspector Mount.

He had known the name was familiar, as soon as he'd heard it. But he'd had to go through nearly two years' worth of back copies of the newspaper to find what he was looking for.

'So he was awarded the Military Cross?' the inspector said.

'Yes, sir. He was one of the first to receive it.'

'And is he from Yorkshire, by any chance?'

'His family are from Derbyshire, sir. That's why he wasn't on my list to start with.'

'Your list!' George muttered under his breath. He had been very sour ever since Charlie made his discovery.

'All the same, it's close enough. It's possible that Hilda Hodges may have been mistaken.'

'That's what I thought, sir.' Charlie remembered the tingle of excitement when he'd come across the name in the *Gazette*. It was as if a missing piece of a particularly difficult jigsaw had suddenly materialised and slotted into place, pulling the whole puzzle together.

'It's certainly a strange coincidence that someone fitting the description of Jean Hodges' boyfriend was at Elizabeth Franklin's funeral,' Inspector Mount said.

'With respect, sir, it's hardly a description!' George said. 'A former soldier from Yorkshire with a Military Cross? There must be hundreds of men who fit the bill.'

'One hundred and twenty-eight, to be precise.' Charlie had found out their names, and then begun the painstaking task of tracking them all down. So far he'd found five who were dead, one who had emigrated to America, eight who had married French girls and remained in Europe, one living on a remote island off the Scotland coast and thirty-six who were in nursing homes, too incapacitated to put on their own boots, let alone murder two women.

Captain Tobias Warriner was the most promising lead they had. And he wasn't prepared to let it go without a fight. Thankfully the inspector seemed to agree with him. 'Nevertheless, it's all we have to go on so far,' he said. He turned to Charlie. 'And this Warriner chap was a friend of the nephew's, you say?'

'That's right, sir. Although . . .'

'What?'

'It seemed like an odd sort of friendship to me, sir.'

'How so?'

'He was very overbearing. And he didn't take kindly to the idea of us talking to Mr Franklin.'

'Why do you think that was?'

'Perhaps he was trying to protect him?' George said.

'Or protect himself.' Charlie hadn't realised he'd said the words aloud until he caught the inspector looking at him keenly.

'From what?' he asked. 'Are you suggesting they might be working together?'

George snorted with laughter. Charlie ignored him. 'I couldn't say, sir. But we know Matthew Franklin was very bitter about his aunt controlling his life, and especially his money. Perhaps his old army friend offered to help get rid of her for a price?'

'A bit convenient, wouldn't you say?' George put in. 'Matthew Franklin just happens to be friends with a gigolo who murders wealthy women for their money!'

'You have a point, Sergeant,' the inspector conceded. George glowed with pride. 'And I suppose if he was the killer, he'd hardly want to be seen with Franklin at his aunt's funeral, would he?'

Charlie fell silent. George was right, he thought. It made no sense when he looked deeper into it.

But there was still something about their friendship that simply did not hit the right note with him.

He tried again. 'What about the man who was seen with Elizabeth Franklin at the Blue Angel?' he said. 'Does he fit Warriner's description?'

'I don't think so.' Inspector Mount consulted his notes. 'Well built, dark hair?'

'Captain Warriner has lighter colouring, from what I can remember.'

'Then it can't be him. Although Dr Spilsbury is still not sure Elizabeth Franklin was at the Blue Angel at all.'

'Can't admit he was wrong, you mean!' George smirked.

'Then how does he explain the witness seeing her?' Charlie asked.

'God knows. I'm still waiting for him to come up with an answer to that one. Inspector Mount rubbed his hand wearily across his face. 'In the meantime, it might be worth finding out what you can about this Warriner character. Even if it's just to eliminate him from our enquiries.'

'Thank you, sir. I thought I might pay a visit to Gloucester Gate this afternoon to speak to Matthew Franklin again, if it's all right with you?'

'Good idea.'

'You're not going on your own,' George said, sitting up straighter. 'If you're going to question a suspect, then I'm coming with you!'

Lydia Franklin was alone in the house when they arrived at Gloucester Gate. She was dressed for dinner in a pale green silk dress that hung in loose folds to just above her ankles. A purple sash fastened around her hips was the only nod towards her figure underneath.

Annie would have told him it was the latest fashion, but to Charlie's untrained eye, it looked horribly shapeless.

'You've just caught me, I was on my way out,' she said breathlessly, as she bent to fasten the buckle on her dainty lavender-coloured shoes. 'What can I do for you?'

'We were hoping to speak to your brother, Miss Franklin,' Charlie said.

'He's not back from work yet. He generally gets home at about six, depending on the trains.' She straightened up, adjusting the band around her fair hair. 'You're welcome to wait for him, if you like? Would you like some tea?' She reached for the bell to summon the maid.

'We won't, Miss Franklin, thank you for asking,' George got in before Charlie could say yes. 'We don't want to keep you, if you're expected somewhere?'

'Oh, I don't mind. Please, won't you sit down?' Lydia seated herself on one of the brocade sofas, and gestured to the other one. 'Why do you want to speak to Matthew anyway? Have you found something out?' She leaned forward. 'Please tell me you've caught the man?'

'I'm afraid not, miss,' Charlie said.

'Oh.' The hope faded from her face. 'So why do you want to see—' She looked up at them with an expression of dawning horror. 'Is it about those dreadful things he's been getting through the post? Oh God, he hasn't had another one, has he?'

Charlie glanced at George's baffled face.

'I'm so glad he decided to call you in the end,' Lydia Franklin went on in a rush. 'I told him he should when the first one arrived, but he insisted there was nothing to worry about. But honestly, I don't think it's a joke at all. Or if it is, it's not very funny.'

'May I ask what you're talking about, miss?' Charlie asked.

Lydia stared at him blankly. 'Those awful things he's been getting. Bloodied handkerchiefs or something. That's why you're here, isn't it?' She looked from one to the other, and the colour drained from her face. 'You don't know anything about them, do you? Oh God, I shouldn't have said anything. Matthew will be furious!'

Before Charlie or George could reply, they heard the sound of the front door opening. Turning, Charlie could see Matthew Franklin in the hall, carelessly tossing his hat onto a chair.

'Don't tell him I told you,' Lydia hissed as he approached the drawing room. 'Say nothing, please!'

Matthew walked in to find the three of them perched on their respective sofas, as stiff and silent as shop window mannequins.

'What's going on?' he asked.

Charlie opened his mouth to reply, but Lydia got in first.

'Don't be angry, Matthew!' she blurted out. 'I didn't mean to say anything, honestly. I thought that's why the police had come, I didn't know—'

'What are you talking about, Lyd? You're not making sense.'

'Your sister tells us you've been receiving some rather disturbing items through the post?' George spoke up. 'Bloodied handkerchiefs, or the like?'

Matthew turned crimson and glared at his sister, who looked helplessly back. 'My sister doesn't know when to mind her own business,' he snapped.

'Can I ask exactly what it is you've been receiving, sir?' George asked.

'It's nothing. Just a stupid prank, that's all,' Matthew mumbled.

'I don't think it's stupid at all. It's very cruel and upsetting.' Lydia sniffed back a tear. 'Show him, Matthew,' she urged. 'You never know, they might be able to help?'

'I don't need help,' Matthew insisted. But after a moment's hesitation, he reluctantly left the room and returned a moment later with what appeared to be a blood-stained rag in his hand, which he tossed to Charlie. 'You see? It's nothing,' he muttered.

Charlie smoothed out the fabric. It was about the size of a pocket handkerchief, stiff with dried blood, with what looked like a hole through the centre of it. The edges of the hole were blackened and scorched.

He lifted the cloth to his nose and breathed in deeply, and was instantly transported back to the battlefields of France, when the smell of cordite hung in the air like a reeking fog, mingling with the meaty, metallic stench of bodies torn apart.

Opposite him, Lydia flinched. 'Is it – real blood?' she whispered.

'I think so, miss. But we'd need to get it tested to find out for sure.' He tossed the cloth to George, who took it gingerly. 'But that's a real bullet hole, all right.'

'It doesn't need to be tested.' Matthew snatched the cloth from George's hands and stuffed it back in his pocket. 'It needs to be thrown on the fire where it belongs.'

'Don't do that, sir. It might be evidence.'

'Evidence of what? That someone likes playing ridiculous pranks?'

'It looks more like a threat to me,' George said.

Lydia nodded. 'That's what I thought.'

'Were there any notes with them, sir?' Matthew shook his head. 'So you've no idea who sent them?'

'No.' The reply came just a fraction too late.

'What do they mean?' Lydia asked.

'I couldn't say, miss. But you really should have reported this,' he said to Matthew.

'Do you think it might be linked to the murder?' Lydia clamped her hand over her mouth. 'You don't think someone's going to kill my brother, do you?'

'Don't be absurd,' Matthew snapped. 'Who would want to murder me?'

'The same person who murdered our aunt?'

They glared at each other for a moment. Then Matthew said, 'Look, I just want to forget about it, all right? It's a stupid practical joke, and not worth taking up the police's time.'

He went over to the cabinet and helped himself to a glass of whisky. Charlie noticed his hands shaking as he gripped the decanter.

His sister eyed him with disapproval, but said nothing. Charlie looked at George to see if he had noticed it too, but he was too busy staring down at his notes.

'I have to go,' Lydia said, rising to her feet. 'Robert will be wondering where I am.'

'Mustn't keep him waiting, must we?' Matthew said in a tight-lipped voice. He downed his drink and refilled his glass, the heavy crystal of the decanter chinking against the glass as he fought to keep it steady.

Lydia hesitated, and for a moment Charlie felt sure she was going to say something more. But the next moment, she turned and abruptly left the room, slamming the door behind her.

Matthew took his glass over to the window and stood with his back to them, staring out into the darkened street. Charlie and George exchanged a puzzled look. He seemed so lost in his own thoughts, Charlie wondered if he had forgotten they were there.

George cleared his throat. 'The reason we're here, sir—' he began.

'It's about Captain Warriner,' Charlie finished for him.

'Warriner?' Matthew Franklin did not turn round, but Charlie saw the muscles in his shoulders tense. 'What about him?'

'You said he was an old friend?'

'I most certainly did not! I scarcely know the man.'

'But he came to your aunt's funeral?'

'So?'

They looked at each other. 'That would suggest a friendship . . .' George ventured.

'Then you don't know Warriner!' Matthew turned round to face him. 'I hadn't seen him in years until he turned up at the reunion. For some reason he decided to attach himself to me for the entire evening. Damned annoying it was too,' he said bitterly. 'He must have read about Aunt Elizabeth, because the next thing I knew he'd turned up at the funeral. Believe me, I was as surprised as anyone.'

That explained why he had seemed to uncomfortable, Charlie thought.

'It seems an odd thing to do,' he remarked.

'Odd? I'll say it's odd. But that's Toby Warriner. He was always something of a law unto himself, even when we were in France. How he didn't face a court martial I'll never know.'

Chapter 40

The following day, it was Spilsbury's turn to visit the house, along with Inspector Mount and Sergeant Stevens. Mary the maid looked dismayed when she opened the door and saw them.

'There's no one at home,' she said bluntly.

'Thank you. We're well aware of that.' Spilsbury swept straight her and into the house.

'It was you we wanted to speak to,' Inspector Mount explained, as he and Sergeant Stevens sidled past into the hall.

'Me?' Spilsbury heard Mary saying. 'But I've already told you everything I— Where are you going?'

Her voice followed Spilsbury as he headed for Elizabeth Franklin's study. There were no lamps lit and the curtains were pulled across the window, plunging the room into darkness. It was as cold as a tomb.

'I see you've given up making the fire?' he commented, as Mary came hurrying into the room after him.

'Yes, well, as you said, there didn't seem much point with Miss Franklin gone.'

'And no evidence to destroy,' Spilsbury muttered.

Mary peered at him, narrow-eyed. 'I beg your pardon, sir?'

Spilsbury sniffed the air. There it was, the same faint soapy scent he'd smelt on Elizabeth Franklin's coat.

'Where are you from, Mary?' he asked.

She looked taken aback. 'I – I don't understand, sir?'

'It's a simple enough question, I would have thought. Where do you come from? Where were you born?'

'Otley, sir. Just outside Leeds.'

'I know it,' he said. 'I once had a case of disputed identity up there. An old woman went missing, only to mysteriously appear a couple of weeks later. Turned out it wasn't her at all, but a distant relative who'd murdered her and assumed her identity. Perhaps you heard of it?'

Mary shook her head. 'I can't say I ever did, sir.'

'Really? You do surprise me. It was in the local newspaper, I understand.'

'I never bother with newspapers, sir.' Mary turned to Inspector Mount. 'You want to speak to me? Only I've got a lot of work to get through before Mr Franklin and his sister come home.'

'Yes, of course. We won't take up too much of your time. I just need you to identify something.' He gestured to the sergeant. 'Could you fetch it for me, Stevens? It's in the car.'

'Yes, sir.'

Sergeant Stevens left. Mary watched him go, a frown on her face.

'Did Miss Franklin ever travel on a bus?' Spilsbury asked. Mary swung round to face him, confusion written all over her face.

'A bus, sir?'

'It's another simple question, Mary. Did she ever travel by bus? The number seventeen bus, in particular?'

'I don't think so.' She looked dismayed at the very idea. 'Miss Franklin always travelled by taxi if she had to go anywhere.' She shook her head. 'I can't imagine her ever getting on a bus.'

'That's what I thought.'

There was a knock on the door. Mary glanced towards the sound. 'Who's that now, I wonder?'

'Probably Sergeant Stevens shut himself out,' Inspector Mount said, with a quick glance at Spilsbury. 'Could you let him in, please?'

Mary looked put out. She stomped off, leaving Spilsbury and Inspector Mount in the study alone.

'Do you really think this will work?' The inspector looked sceptical.

'Of course it will.' Spilsbury picked up a paperweight from the desk, examined it then put it down again.

'I hope you're right. Otherwise we'll look like fools.'

'Oh, I'm right.'

Just at that moment there was a scream from the hall.

Spilsbury looked at Mount. It was all he could do to keep the knowing smirk from his face. 'What did I tell you?' he said.

Chapter 41

'I – I don't understand!' Josephine Rogers stood in the hall, looking nonplussed. 'Lizzie, darling. I thought you were dead?'

Spilsbury looked at Mary. He had certainly seen cadavers on his mortuary slab with more colour than her. Her skin was ashen, her mouth hanging open. Her eyes had the glazed, terrified look of a cornered animal.

'I take it you two have met?' Inspector Mount said.

'Of course.' Josephine tore her gaze from Mary to the inspector and then Spilsbury. 'Can someone please tell me what's going on?'

'I'm sure Mary can explain it better than we can.'

'Mary?' Josephine Rogers looked perplexed. Mary said nothing, her head hung.

And just as it appeared the situation could not possibly get any more wretched, Sergeant Stevens came in, carrying an armful of black fur.

'Do you recognise this coat, Miss Rogers?' Inspector Mount said.

'Of course I do, I gave it to you. Elizabeth left it in my club the night she—'

Josephine Rogers looked from one to the other, her expression darkening from bafflement to anger. 'Look, can someone please explain what the hell is going on?' she demanded.

Inspector Mount turned to Mary. 'Have you ever seen this coat before?' Mary did not reply. 'Mary?' he prompted.

'You know I have.' Her voice emerged as a low growl in her throat.

'Does it belong to you?'

'No.'

'Then who does it belong to?'

Mary glared at him, full of hatred and humiliation. 'It's Miss Franklin's,' she mumbled.

'But you're Elizabeth Franklin?' Josephine Rogers' voice had lost its confidence.

'I'm afraid you've been misled, Miss Rogers,' Inspector Mount said. 'This is Mary, Elizabeth Franklin's maid. We have reason to believe that she impersonated her mistress on the night she was murdered.'

'Don't say it like that!' Mary turned on him. 'You make it sound like I did something wrong!'

'Didn't you?'

She lifted her chin. 'I didn't commit any crime.'

'The inspector would know more about that than me,' Spilsbury said. 'But I'm sure wasting the police's time and wilfully impeding an investigation might be considered felonious.'

Colour rose in Mary's face. 'I didn't set out to defraud anyone. And I certainly didn't have anything to do with her murder!'

'Then why did you do it?' Spilsbury asked.

'You wouldn't understand,' Mary muttered. 'You don't know what it's like to be—'

'What?'

'Invisible.' She looked at him accusingly. 'You don't know what it's like, do you? Everyone knows who you are. You're famous. And even if you weren't, people would still treat you with respect because of the way you look and how you act. You have no idea what it's like to be treated as if you're invisible, or part of the furniture. But I'm no one, especially in this uniform.' She looked down at herself. 'I could pass a hundred people on the street and not one of them would notice me. I'm just a maid, not worth a second look. I just wanted to see what it was like to be noticed for once.'

'So you stole your mistress's coat?'

'I borrowed it!' Anger flared in Mary's eyes. 'I've never stolen anything in my life. It wasn't as if she missed it, anyway. It was a present from her brother, and she never wore it. Said it was too showy for her liking. It just got stuffed into the back of the cupboard.'

Hence the smell of mothballs, Spilsbury thought. And the soapy scent he thought he'd detected in Miss Franklin's study had actually come from Mary herself. He realised he'd only been able to smell it when she was in the same room.

He recalled Elizabeth at her brother's funeral, and the plain black coat she wore. He should have known she would never be seen in anything as extravagant as black astrakhan.

'One day when she was out, I thought I'd try it on,' Mary said. 'I've never owned anything like it. I wondered if I'd feel different if I was wearing it.'

'And did you?'

'Oh, yes.' Mary smiled reluctantly at the memory. 'But it wasn't just that. I got treated differently, too. People who would never have given me the time of day were smiling and greeting me on the street. I wasn't invisible for once.'

'So you decided to take it one step further and go up west?' Spilsbury said.

Mary's smile slipped. 'I was just curious,' she defended herself. 'I would never have dared go into a place like that in the normal way of things. But when I was pretending to be someone else, I had the confidence to do anything.'

'Including impersonating someone else?'

'I didn't mean to do it. When someone asked my name, I just panicked and came out with it. The minute I said it I wanted to take it back, but how could I?'

'So you became Elizabeth Franklin?'

'No,' Mary insisted. 'I was me all the time.'

'But you told everyone your brother was a respected physician, and that you lived here?'

'I tried not to tell them anything about myself,' Mary said in a low voice. 'I didn't want to lie to anyone. Anyway, all the time I was there, I kept expecting someone to see through me and throw me out, but everyone was so nice and welcoming, and I had so much fun . . .'

'I wish you'd told me.' Josephine looked reproachful.

'Would you have welcomed me into your club if you'd known I was just a maid?'

Josephine Rogers was silent, but her expression gave her away. Mary was right, Spilsbury thought. For all her worldly talk, and holding socialist meetings, underneath it all she was as snobbish and small-minded as the rest of them.

'I knew none of it was real,' she said. 'And I knew it couldn't go on forever. But it was just nice for a while, to be someone else. Someone . . .'

'Different?'

'Important,' Mary said.

'Well, your little charade has cost us dear,' Inspector Mount said. 'We've spent a great deal of time chasing a false lead, thanks to you.'

'You wouldn't have if you'd listened to me in the first place,' Spilsbury could not resist pointing out.

'Did he know who you were?' Josephine Rogers asked. 'Your friend, from the club?'

Panic flared in Mary's eyes. Then she nodded.

'So who is this man?' Inspector Mount asked, turning over a page in his notebook.

'He's just someone I know.'

'And his name?'

'I called him Eddie.'

'Surname? I suppose he had another name?' Inspector Mount prompted, when Mary looked blank.

'I suppose he must. But I don't know it.'

'You don't know his name?'

'He was just a casual acquaintance.'

'Where did you meet him?'

'He came to the house selling brushes and we got talking.'

'Do you have his address?'

Mary shook her head. 'He moved about.'

'What happened on the night Miss Franklin was murdered?' Mount tried again.

'I brought her some supper on a tray, and I told her I was going out. She said she was expecting a visitor, and I asked if she wanted me to stay and let them in, but she said no. So I went down to my room and got changed, and caught the bus up west.'

'Hence the bus ticket I found in the pocket of the coat,' Spilsbury said. That was when he had known for sure that Elizabeth Franklin had not visited the Blue Angel that night. The idea of her visiting a nightclub might have been absurd, but the idea of her travelling on a bus was utterly fantastical.

'I was supposed to be meeting Eddie but he didn't turn up. I was going to go home early, but I thought I might as well stay and have a drink first, since I'd come all that way.'

'And what about the other man you were seen with that night?'

'Oh, him.' Mary pulled a face. 'He came over and asked if he could join me. I said no, but he sat down anyway. Really making a nuisance of himself, he was. Quite spoiled my evening.' She frowned at the memory. 'I couldn't get rid of him, so I said he could escort me home. Then I waited until he'd gone to the cloakroom, and ran.'

'Leaving your coat behind?'

'I couldn't very well fetch it, could I?'

'Like Cinderella,' Josephine Rogers spoke up. 'I used to call you that, didn't I? Because you always ran off before midnight.'

'I had to catch the last bus.' Mary looked rueful. 'You weren't far wrong, anyway. About my riches turning back into rags.'

The two women looked at each other.

'I wish you'd been honest with me,' Josephine said sadly. 'I know what it's like to come from nothing, you know.'

'Yes, but you're one of them now. I'm still nothing.'

'So you didn't leave with him?' Inspector Mount interrupted. Mary shook her head. 'Not a chance. I came straight home.'

'And what time was that?'

'Just after midnight.'

'And then you both went to bed?' Mary nodded.

'What about the letters?' Spilsbury asked.

'What letters?' Inspector Mount and Mary both said together.

'The letters I saw you throwing on the fire the morning Miss Franklin's body was discovered.'

Spilsbury caught the inspector's astonished look out of the corner of his eye. But his attention was fixed on Mary. She was squirming like a worm on the end of a fishing hook.

'I don't know what you're talking about,' she said tightly.

'I think you do.'

For a moment she did not meet his eye. Then she blurted out, 'It was just some correspondence, that's all. Personal letters and such. Miss Franklin wouldn't have wanted them falling into the wrong hands.'

'What kind of personal letters?'

'I don't know, do I?' Mary snapped. 'I'm not in the habit of going round reading other people's correspondence.'

'Then how did you know they were personal?' Spilsbury asked.

She glared at him. 'I know they were personal because Miss Franklin kept them locked away. If she didn't want anyone in the family seeing them, then I'm sure she wouldn't want the likes of you lot getting your hands on them!' Her eyes were bright with anger. 'I only did it to protect her.'

Chapter 42

'Was she really trying to protect Miss Franklin, I wonder? Or someone else?'

Inspector Mount posed the question when they were in the car heading back to Scotland Yard. Once again, Spilsbury would have preferred to travel alone, but it was either go with the police or share a car with Josephine Rogers, and the thought of making awkward conversation with a woman he scarcely knew did not appeal to him.

'She was definitely hiding something,' Sergeant Stevens said. 'She was squirming all the way through the interview.'

'Not all the way,' Spilsbury corrected him. 'Her words became less stilted and her muscles relaxed towards the end, when she was talking about the events of that particular evening. Which means she had started to tell the truth.'

'So she was lying about this Eddie character?' Inspector Mount said.

'Most certainly. She was at her most uncomfortable when she was talking about him. Her colour was heightened and she blinked rapidly throughout.' He shook his head. 'She knows far more about him than she is letting on. And what she told us was not necessarily true.'

'Then who is he, I wonder?'

They were all silent, but Spilsbury knew what they were thinking.

'The Lonely Hearts Killer.' As usual, it was Sergeant Stevens who'd broken the silence. Spilsbury saw the inspector wince at the ridiculous epithet. 'Are they in it together, do you think?'

'It's possible,' Mount said. 'It certainly seems more than a coincidence that he and Mary were friends.'

'Perhaps he used her to gain access to Elizabeth Franklin?' Stevens suggested.

'But why would he need her for that? He had already made contact with Miss Franklin himself through the newspaper.'

'That's true.' Sergeant Stevens thought for a moment. 'Although he might have used her to help cover his tracks? If those letters contained clues to his identity, he wouldn't want them lying around for us to find.'

Inspector Mount turned to Spilsbury. 'I must say, doctor, I do wish you'd mentioned earlier that you'd found her burning letters. It was rather an important piece of information, don't you think?'

'I would have if I'd known for certain that was what she was doing,' Spilsbury replied.

'But you just said—'

'I only *suspected* they were letters she was burning. She had made a point of lighting a fire in a room that was unoccupied. And yet she was most reluctant to go to the trouble of lighting the gas lamp in the same room. I assumed she needed the fire to destroy something. Had anyone challenged her at the time she would have denied everything, I believe. It was only when I caught her off-guard earlier on that she confirmed my suspicions.'

'All the same, you should have mentioned it,' Sergeant Stevens grumbled.

'Yes, well, never mind that now,' Inspector Mount dismissed. 'This man, whoever he was, arranged to meet

Mary that night in the Blue Angel, but he didn't turn up. Do you think he wanted her out of the house while he did the deed?'

'Either way, you know she wasn't the one who murdered Elizabeth Franklin,' Spilsbury pointed out. 'Thanks to her secret life, she has an alibi for the evening in question.'

'But she might know who did,' Stevens said.

'Or she might think she does.'

The inspector sent him a sideways look. 'You don't seem very certain, doctor?'

'I don't like wild speculation, Inspector. I prefer demonstrable facts and evidence.'

'And yet you reckon you can tell someone's lying from the way they speak?' George Stevens muttered.

Spilsbury turned to him. 'The constriction of muscles, dilation of blood vessels and increased levels of perspiration are physiological evidence, as much as a fractured skull or a bullet wound in a dead body.'

'But sometimes you have to start with speculation,' Inspector Mount pointed out. 'You make certain assumptions and then look for the evidence to back them up.'

'As long as you don't close your mind to other possibilities.'

'So you don't think Mary is working in cahoots with the Lonely Hearts Killer?' Stevens said.

Inspector Mount gave a pained sigh. 'Must you call him that, Sergeant? Save the headlines for the newspapers.'

'I know she suspects this friend of hers is involved in something illegal,' Spilsbury said. 'She certainly wants to protect him and his identity. But whether she believes he's a murderer, I could not say.'

'Either way, the family will have to be informed,' Inspector Mount said.

'Why?' Spilsbury asked.

'She's been helping herself to their belongings,' Sergeant Stevens answered for him. 'She deserves to get the boot for that.'

'Belongings that no one knew or cared about,' Spilsbury said.

'Nevertheless, she is guilty of deception, and she has betrayed their trust,' Inspector Mount said. 'Surely they deserve to know what she's really like?'

'I know I wouldn't want a thief under my roof,' Stevens muttered.

'She hasn't stolen anything,' Spilsbury pointed out. 'All she's done is indulge in a harmless fantasy from time to time.'

'She deceived her employers.'

'A mistake I don't believe she will repeat.'

'You think she's learned her lesson?'

'She has no reason to continue with such a charade. Any pleasure she took in it has now gone.'

Inspector Mount smiled. 'Why Spilsbury, I do believe you pity her.'

'I have no idea what you mean,' Spilsbury snapped. 'I never allow emotion to cloud my judgement. But I do believe you would be making a grave mistake by exposing her. Think about it, Inspector,' he reasoned. 'If she does know who Elizabeth Franklin's murderer is, then surely she would be better off where you can keep an eye on her?'

Mount considered it for a moment. 'You have a point,' he conceded. 'We've clearly rattled her cage. If she's concerned, she might try to make contact with this Eddie character at some point, if only to reassure herself.'

'But she said she hadn't heard from him since the night of the murder?' George Stevens said.

'You only have her word for that,' Spilsbury said.

'You think she's been in contact with him?'

'Perhaps not yet. But she will.' Spilsbury shifted his gaze from Stevens to Inspector Mount. 'And if this man really is your killer, then I believe Mary will lead us right to him.'

'If he's our killer?' Mount said. 'You still think we're on the wrong track?'

'I still believe there are other people with an equally sound reason to want her dead.'

'Like her nephew?' Sergeant Stevens said. 'We've talked to him. He reckons their argument was nothing to do with money.'

'There are more motives to murder someone than money, Sergeant.'

'You mean the widow?' Stevens nodded. 'I must say, I've never liked her. A bit too uppity for her own good, I reckon. And she comes from a criminal family.'

Spilsbury felt a pang of guilt, remembering the conversation he and Violet had had in the back of his car coming home from the funeral.

At least I've never been ashamed about where I came from. You know what you're getting with me.

Did he really know? She had seemed so honest, but he had a feeling Violet Franklin concealed more than she ever revealed.

'I was thinking more of Dr Dillon,' he said.

'Who?' Sergeant Stevens looked blank.

'Lydia Franklin's former fiancé,' Mount said. 'What does he have to do with this?' he asked Spilsbury. 'Surely he was out of the picture by the time Elizabeth Franklin died?'

'He was. And I'm afraid that was very much her doing. Robert Dillon had high hopes for his marriage to Lydia. He would be joining the minor aristocracy, and her father was planning to make him a partner in his private practice. But Elizabeth Franklin put an end to all that. I would say that might be a good motive for murder, don't you think?'

'It's possible,' Inspector Mount conceded. 'But I still believe the mystery admirer is our strongest lead. And it seems we have two possible suspects: this Eddie character, and Matthew Franklin's friend Tobias Warriner.'

'And neither of them are anywhere to be found,' Sergeant Stevens muttered.

'Quite. But PC Abbott is going up to Derbyshire tomorrow to question Captain Warriner's family. They might give us a clue as to where he might be.'

'I'm still not sure it's a good idea, sending him on his own, sir,' Sergeant Stevens grumbled. 'He's got no experience.'

'He's a bright lad,' Inspector Mount said.

Spilsbury noticed Sergeant Stevens' jaundiced expression. Jealousy was written all over his face.

'And let's not forget what's also happening tomorrow,' Mount said.

'And what is that, Inspector?'

'Elizabeth Franklin's will is being read. Perhaps that might give us more of a clue as to who had reason to want her dead?'

Chapter 43

The first Violet knew about Elizabeth Franklin's will reading was when she received a letter from the solicitor, summoning her to his office.

Naturally, she ignored it. She'd had no interest in hearing what Elizabeth Franklin had to say before her death, so she certainly didn't need to listen to her after it, either. Besides, she was certain her sister-in-law would have contrived some way to slap her in the face and deliver a final insult from beyond the grave.

And so, when the morning of the will reading came, Violet put on her coat and boots and took Thomas to Borough Market.

He loved the hustle and bustle of the place, the porters going back and forth, pushing trolleys laden with sacks of fruit and vegetables, their wheels trundling over the cobbles, mingling with the sound of laughter and good-natured cursing from the wholesalers as they plied their trade.

And then, on the fringes of the market were a few coster-mongers' stalls. Thomas knew them all and would greet them with a cheery wave. They, in turn, would ruffle his hair and pinch his cheek and slip him apples and oranges from their stalls.

Violet usually enjoyed their early morning walk as much as her son, but this morning she was too preoccupied by her thoughts to respond to the costers' greetings.

Violet had lain awake half the night, her arm around her sleeping son, listening for the sound of her brother's key in the door. She must have drifted off to sleep eventually because by the time she crept out to work in the morning her brother was sprawled out on the sofa, snoring gently.

But it wasn't just his late-night activities that concerned her. He had become very irritable and moody recently. But when Violet tried to talk to him, he had practically bitten her head off, snarling that he was a grown man and it was none of her damn business.

He was right, she told herself. He was a grown man, and he could sort out his own problems, whatever they were. But that didn't stop her worrying.

But then again, she had her own problems to worry about. Like how she was going to make some money. Most of her best clothes had already gone to the pawn shop to help pay the rent, so she needed to find another job soon.

She refused to touch the small inheritance James had left her. That was all in the post office, waiting for Thomas when he was old enough to need it. She wanted to be able to tell her son that his father had remembered him, even in a small way.

Her neighbour, Nan, said they were taking on girls at the Cross and Blackwell factory. Violet didn't fancy working on the pickle production line, coming home every night with her limbs aching, reeking of vinegar. But she also knew beggars could not be choosers.

Since when did you become too grand for factory work, girl?

She thought about her small, cosy office at St Mary's. She had so enjoyed working in the Pathology department. Even the grim prospect of being surrounded by death all day had not fazed her because she had found it all so fascinating. And all the doctors had been so kind to her, especially Dr Willcox.

The least said about Dr Spilsbury, the better. His aloof arrogance had been hard to take at first, until she realised he treated everyone with the same dismissive contempt. As Dr Willcox had explained to her in a hushed voice, 'It's just his way, my dear.'

Anyway, she would not find another job like it, so the pickle factory it had to be. Either that, or go back to her old life, the one she'd had before the war, before James, before she had found the strength to walk away . . .

Alice Diamond would welcome her back, she was sure of it. She would be furious that Violet had abandoned her, and she would no doubt suffer for that. But even though she could be petulant, Alice was also a very shrewd woman, and she knew very well what an asset Violet was to the gang.

Thieving came so easily to her. It was in her blood. It would be so easy to go back, to walk into one of the big department stores on Oxford Street and just help herself to whatever she wanted . . .

She shook her head, dismissing the thought. What on earth was she thinking? She'd hated that life. Sometimes she could hardly face her own reflection in the mirror, she loathed herself so much for who she was and what she did.

It was being here, south of the river, she thought. It was beginning to creep into her veins.

She had to make a plan, a proper one. She couldn't stay in Scovell Road forever. Perhaps that was why Mickey was so irritable, because he was used to having the place to himself? It was bound to be difficult for him, having a nipper in the house, even though Thomas was a good little boy, and Mickey seemed to dote on him.

They did two circuits of the market, then crossed London Bridge so Thomas could look at the river. As they returned home, she met her neighbour Nan in the courtyard, hanging out her washing.

'There was a bloke here, looking for you,' she said, her teeth gritted around a couple of clothes pegs.

'Who?'

She took the pegs out of her mouth and pinned up a shirt on the line. 'Some solicitor. Very posh, nice suit. He said you had an appointment this morning?'

'Oh, that.'

'What would a solicitor be wanting with you? Here, you're not in trouble, are you, Vi?'

'Not as far as I know.'

'You make sure it stays that way!' Nan winked at her. Violet felt a guilty flush rising in her face. *If only you knew*, she thought. How tempted had she been just now to walk down Stamford Street and seek out Alice Diamond?

She made her way up the three flights of stairs and along the narrow outside walkway that joined the front doors of various flats. As she rounded the corner, she saw a man in a dark suit standing outside her own front door.

He turned to look as she approached, and she recognised Frederick Marchmont himself, his haughty face stiff with disapproval.

'You did not come to the will reading as you were instructed, Mrs Franklin,' he said.

'I don't take kindly to being instructed by anyone.' Violet moved past him to put her key in the door.

'That's a great pity. I believe you would have heard something to your advantage.'

'Believe me, Mr Marchmont, I heard enough from my sister-in-law when she was alive. I don't want to hear anything from her now she's dead.'

'Nevertheless, I believe you're going to want to hear this.'

He produced a slim brown envelope from his inside top pocket and handed it to her.

Violet kept her hands by her sides and refused to take it. 'What's this?'

'As I said, it's something to your advantage.' The thinnest of smiles crossed the solicitor's face. 'Read it, Mrs Franklin. I think you might be pleasantly surprised.'

Matthew helped himself to another drink. He could feel the weight of his sister's disapproval from across the room, but he didn't give a damn. He needed a drink and he was going to have one.

'I still can't believe it,' Robert Dillon said in a dazed voice. 'She got almost everything.'

'Violet didn't get anything,' Lydia pointed out. 'It was left to Thomas.'

'In trust until he turns twenty-one,' Robert said. 'She controls the money until then.'

Twenty-one. That was another kick in the teeth, Matthew thought as he lifted the glass to his lips. He and Lydia had to wait until they were twenty-five to get their hands on their paltry bequests.

Not that they were worth having.

He took another gulp of his drink. *The nasty old bitch*, he thought. Every single line of that will had been cruelly crafted to twist the knife.

'At least she left us the house,' Lydia said. 'We'll still have a roof over our heads.'

'But not a pot to piss in!' Matthew snapped.

His sister flinched. 'Steady on, old boy,' Robert said, reaching for her hand. 'There's no need for that sort of language.'

'Who asked you?' Matthew turned on him. 'And what are you doing here, anyway? You're not part of this family.'

Colour crept up from Robert's starched collar. 'Lydia wanted me here,' he said. 'Someone has to look after her. Because frankly, old man, you're not doing a very good job of it.'

Matthew lip curled. What a fraud he was! Did he really think that affected accent fooled anyone? They could all see him for the jumped-up little farm labourer's son he really was.

Everyone except Lydia, apparently. He had wasted no time in wheedling his way back into her affections. Much good it would do him.

'I wonder how long you'll want to go on looking after her now her fortune's gone?' he sneered.

'Don't be so beastly, Matthew!' Lydia cried. 'Just because you're upset about Aunt E's will, there's no need to take it out on the rest of us.'

Upset! If only it was as simple as that. Matthew wasn't upset, he was utterly desperate. Aunt Elizabeth's money had been his last lifeline, and it had been cruelly snatched away from him.

'You must appeal,' Robert said. 'There's something very wrong here. Everyone knows how much your aunt loathed Violet. She wouldn't possibly leave all her money to her, unless she was coerced into it.'

'Violet would never coerce her,' Lydia said.

Robert sent her a pitying look. 'My darling, I know you like to think the best of everyone, but you must see your stepmother for what she is. She has somehow manipulated your aunt into changing her will in her favour.'

'Can you really imagine anyone manipulating Aunt E?' Lydia said.

'Nevertheless, you and Matthew must go and see Frederick Marchmont tomorrow, and lodge a formal appeal against this will. I can scarcely believe your aunt was in her right mind when she made it.'

'But it just doesn't seem right . . .'

Matthew listened to them talking. He knew exactly why Aunt Elizabeth had changed her will. And he knew she had been in her right frame of mind when she did it, too.

If only he had kept his mouth shut, none of this would have happened. But he was so sure she would understand, that she would approve of what he had done . . .

But instead she had turned on him. And this was her way of punishing him from beyond the grave.

Only she had no idea how much damage she had truly done.

Chapter 44

Charlie had never been further afield than his family's annual hop-picking trip to Kent. So it was quite an adventure for him to catch a train all the way up to Derbyshire.

He had been travelling so long, he almost felt as if he had arrived in another land when he stepped out of Chesterfield Station. He half expected the locals to have green skin, or to be speaking in a foreign language. But even though their accent took some getting used to, Charlie found the town centre to be comfortingly like his own beloved city, with its shops, electric trams and busy marketplace, albeit far less brash and busy.

Tobias Warriner's family lived on the outskirts of the town. Charlie was aware that he was travelling on Metropolitan police expenses, so he decided to make the two-mile journey on foot, rather than running up the cost of a bus or taxi. But he began to regret it after he had got lost for the third time. Every time he consulted a local, they seemed to tell him to go a different way. Or perhaps it was his fault for not understanding them properly, he decided.

He was very conscious that he wanted to get everything right, since Inspector Mount had trusted him to carry out the mission alone.

George had wanted to go with him, of course. But Inspector Mount had insisted Charlie should go alone. Charlie couldn't help wondering if Tobias Warriner was really a serious lead, or if the inspector was just humouring him. Surely if he'd thought there might be anything in it, he would have sent a proper detective with him?

The clouds that had threatened overhead finally broke and Charlie was a sorry sight by the time he arrived at the Warriners' house. He looked more like a drowned dog than an officer of the Metropolitan police force.

Mr and Mrs Warriner lived in a large Edwardian villa, set back from the road in a broad, leafy avenue. It was a solid, respectable-looking redbrick building, with angular bay windows and a pointed gable trimmed with black and white mock Tudor beams. As Charlie approached up the wide gravel drive, he had the feeling that he was being watched. But when he looked up at the windows, he caught only the twitch of a curtain.

The maid stared at him, dripping on the doorstep, and seemed reluctant to let him in at first. But finally she relented and ushered him into wood-panelled drawing room, where the Warriners were waiting for him.

Mr Warriner was an elderly man in a wheelchair, but there was nothing frail about him. Charlie could see straight away the resemblance between father and son. They had the same commanding presence, square jaw and piercing blue eyes, although Mr Warriner senior's leonine head of thick curls had turned to grey.

'What do you want?' he demanded brusquely.

'It's about your son Tobias, Mr Warriner.'

His wife spoke up. She was, by contrast to her husband, a timid-looking little creature; pretty in a faded, insipid kind of way. She was much younger than her husband – possibly no more than mid-forties – but time had not been kind to her. Her fine light brown hair was threaded with grey, and there was a network of lines around her brown eyes.

'Tobias? What's happened to him?' she said.

Her husband turned his face away. 'Whatever it is, I'm not interested.'

Charlie saw the way his big hands closed around the arms of his wheelchair. He seemed too dominant and powerful to be so confined, with a tartan rug tucked pathetically around his knees.

The woman looked crestfallen.

'Leonard—' she pleaded, but her husband cut her off.

'I mean it, Daphne. Tobias is dead to me.'

The woman lapsed into silence, her lips pressed together. Charlie thought she looked as if she might cry.

'When was the last time you saw Tobias, Mr Warriner?' he asked.

The man kept his face stubbornly averted and said nothing.

'Not since he came home from France,' the woman answered for him quietly. 'Tobias is no longer welcome here,' she added, with a quick sideways look at her husband.

'May I ask why?'

A muscle flickered in Mr Warriner's clenched jaw, but he stayed silent. He wife stared at Charlie with anxious, helpless eyes.

Charlie looked at the photographs arranged on the mantelpiece. The one in the centre showed a schoolboy rugby team proudly lifting a trophy aloft. In the middle a tall, lean boy in striped kit squinted into the camera with a broad, lopsided smile, his messy dark hair falling into his eyes.

The same boy appeared in another photograph, this time dressed in a smart suit and standing between Mr and Mrs Warriner. Leonard Warriner was on his feet, and his wife looked so young and pretty, Charlie had to look twice to make sure it was the same woman. The last few years had not been kind to either of them, he thought.

There was no sign of Tobias in any of the photographs.

He got up to examine them more closely. 'Who's this?' he asked.

'Our son, Edgar.' There was pride and sadness in Mrs Warriner's voice. 'That one was taken after he captained his school's under-sixteen team. He was a very promising rugby player.'

Was. Charlie looked back at the photograph. He almost had no need to ask the question.

'What happened to him?'

'He – he –'

'He died in France.' The old man abruptly finished the sentence his wife could not.

'I'm sorry.' Charlie looked at the boy, his smile so full of joy, and felt the usual tug of emotion for him and all the other young men who did not come home.

There but for the grace of God, he thought. Sometimes he almost felt guilty that he had been one of the lucky ones.

'Tobias was in France too, wasn't he? He won a Military Cross—'

'Tobias is no hero!' Mr Warriner spat out the words. 'He never deserved that medal.'

'Leonard!' His wife rebuked him mildly, but the old man ignored her. He turned to Charlie, anger blazing in his blue eyes.

'I've said all I have to say,' he declared. 'Whatever trouble Tobias has got himself into, it's no concern of ours.'

'What makes you think he's in trouble?'

The man's lips tightened, but he remained obstinately silent.

'So you've no idea where he might be?' Charlie persisted.

'I don't know and I don't care. I told you, he is dead to me.'

His wife rose to her feet. 'I'll show you out,' she said.

'But I haven't finished my questions . . .'

'You heard my husband. We've said all we have to say on the matter.'

But her eyes told a different story. Charlie read the unspoken message there, and put his notebook away.

'Very well,' he said, standing up. 'Thank you for your time, Mr Warriner.'

The old man said nothing.

Mrs Warriner ushered him out into the wood-panelled hall.

'I'm sorry about my husband,' she whispered. 'He just finds it very difficult to talk about his son.'

Which one? Charlie thought.

'Edgar was only seventeen,' she went on. 'He lied about his age so he could join up.' She smiled sadly. 'He couldn't wait to go and fight for his country. He was afraid it might be all over by the time he was old enough to go.' Her eyes, full of raw despair, met Charlie's. 'How I prayed it would be too late. I suppose your mother was the same?'

Charlie thought about his own mother, the pride in her face as she waved him off to war. But she didn't know what it was going to be like. None of them did.

'But he wanted to be like Toby,' Mrs Warriner went on. 'He always looked up to him so much. And Toby used to write him letters, telling him about his adventures. I think Ed just imagined it would be a big lark.'

'There's quite a big age different between them?' Charlie remarked. Daphne Warriner blushed.

'Toby was practically a man when Edgar was born. I was Leonard's second wife, you see. We married when Toby was sixteen. But there was no resentment there,' she said quickly. 'Edgar adored his brother from the moment he was born. And Tobias doted on him, too. I think he'd always wanted a brother. He had such a lonely life, away at boarding school while his mother and father travelled the world for Leonard's military career. Toby would have done anything for Ed.' Her eyes filled with tears.

'Why did your husband disown him?' Charlie asked.

'He blames him for Edgar's death. He was supposed to look after him.' She gave Charlie a feeble smile. 'I know it sounds ridiculous, but Tobias promised, you see. When we found out Edgar had signed up without telling us, Leonard wrote to Toby and asked him to watch out for him.

'I know he did his best to keep his promise. Edgar joined Tobias's regiment, and they ended up in the same place. It seemed like a miracle. We were comforted because we knew Toby would try to keep his brother safe. But of course he couldn't really, could he?'

'No,' Charlie said. 'He couldn't.' He remembered the chaos of war, of life in the trenches. A man couldn't even take care of himself, let alone anyone else. It would have been an unbearable burden.

'I knew that, deep down,' Daphne Warriner said. 'But I suppose I wanted to go on believing that there was someone watching over Edgar. He was so young, barely more than a boy. But Leonard put all his faith in Toby. And then, when it happened . . .' She broke off, emotion choking her words.

'Your husband blamed Tobias?'

'I tried to reason with him, to show him how unfair he was being, but he wouldn't have it. I couldn't understand how he could just cut him off like that so coldly. But I suppose they were never that close to start with. As I said, Tobias spent most of his childhood at boarding school in England while Leonard was in the army.'

'But it was different for Edgar?'

Mrs Warriner blushed. 'I always felt rather guilty about that,' she admitted. 'Leonard had retired from the army when we married. He had more time to devote to our son. Not that Toby resented it,' she added quickly. 'I was devoted to Edgar, just like the rest of us. And I tried to be a mother to Toby, even though he was too old to need one,' she said. 'I made it clear that he and Edgar were the same in my eyes, that this was his home and he was always welcome, even after Edgar—' She broke off, biting her lip.

'But your husband didn't feel the same?'

'My husband was heartbroken, he didn't stop to think about what he was saying,' Mrs Warriner said sadly. 'He lashed out and now I sometimes wonder if he regrets his hasty words. But they're both cut from the same cloth,' she sighed. 'He and Toby are both too stubborn and proud to make amends.'

She turned to Charlie. 'Why did you come? Is Toby in trouble?'

'I'm just following up on an inquiry, Mrs Warriner.' It was a meaningless sentence, and he prayed she would not ask any more. Thankfully, she didn't.

'I hope he's all right. I often think about him.'

'But you don't have any idea where he might be?'

'I wish I did. The poor boy deserves to be able to come home.'

She looked on the verge of tears. Charlie cleared his throat, 'I wonder, do you have a photograph of him I might borrow?'

'Well . . .' Daphne Warriner glanced towards the drawing room. 'My husband had the maid throw them all on the fire when he and Toby fell out. But I did manage to keep hold of one, just because it had Edgar in it, too. Wait a moment.'

She hurried upstairs. Charlie stood in the hall, looking around him. There was a painting on the stairs of a man in military dress uniform. At first he thought it was Tobias Warriner, but then he looked closer and realised it was actually his father.

They were so strikingly similar, he thought. It was a terrible shame that they were so estranged.

Mrs Warriner returned, carrying a dog-eared photograph. 'Edgar sent it to me,' she said. 'He was so proud of it. He and his brother, both in uniform.' Her gaze lingered on it for a moment, then she thrust it at Charlie.

There were half a dozen young men in the photograph, all sitting outside a village café. Charlie had visited many such places during his time in France. It was a chance to briefly escape the unrelenting grimness of the trenches, where death stalked in the shadows.

He recognised the look of determined gaiety on the men's faces as they clutched their glasses of beer and grinned for the camera. Tobias Warriner sat beside his brother, his arm slung carelessly around the boy's skinny shoulders. They looked so different, no one would have ever thought they were brothers.

Anyone could see Edgar Warriner was just a child. How had they ever let him join up at the recruiting office? Charlie wondered. Or perhaps they just didn't care. It was the height of the war by then and they were taking anyone they could get for cannon fodder.

He flipped the photograph over. The men's names were scrawled in pencil on the back of the photograph.

'You will tell Tobias I'm thinking of him, won't you?' Daphne Warriner's anxious voice broke into his thoughts. 'Tell him I don't bear him any ill will. Tell him—'

But Charlie wasn't listening. He was too busy staring at the list of names. Trent, Parrish, Jeevons, Conway, Toby W – and Eddie.

Chapter 45

'So let me get this straight,' George said. 'You think Tobias Warriner's dead brother is the man Elizabeth Franklin met at The Blue Angel?'

'I don't know what to think.' Charlie had been turning it over and over in his mind all the way back from Derbyshire. 'Surely it must be more than a coincidence that Tobias Warriner's brother is called Eddie?'

'I don't see why. It's a common enough name. I can think of at least two of my cousins who are called Eddie.'

'I know, but there's just something about it . . .'

He felt like a fool, saying it out loud. What must Inspector Mount think of him, chasing shadows? He had been brought in to help with the menial slog, the donkey work, not to run up and down the country on wild goose chases that helped no one.

But the inspector was very encouraging.

'Follow it up, if you think there's something in it,' he said. 'Get hold of Edgar Warriner's death certificate, find out exactly where and when he was killed.'

'I'd also like to show this photograph to Hilda Hodges, sir, if you don't mind?'

George sighed and rolled his eyes heavenwards. 'Another waste of time!' he muttered under his breath.

'I suppose it might be worth a try,' Inspector Mount agreed.

'I don't see how, if she's never met the man!' George said.

'As far as she knows. But she might have seen him and not known about it,' Charlie reasoned. 'This might help jog her memory, at least.'

'Good idea, constable. Tobias Warriner is still our main suspect, and since he seems to have disappeared off the face of the earth, we might as well pursue whatever leads we can, no matter how tenuous.' Inspector Mount turned to George. 'I take it you've still had no luck tracking down the elusive captain?'

'No, sir. I can't find any address for him, nor any place of work. He's entitled to an army pension, but he's never bothered to collect it.'

'Well, he must do something, otherwise how can he live?' Inspector Mount turned to Charlie. 'See what you can come up with, constable. In the meantime, I have to go and talk to another suspect who has entered the fray. I'm glad to say this one is a little easier to find.'

'Who's that, sir?' Charlie asked.

'The Black Widow,' George answered for him. 'She's certainly living up to her name, I must say.'

'You won't have heard, will you, constable? Violet Franklin's son Thomas has been named as the main beneficiary in Elizabeth Franklin's will.'

'With Violet in charge of the money until he's twenty-one,' George put in. 'If there's anything left by then,' he added. 'I daresay she's spending his inheritance as we speak!'

But Charlie was scarcely listening to George. His mind was racing too fast.

'I don't understand . . . How could that happen?' he murmured.

'That's what I'm going to find out,' Inspector Mount said firmly.

Charlie hesitated. He was still holding onto the information Annie had given him about Violet Franklin. He wasn't sure why he hadn't shared it with anyone. Perhaps it was out of some kind of compassion for Violet and everything she had been through? He had seen the weary pride in her face, the way she had refused to allow her circumstances to beat her down, and that had sparked something in him. Deep in his heart he believed she was innocent of murder.

But this revelation had changed everything. It made him remember that Violet was a con artist and a thief, skilled in the art of making people believe she was something she wasn't.

And there he was, thinking he was too clever to be fooled.

He took a deep breath. 'Before you go, Inspector,' he said. 'I think there's something you ought to know about Violet Franklin . . .'

It was the second time the police had come to her door in as many weeks, and Violet did not like it.

The lanky young constable was not there this time. Instead the cocky little sergeant was with an older man, lean with light grey eyes and thinning brown hair springing from a high, domed forehead. He had a pleasant manner, but Violet was not fooled. He was still police.

'I'm in the middle of cooking tea,' she said, leading the way into the flat. 'If you want to talk to me, you can do it while I work.'

Thomas was sitting at the kitchen table, fiddling with the strings of a wooden puppet Mickey had bought for him. Violet gave her son's hair a quick, reassuring ruffle then went back to the stove.

'It smells good,' the older man commented. 'What are you cooking?'

'Pease pudding and boiled beef.'

'I'd have thought it would be caviar and champagne all the way for you now?' the sergeant said with a sneer.

'That's what you think, is it?' Violet sent him a long, hard look until he dropped his gaze.

'Sergeant Stevens has a point,' the older man said. 'You're a wealthy woman now, Mrs Franklin.'

'The money was all left to Thomas. It's not mine to spend.'

'Yes, but it's yours to control until he's twenty-one.'

'And when he's twenty-one, it will all be there waiting for him.' Violet tucked a stray lock of hair behind her ear and went back to stirring the bubbling pan of split peas on the hob.

She didn't say that the reason she didn't want to touch the money was because she was afraid it was tainted in some way. She had not earned it, she was not entitled to it, and if she even thought about it, she would feel Elizabeth Franklin's cold, dead hand reaching out from the grave.

Not that these two would ever understand it, or even believe it. She caught sight of their reflection in the cracked fragment of mirror above the sink that Mickey used for shaving. They were sitting side by side on the couch, their bowler hats perched on their knees, looking around them as if they could not quite believe that anyone could live in such squalor.

Certainly not someone who had just inherited a sizeable fortune, at any rate.

'Did you know Miss Franklin was leaving the money to you?' The older man, Inspector Mount, asked.

'She didn't leave anything to me,' Violet insisted stubbornly. 'I told you, she left it to Thomas.'

'But you never discussed it?'

Violet hesitated for a moment, watching her hand dragging the spoon through the thick, bubbling mixture. 'No,' she said finally. 'We never discussed her will.'

'So it came as a surprise to you?'

'Yes.'

'And would it also surprise you to learn that Miss Franklin only changed her will two days before she died?'

No, she thought. *It wouldn't surprise me.*

'Why do you think she might have done that, Mrs Franklin?'

Violet caught his eye in the mirror. She could have told him. But she didn't.

'I have no idea,' she said.

She took a pie dish from the cupboard and began spooning the mixture into it, ready to keep warm in the oven.

'It's a funny thing, isn't it?' Sergeant Stevens said. 'You two never got on, and yet she changed her will in your favour two days before she was murdered. Very suspicious, wouldn't you say?'

'She didn't change it in my favour—'

'Oh, come on, Mrs Franklin!' the inspector raised his voice, startling her. 'Don't take me for a fool. You can play around with words as much as you like, but the fact of the matter is you're now a rich woman, even if you don't choose to take advantage of it. Now, what we're trying to work out is why a woman who made no secret of the fact that she disliked you then left most of her fortune in your control?'

'You'd have to ask her that,' Violet said.

'If only we could, Mrs Franklin. If only we could.'

'At least you got what you wanted this time,' Sergeant Stevens said. 'I'm sure it made up for the disappointment of your husband not leaving you anything, eh?'

Heat rose inside her, bubbling to the surface. Violet opened her mouth to retort, then closed it again when she saw the sergeant's eager expression.

Keep your head, girl, she told herself over and over again. *Don't let them make you say something you'll regret.*

With all the composure she could muster, she grabbed a tea towel from the side and bent to put the pease pudding in the oven.

'Tell me about your husband, Mrs Franklin.'

The inspector was smiling when he said it. But Violet still did not trust him.

'What do you want to know?' she asked cautiously.

'What sort of man was he?'

'You already know that –'

'No, Mrs Franklin. I mean your first husband.'

The world tilted wildly on its axis, and Violet almost felt the ground shift under her feet. 'What?'

'You were married before, weren't you?' The inspector was still smiling as he consulted his notes. 'To – let's see – ah, here it is. Harold Henry Baines. Harry the Blade, to give him his more colourful nickname.'

Violet glanced at Thomas, but her son seemed oblivious to everything as he jiggled his puppet up and down, making it dance on the end of its strings.

Fighting to stay calm, she said, 'It sounds as if you already know about him.'

'Except what happened to him,' Sergeant Stevens said.

'He died.'

'He was murdered,' Inspector Mount corrected her. 'Pulled out of the Thames with a fractured skull. Isn't that right?'

'If you say so.'

The inspector looked back at his notes. 'Was it a happy marriage, Mrs Franklin?' Violet did not reply. 'You were very young when you married him, weren't you? Barely eighteen. And he was . . .' He flicked through his notebook. The rustle of the pages skittered across her nerves.

'Twenty-five,' Violet said.

'Twenty-five,' Inspector Mount said. 'And he'd already done four stretches in prison.' He laughed. 'I bet you hardly saw him during your married life?'

Oh, I saw him enough, Violet thought. *Believe me.*

Harry Baines was the man all the girls in Alice Diamond's gang wanted to be with. He was handsome, charming when he wanted to be, and powerful with it. Violet was young, desperate to escape from her father and brothers, and thought she'd landed a real prize when he chose her.

Talk about out of the frying pan into the fire. Even Patrick Malone, never the most caring father in the world, had tried to warn her in his own way.

'I hope you know what you're doing, girl,' he had said. 'Just don't put a foot wrong, that's my advice.'

But it was hard not to put a foot wrong with Harry. Violet soon found out that his violent reputation extended into their private life.

She couldn't allow herself to go to that dark place where her memories lurked. A place of beatings and humiliation and having to do everything he demanded of her or pay a terrible price.

'Did you kill him?'

Inspector Mount's question took her by surprise, as she was sure it was supposed to.

'No,' she said.

'Are you sure?'

'I would have had a job, wouldn't I? Considering I was locked up in Holloway at the time.'

Now it was their turn to be surprised. She could see it in their faces. 'You're telling me you didn't know?' she said. She shook her head, tutting softly. 'Blimey, Inspector. All those pages and pages of notes and you didn't even bother to check that.'

'You were in prison?'

'A six-month stretch for stealing jewellery in Bond Street. Perhaps you'd better write it down, in case you forget?' She pointed to his notebook.

They didn't stay for much longer after that. Violet stood in the doorway and watched them until they had disappeared out of sight down the stairs. Then she moved to the walkway to watch them crossing the courtyard. She did not take her eyes off them until she was certain they were gone. Only then did she feel safe to return to the flat.

She closed the door and allowed the breath she had been holding to escape her in a long sigh of relief.

Thank God. Thank God she had not allowed her mask to slip. Thank God she had not told them it was her older brother Frank who had put Harry the Blade in the Thames – not out of any loyalty to her, but over a stupid gambling debt. He was every bit as violent a bully as her husband, and he had suffered the same fate soon enough. But Violet still felt she owed him.

And thank God she had not revealed what she really knew about the night Elizabeth Franklin died.

'Mama?' Thomas clambered down from the kitchen chair and came over to her, the puppet dangling from its strings. 'It's got all muddled again, look.'

'Here, let me fix it for you.' Violet bent down and put her hand out to stroke her son's head. Little Thomas, the light of her life. The only man who had never let her down. She would die for him, and she would kill for him.

'Mama will sort it out,' she said, taking the puppet from him. 'You'll see. Mama will make it right.'

Chapter 46

'You want what?'

Spilsbury did not blame Professor Bartlett for his bemused reaction. He tended to go out of his way not to cross paths with any of his colleagues at St Mary's. And any interaction he was forced to have was usually kept brief and to the point.

And yet here he was, in the dining room – somewhere else he rarely ventured – approaching the venerable physician with a cup of tea in his hand. No wonder the poor old man looked startled.

'To speak to you, if I may? About one of your former students?'

'I see.' Luckily Professor Bartlett was one of the more amiable consultants at the hospital. 'Well, let's sit down, shall we? I shall get a neck ache if I have to stand here talking to you.'

He chuckled at his own joke. He was short and stout, his polished bald head barely coming up to Spilsbury's shoulder. His lack of stature, along with his beady, bespectacled gaze and round, smiling face, gave him the appearance of a benevolent gnome.

They found two armchairs in the corner of the dining room and settled themselves. Spilsbury was aware of the other doctors watching them with interest, but Professor Bartlett was completely oblivious as he helped himself to a biscuit from the plate and said, 'Now, who is it you'd like to talk about?'

'Robert Dillon.'

The professor's face lost its smiling softness. 'What about him?'

'He was one of your students, wasn't he?'

'For a while, yes. I do hope you don't want a character reference?'

He looked dismayed at the idea, Spilsbury noticed. 'I take it you wouldn't be willing to give me one?'

'Oh, he has some admirable qualities. He's extremely determined, tenacious and single-minded. If he sets his mind to a task then he will move heaven and earth to achieve it.'

'A rather dubious trait,' Spilsbury observed. 'If the best you can say about a man is that he is single-minded . . .'

The older man looked amused. 'It's what people say about you, Dr Spilsbury.'

Spilsbury was only too aware what his colleagues thought of him. Single-minded was probably a compliment from them.

'But then I suppose he had to show a certain amount of determination to get where he is today,' Professor Bartlett continued. 'It can't be easy to battle one's way up through school and university solely on scholarships.'

'You knew about that?'

'Of course. I found it rather admirable. But I gather Dr Dillon is rather sensitive when it comes to his humble beginnings.'

Spilsbury could imagine why. From his experience, boarding school was a brutal place, and boys were bullied mercilessly over the slightest things. The scholarship boys were always the easiest targets, as he recalled.

'May I ask why you want to know about him?' He frowned. 'You're not thinking of taking him on as your assistant, I hope?'

'My assistant?'

'Willcox tells me you're considering taking someone on.'

'Did he indeed?'

'He seems to think you're doing too much. He asked me to keep an eye out for a suitable candidate, as a matter of fact.'

'Please don't bother on my account,' Spilsbury said through gritted teeth. 'I'm not considering an assistant. And if I was, it wouldn't be Dr Dillon.'

'I daresay it wouldn't,' Dr Bartlett said. 'He's gone on to bigger and better things at Bart's, so I understand. I suppose it was inevitable that he would move on, once he'd lost his patron.'

'Are you talking about Franklin?'

Professor Bartlett helped himself to another biscuit. 'James was very generous to his future son-in-law. He had very high hopes for him.'

'I think Dillon had very high hopes for himself,' Spilsbury muttered.

'Well, quite.' Professor Bartlett helped himself to another biscuit. 'Private practice, indeed. At his age! I don't know what Franklin was thinking. But of course, once the girl jilted him it was all over. I do believe Dillon faced rather a lot of ribbing from his peers over that. But he only had himself to blame, of course. If he had ever shown the slightest humility, perhaps they might have had more sympathy for him. But as it was, some of them took positive glee in his downfall.'

'So he decided to seek advancement elsewhere?'

'Well, I rather think he had to. After what happened.'

'What happened?'

'Surely you must have heard about it?' Professor Bartlett frowned.

Spilsbury suppressed his irritation. Did everyone really think he had nothing better to do than gossip? 'Perhaps you could refresh my memory?' he said.

'Well, as I said, he faced rather a lot of ribbing after the engagement ended. How the mighty are fallen, that sort of thing. Most of it was fairly good-natured, but there was one particular chap who took it too far. They'd always rubbed each other up the wrong way. This particular young man came from a very well-to-do background, and he was forever teasing Dillon about his accent, and his manners, that sort of thing. Anyway, this chap must have said something out of turn, because Dillon took offence and lashed out. The unfortunate young man ended up with a broken nose, concussion and several stitches in his upper lip, as I recall.'

'That sounds more like a sustained beating than someone lashing out.'

'I'm afraid you may be right,' Professor Bartlett said. 'The young man's family did not take kindly to the matter, and there was a great deal of unpleasantness. Everyone thought it might bring the hospital into disrepute. But luckily it was settled quietly, on the condition that Dr Dillon transferred to another hospital.'

'I see.'

Professor Bartlett looked earnestly at Spilsbury. 'I wouldn't want to give you the impression he is a violent young man,' he said.

'Then what would you call him?'

He thought for a moment. 'Oversensitive, perhaps,' he said finally.

And how might an oversensitive young man react to being publicly humiliated? Spilsbury wondered. If he could turn on a colleague for teasing him, then surely he could plot the murder of the woman who stood between him and his dreams?

Chapter 47

It was half past six and long past closing time. But there was still a light burning in the window of the grocer's shop as Charlie approached. Peering through the glass, he could see Hilda Hodges behind the counter, surrounded by boxes.

He tapped on the glass and she looked up, distracted.

'You'll have to come back another time,' she called out. 'I'm busy.'

'Open the door, Miss Hodges. I need to speak to you.'

It took her several minutes to find the key and unlock the door. She didn't seem like her usual self at all: her curls were uncombed, and her cardigan was buttoned up the wrong way. She looked tired, her eyes red-rimmed as if she had been crying.

She looked so dreadful, Charlie immediately forgot why he'd come.

'Are you all right, Miss Hodges? You don't look well,' he said.

'I'm surprised I've not had a heart attack with everything that's going on. Look at this mess,' she gestured to the boxes. 'These deliveries were supposed to go out today, but the boy didn't turn up this morning. And when he did show his face yesterday he was worse than useless.' Her words came out in a torrent. 'I've had people knocking on my door all day long, asking where their orders are. And most of this lot will have to be thrown away because it's all spoiled. Such a waste,' she shook her head, 'and all because our stupid new delivery lad doesn't know his backside from his elbow!'

She leaned on the counter, her shoulders slumped.

'What happened to the last bloke? Is he on holiday?'

'He left.' A sour look crossed Hilda's face. 'Just walked out last week without a by your leave. I don't think I've slept a wink since. So if you're going to vex me even further, I'd advise against it,' she warned as Charlie opened his mouth to speak. 'I'm not in the mood for it.'

'I only wanted to show you something. I won't keep you too long, I promise.' Charlie took the photograph from his top pocket and handed it to her.

'What's this?' Hilda lifted her spectacles from their chain and peered at it. 'What am I supposed to be looking at?'

'I was hoping you could tell me. Do you recognise any of them?'

'No. Should I?'

'Well, I'm not sure. We have reason to believe one of them might be your sister's boyfriend.'

Hilda looked again. Even with her spectacles on, she held the photograph almost to the tip of her nose. 'I can't say any of them looks familiar,' she said. 'But then as I told you before, I never met the man.'

'Are you sure? It might be possible you've seen him and not known who he was. He might even have come into the shop . . .'

'As if I remember everyone who comes in here!' Hilda thrust the photograph back at him. 'No, I'm sorry. I can't help you.'

'But—'

'Look, I said can't help you, all right?' Hilda snapped. Behind her spectacles her eyes glittered with tears. 'I'm sick of talking about Jean, anyway. It's all anyone cares about. She caused me enough trouble when she was alive, and she's causing me even more now she's dead!'

'In what way?' Charlie asked.

'What?'

'How is she causing you trouble?'

'Well you keep coming in here for one thing!' Hilda regarded him angrily. 'As if I didn't have enough on my plate as it is.' She looked around the shop. 'My father would turn in his grave if he could see the place in this state. I promised him I'd keep it going as he would have wanted, and now look at it!'

'I'll leave you to get on with it then, shall I?' Charlie said, beating a cautious retreat towards the door.

'Why not? That's what everyone else does,' he heard her mutter as the door closed behind him.

It was a fine spring evening, and as Charlie was walking down Arlington Road, he noticed the men had started to gather outside Rowton House. They did not seem quite so desperate as they had when he'd first seen them in the depths of a bitter winter. They were chatting to each other, passing a bottle between them.

Except for one. A terrified young man near the end of the queue, still huddled in a blanket, his teeth chattering in spite of the pleasant evening.

His wild eyes met Charlie's, and he instantly knew who he was. It was the boy who had sprung at George the last time they had been there.

Almost immediately, another image came into his mind, like the final piece of a jigsaw slotting into place.

Charlie doubled back on himself and ran the length of the queue, scanning all the faces as he went. Then he went up to the front door and hammered on it with his fist.

'Doors are unlocked at seven,' the voice growled from inside.

'Police! Open up!'

Bolts slid back and chains rattled on the other side. Then the door slowly opened, and Mr Frazer, the superintendent, stood there, his arms folded across his burly chest.

'What do you want this time?' he said.

'Do you know this man?' Charlie pulled the photograph from his inside pocket and passed it to him. The Superintendent studied it for a moment, then a slow grin spread across his face.

'Of course I do,' he said, handing it back to Charlie. 'Everyone knows Eddie.'

Chapter 48

'I wondered when you'd realise who I was.'

He regarded them all across the table, one by one. He didn't seem in the slightest bit intimidated to be sitting in a police interview room. In fact, he seemed rather amused by the whole affair.

'When I saw you at the funeral, I felt sure you'd know me straight away,' he said.

Charlie looked at him. The suit he wore was well-cut and expensive, but the knees and elbows were worn shiny with age. His shoes were carefully polished, but showed signs of mending. This was a man who was not all he seemed in more ways than one.

How had he not remembered his face, from the first time he saw him at Rowton House? It seemed so obvious now.

'I knew your face was familiar, but I couldn't work out where from until I saw that boy again. The one with the shell shock?'

'You mean Joe?' He shook his head. 'It's a terrible business. By rights he should be in hospital, not living on the streets.'

'You're not an easy man to find, Captain Warriner,' Inspector Mount said.

He winced. 'Please, I go by the name Edgar French now. I left Tobias Warriner on the battlefield years ago.'

'May I ask why?'

'Because that isn't who I am anymore.'

'Edgar,' Charlie said. 'You chose your brother's name?'

'How did— Of course, I suppose you've been to see my father. That must have been a treat for you. Did he curse my name and tell you never to speak of me in his presence again?' His mouth twisted mockingly. 'I chose my brother's name because I wanted people to remember him. And I also took my mother's maiden name.'

'To remember her?'

'To enrage my father mostly. And to remind him of the wife he betrayed right up until her death with his secretary, the delightful Daphne. Although that rather backfired, since he was probably relieved I wasn't bringing shame to the family name anymore.'

'You didn't bring shame to anyone,' Charlie said. 'I read the despatches in the *London Gazette*. You saved those men—'

'Please.' He held up his hand. 'I told you, I'm not that man any more, thank God.'

'But you won the Military Cross?'

'A pathetic bit of tin! What does it mean, anyway? My brother didn't get a medal, did he? He was a damn sight braver than I was, but all he got was a bullet through the heart.' He leaned forward towards them. 'Do you know what I did with my precious medal? I gambled it away in a game of cards. That's how much it meant to me.'

A heavy silence descended on the room. Charlie could see Tobias Warriner fighting to regain his composure as he lit up a cigarette.

'Let's talk about something else, shall we?' Inspector Mount said.

'Let's.' The facade was back in place. Warriner relaxed back in his seat and blew a smoke ring at the ceiling. 'What do you want to know, Inspector?'

'What were you doing at Elizabeth Franklin's funeral?'

'I went to pay my respects.'

'But Matthew Franklin said he hardly knew you,' George said.

'That's correct. I haven't seen him in years. Not until I met him again at the regimental reunion.'

'Why did you go, if you hate the memory of the war so much?' Charlie asked.

A slow smile spread across the other man's face. 'Very astute, constable.' He leaned back in his seat. 'I had some business to attend to.'

'What kind of business?'

'I'm afraid that's confidential.'

'The devil it is!' Mount's patience was wearing thin. 'What's your business, Warriner?'

He winced, but he did not correct him. 'I'm a private investigator.'

He looked round at their stunned faces. 'Believe me, my father had the same look on his face when I told him. If he hadn't already disowned me, I'm sure he would have done so at that moment.'

'What do you investigate?' Inspector Mount asked.

'Oh, I'm sure you can imagine: marital infidelities, mostly; missing people, evidence for court cases, double-dealing among business partners. I deal in secrets,' he said.

'How ironic, when you're living under an assumed identity yourself,' Inspector Mount said.

Warriner laughed. 'Me? I'm an open book, Inspector.'

'So who were you investigating that night at the reunion?' Mount asked.

'In the normal way of things, I would never break client confidentiality, but given that my client is now dead I suppose it hardly matters. I was there to keep an eye on Matthew Franklin.'

'Elizabeth Franklin sent you? Why?'

He ground out his cigarette in the ashtray. 'She wanted to make sure he was at a regimental reunion, and not in some club in St James Street, running up gambling debts.'

'So you were with him all evening?' Inspector Mount asked.

'Unfortunately, yes.'

'Unfortunately?'

'I had to listen to him and his friends laughing and joking about their glory days in GHQ. As if there was anything glorious or honourable about what they did,' he said bitterly.

'You don't have a lot of respect for them, then?'

'Did you serve, Inspector?'

'Yes, I did.'

'Then you'll know why I have no respect for them.'

'They had a job to do, just like the rest of us.'

'Recruiting schoolboys to fight, and organising for their graves to be dug when they were slaughtered.' His mouth tightened. 'Yet to listen to them talk, you'd think they'd been side by side with them in the trenches, instead of miles away out of harm's way. Matthew Franklin and his cronies never knew what it was like to face death, otherwise they might not have been so keen to punish those who did.'

He reached into his pocket and pulled out his cigarettes again. Inspector Mount automatically reached across with a light.

'You didn't like Matthew Franklin?'

'I found him utterly repellent. Greedy, selfish, without a shred of compassion for anyone but himself. That's what I thought when I first met him, and the years had not changed him at all.'

'You seemed very protective of him at Miss Franklin's funeral?' Charlie said.

Tobias Warriner grinned. 'I was teasing, constable. I could tell Franklin didn't want me there, and I enjoyed making him feel uncomfortable.'

'Why were you there?' Inspector Mount asked.

'I told you, I went to pay my respects. Miss Franklin was one of my best clients.'

'You'd worked for her before?'

'Oh yes, many times.'

'What sort of work?'

'Mainly delving into people's backgrounds, making sure there were no dark secrets lurking there.'

'Whose background did you look into?'

'It would be easier to tell you who I didn't investigate. Elizabeth Franklin was not a terribly trusting soul,' he said wryly.

'With good reason, given what happened to her,' George commented.

'I suppose you might be right.' Tobias Warriner looked thoughtful as he drew on his cigarette. 'Yes, I never thought about it like that. Poor Elizabeth.' He shook his head.

'You were telling us about your investigations?' Inspector Mount prompted.

'Let me see . . .' He thought about it for a moment. 'She first wrote to me just after her brother returned from the war with his new bride in tow. Miss Franklin was rather concerned about her sister-in-law, and she asked me to find out more about her.'

'And did you?'

'I did indeed.'

'And what did you find out?'

'Nothing that you gentlemen haven't already discovered, I'm sure. It just might have taken you a bit longer,' he smirked. 'I discovered Violet Malone came from a somewhat notorious family, that she had a criminal record and that she had been married before, to a gangster who somehow found himself murdered.'

'And what did Miss Franklin make of that?'

'She was utterly delighted. I believe she ran straight off to tell her brother the good news, only to find he already knew all about it. Turns out his new bride didn't have any secrets from her husband after all. It rather took the wind out of her sails, I think. I didn't hear anything more from her until a few weeks later, when her niece took up with that doctor fellow.'

'Dr Dillon?'

'That's the chap. Miss Franklin definitely didn't like the cut of his gib. She had him down as a fortune hunter right from the start.'

'And was she right?'

'That's not for me to say. But Miss Franklin was horrified when I told her what I'd found out, appalling old snob that she was,' he laughed. 'And then there was the latest investigation I carried out on Miss Franklin's behalf. I would have thought that was the one you were most interested in? It's why you've been looking for me, after all.'

'You mean the Lonely Hearts Killer?' George blurted out.

Warriner grinned. 'What a ridiculous name. Who came up with that, I wonder?'

'Not us.' Inspector Mount shifted in his seat. 'So what do you know about it?'

'Only that Miss Franklin asked me to look into who had been placing certain advertisements in *The Times*.'

'And did you find out who it was?'

'I tried. But alas, as you discovered yourselves, the files had been stolen.'

'You didn't steal them?' Inspector Mount asked.

'Now why on earth would I do something like that?'

'To cover your tracks, if you were the killer,' George muttered.

'Would I be sitting here if I was? Believe me, I was as disappointed as you to find those files had been stolen. It meant I couldn't carry out my investigation. Miss Franklin was not best pleased when I drew a blank, I can tell you.'

'Why did she need you to find out who had placed the advertisements?' George asked. 'Surely she already knew who her mystery man was?'

'I'm afraid I can't help you there, Sergeant.' Warriner shrugged. 'Your guess is as good as mine.'

'Did you call on her the night she was murdered?' Mount asked.

'How could I? I was babysitting her nephew all evening.' He leaned forward. 'Why? Did she have a visitor?'

'We believe so.'

'Well, then, I'm sure you have your man.' Warriner looked at his watch. 'Now, if you'll excuse me, I have an illicit liaison in a hotel in Marylebone.'

As they all rose to their feet, Inspector Mount said, 'We'll need your address, just in case we need to get in touch with you again.'

'You'll generally find me at Rowton House.'

'You don't have a permanent place of residence?'

'Rowton House is as good a place as any.' He held out his hand and shook the inspector's firmly. 'Goodbye, Inspector. I'm sure we'll be speaking again very soon,' he said.

'I'm sure we will,' Inspector Mount replied.

Chapter 49

'I don't like him,' George said, as they walked back together down the corridor. It was late in the evening, and most of the offices leading off the passage were in darkness. Only a light glowed at the far end, in the tiny cubicle that Charlie shared with George and two detective constables.

'He seemed very sure of himself,' Inspector Mount commented. 'He was either telling the truth or he's a very accomplished liar.'

'My money's on the latter,' George said. 'He certainly knows more about those missing files than he's letting on. Did you see the way he was smirking? As if he'd got one over on us and he knew it. He was too clever by half.'

'He's certainly clever,' Charlie said.

George turned on him accusingly. 'You sound as if you admire him?'

'I did.' In spite of everything, Charlie couldn't help it. 'He kept us guessing for long enough, didn't he?'

'That's why you'll never be one of us,' George said sourly. 'Detectives have to take a balanced view.'

'You just said you didn't like him. That's hardly a balanced view, is it?'

'Sergeant Stevens is right about one thing,' Inspector Mount spoke over them. 'Warriner certainly knows what happened to those files. But why would he want to hide that information?'

'Because they implicate him,' George said. 'He's Elizabeth Franklin's mystery man.'

'Or he knows who is,' Charlie said.

Mount sent him a curious look. 'You think he might be working with someone?'

'I don't know about that, sir. He might be. But he told us himself, he deals in secrets. What's to stop him using that information to his advantage?'

'Blackmail, you mean?' The inspector considered it for a moment. 'That would be rather risky. If this man has killed twice, then he'd almost certainly kill again to keep his secret.'

'Captain Warriner strikes me as the sort of man who might enjoy taking risks, sir.'

'I tend to agree with you, constable. Perhaps we'd better keep an eye on him for his own good, if nothing else.'

'At least it means we can eliminate Matthew Franklin from our list of suspects,' George said, determined not to be outdone.

'What makes you say that, Sergeant?'

'Well, it stands to reason, sir. It's clear Warriner can't stand him. If he'd had any chance to put him in the frame for his aunt's murder then I don't doubt he would have taken it. But instead he gave him an alibi.'

'That's true. Good thinking, Sergeant.'

'Thank you, sir.' George puffed up with pride. 'But I do wonder why he hates him so much. What was so wrong with what he did in the war?'

Charlie caught the inspector's eye. George would never understand, he thought. Not unless he had been there.

'General Headquarters weren't very popular,' Mount explained. 'Lots of us felt they had far too easy a time. They were kept well away from the fighting.'

'So there was a lot of jealousy?' George said.

'It was partly that. But some of the duties they carried out weren't popular, either. The Adjutant-General's section in particular were in charge of pay and punishments. I suspect Captain Warriner may have fallen foul of them, if his attitude today was anything to go by. Wouldn't you say so, constable?'

'I'm sure he did, sir.'

'Anyway, get on to Y Division and make sure we get a couple of men posted outside this Rowton House place, just in case he decides to disappear again.' He smiled wearily at them. 'Now go home,' he said. 'It's been a long day.'

'Yes, sir,' they chorused.

As soon as he was out of earshot, George turned on Charlie and said, 'You didn't think you're going anywhere, Beanpole? Not until you've tidied up that office.'

'What? That's not fair. Why should I be the one to clear it up?'

'Because you're the one who makes all the mess! It's never been in such a state since you arrived, piles of old magazines everywhere.'

'I can't help that. They're for my research.'

'I don't care what they're for, I want them all out of that office before tomorrow morning. All right?'

He left, and Charlie regarded the teetering pile in despair. George was right, he thought, he had rather taken over the tiny office since he'd arrived. So much for trying to fit in! He was surprised the other lads in the office hadn't complained about it too.

He picked up an armful of magazines from his desk, then looked around for somewhere to put them. There was barely any floor space, with four desks crammed into the tiny office. He wondered about asking Inspector Mount if he could store them in his office, then decided against it.

He'd found out all the information he could from the *London Gazette*. Now it was time for them to go back to the library.

But the thought made him panic. Because he knew when the gazettes went back to the library, it would also be time for him to return to his old division. With his research over, there would be no more reason for him to stay.

All good things must come to an end, Charlie boy, he thought.

He dumped the magazines out in the corridor, then returned for another armful. As he lifted them from his desk, he noticed the letter lying underneath. How long had that been there? he wondered.

He picked it up and examined it. It bore the postmark of Somerset House.

It must be Edgar Warriner's death certificate. Charlie had ordered it after he returned from Derbyshire. He tore open the envelope out of idle curiosity more than anything else. He already knew how the young man had died, after all.

Edgar Rupert Warriner. Date of birth: 15 March 1898. Date of death: 28 July 1916.

The Somme.

Poor kid, Charlie thought. To die in a hellhole like that, at barely eighteen years of age.

His eyes skimmed past the cause of death before he realised what he seeing. He read it again. And again.

And suddenly he understood.

Chapter 50

'A private investigator?'

'I know. Isn't it horrible?' Lydia shuddered. 'Just think, all this time Aunt E was spying on us all. What sort of person would do that to their own family?'

Violet wished she could have shared her stepdaughter's surprise. But she was only too aware of Elizabeth Franklin's capabilities.

It all made sense to her now. She and James had only been married a matter of weeks before Elizabeth went to her brother and exposed all the secrets of Violet's past. Secrets so shameful she had kept them hidden for years. And yet somehow Elizabeth had discovered every detail, from her prison record to her ill-fated marriage.

Violet had been deeply shocked at the time and wondered how she could have found out so much about her. Now she knew.

Thankfully she had already told James everything about her past, otherwise it might have been utterly devastating. But she had never forgiven Elizabeth for trying to destroy their marriage. And Elizabeth had never forgiven Violet for the fact that she did not succeed.

'That dreadful man must have kept files on all of us,' Lydia said. 'All the details of where we went, who we were seen with. And he was reporting everything back to her. And do you know the worst of it? I knew him. He lodges in Rowton House. I remember him, always in the library. I even used to talk to him about what he was reading. Little did I ever imagine he was spying on me . . .' She paused. 'It doesn't bear thinking about, does it?'

'No, it doesn't.'

The front door slammed, making Lydia flinch.

'It's all right. It's just my brother gone out,' Violet said. She only hoped Mickey hadn't heard their conversation. If this Warriner character had been spying on her then he most likely would have been spying on Mickey, too. She couldn't imagine what he would say about that.

'In this rain?' Lydia peered out of the window. Water streamed down the glass.

'He probably had an errand to run.'

'Or can't wait for me to leave.' Lydia looked rueful.

Violet opened her mouth, then closed it again. There was no point in denying it. Mickey had retreated to the bedroom as soon as Lydia arrived, taking Pistol with him.

'It's more likely me he's trying to avoid. We've had a falling out,' Violet explained.

'Oh? What about?'

'Something and nothing.' At least, she hoped it was nothing. Mickey had been out all night again. Violet had been waiting for him when he stumbled in just before dawn, looking rough and unshaven. Nevertheless, he insisted that he was still working as a watchman at the docks, but she knew when her brother was lying to her.

Lydia smiled. 'He's like that dog of his, laying low when he knows he's in trouble!'

'That's true.'

'Lyddy?' Thomas claimed Lydia's attention, his hands resting on her knees, his face in front of hers. 'Will you play soldiers with me?'

'Of course I will, sweetheart.' She gave Thomas's cheek a gentle pinch. 'You go and fetch them.'

As Thomas ran off, Violet said, 'You don't have to stay and entertain him, you know.'

Lydia's brows arched. 'Are you trying to get rid of me?'

'Not at all. I just thought you must have better things to do with your time.'

'Nothing I'd rather do than this.' Lydia beamed at Thomas as he returned with his boxful of soldiers. 'I miss him so much, you know. The house seems empty without him.'

Violet watched as her stepdaughter carefully tipped the tin soldiers out onto the rug. She looked so sad. She was always such a sunny, optimistic girl, but now she seemed to have the weight of the world on her shoulders.

At least she seemed happy enough, playing with Thomas. She had always been so fond of him.

'I wonder what else Elizabeth's detective found out?' Lydia said suddenly.

'What do you mean?'

'I do wonder . . .' She lifted her grey gaze to Violet's. 'I wonder if perhaps she unearthed something she shouldn't have? A secret, perhaps?'

'One that got her killed?'

Lydia shuddered. 'It hardly bears thinking about, does it?'

'No,' Violet said. 'No, it doesn't.'

She left Lydia and her son re-enacting a noisy battle on the rug as she went to peel potatoes for their tea. But Lydia's remark still haunted her.

What if Elizabeth's mysterious investigator had discovered something? A secret so terrible that someone would go to any lengths to keep it hidden?

In which case, her murderer had to be someone she knew.

'I've got something to tell you.' Lydia spoke up suddenly, interrupting her thoughts.

'What's that?'

Her stepdaughter stared down at the battered little tin soldier in her hand.

'It's about—'

No sooner had she started to speak than there was a sharp rap on the front door.

'Who's that?' Violet wiped her hands on her apron as she went to answer it. No one ever knocked in Queen's Buildings. Not unless it was the rent man or the police.

But it was neither.

'Where's Lydia?' Robert Dillon stood on her doorstep, sheltering under a huge black umbrella. He did not even bother to meet Violet's eye as he craned his neck to look beyond her into the flat. 'She said she'd be here.'

He shifted as if to take a step inside, but Violet barred his way. 'Did I say you could come in?' she said.

He looked her up and down, his lip curling. 'I'd need to burn all my clothes if I stepped inside there.'

'Lucky I ain't inviting you, then, ain't it? What are you doing here, anyway?'

'He's looking for me.' Lydia appeared behind her. 'Hello, Robert.'

'There you are!' He reached for her, dragging her into an embrace. 'You told me you'd be back by two o'clock. I was worried about you.'

'I'm sorry. I was talking to Violet and I lost track of time.'

'What a silly goose you are! We'll be late for our meeting with the registrar.'

'Registrar?' Violet looked from one to the other.

'Didn't Lydia tell you?' Robert laughed. 'Good lord, my dear, you've been gossiping all this time and yet you forgot to mention the most important piece of news.' He reached for her hand. 'We're getting married,' he announced.

'I was just about to tell you,' Lydia said quietly.

'When did this happen?'

'A few days ago.'

Violet looked at Lydia's bare left hand. 'I don't see a ring?'

'Yes, well, that's not my doing. I tried to give her ring back, but she won't wear it. Superstitious nonsense!' Robert scoffed.

Violet flashed a look at her stepdaughter. Above her fixed smile, Lydia's eyes were expressionless.

'I suppose it could be considered bad luck,' she said. 'So when's the big day?'

'That's why we're seeing the registrar. We're hoping for the end of the month.'

'Two weeks? That ain't long to plan a wedding.'

'Robert didn't want to wait.' Lydia shot him a wary sideways glance.

'I let her slip through my fingers once. I'm not risking it again!' His hand still held Lydia's, his fingers wound tightly around hers. 'We decided it was for the best. Didn't we, darling?'

Lydia nodded. 'Robert is going to take over my father's practice. Everything has been such a muddle since Aunt Elizabeth died.' She spoke in a strange, almost wooden tone.

'Anyway, we'd best go if we're going to get to the register office in time.' Robert moved to pull Lydia under the shelter of his umbrella, but Violet put her arms around her instead, hugging her close. She could feel all the bones in her slender frame.

As she pulled away, Violet thought she caught the glint of tears in her eyes. But the next moment she was smiling again.

'I'll see you soon,' she promised.

'Oh, I don't know about that!' Robert gave a forced laugh. 'I expect you'll be far too busy getting ready for your wedding.'

Thomas joined her at the door as she stood, watching them go.

'Has Lyddy gone?' he said.

'Yes, my love.' Violet put her arm around his small shoulders, holding him close. 'Yes, I'm afraid she has.'

Chapter 51

'You're sure about this?'

'I'm certain, sir. I double-checked the name in the *Police Gazette*. Edgar Warriner did not die on the battlefield in 1916. He was shot as a deserter.'

A bullet through the heart, was all his brother had said. They had all assumed the rest.

'Did you find out anything else?'

'Yes, sir. There were two of them went missing, Warriner and another fellow. Just boys, barely eighteen years old. According to the report, their unit had been pinned down by heavy artillery barrage for several days. When it finally stopped, they ran.'

'And they were caught?'

'No, sir. They came back of their own accord a day later. They'd spent the night sheltering in a deserted farmhouse. They said they'd only wanted to calm their nerves.'

He could almost imagine them, two skinny, trembling kids, terrified out of their wits by what they had endured. Who could blame them for running away? If it had been him, he might not have stopped running until he reached Blighty.

But these boys had mustered the courage to return, only to find themselves facing a court martial and sentenced to death by firing squad.

'I think I can guess who was in charge of that court martial,' Inspector Mount said.

'Indeed, sir.'

Tobias Warriner's bitter words came back to him. *Matthew Franklin and his cronies never knew what it was like to face death, otherwise they might not have been so keen to punish those who did.*

No wonder he hated Franklin so much.

'I suppose that explains the blood-stained cloths he's been receiving?' Mount said.

George Stevens looked from one to the other. 'I'm sorry, sir. I don't follow?'

'When deserters faced a firing squad, a piece of white cloth was pinned to their chests, over their hearts,' Charlie explained. 'It gave the other soldiers something to aim at.'

He had never had to perform such a grisly task himself, thank God. He couldn't imagine what was going through those poor men's minds as they lined up in the cold light of dawn and pointed their rifles at two shivering boys, lads they had lived and fought beside for weeks. Even amid the hell of war, with all its blood and death and chaos, it seemed like a ghastly, inhuman thing to make a man do.

'Warriner didn't want him to forget what he'd done, did he?' Inspector Mount said grimly.

'Nor would I, sir, if it had been my brother.'

'But it wasn't Franklin's fault those boys ran away, was it?' George Stevens spoke up. 'He was only doing his duty, surely?'

Charlie and Inspector Mount looked at each other, and Charlie knew the senior officer was thinking exactly the same as him.

'And there's another thing I don't understand,' George went on, oblivious to the sudden tension in the room. 'If Matthew Franklin knew Warriner was the one threatening him, why didn't he report it to us? Why would he keep quiet about it?'

'Perhaps he also had something to hide?' Inspector Mount said. 'Let's bring them both in for questioning and find out, shall we?'

As he turned away, Charlie said, 'Excuse me, sir?'

'Yes?'

'Before you speak to Captain Warriner, I think there's something else you should know. It's about the other soldier who was executed . . .'

Tobias Warriner looked out of the window of his room to the street below. The policeman was still there, illuminated in a pool of light from the street lamp. He stood out like a sore thumb on the empty street. God knows what the other men at the hostel must be thinking. Many of them had good reason to be wary of the police.

The only sound was the rumble of traffic under the viaduct, and the barking of a dog somewhere in the distance.

It wouldn't be long before they were knocking on his door, he thought. They already knew he must have been the one to steal the files from the newspaper office, even though he'd denied it.

But they wouldn't find anything because it was all locked up in a bank safe deposit box.

He sat down on the bed, the horsehair mattress yielding only slightly under his weight. He always shelled out half a crown for a 'special', a proper bedroom to himself, preferring the privacy to the sixpenny cubicles most of the other men preferred. He changed rooms every night depending on where he was in the line when the doors opened, but it was as good as any hotel, and he liked the camaraderie among the other men. He spent many happy hours reading, or playing dominoes with the other men, or just talking and having a laugh.

He closed his eyes for a moment, listening to the men's voices outside in the passageway. It gave him comfort, made him feel less alone.

It was a pity it all had to come to an end. But he had a feeling he would not be so welcome in Rowton House now he had brought the police to their door.

His career as a private investigator would probably have to come to an end, too. But Tobias felt less sorrow about that.

It was a grubby little trade, to be sure. Unfaithful spouses, sordid affairs, cheating business partners, employees with their hands in the till, a peer of the realm's child born out of wedlock. He found them all out in the end, thanks to his cunning, his contacts, and his ability to charm all kinds of things out of people.

He despised the tawdriness of it all, but at least he had the satisfaction of knowing how much shame he was bringing to his family. His father's rejection did not even hurt him anymore because Tobias knew he would be wounding him in return, and in the place where it would hurt most – his pride.

But lately, all the secrets he carried had become a burden to him. Elizabeth Franklin had died because of what he had discovered, and now Tobias suspected he was in danger too. The sooner he rid himself of the secrets, the more chance he had of living to tell the tale.

Or rather, not telling the tale.

He made up his mind. When it was safe, he would go down to the safe, take out every one of those wretched files and burn them. He would have done it straight away, but he knew the police would probably be following his every move, at least for a while. Far better to lay low until they had lost interest, and then get rid of the evidence.

All he had to do was stay out of trouble until then.

He tensed at the sound of a knock on the door.

Slowly, he stood up and crept over to the window to look out into the street. The policeman had gone.

There was another knock on the door. Tobias smiled to himself. So they'd come already, had they? They must have knocked on a few magistrates' doors to get a warrant so late.

Tobias tucked the key to the safe deposit under the mattress and went to the door.

'Good evening, officer,' he said, as he flung open the door. 'I hope you haven't got too cold, standing on that corner—'

Then he looked up and saw the figure standing before him, and the words died in his throat.

Chapter 52

Violet was waiting when Mickey came home in the early hours of the morning. She sat on the couch, an old blanket around her shoulders to keep out the cold.

He didn't see her sitting there in the darkness. Violet watched his tall, dark shape as it lumbered past her towards the kitchen, Pistol at his heels. The dog stopped for a moment, sensing Violet in the shadows. Then he turned and trotted after his master.

Violet waited as Mickey stood at the sink and ran the tap, hissing as the cold water ran over his hands.

'Where have you been?' she asked.

Mickey swung round. 'Bloody hell, Vi, you gave me a start! What are you doing, sitting in the dark?'

'Waiting for you.' Violet stood up, easing her limbs which had become stiff and cramped after sitting for so long. 'You ain't answered my question. Where have you been?'

Mickey turned back to the sink. 'Don't start,' he growled. 'It's been a long night, and I want to get to bed.'

'No, Mickey, you ain't putting me off so easily this time.' Violet lit the gas mantle and went to stand beside him. 'Where have you been? And don't bother giving me any old nonsense about a watchman's job, because I've been asking down at the docks and no one's heard of you.'

'You've been checking up on me?' His voice was sharp.

'What else was I supposed to do, when you won't give me a straight answer?'

'You had no right.'

'I'm your sister and I've got every right to know if my brother's in trouble. Mickey?' She seized his arm and swung him round to face her. 'For Christ's sake, look at me when I'm talking to—'

She stopped dead at the sight of his battered face. His nose was caked in dried blood and his left eye was little more than a slit amid an ugly, swollen purple mess.

'Oh my God, Mickey! What happened to you?'

He turned away. 'I gave worse than I got,' he muttered, leaning over the sink to rinse his face. Violet saw him wince as he uncurled his right hand. His knuckles were scraped and caked in more dried blood.

Fear and dread clenched her chest.

'What have you done?' she whispered. 'Are you in trouble?'

'No.'

There was a fraction of hesitation before he answered. Anyone else might not have spotted it, but Violet knew him too well. Over the years, she had learned to read his every move.

'Tell me, Mickey. Because I swear whatever it is, it can't be worse than what I'm imagining!'

'All right!' He shook off her restraining arm. 'If you must know, I've been back in the ring.'

'But how? You told me your trainer wouldn't get you any more fights because of your injured hand . . .' Then she looked back at the grazes across his hands. 'Oh Mickey, no! Not bare-knuckle fighting?'

He turned away from her. 'It's all I can get,' he mumbled.

'But you're better than that!'

'Not anymore. I lost any chance I might have had of turning professional after this.' He flexed his right hand, wincing as his clawed fingers refused to straighten. 'Besides, I needed the money for you and the kid.'

Violet looked up into her brother's bruised and battered face. Then, with a sigh, she took down the tin from the shelf over the sink, where they kept the Beechams Pills, aspirins, Sloan's Liniment and various other remedies.

'Here. Let me see.' She found a clean cloth and bathed the dried blood carefully from his face. 'Blimey, Mickey, keep still. Don't be such a baby!'

'It stings.'

'Yes, well, you shouldn't have been fighting, should you? There, it's done. Now let me look at your hands.'

He stood meekly while she bathed and bandaged his hands.

'That was the last fight?' she said. He nodded. 'You swear to me, Mickey?'

'I swear.'

She looked at him. 'And you would tell me if there was anything else, wouldn't you? I mean, if you were in any sort of trouble?'

'Yes,' he said. And there it was again, that hesitation.

Violet thought about saying something, but then she went on with her bandaging. Whatever it was, she had to hope she could trust her brother to keep his promise to her, and not go back to his old ways.

But sometimes she wished she did not know him so well.

Chapter 53

'He's missing, you say?'

Matthew Franklin lounged in one of the wing chairs that flanked the marble fireplace, a glass of whisky in his hand. He appeared indifferent, but even from across the other side of the drawing room Charlie could sense the tension in him.

'And what does that have to do with me?' he said.

'We wondered if you had any idea where he might have gone, sir, since you and he are acquainted?'

'I'd hardly call us acquaintances. I've already told you, I hadn't seen him for years before he turned up at the reunion.'

'Indeed,' Inspector Mount said. 'We've spoken to a number of other men who were at the reunion. They all tell us the two of you were in close conversation for much of the evening. Now why would that be, I wonder, if you barely knew each other?'

A muscle flicked in Matthew Franklin's cheek. 'We spent some time catching up on old times,' he said.

'I wonder there was much to catch up on, since you were in different regiments.' Inspector Mount's face was completely bland. Charlie wondered if he would ever master such a deadpan expression. 'But then, your respective units did spend some months at the Somme together, isn't that right?'

'That's correct.' Matthew's hand trembled a fraction as he lifted the glass to his lips.

'Is that what you were talking about, Mr Franklin? Your days at the Somme?'

'I suppose so.' He took another gulp of his drink.

Inspector Mount allowed the silence to stretch between them. Watching him, Charlie was lost in admiration. He was a master of interrogation, understated but very effective.

'But you say you haven't seen him recently?'

'No. No, I haven't.'

'Or heard from him?'

Matthew looked at him sharply over the rim of his glass. 'I've already told you,' he said.

'So he hasn't written to you at all? To let you know of his whereabouts?' Inspector Mount said.

'No.'

Once again, the silence lengthened. For all his studied indifference, Matthew was as tense as a coiled spring.

'We have reason to believe Captain Warriner might have come to some harm,' Inspector Mount said at last.

'Good God!' Matthew sat bolt upright. 'You mean someone's killed him?'

'We can't be certain of anything. But there is evidence that someone broke into Captain Warriner's room on the night he went missing and stole certain items.'

'What items?'

'Information relating to some cases that Captain Warriner was working on.'

'Secret information,' George Stevens put in helpfully. 'Highly sensitive.'

The flicker of fear in Matthew Franklin's eyes gave him away. Charlie could almost see the calculation going on in his brain.

'You wouldn't know anything about that, would you, sir?' Mount asked.

'Of course I wouldn't! What on earth would I know about it?' Then he added, 'Do you know who stole these things?'

'I'm afraid not. We're not even sure if they have fallen into the wrong hands yet. That's why it's important we find him and speak to him.'

'Yes. Yes, of course.' But Matthew Franklin was no longer listening. He was staring into the depths of his empty glass, his thoughts miles away.

'I don't suppose you know of anyone who might have wanted to cause Captain Warriner harm?' Inspector Mount asked.

'No, Inspector, but I can imagine there might have been quite a long list.' Matthew's voice was bitter. 'Tobias Warriner had a habit of rubbing people up the wrong way.'

'Including you, sir?'

'Me?' He looked startled. 'I hope you're not implying I had anything to do with his disappearance?'

'I'm not saying anything of the kind, sir. What possible reason might I have to think something like that?'

The two men stared at each other across the room. Charlie saw the look of fear on Matthew Franklin's face and for a moment he thought he might crack and confess the secret he had been keeping.

'No reason at all,' he said tightly.

Mary was busy polishing the longcase clock in the hall when the policemen came down the staircase.

'May I see you out, sir?' She put down her duster and wiped her hands down her apron, ready to show them to the door. But Inspector Mount said, 'I wonder, Mary, is there somewhere we could speak in private?'

'To me, sir?' Mary flicked an anxious glance towards the drawing room above.

'If you wouldn't mind?'

She hesitated a moment, then said, 'You'd best come down to the kitchen.'

She led the way down a short, narrow flight of stairs at the back of the hall, and pushed open a heavy green baize-covered door into the kitchen.

It was a large room, immaculately kept, with the faint scent of freshly baked bread and beeswax polish. A large copper boiler bubbled away in the corner.

'You'll have to excuse the state of the place,' Mary said. 'It's laundry day today.'

She glanced towards the window. Out in the yard, freshly washed sheets billowed like sails on the washing line.

'It must be hard work, keeping up a place like this?' Inspector Mount commented.

'It's all right.' Mary shrugged. 'Miss Lydia and Mister Matthew are hardly ever home these days. And they're not difficult to please. Not like—'

'Not like Miss Franklin? I can imagine she was rather a hard taskmaster.'

'She wasn't that bad. She just liked things done a certain way, that's all.'

'All the same, it must have been rather a shock having to take orders from someone after running your own home.'

Mary said nothing. She lifted the lid on the copper and inspected the washing bubbling inside.

'Where is it you come from, Mary? Yorkshire, isn't it?'

'That's right, sir.'

'And your husband still lives there?'

Charlie saw the muscles in her narrow shoulders tense. 'As far as I know,' she said shortly.

'But you have nothing to do with him? Not since the death of your son?' She did not reply. 'That's what caused the end of your marriage, isn't it, Mrs Jeevons? Terence's death?'

Mary turned to face them. Her eyes darted from one to the other, like a cornered animal.

'He wouldn't have Terry's name mentioned in the house,' she said finally. 'He said he was a shame to the family.'

'Because he was shot as a deserter?'

'My son was no coward!' Pain and anger flashed across her face. 'He was just a boy, he shouldn't have even been there. He was too young.'

The kitchen was silent, except for the low bubble of the copper and Mary's deep, unsteady breathing.

'They couldn't take it,' she said. 'Day after day, nothing but endless gunfire and bombs going off. Seeing their friends killed all around them and not knowing if they were going to be next.' She looked at them, her eyes full of appeal.

'So they ran away?'

'They went back! They could have carried on running, but they didn't. Terry knew he'd done wrong, and he went back to face the music, just like I'd taught him.'

'Did you know about Matthew Franklin when you came to work here?' Inspector Mount asked.

Mary shook her head. 'I just answered an advertisement in the newspaper,' she said. 'I had to get away from my husband, I couldn't stay with him anymore. I needed a new start, and this was as good a place as any. I knew nothing about any of it until Eddie told me.'

'Eddie? You mean Captain Warriner?'

'I only know him as Edgar French.'

Charlie looked at the others, and saw the realisation dawning on their faces.

'You met him when he came to see Miss Franklin?' Inspector Mount said.

'He used to come quite often. She was always wanting him to look into something or other. She had him investigate me, too. And that's how he found out who I was.'

'She hired a private investigator to check up on you?' Charlie couldn't help blurting out.

'I daresay she was worried I was going to steal the silver,' Mary said bleakly. 'Imagine, living your whole life not trusting anyone. Much good it did her in the end,' she muttered.

'So Captain – Edgar French found out you were Private Jeevons's mother?' Inspector Mount said.

Mary nodded. 'I was so shocked, hearing his name after so long. But Eddie didn't talk about him like he was a coward. He told me what really happened. Did you know those boys were entitled to a trial? They should have had a proper lawyer to speak up for them. But they weren't told any of that. Eddie tried to speak for them. He wanted to get it stopped, at least until he could make sure it was all done fairly. But it was rushed through. Apparently some general or other was leaving the next day, and they wanted to get the paperwork all signed off before he left.'

'You mean the Adjutant-General's section?'

'I mean Matthew Franklin.' Mary's face was bitter. 'Just another day or two, and my boy might have been saved. There was no reason to shoot him. He was over there, fighting for his country like everyone else. He died because of a bit of paperwork.'

'You have good reason to hate Matthew Franklin, then?'

'Wouldn't you? My boy's dead, and I'm not allowed to mourn him because he was a coward. And there's him upstairs, preening himself and polishing his medals, and going off to his reunion to laugh about the good old days with his army pals. He's the one who should be buried in a coward's grave, not my Terry!'

'Is that why you decided to blackmail him?'

She paled. 'I don't know what you mean. I'm not black-mailing anyone.'

'Mary, we know you and Captain Warriner were working together.'

Colour rose in her face. 'I'll admit he asked me to pass on the the packages. But I never knew why, or what was in them.'

'But you knew Captain Warriner was blackmailing him?'

'All I know is that Eddie told me he'd found something out about Mister Matthew, and he planned to use it to his advantage.'

'And when did this start?'

'The night of the reunion. I was supposed to meet Eddie at the Blue Angel, but he went off to confront him instead. He'd already started sending the notes by then, and he said it was time to meet him face to face and tell him what he knew.'

'But you don't know what it was?'

'No, and I didn't want to know, either. I told Eddie – Captain Warriner – that I wanted nothing to do with it.' She turned to Inspector Mount. 'You might not believe this, Inspector, but I didn't want revenge. Yes, I'll always hate that man for taking my son, but he's a miserable, wretched excuse for a human being, and he knows it. That's punishment enough in my eyes.' She took a deep, steadying breath. 'I got what I wanted the day Eddie told me my Terry wasn't a coward. That was enough for me, and I'll always be grateful to him for that, whatever else he's done.'

'And do you know where Edgar French is now?'

She sent him a long, steady look. 'No,' she said. 'I don't. But even if I did, I wouldn't tell you.'

Chapter 54

How the woman was not dead yet, Spilsbury did not know.

'Mrs Celia Beckett, aged forty,' the nervous-looking young houseman recited from his notes. 'Admitted at ten minutes past ten this morning, suffering from a large scalp wound. Her husband came home from work and found her semi-conscious on the floor, with blood everywhere. On the way to hospital she started suffering from convulsions.'

It was rare that Spilsbury was called to a patient who was still living. But he had been summoned by the police to St Pancras North Infirmary at Highgate that morning to confirm a case of poisoning. Apparently the doctor treating Mrs Beckett had become suspicious and called them in.

He was quite right to be suspicious, Spilsbury thought. Even under the calming veil of chloroform, the woman's face was strained and anxious, her eyes wild, pupils unnaturally dilated, as if she was staring into the gates of hell. Her skin was dark and dusky, her lips livid.

'We've washed out her stomach and administered twenty grains of chloral hydrate subcutaneously,' the doctor said. 'It seems to be holding her stable so far.'

'Let's hope it continues.'

But Spilsbury did not hold out much hope, judging from her prostrate and exhausted appearance as she lay in her hospital bed in the dimly lit room. He had a strong feeling it would not be long before Mrs Beckett joined his usual roster of patients.

He went outside, where the police inspector was waiting for him. Inspector Jones was an affable Welshman in his forties, sturdily built with a bristling moustache and a ruddy farmer's face. He reminded Spilsbury of his old friend Willcox.

'Well?' he asked.

'From what I can see of the patient, I would say it's almost certainly strychnine poisoning.'

Inspector Jones blew out a long breath. 'I was afraid you'd say that.'

'What time was she found, exactly?'

'Her husband got home about half past nine. She usually had a cup of tea waiting for him, but this morning he found her on the kitchen floor, semi-conscious with blood everywhere. He thought she'd had a fall but then when he went to help her she started having convulsions.' He paused, his head tilting to one side. 'You don't look convinced, Dr Spilsbury?'

'In my experience, strychnine is a quick killer. Symptoms can start within minutes, and death often comes soon after. Either way, most people are dead within two hours of ingesting it.'

He looked at his pocket watch. It was nearly half past eleven.

'So you're saying it's not possible she could have been like it for hours, as her husband says?'

'I wouldn't say it's impossible, but I'd say it was most unlikely. I've heard of a case in Australia where a man had lasted for five hours, but that was quite extraordinary.' He tucked his watch back into his waistcoat pocket. 'It's more likely it happened just before her husband came home, or—'

'Or he did it,' Inspector Jones finished for him.

'Is there any reason to suspect him?'

'Not as far as I know. I've got men out questioning the neighbours, and I'm just about to go down there now and talk to the husband. I don't suppose you'd care to come with me, doctor?'

Spilsbury glanced back towards the room where Mrs Beckett lay, suspended precariously between life and death. There was not much he could do for her until she took that final step one way or another.

'I would like that,' he said.

The Becketts occupied the bottom floor of a tall Victorian terrace just off Holloway Road. A uniformed constable was standing at the door, rocking back and forth on his heels to keep the life in his legs. He straightened up to attention when he saw Spilsbury and the inspector getting out of the car.

'Good morning, constable. Is Mr Beckett still inside?' Inspector Jones asked.

'Yes, sir. Constable Fletcher is with him.' The constable addressed the tip of his nose rather than looking at them.

'Have you spoken to the neighbours?'

'Yes, sir. No one saw anyone going in or out of the house before the husband came home from work.'

'And did he always come home at this time?'

'Not usually, sir. But he says he came home today on account of it being their wedding anniversary.'

'Very touching, I'm sure,' the inspector said dryly.

'They've not long lived here, sir,' the constable said. 'They moved in about a month ago.'

'Really? That's interesting.' The inspector glanced past him towards the house.

'Mrs Beckett told a neighbour it was a new start for them,' the young officer went on. 'Apparently her husband had just got a new job as a postman.'

'Let's go and see what he's got to say for himself, shall we?'

Mr Beckett was sitting at the kitchen table, a uniformed constable standing over him. As soon as Inspector Jones entered the room, Mr Beckett jumped to his feet and started to protest.

'You can't keep me here!' he insisted. 'I've done nothing wrong. I want to see my wife!'

'All in good time, Mr Beckett. Let's have a chat first, shall we?'

He sank slowly into his chair, but he did not look convinced.

'How's my Celia?' he asked, looking from one to the other. 'Is she all right?'

'She's holding on, Mr Beckett.'

'Barely,' Spilsbury muttered.

Mr Beckett sent him a sharp look. 'What do you mean? She ain't dying, is she?'

'Can you tell me how you came to find her?' Jones quickly asked, before Spilsbury could reply.

'I came home from work and found her on the floor, bleeding.'

'And you say she was unconscious?' Spilsbury cut in.

The man shook his head. 'She was talking, but she wasn't making a lot of sense. I thought she must have had a fall and banged her head. But then as soon as I touched her, she went all sort of stiff, and the next minute she was bent back, like this – ' He arched, his head thrown back. 'It was frightening, I can tell you. Like she'd been – I don't know, possessed. I'd never seen anything like it.'

'That will be the poison hitting her spinal cord,' Spilsbury said.

'Poison?' Mr Beckett shot to his feet. 'She's never been poisoned?' He looked from Spilsbury to the police inspector and back again. Either he was a remarkable actor, Spilsbury thought, or the shock on his face was genuine.

'Can you think of anyone who might want to harm your wife?' the inspector asked.

'No.' He frowned. 'Everyone thought the world of Celia.'

Spilsbury watched him carefully. There was a tightness in his jaw that hadn't been there before.

'Including you?' Inspector Mount asked.

Mr Beckett shot him a narrow-eyed look. 'What's that supposed to mean?'

'You've just moved to the area, I understand?'

'That's right. I got a new job.'

'Where were you living before?'

'Camden Town.'

'That's not a million miles away, is it? I wonder you didn't stay where you were.'

'Celia wanted to move.'

'For a new start?'

He looked sharply. 'Who told you that?'

'Your wife mentioned it to one of the neighbours. Now why would you need a new start, Mr Beckett?' Inspector Jones asked mildly. 'Were you not getting on before?'

Mr Beckett sent him a truculent look. 'All right, I'll admit it. We hadn't been getting on lately. But we're right as rain now.'

'And why was that, Mr Beckett?' Inspector Jones's sing-song voice took the edge off the directness of his questions. 'Why weren't you getting on?'

'Just the usual things,' Mr Beckett mumbled. 'I wasn't the husband she thought I should be.'

'And was she right?'

'Maybe she was.' He looked down at his hands. 'Anyway, like I said, we've sorted it all out, made a fresh start. We're happier than we've ever been.'

Spilsbury got up and began to prowl around the kitchen. It was neat and well kept, with a place for everything. A teapot sat on the draining board, with two cups and saucers beside it. He removed the lid from the china pot and peered inside. It was clean and empty, but Spilsbury sniffed it anyway, just to be sure.

'I understand it was your wedding anniversary today?' Inspector Jones said.

'That's right.'

'Did you buy her a present?' Spilsbury asked.

Mr Beckett looked at him blankly. 'A present?'

'Some flowers, perhaps?'

'I didn't have time. I was going to get her something later. That's why I came home – I thought I'd surprise her.'

'But you came home empty-handed?'

'I told you, I didn't have time to get anything!'

'So you weren't in the habit of coming home at that time?' Inspector Jones cut in.

He shook his head. 'Look, when can I see Celia?' he changed the subject abruptly. 'If she's as sick as you say, I need to be with her.'

'Inspector?' A constable appeared at the back door, holding a flat blue box in his hand. 'I found these in the parlour.'

'What have we here?' As Inspector Jones went to take the box, Spilsbury looked at Mr Beckett. His face was rigid, impassive. 'Milk Tray, eh? Very nice.' He eased the lid off. There was a watercolour of an Alpine scene on the front. 'Only two have been eaten. Oh, and there's a note inside the lid.' He took it out and peered at it. *'To my only darling, from your loving boy Billy.'*

Spilsbury shook his head. 'I thought you said you hadn't got her a present?'

Mr Beckett shot to his feet. 'I've never seen those before in my life!'

'I'm sure it will be easy enough to verify your handwriting, Mr Beckett.' Once again, the inspector's sing-song voice belied the gravity of his words. He handed the box to Spilsbury. 'The murder weapon, doctor. If I'm not very mistaken.'

Chapter 55

'But they can't do that!' Annie was outraged. 'They can't just send you back to uniform!'

'I was only brought in to help with donkey work,' Charlie reminded her. 'Now that's all finished they've got no more use for me.'

'But after all you did! They'd be nowhere near finding out who killed those poor women if it weren't for you.'

'Much good I did them! They still haven't found the killer.'

'And they never will with that useless article George Stevens on the case!'

Charlie smiled. He could always rely on his wife to be furious on his behalf. Listening to Annie venting her rage acted like a salve on his own hurt pride.

He had been very disappointed when Inspector Mount broke the news to him the previous evening that he would be returning to his old division. He believed the inspector had sounded rather deflated too, but that might have just been his own wishful thinking.

'So that's it, then?' Annie said.

'It looks like it.'

'I hoped they might keep you on after it was all finished?'

So did I, he thought. 'All good things must come to an end, as they say. Besides, those missing cats won't find themselves!'

He tried to keep his smile bright, but his dejection must have shown in his eyes because Annie patted his arm comfortingly and said, 'Never mind, love. There'll be other chances, you'll see. I reckon they'll soon find out they can't do without you!'

'You're right.' He planted a kiss on her cheek. But deep down he knew his only chance had passed him by.

He tormented himself with the thought as he walked to the police station. It was a fine, bright March morning and the street was busy with early morning shoppers and buses carrying workers to the city.

Had he made the most of his chance? he wondered. Perhaps if he'd pushed himself forward more, he might have made a better impression.

Or perhaps he'd pushed too much? Had he asked too many questions, made his voice heard too often? He had thought he was being helpful, but perhaps he'd overstepped the mark without realising it?

And the most frustrating thing of all was, they were still no nearer finding the killer.

Any hope of finding out who had placed the advertisements had disappeared with Tobias Warriner. After nearly a week they were still looking for him, but he had gone to ground. Inspector Mount was still toying with the theory that he had faked his own death and disappeared with the evidence to deflect suspicion away from himself.

Tobias had certainly been guilty of blackmailing Matthew Franklin, although Franklin was still being tight-lipped and refusing to admit it had ever happened. Whatever Warriner had discovered about him, Franklin certainly did not want the police knowing about it.

Was it murder Warriner had uncovered? Inspector Mount did not think it likely. The blackmail had begun before Elizabeth Franklin met her untimely end. And Matthew had an alibi for the night of her murder. And frankly, he seemed like such a craven coward Charlie could not imagine him having the stomach to kill.

But that didn't mean he was innocent. There was still the chance he might have got someone else to do his dirty work for him.

It wouldn't be the first time. A picture of those bloodied handkerchiefs came into Charlie's mind. What must it have been like for those poor men, he wondered, having to shoot one of their comrades? The guilt and mental anguish they suffered afterwards must have been unbearable.

And yet Matthew had always managed to keep his own hands scrupulously clean. Had he done the same now? Charlie wondered. With so many old soldiers out of work and desperate for money, how difficult would it be to find someone to kill his aunt while he sipped claret at the regimental reunion?

Which sent Charlie's mind straight back to Tobias Warriner. He certainly needed the money, there was no doubt about that. According to those stubs in his chequebook, he had barely been keeping his head above water as a private investigator.

Charlie thought about his suit with its worn patches, and how he had eked out his tobacco with those thinly rolled cigarettes. This was not a man with a lot of money. But surely he was not desperate enough to do the bidding of a man he detested? Blackmail was far more his style.

And besides, there were easier ways to make a living. Warriner was personable, and he could charm the birds from the trees. It wasn't difficult to imagine him wooing a lonely woman. He certainly fit the bill of the man Jean Hodges had been seeing, too.

Charlie made a mental note to suggest they look into his financial affairs, until he remembered with a jolt of disappointment that it was no longer anything to do with him.

There was a fair amount of good-natured joshing from his old colleagues when he reached the station.

'What are you doing back here? I thought you were Abbott of the Yard now?' they jeered.

'What happened? Did you blot your copy book?'

'You must have done something shocking for them to send you back here.'

'No, he just missed us, that's what it is.'

The duty sergeant gave him a friendly slap on the shoulder. 'Never mind, son. We want you, even if that lot don't.' He dumped a pile of files down on the desk with a thud. Charlie stared at them.

'What's all this?'

'Filing. We kept it for you because we know how much you enjoy it.'

Charlie looked around at the leering faces of his fellow officers. This was his punishment, he realised, for daring to get above himself.

'It will take me till next Christmas!' he groaned.

'Best make a start on it then, eh?' The sergeant grinned.

Charlie had no choice but to grimly buckle down to it. But faced with such a tedious and lengthy task, it wasn't long before his mind wandered back to Scotland Yard.

He couldn't stop thinking about the dog hairs they had found in Warriner's room. Even though most of the men were reluctant to speak to the police, a couple had admitted seeing a man with a dog going about the building. But if they knew any more than that, they weren't saying.

The image of a large, snarling brown dog came into Charlie's mind. Of course, there were hundreds, if not thousands, of dogs just like it all over the city. But this one, with its powerful, muscular body and murderous yellow eyes, kept coming back to him.

Mickey Malone. Now there was a man who was capable of doing someone's dirty work. But whose, that was the question.

It was possible that Matthew Franklin had taken him on to get rid of his aunt. Possible, but not likely. Why on earth would he entrust such a task to his stepmother's brother? No, Franklin wasn't that stupid. If he was going to get someone to kill his aunt, he would far more likely choose a stranger, someone with no connection that could be traced back to him.

Which left Violet.

Mickey would have known how Elizabeth had treated his sister all through her marriage. And then to see her suffer that final indignity of losing everything, the inheritance that should have rightly been hers . . .

Of course he would have been furious on her behalf. What brother wouldn't? But furious enough to kill for her? Charlie did not doubt it for a moment. But did he do it off his own bat, or did Violet ask him to kill her? That was the question.

The door to the station banged open as two officers came in, dragging a man between them. He was protesting loudly as he was manhandled towards the cells.

'But I didn't do it!' he was shouting. 'I had nothing to do with it, I swear.'

'You can tell that to the inspector,' one of the officers muttered, tightening his grip as the man wriggled and twisted.

He let out a yell of protest. 'You're going to break my arm!'

'Better stop struggling, then.'

Charlie looked up as the man was bundled past them and through the door that led to the custody area. He caught the man's eye. His face was ashen and full of fear.

Somewhere in the back of his mind a spark of recognition flared.

'Who was that?' he asked one of the constables when they returned a few minutes later.

'Some bloke tried to poison his wife. She's still in hospital, and it's touch and go. We might be looking at murder.' He grinned at Charlie. 'And there you were, thinking we weren't nearly as exciting as Scotland Yard!'

Charlie looked back at the door that led to the cells. The spark of recognition was kindling, glowing in the back of his mind. But he couldn't think where he'd seen him before.

'What's his name?'

'William Beckett. Why? Do you know him?'

Charlie shook his head. 'Can't say I've heard of him.'

And yet . . .

He shook the thought from his mind and went back to his filing. But William Beckett was still troubling him, no matter how much he tried to focus on his work.

At least it made a change from thinking about what was happening in Scotland Yard, he thought.

It was the middle of the afternoon and Charlie had almost finished the filing when the sergeant summoned him again.

'We've had a call,' he said. 'Some bloke's making a nuisance of himself round Regent's Park.'

'Surely that's one for the Royal Park Keepers, Sergeant?'

'Unfortunately this one's on our side of the railings, over by Gloucester Gate. One of the residents reckons he's seen him lurking about outside. And not for the first time, he says.'

Charlie's stomach began to sink. 'This resident – he wouldn't be called Bainbridge, by any chance?'

The sergeant grinned. 'You know him? That's a bit of luck, isn't it?'

Chapter 56

'You took your time,' were Cecil Bainbridge's first words when the maid showed him into the house. 'I could have gone and apprehended the blighter myself while I've been waiting for you to arrive.'

Charlie eyed the old man's daughter, who stood nearby, nervously fiddling with her pearls.

'I'm so sorry,' she said. 'I wouldn't have troubled you, honestly, but Father wouldn't shut up about it.'

'Yes, well, I'm here now,' Charlie said bracingly. 'So what seems to be the trouble?'

'Hell's teeth!' the old man let out an explosive sigh. 'Am I surrounded by imbeciles? I've seen him again.'

Charlie frowned. 'Seen who, sir?'

'Who? Who?' Mr Bainbridge rapped his stick impatiently against his armchair. 'Him, of course! That man I saw hanging about the house on the night that Franklin woman was murdered. Good gracious, doesn't anyone pay attention?'

'Father, please . . .'

'Oh, do stop hovering, Marjorie! You're like an annoying gnat.'

'I'm afraid the Franklin case is nothing to do with me anymore, sir,' Charlie explained. 'If you'd like to get in touch with Inspector Mount at Scotland Yard—'

'Dash it all, man! Do you want to catch this villain or not?' Mr Bainbridge interrupted him. 'I haven't got time to go round to every police station in the city. It's taken me this long to get Marjorie to telephone you!'

He glared at his daughter, who looked suitably apologetic.

'I didn't want to waste your time,' she said. 'But he insisted. He hasn't shut up about it for weeks. In the end he was driving us so mad, my husband said I either had to call you or he'd put him in the workhouse.'

'I'd like to see him try!' The old man's rheumy eyes blazed with anger. 'This house still belongs to me, Marjorie, even if your pompous ass of a husband likes to think otherwise. And if anyone's going—'

'Weeks?' Charlie cut in. 'So you saw him again some time ago?'

'I told you!' Mr Bainbridge said. 'He's been there on and off for weeks. Just standing there, watching the house.'

'It's not a crime to stand in the street, sir.'

'He's loitering with intent, I tell you. Surely you can do something about that?'

'You know, I do believe there is someone there.'

They both turned at the sound of Marjorie's voice. She was standing at the window, peering out of a crack in the lace curtains down to the street below.

'Look,' she said. 'He's just peering out from behind that tree. He doesn't look as if he wants to be seen, either. Look at the way his hat's pulled down to cover his face.'

But that did not stop Charlie recognising him.

'That's what I've been trying to tell you!' Mr Bainbridge spluttered. 'But of course no one listens to me. I'm just a senile old man, what could I possibly know—'

Charlie did not stay to hear the rest of what he said. He was already thundering down the stairs, heading for the front door.

*

313

'It's all been a dreadful misunderstanding, constable.'

Robert Dillon had divested himself of his heavy coat and trilby hat, and seemed perfectly at ease as he sat in the Franklins' drawing room, Lydia at his side. But behind his confident smile, Charlie could see a flicker of anxiety in his eyes.

'Perhaps you'd care to explain then, sir?' he said.

'I was just worried about Lydia, that's all. There's a murderer on the loose, and I wanted to make sure she was safe.' He smiled at the young woman beside him and patted her hand. 'She means everything to me.'

Lydia smiled back. She was wearing an engagement ring, Charlie noticed.

'So you've been watching the house?'

'Gracious, constable, you make it sound so sinister!' Robert smiled.

'And what would you call it, sir?'

'Looking after my fiancée. Lord knows, her brother hardly takes care of her.'

'Surely you could have knocked on the door?' Charlie said.

'Yes,' Lydia said quietly. 'Why didn't you just call, Robert?'

'To tell the truth, I was afraid you'd laugh at me.' Robert looked rueful. 'I didn't want you to know how much I worried about you.' He looked down at their hands entwined. 'But hopefully we'll be married soon, and then I won't have to lurk outside in the bushes!'

His thumb absently grazed the engagement ring on her finger. Charlie looked at Lydia. She looked positively sick at the prospect.

'But you didn't know there was a murderer on the loose the night Elizabeth Franklin was killed, did you?' he said. 'Yet your neighbour reported that he had seen you outside then.'

'He must have been mistaken—' Lydia started to say, but Robert interrupted her.

'There was no mistake,' he said. He looked at Charlie. 'Yes, I admit I was outside the house that night. I followed Lydia home from Rowton House. I'm sorry, my darling,' he turned to her, 'but you know I've never approved of you going to that place, mixing with those ruffians. I was always so worried one of them would follow you home.'

'So you followed me home instead?' Lydia said tightly.

'I wanted to make sure you were safe, that's all.'

'And then what did you do?' Charlie asked.

'I watched her go inside and then it started to rain, so I left.'

'And what time was this?'

'It would have been about ten o'clock. That's right, isn't it, darling?' he looked at Lydia.

'Yes,' she said quietly. 'It was ten o'clock.' She had gone rather pale, Charlie noticed.

'And you didn't see anyone else coming or going from the house?'

'Not a soul. I would have certainly told the police if I had.'

But you didn't tell them you were outside that night, did you? Once again, Charlie had to remind himself that the case was none of his business.

'Is that it?' Robert said, as Charlie put away his notebook. 'That's all you wanted to know?'

'That's all for now, sir. But if I were you, I'd stop loitering in bushes, otherwise we won't hear the end of it from your neighbour.'

'Oh, I will, Sergeant. Don't you worry about that!' Robert laughed, a trifle too heartily.

'I'll show you out.' Lydia rose to her feet.

'Surely that's the maid's job, darling?'

'Mary's out on an errand, isn't she?' Lydia snapped back, a little too quickly. 'I thought you might have noticed that, since you've been watching us all so closely.'

Robert's face reddened, but he said nothing.

'I'm sorry to have wasted your time, constable,' Lydia said as she followed Charlie down the stairs. 'You must be tired of calling here all the time?'

'Not at all, Miss Franklin.' Charlie paused at the bottom of the stairs and turned to look at her. Her pretty face was pale and strained. She did not look like a young woman in love, that was for sure.

He thought about Robert Dillon's hand, the possessive way it had gripped hers. On impulse he said, 'Are you sure there's nothing more I can do for you?'

She looked up at him, and for a fleeting moment he thought he saw panic in her soft grey eyes. But the next moment her bracing smile was back in place.

'I think we've wasted enough of your time already, constable,' she said.

Chapter 57

'Can you believe it? All this time he's been following me, watching me. It's so bizarre, isn't it?'

Lydia was smiling as she said it, but the strain showed on her face as she sat on the floor beside Thomas, watching him play with the clockwork train she had just bought him.

She had arrived just after tea, the gift tucked under her arm. She claimed she had come to see Thomas, but it wasn't long before Violet had got the full story out of her. How a policeman had marched into the house earlier on, practically brandishing Robert by the collar, and announced that he had been loitering outside the house watching her every move.

She seemed surprised, but Violet wasn't.

'And what did he have to say for himself?' she asked.

'He says he was worried about me after Aunt Elizabeth was killed. He says he cares about me.'

'And how does he explain spying on you before she died? While you were apart?'

'He wanted to make sure I was all right.'

'Couldn't accept it was over, more like!'

'I think you might be right.' Lydia bit her lip. She wound up Thomas's train and set it back on the rails. 'He said as much when I ended our engagement. He said he would win me back in the end. "No matter what it takes," he said.'

No matter what it takes. It sounded more like a threat than a tender declaration of love.

317

'And so he did.' She looked at the engagement ring on Lydia's finger.

Lydia followed her gaze. 'You're angry, aren't you? Please don't be angry with me,' she begged. 'I couldn't bear it.'

'Why should I be angry, if it's what you want?' Violet paused. 'It is what you want, ain't it?'

Lydia watched the train going round and round on the track. 'I don't know what I want any more,' she sighed. 'But Robert says it's for the best.'

'I'm sure he does.'

'He does care about me, you know,' Lydia insisted. 'He's been such a help since Aunt Elizabeth . . .' She faltered and looked down at her hands. 'Anyway, it's all arranged. We're going to be married next month, and then Robert is going to move into the house and take over Father's practice.'

Talk about dead men's shoes, Violet thought. Although Robert Dillon could never match up to her husband in a million years.

'Sounds like a sensible arrangement,' she remarked.

'It is.' But Lydia's wistful face told a different story as she reached out to smooth Thomas's dark curls.

'Are you happy, Lyd?' Violet looked at her searchingly.

'I'm fine.'

'You don't look it.'

'I'm happy as long as Robert is happy.'

And I'll bet he's like a pig in muck, Violet thought. He was about to marry into the Franklin family, and he had his private practice in Harley Street. He finally had the respectability and standing he had always felt he deserved.

But then Lydia turned her head and Violet saw the tears glinting in her eyes.

'Lydia! What's wrong, love?' She knelt down beside her and put her arm around her. 'Come on, you can tell me.'

'Oh Violet, I'm in such a mess.' The next moment Lydia was sobbing in her arms like a child while Thomas looked on, wide-eyed. 'I wish I'd never let him back into my life! I was such a fool to do it, I should have known how it would end. But I was so confused and upset after what happened to Aunt Elizabeth, I don't think I was quite in my right mind.' She pulled away and fumbled in her bag for her handkerchief. 'Then out of the blue I received such a lovely letter from Robert. He was so kind and thoughtful, and he said all he wanted was to look after me and to be my friend and – and I was so lonely . . .'

A fresh flurry of tears sprang from her eyes and ran down her pale cheeks.

Poor Lydia. Violet felt a pang of guilt that she hadn't looked after her stepdaughter better. She was so close to her aunt, of course she was bound to feel alone and vulnerable. And God knows, her selfish brother would never have done anything to protect her.

No wonder Robert Dillon had managed to worm his way in so easily.

'Let me guess,' she said. 'Friendship wasn't enough for him?'

'He was so kind at first,' Lydia said. 'But then he started talking about our engagement, saying he wanted everything to go back to the way it was. I kept trying to tell him it wasn't what I wanted, but he wouldn't give up. In the end it was just easier to go along with it.' She sat up straight and drew in a long, bracing breath. 'I'm just being silly,' she said. 'As Robert says, this is the best way.'

Best for him, Violet thought. 'Do you love him?'

Lydia looked startled at the question. 'I – I'm not sure. I thought I liked him at least. But now, after finding out what he's been doing . . .' She bit her lip, as if she was trying to hold back her next words. Then they all came out in a rush. 'Violet, I'm rather frightened of him,' she said.

'Frightened?'

'He has – a temper.' Lydia seemed to be choosing her words carefully.

Violet stared at her. 'What's he done, Lyd? Has he laid a finger on you? Because if he has . . .'

'Oh no.' Lydia shook her head, then added quietly, 'Not yet, anyway.'

'But you're afraid he might?'

'He can be so forceful sometimes, especially if he doesn't get his own way. Sometimes he scares me.'

'Well, he doesn't scare me!' Violet knew only too well what it was like to live with a violet man, and she would never wish that on anyone. Especially not someone as sweet and vulnerable as poor Lydia. 'And if you don't get rid of him, then I will!'

Lydia gave a little laugh. 'I wish I was as fearless as you.'

If only you knew, Violet thought. She'd always thought her upbringing made her tough, but there were times when she had cowered in fear herself.

'Then let me help you,' she urged. 'Believe me, nothing would give me greater pleasure than telling the almighty Dr Dillon where to go!'

She savoured the thought of putting him in his place. It would go some way to making up for all the insults and snide remarks she had had to endure from him over the years.

'Would you really?' Lydia's face brightened.

'If that's what you want?'

'Oh, thank you, Violet.' Lydia flung her arms around her, hugging her close. 'I'd feel much braver if you were there, honestly.' She drew back, looking shame-faced. 'I suppose you must think me very feeble, not being able to face him on my own?'

For a moment Violet thought about Harry the Blade. Her own bravery had deserted her when his fists started raining blows on her.

'Not at all,' she said.

Chapter 58

'Each chocolate contains half a grain of strychnine.' Willcox handed Spilsbury a piece of paper containing the results of his analysis. 'There's enough in the whole box to kill a donkey.'

'But not Mrs Beckett, apparently,' Spilsbury said.

'She's not dead yet?'

'On the contrary, she seems to be making a remarkable recovery.' Spilsbury scanned through the results. They were exactly what he had been expecting.

Celia Beckett should thank her lucky stars she did not have a particularly sweet tooth. Had she eaten more than two of the chocolates she would definitely not have lived to tell the tale. As it was, it was a miracle she was still alive, since half a grain of strychnine was commonly held to be a fatal dose.

'Is the husband still denying everything?' Willcox asked.

'He's adamant he did not give them to her, but all the evidence points to him. The police have checked the card against a sample of his handwriting and it's definitely him.'

'No getting away from that, then. Any prints on the box?'

'Several, but none clear enough to use.' He paused. 'There was also a packet of Butler's Vermin Killer in the cupboard.'

'Ah. Rather damning evidence, I'd say. So are they charging him?'

'It seems so.'

Willcox looked at him. 'You seem hesitant to condemn the man, old boy?'

'I am rather. Who would be stupid enough to sign the murder weapon? Beckett must have known his wife would leave them lying around.'

'You forget how stupid people can be,' Willcox said. 'Besides, he might have meant to dispose of it, but forgot in all the panic that ensued? Seeing someone in the throes of strychnine poisoning can be very alarming, no matter how much you think you're prepared for it.'

'You may be right, of course.' Spilsbury had himself seen a patient in the throes of opisthotonus, their spine arched into a bow, head thrown back at an unnatural angle, nearly touching the heels. The rigid contortion of the body was terrifying to behold.

'But you doubt it?' Willcox looked amused.

'I just wonder what he stood to gain,' Spilsbury said. 'I might understand if he wanted to get rid of her so he could run off and marry a mistress. But according to him, he and his wife had reconciled.'

'Unless she wouldn't let him forget it? Their wedding anniversary might have brought unpleasant memories. I know Mildred finds it very difficult to let go of a resentment,' he said ruefully. 'They might have argued . . .'

'In which case, he would have struck out in anger,' Spilsbury said. 'He wouldn't have gone to all the time and effort to poison a box of chocolates.' He paused. 'I wonder . . .'

'What?'

'No, it's too fanciful.' He shook his head.

'It's not like you to be given over to flights of fancy, old man. Go on, spit it out. Let's hear it.'

Spilsbury hesitated for a moment. 'I wonder if this has anything to do with the other Camden Town cases?'

'The Lonely Hearts Killer, you mean?'

He winced at the name. 'Two women from the same area, both poisoned with strychnine.'

'But they were both spinsters.'

'Mrs Beckett might have believed her marriage to be over?'

'So she decided to look elsewhere? The Personal column of *The Times*, perhaps?' Willcox considered it for a moment. 'It's possible, I suppose. So why didn't she end up in the canal like the others?'

'Because she didn't die. He might have panicked when death did not occur immediately, and decided to flee the scene.'

'Leaving the evidence behind?'

The two men looked at each other for a moment.

'There's only one way to find out,' Willcox said. 'Let's go and pay a visit to Mrs Beckett, shall we?'

Spilsbury was surprised to see PC Abbott, the lanky red-haired constable from the Franklin case, standing guard outside Mrs Beckett's door.

'What are you doing here?' he asked.

'I've been sent back to Division, sir.'

'That's a pity. I seem to recall you made some useful observations on the Franklin case.'

'Thank you, sir.' Colour rose in the young man's face.

'I'm sure you didn't expect to find yourself on another attempted murder case so soon?'

'No, sir.'

Spilsbury glanced at the door. 'Perhaps you'd care to be present while I speak to Mrs Beckett?'

'Well, I . . .' PC Abbott looked up and down the deserted passageway. 'I was told to guard the room, sir.'

Spilsbury caught the look of longing on his face, and wondered at the sense of sending him back into uniform.

He was such a bright young chap, utterly wasted keeping guard over an empty corridor. That was far better left to a blockhead like Sergeant Stevens.

'If Inspector Jones wishes to query the matter, then he can take it up with me. Come along.' He swept into the room, knowing the constable would follow.

Celia Beckett looked taken aback to see Dr Spilsbury at the end of her bed.

'Blimey,' she murmured. 'It's you, isn't it? The bloke from the newspapers?' She managed a faint smile. 'I'm not dead, am I?'

'No, but you should have been.'

The woman looked startled, but Willcox stepped in quickly.

'How are you feeling, my dear?' he asked.

'All right, thank you.' Mrs Becket shot Spilsbury a wary look. The livid, dusky hue had gone from her face, leaving her ashen pale. She looked weak and tired, but in remarkably good spirits. As well she might be, given that she had cheated death.

'You know your husband is in custody, charged with your attempted murder?' Spilsbury said.

Celia Beckett flinched. 'You're direct, I'll give you that.' She took a deep breath. 'I've been told they've locked him up,' she said quietly. 'But I don't understand it. He told me he wanted us to have a new start. We were going to Southend.'

'Those chocolates he gave you were poisoned with strychnine.'

Out of the corner of his eye he saw PC Abbott wince. But Mrs Beckett did not seem upset by it.

'Is that how he did it? I thought it was strange, him sending them to me. It ain't like Bill to remember to buy me a present, even if it was our wedding anniversary.'

'So he didn't give them to you himself?'

325

'Oh no, they were waiting on the doorstep for me in the morning. I thought he might have dropped them off while he was on his rounds.' She shook her head. 'I still can't believe it,' she said. 'We were getting on so well since we moved away.'

'Away from what?' Spilsbury asked.

A look of stubborn reluctance crossed her face. 'From our troubles,' she muttered.

'And what sort of troubles were those?'

'Use your imagination, doctor.'

Spilsbury frowned. Imagination was not usually a requirement for a forensic pathologist. Wild flights of fancy were no substitute for the evidence that analysis of blood and bones could provide.

Thankfully, PC Abbott seemed more given to such imaginings.

'Another woman?' he spoke up behind him. Mrs Beckett nodded.

'Yes, but it's all over now. He came back to me.'

Spilsbury glanced at Willcox, standing at his shoulder. 'And what about you, Mrs Beckett?' he asked.

'What about me?'

'Did you have a lover?'

What little colour she had drained instantly from Mrs Beckett's face. Behind him, he heard Willcox groan.

'Certainly not! Why would you ever ask such a thing?'

'I'm merely suggesting that if you thought your husband was going to leave you, you might have thought it prudent to find someone else yourself. It would make sense, wouldn't it?'

He looked around. Willcox was rubbing his temples as if he had developed a sudden headache, while the young policeman was staring fixedly at the ceiling. Spilsbury followed his gaze but saw nothing of interest.

Mrs Beckett gasped. 'Well, I most certainly did not!'

'So you didn't answer an advertisement in any Lonely Hearts column?'

'Good gracious, no! Anyway, I never thought my Bill would leave me,' she said. 'I knew it was just a fling. On his part, anyway. But she took it too far, he said. She kept pushing him to leave me. I think he got a bit frightened, to be honest. Came back with his tail between his legs, just like I knew he would.'

She glared at Spilsbury. 'And to think you'd ever imagine I'd do something like that. What sort of woman do you take me for?'

He might have told her, if PC Abbott hadn't stepped in.

'Why did he start a new job?' he asked. 'Is it because he worked with this woman?'

Celia Beckett's mouth tightened. 'Yes, he did,' she said. 'And that worked out for the best, too. I've been telling him for years he should join the Post Office. That's a proper career for a man, isn't it? I said to him, he's too old to be cycling around delivering groceries. That's what kids do, isn't it?'

Spilsbury saw the young constable shift, his body tensing, suddenly on high alert.

'Did you say your husband delivered groceries, Mrs Beckett?' he said quietly.

'That's right. Hodges, on Camden High Street. He worked for them for years.' She looked from one to the other. 'Why? Do you know it?'

Chapter 59

Inspector Jones would never have agreed to it if it hadn't been for Dr Spilsbury.

'Just give him a chance,' Charlie had heard him urging on the telephone. 'You never know, he might be onto something. And if nothing else, it might help to tie up a few loose ends?'

He could tell just from one side of the conversation that the inspector was reluctant. As far as he was concerned, they already had their man safely in custody.

But the Home Office pathologist clearly brought all his considerable clout to bear, because the next thing Charlie knew, he and Inspector Jones were walking along Camden High Street.

'You can do the talking,' he said to Charlie. 'I've got nothing to say to her.'

The senior officer stomped along the street, his hands thrust into the pockets of his raincoat, clearly in bad grace about the whole thing. Charlie was beginning to regret he had ever spoken up. The last thing he needed was to blot his copybook at the station, otherwise he might never make it back to Scotland Yard.

It was teatime and Hilda Hodges was just shutting up the shop when they arrived.

'What's all this, then?' Hilda Hodges folded her arms and looked from one to the other. She looked every bit as irritable as the inspector.

'Hello, Miss Hodges,' he greeted her, trying his best to calm things down. 'Can we come in? We'd like a word, if that's all right?'

She rolled her eyes. 'If it's about Gwen, I've already told you . . .

Charlie slid past her into the shop. It all seemed a lot more orderly than the last time he'd seen it. The shelves were neatly arranged, and there was a broom in the corner where Hilda had been sweeping.

'You seem to have it all a bit more sorted out now,' he commented.

'Eh?'

'Last time I visited, you were in a bit of disarray?'

'Oh right. Yes.'

'Your new delivery boy is up to scratch now?'

'He'll do, I suppose,' Hilda sniffed.

'But he's not as good as the last one?'

She sent him a sharp look. 'What?'

'He knew the job, didn't he? It must have been inconvenient when he left.'

'It was. He left me in a right pickle.'

'Why did he leave so suddenly, do you think?'

'I'm sure I have no idea.'

'Don't you?'

Hilda met his eye for a moment, then her gaze slid away. 'I never bothered to ask,' she muttered. 'I daresay he had his reasons.'

Charlie took out his notebook. 'What was his name again?'

'Beckett.' The name came reluctantly from between tight lips.

'That's right. William Beckett. You know he's been arrested for trying to kill his wife?' Hilda did not react. 'You don't seem very surprised?'

'I don't poke my nose into anyone else's business.'

'Would you say he was capable of murder?'

'How should I know? All I can say is that he was a good worker. He was always very punctual with the deliveries.'

Charlie sensed Inspector Jones growing restless beside him. 'How long had he worked here?' he asked.

'Ten years. Since Father ran the place.'

'So you knew him well?'

She shrugged. 'We passed the time of day.'

'We think he might have been having an affair with your sister.'

Finally, there was a flash of emotion. 'Never!' she snapped.

Inspector Jones caught her change of tone too. He was suddenly alert, his eyes fixed keenly on Hilda Hodges.

Charlie forced himself to stay calm. 'You seem very sure, Miss Hodges? I thought you knew nothing about your sister's mystery man?'

'I know it wouldn't have been Bill.' Hilda shook her head firmly. 'Of course, Jean was always trying to flirt with him whenever she met him in the shop. But he never looked twice at her. She wasn't his type.'

'How do you know?' Charlie said. 'Is it because he only had eyes for you?'

'Don't be ridiculous! I don't know what you're talking about.' But Hilda's fiery red face gave her away. 'I'd like you to go now, if you wouldn't mind.'

But the two men stood their ground. 'That was why he left, wasn't it?' Charlie said. 'Because his wife made him choose between you, and he chose her?'

'That's not true.'

'Is that why you decided to get rid of her?'

'I don't know what you're talking about. Now I'd like you to leave.' She went to open the door but neither Charlie nor the inspector moved.

'I see you stock Milk Tray in your shop?' Inspector Jones nodded towards the small display of chocolates on one of the shelves.

'So does the Co-op round the corner,' Hilda snapped. 'Are you going to go and question them, too?'

'It seems like a coincidence, doesn't it? It wouldn't be difficult to leave a box on her doorstep.'

'And how do you account for the note?' Hilda's mouth shut abruptly, like a trap. But it was too late.

'How did you know there was a note?' Inspector Jones asked quietly.

'I don't know, do I? I just assumed there would be, since you know they came from him . . .' Her words came out in a rush, tumbling over each other.

To my only darling, from your loving boy Billy.' Inspector Jones quoted the inscription from his notes. 'Come to think of it, it's not exactly specific, is it? I mean, it doesn't mention his wife by name, does it?'

Charlie quickly picked up on his meaning. 'You kept all his notes as keepsakes, didn't you? Little did you ever imagine they'd come in useful.'

'I don't know what you're talking about,' Hilda said, but more feebly this time. She knew she was trapped, and she no longer had the passion to fight it.

'How long did it go on for, this affair of yours?' Inspector Jones asked.

His comment roused her. 'It wasn't an affair!' she snapped back. 'He loved me. He'd always loved me. We had it all planned: when Father died we were going to be together. But then she ruined it all.' Her face darkened. 'If it hadn't been for her, he would never have left me.'

'His wife?' Inspector Jones said.

Hilda stared at him, a strangely blank look in her eyes. A chill crept up the back of Charlie's neck.

'He didn't want to be with her,' Hilda said quietly. 'She forced him into it. She clung on, wouldn't let him go . . .'

Inspector Jones leaned forward. 'So you decided to kill her?'

'He would never have walked out on me,' Hilda mumbled. 'Not after everything we'd planned, everything I'd done for him . . .'

The inspector drew himself up to his full height. 'Hilda Hodges, I am arresting you for the attempted murder of Celia Beckett. You do not have to say anything—'

'What did you do?' Charlie interrupted him.

Hilda turned to look at him silently. The chill at the back of his neck turned his spine to ice.

'Constable—' Inspector Jones started to say, but Charlie ignored him.

'You just said, "after everything I did for him". What else did you do, Miss Hodges?'

Chapter 60

Violet was nearly an hour late getting to Gloucester Gate.

She had almost not gone at all. Thomas had woken up that morning with a cold and fever, and Violet had spent all day at his bedside, playing cards and reading to him, sponging him with tepid washcloths and bringing him endless cups of honey in hot water to soothe his sore throat.

Some time in the middle of the afternoon, she made up her mind that she would not be going out that evening after all. She might have promised Lydia that she would be there when she confronted Robert, but her son's welfare came first. She was certain her stepdaughter would understand.

But by teatime Thomas suddenly rallied, as small children so often did. He woke up from his nap, his fever gone, and insisted he wanted to get up and play. He had been roaring around the flat ever since, playing at being a train driver and getting under Violet's feet.

It was almost a relief for her to be able to put on her coat and leave him in the care of her neighbour Nan.

'He seems right as rain to me,' Nan had said cheerfully, as Thomas ran past her, narrowly missing her ankles. 'And I've bought some toffee, too, so that should cheer him up!' She looked around. 'Mickey not about?'

'He ain't been home all day.'

Nan nodded. 'I saw him going off on his bicycle first thing. I said to my Eric, he's a bit keen!' She looked carefully at Violet. 'Everything all right with you two, love?'

'It's fine,' Violet lied. Nan must have heard them arguing the previous night, she thought. The walls of Queen's Buildings were as flimsy as everything else.

The truth was, she had no idea where her brother was, since neither of them were speaking. She had heard him slamming out of the flat before dawn that morning, with Pistol at his heels, as she sat by Thomas's bedside. He hadn't wished her his usual cheerio, and she certainly hadn't chased after him to say goodbye. Let him sulk if he wanted to, she thought.

But it had been such a silly argument, coming out of nowhere. And after they had made peace again, too.

The day Lydia had called round, Violet had made up her mind that she couldn't allow things to continue as they had. Mickey was her brother, after all, and the last thing she wanted was to drive him away.

So she had waited up for him, and they had talked, and everything was sorted out between them.

Then, last night, she'd happened to mention that she had arranged to see Lydia at Gloucester Gate the following day so she could be there when she ended things with Robert.

She had never expected Mickey to react the way he did. He had practically exploded with anger.

'You promised me you'd never set foot in that place again,' he had shouted.

'But Lydia wants me to be with her.'

'Why does it have to be you? Why can't someone else help her?'

'She asked me.'

'And you always have to do her bidding?' His face was bitter. 'She calls and you come running, is that it?'

334

'She's family, Mickey.'

'So am I, and so is Thomas. But you don't think about us, do you?'

'That's not fair,' Violet said. 'You know you and Thomas will always come first. But Lydia's only got Matthew, and he's no use to anyone. Besides, he's gone away so she's all alone.'

Their eyes met across the room, and for a moment Violet glimpsed another emotion under that mask of anger.

Fear.

'What's going on, Mickey?' she said. 'This ain't like you. Talk to me, please.'

'I just think you should stay out of it,' he muttered, turning away from her. 'That family's never brought us anything but trouble.'

And that was it. After that, there had been nothing but sullen silence.

Well, let him sulk, she thought. There would be time enough to make their peace later.

She was nearly an hour late getting to Gloucester Gate. As she turned the corner and saw the long, imposing Nash terrace, Violet's nerve began to fail her. There was something truly repellent about the house. It was almost as if the spirit of Elizabeth Franklin was standing on the threshold, trying to stop her coming in.

'Believe me, I don't want this any more than you do,' she muttered under her breath as she forced herself to climb the stone steps and lifted the heavy brass knocker.

As soon as she knocked, she remembered there was no maid to answer the door. Mary had handed in her notice out of the blue a few days earlier, and promptly gone off to stay with a relative somewhere in Kent. She doubted if Lydia had engaged anyone new yet. Her stepdaughter was a novice at household management.

She knocked again. There was no answer. Violet felt her annoyance growing. She hoped she hadn't come all the way across London on a fool's errand.

She would not have put it past Lydia to forget all about their plan. Robert Dillon could be very persuasive when he wanted to be. There was every chance that the pair of them were at this very moment having dinner or dancing in the West End, leaving her standing like a fool on the doorstep.

She knocked again.

'Lydia!' she called out. 'Lyd, are you in there?'

No reply. Violet was about to give up when she heard a faint cry from inside the house.

'Lydia?'

She bent to look through the letterbox. Lydia was slumped on the staircase, pale as a wraith, her dishevelled hair hanging loose around her face. The front of her pink dress was soaked crimson from the body she cradled in her arms.

'Help me,' she whispered.

Chapter 61

Miss Franklin's injuries looked far worse than they were. There were scratches running down both her cheeks, and livid fingermark bruises on her milky white throat, with two particularly large thumb prints on either side of her clavicle. There were also a number of minor bruises on her upper arms. She was clearly shaken by her ordeal, but relatively unhurt.

Which was more than could be said for the body at the foot of the stairs.

Spilsbury watched as the police photographer snapped away at the victim's face, lifeless under its blood-streaked mask.

Robert Dillon lay half on his side, sprawled down the last three stairs, his feet splayed out on the black-and-white tiled hall floor. He wore no tie, and his white shirt was crimson with blood. He stared unseeingly up at the chandelier above him, his mouth slightly open, as if uttering his final cry. A large bruise crowned his left temple.

Even without examining him, Spilsbury could see his head wound was extensive. He tracked the bloody trail back up the carved newel post, which was an ugly mixture of gore and shattered bone fragments.

'Inspector Mount says Miss Franklin is ready to talk now, sir, if you'd like to join us in the drawing room?' Sergeant Stevens said behind him.

'Just a moment.' Spilsbury looked up the staircase. It was wide and sweeping, with a curve just before it reached the top landing. There were traces of blood on several of the steps above.

Spilsbury followed them, taking a careful note of each one. They went almost to the top.

'Make sure you take pictures of those,' he instructed the photographer. 'And be careful not to tread in them yourself.'

He looked around him at the scene, trying to piece it all together in his mind. Fragments of a vase lay shattered on the parquet floor, under a small polished table. It must have fallen off during a struggle, Spilsbury thought. There was a smear of blood on the wall just beside one of the doors, too. He peered at it closely.

'Sir?' Sergeant Stevens broke into his reverie again. 'Will you be joining us?'

Spilsbury looked up, as if noticing him for the first time. 'Yes, indeed,' he said. 'I'd be most interested in what she has to say.'

'I don't know what I can tell you, Inspector. It all happened so fast.'

Lydia Franklin spoke in a quiet, hoarse voice, hardly surprising given the injuries to her throat. Her hand kept going to her neck, massaging the livid bruises on her tender white skin. Her delicate fingers were still caked in dried blood.

Violet Franklin sat beside her, holding the girl's other hand. She looked as if she was in shock herself, her face ashen against her dark hair.

'Take your time and just tell us what you remember, Miss Franklin.' Inspector Mount spoke gently, as if to a child. 'You say you invited Dr Dillon to the house?' Lydia nodded. 'Was this a social call?'

'Not exactly.' Lydia swallowed hard, wincing at the pain. 'I wanted to end things with him.'

'I see.' Inspector Mount scribbled in his notebook.

'I was afraid he might not take it very well, so I asked Violet if she would be with me.'

She turned her gaze towards her stepmother, who shifted uncomfortably.

'I should have been here,' she said quietly. 'But my little boy was ill, so I was delayed . . .'

She looked wretched, Spilsbury thought. And no wonder. It was quite possible her presence could have avoided bloody murder.

'And why did you think he might not take it well?' Inspector Mount asked.

'He – he –'

'She was afraid of him,' Violet Franklin spoke up for her.

'Is that right, Miss Franklin?' Inspector Mount turned to her. 'Had he been violent towards you in the past?'

Lydia Franklin shook her head, but her anxious expression told a different story.

'I was waiting for Violet,' she whispered. 'I kept looking out of the window, hoping she would arrive before Robert got here. But then he knocked on the door, and I had to let him in.'

'Oh, Lyd, I'm so sorry.' Violet Franklin squeezed her hand.

'And what time was this?' Inspector Mount asked.

'I – I'm not sure. I asked him to come at six o'clock, and Robert is – was – always very punctual, so I suppose it must have been then.'

'So you're saying he died after six?' Spilsbury cut in.

Lydia Franklin flinched, then started to weep. Her stepmother immediately put her arm around her.

'It's all right, Lyd,' she said softly. 'It's all right.'

'But he's dead,' the girl whimpered. 'And it's all my fault!'

'Can you tell us exactly what happened, Miss Franklin?' Inspector Mount prompted. Violet Franklin turned on him.

'Give her a minute!' she snapped. 'Can't you see she's beside herself?'

They all sat in silence, waiting for Lydia Franklin's noisy sobbing to subside. Inspector Mount fiddled with his pencil. Spilsbury passed the time staring at the ornate clock on the mantelpiece and doing some rapid calculations in his head.

Finally, Lydia composed herself enough to continue with her story.

'I was very nervous,' she said. 'Robert must have noticed because he kept asking me what was wrong. I was still waiting for Violet, so I kept him talking for as long as I could.'

'Is that when you drank the champagne?' Spilsbury asked. 'I see an open bottle over there.' He pointed to the table beside her. 'From the look of it, I would say it was half empty.'

Lydia stared at him. 'Robert brought it,' she said. 'He thought we were going to celebrate.'

'Celebrate?'

'He thought he was here to set a date for the wedding.'

'And you let him open a bottle of champagne, knowing full well you intended to break things off?'

'I told you, I was waiting for Violet to arrive,' Lydia said. 'I had to keep him talking. I didn't know what else to do.'

Violet squeezed her hand. 'I'm sorry, Lyd,' she said. 'I should have been here. You shouldn't have had to face this on your own.'

'But in the end you couldn't put him off any longer?' Inspector Mount said. Lydia Franklin nodded. 'How did he take it?'

'He was very angry. He said I'd promised him, and – and he wouldn't let me make a fool of him in front of everyone again. Not after everything he'd done to get us back together.'

'And what did he mean by that?' Inspector Mount asked.

Lydia was silent for a long time. For a moment, it felt as if everyone in the room was holding their breath, waiting. Finally, she spoke.

'He told me that he'd killed Aunt Elizabeth,' she said.

The whole room went very still.

'He confessed to killing your aunt?' Inspector Mount said slowly.

Lydia put her hand up to her throat again, wincing as her fingers found the bruises.

'He said he came to the house that night while Matthew and I were out,' she said. 'He wanted to plead with her to give him another chance. But she laughed in his face and told him he would never be part of this family as long as she lived.'

Spilsbury looked at Violet Franklin. She had turned even paler, he noticed.

'And so he killed her?' Inspector Mount said. His voice betrayed no emotion but Spilsbury could see the glint in his eyes.

'He already knew she would say no,' Lydia said quietly. 'It was really just an excuse to get back into the house. He told me he'd already planned to kill her.'

'How?'

She blinked at him. 'What?'

'How did he kill her?'

She frowned at the question. 'I – I don't understand . . .' She looked from one to the other.

'Did he bring the poison with him?'

341

Lydia shook her head. 'He knew Aunt Elizabeth had been taking some kind of medicine for her nerves. A tonic of some kind, I don't know. He poured it into her cocoa when she wasn't looking.'

'I see.' Spilsbury looked at the inspector. It all made sense on the face of it.

'Robert didn't like to be humiliated,' Lydia said. 'He could be utterly charming, but if he thought he was being slighted, then he could turn very quickly.'

Once again, she put her hands up to the bruises at her throat, wincing with pain.

'So what happened after Dr Dillon made this confession to you, Miss Franklin?' Inspector Mount said.

She paused for a moment. 'I was terrified, of course. I started to think, if he could do that to poor Aunt E, then I wasn't safe. And now I knew everything, so . . .'

She swallowed. 'All I could think was that I had to get away from him. I ran upstairs.'

'You didn't try to leave the house?' Spilsbury asked.

Lydia stared at him blankly. 'What?'

'Surely if you were running for your life it would make sense to run downstairs, to try to get out of the front door?'

'I – I –'

'Perhaps she wasn't thinking straight,' Violet Franklin cut in. Lydia gave her a shaky smile.

'Dr Spilsbury's right, of course,' she said. 'Looking back on it, of course I should have tried to get out. But I was so scared.' Her voice trembled with emotion. 'I just wanted to get away. I ran upstairs and tried to get into my bedroom, but he caught up with me. He put his hands around my throat. I – I was sure he was going to kill me. I remember looking up into his eyes, and thinking how mad he looked, and thinking this was how I was going to die.'

'Oh, Lyd!' Violet Franklin whispered.

'Then what happened?' Inspector Mount asked.

'I fought him. He had me pinned against the wall, his hands around my neck. I knew if I didn't do something I would die, so somehow I found the strength to fight him off. There was a struggle at the top of the stairs, just out there.' She nodded towards the drawing-room door. 'And then – he fell.'

She closed her eyes briefly. 'I must have fainted from where he'd hit me, because when I came to, he was lying at the bottom of the stairs.'

'Then what did you do?'

'I didn't know what to do. I sat there for a moment, too stunned to move. Then I gathered myself together and ran downstairs to see if he was still alive. But there was so much blood, I knew – I knew he must be gone.' Her face crumpled and she started to cry again. 'Poor Robert. I know he did a dreadful thing, but he didn't deserve to die like that.'

Spilsbury turned to Violet Franklin. 'Where did you find her?'

'She was sitting at the foot of the stairs, cradling him in her arms,' she said in a toneless voice.

'And what time was this?'

'Just after seven o'clock.'

'But you were expected an hour earlier?'

'I was.' She was looking at Lydia as she said it.

'Do you have anything you wish to add, Mrs Franklin?' he asked.

Their eyes met. Her gaze was bold and direct. 'No,' she said. 'I have nothing to add.'

Chapter 62

At Inspector Mount's suggestion, they left the police at the house and Violet took Lydia by taxi to a small commercial hotel in St John's Wood for the night.

'What an awful place.' Lydia pulled aside the grubby lace curtain and looked listlessly out into the street below.

'It's all the police could find at such short notice.' Violet pulled open the top drawer and was met with the strong scent of mothballs. 'Beggars can't be choosers.'

'I suppose not,' Lydia sighed, letting the curtain drop. 'I just wish it wasn't so dismal. I feel wretched enough already.'

Violet looked around at the faded wallpaper and yellowing paintwork. There were tenants in Queen's Buildings who would have thought this place a palace. At least there were no mice in the woodwork, or cockroaches scuttling up the walls.

'Better this than staying at the house,' she said.

'You're right.' Lydia shuddered. 'I don't know if I can ever face that place again.' She turned to face Violet. 'How long do you think the police will be there?'

'I don't know. Until they get all the information they can from the scene, I suppose.'

'But I told them exactly what happened. Don't you think they believe me?'

'I'm sure they do,' Violet said. 'It's just routine, that's all. They have to gather all the evidence.'

'I don't think Dr Spilsbury believed me.'

'Why wouldn't he?' Violet was carefully non-committal as she lifted a pile of Lydia's neatly pressed silk underwear from the valise and placed it in the top drawer.

'I don't know. It was just all those questions he kept asking me.' The ancient bedsprings groaned as Lydia sat down on the bed. 'I'm sure he doesn't like me.'

'I get the impression he doesn't like anyone,' Violet said.

'I don't know why everyone makes such a fuss about him. He seems like a horrible man to me.'

Violet caught her stepdaughter's reflection in the looking glass. Lydia was hunched on the bed, her elbows propped on her knees, her chin in her hands. She looked very young, her face scrubbed clean of rouge and powder. Thankfully she had been allowed to wash and change out of her blood-soaked dress. The police had wrapped it up and taken it away for evidence.

The sight of her, sitting at the foot of the stairs covered in blood, had been so shocking and horrific, for a moment she hadn't seemed like the young girl Violet knew and loved.

'Matthew will have to be told,' she said.

'Oh God! I'd forgotten all about him.' Lydia looked panic-stricken. 'I don't even know where he is.'

'Don't worry, I'm sure the police will be able to track him down.'

'I hope so. He'll blame me too, won't he? He's bound to think all this is my fault. He'll say I was a fool to get involved with Robert again.' She looked up and met her gaze in the looking glass. 'Do you think I'm a fool, Violet?'

Their eyes held for a moment in the mirror.

She's hiding something. Violet pushed away the thought that had been ticking away in her brain ever since she had arrived at the house. She didn't want to think that way, did not want to believe her stepdaughter could be lying. And yet . . .

She looked away and went back to her packing. 'You didn't know what Robert was like,' she said.

'But I did, didn't I? I knew he had a horrible temper.'

'But you didn't know he was capable of murder.'

'No,' she said. 'No, I didn't. I keep thinking of his face when he was attacking me. He wanted to kill me, Violet. Just like he killed Aunt Elizabeth.'

She started sobbing again, her face buried in her hands.

'Come on,' Violet said gently. 'Let's get you into bed.'

'What's the use? I won't be able to sleep.'

'I'll give you one of your sleeping pills.' Violet crossed to the dressing table, where she had already set out Lydia's hairbrush, comb and pearl-backed hand mirror, along with her other toiletries. 'Oh, they're not here. We must have left them behind.'

'They're in my bag,' Lydia said. 'Over there, with my coat.'

Violet went to fetch them, then helped Lydia into her nightgown. Her slender limbs were covered in bruises. The poor girl must have been through hell.

And yet . . .

'Will you stay with me?' Lydia asked, as Violet tucked her in like a child.

'I can't, love. I have to go home to Thomas.'

A tear rolled down her cheek, and Violet's heart ached for her. 'You'll come and see me tomorrow though, won't you? You won't abandon me, Violet?' She clutched her hand.

'I'm not going anywhere,' she promised. 'Now take your pill. It'll help calm you down.'

She handed her the tablet. As she was filling a glass of water from the pitcher, Lydia suddenly said, 'Do you think I'll go to prison?'

346

Violet looked over her shoulder. The girl was shaking, her face full of fear.

'Not if it was self-defence,' she said.

'But what if the police don't believe me?'

'Why shouldn't they?'

'You believe me, don't you?'

Violet placed the glass in her stepdaughter's hand.

Say it, the voice in her head whispered.

'Violet?' Lydia's voice was urgent. 'You do believe me, don't you?'

She took a deep breath. *Say it.*

'The blood was dry,' she said.

'What?'

'When I found you cradling Robert's body, you said he'd only been dead a matter of minutes. But when I tried to pull you away, I saw him, and the blood was dry on his face.' She looked at her stepdaughter, still hunched on the bed.

Lydia was very still. 'What are you saying?'

'I'm saying it can't have happened just before I arrived.'

The silence stretched between them. Lydia stared at her, her face giving nothing away. Violet desperately willed her to speak, to say something, anything she could believe.

'You're right,' Lydia said.

The room began to spin. 'Lydia . . .'

'But I didn't kill him, Violet. You must believe that. Truly, it wasn't me.'

Violet looked down at her and suddenly it all made sense. Lydia's odd manner, the coldness of the body, the dried blood on her hands. 'You're protecting someone,' she realised. 'Who, Lyd? Who are you protecting?'

Lydia looked at her, her eyes wide and luminous in the dim lamplight.

'Do you really want to know?' she whispered.

Chapter 63

'We started writing to each other while he was in France. I was writing to a few other soldiers as part of my charity work with the church – sending them gifts, trying to keep their spirits up, that sort of thing. But he was special. I found I was looking forward to his letters, more than any of the others. We really opened our hearts to each other. I felt as if I could tell him secrets I'd never told anyone else.'

Violet watched Lydia's mouth moving, but she barely heard a word she was saying. Her heartbeat thrummed deafeningly in her head, blocking out any other sound. She put her hand out to grasp the iron bed knob in an effort to anchor herself. It felt as if she was floating, lost in a nightmare. Everything seemed to be unravelling around her.

'I knew I had feelings for him, but I tried to ignore them. I was engaged to Robert by then, and I knew it was wrong to feel the way I did about another man. But I couldn't help myself.'

Lydia sat up in bed, her knees drawn up to her chin, her arms wrapped around them. With her long white nightgown tucked under her bare feet, she reminded Violet of a child listening to a bedtime story.

Except she was the one telling the story. And the tale she was telling sounded too fantastical to be real.

'Anyway, I didn't expect it would last. I thought once the war was over we would stop writing and forget about each other. I suppose it was naïve of me, wasn't it? I mean, it was inevitable that we would meet.' She smiled. 'Then one day, I came out of the house and there he was, standing across the road by the railings to the park. He was smiling that smile of his – you know the one? I just looked at him and I knew my heart belonged to him forever.' She looked shyly at Violet. 'But I don't need to tell you that, do I? You love him too.'

Yes, she did, God help her. Although she barely recognised him from what Violet was saying.

And it was all her fault – she had been the one who had encouraged Lydia to write to her brother. She wrote to him herself every week, but she could tell he was struggling, and she thought that receiving some other letters from home might cheer him up a bit.

If only she had known.

Even now, she didn't want to believe it. But at the same time, everything began to make sense. Loose ends in her mind that had troubled her without her really knowing why suddenly began to connect themselves.

The way Pistol, always so protective and wary of strangers, lay as quiet as a lamb when Lydia came to visit. The way she was so confident about walking around the area at night. She knew she could go anywhere because she had the protection of Mickey Malone.

And then there was the way her brother acted when Lydia was around. Violet knew Mickey could be a surly sod, but she had never seen him treat anyone with the cold contempt he did Lydia. It must have all been play acting for her benefit, she realised.

He's like that dog of his, hiding away when he knows he's in trouble. Lydia's words came back to her. Why would she say that, if she didn't know and love Mickey as much as Violet did?

'He killed Robert.'

'He was only doing it to protect me,' Lydia said. 'Robert turned nasty, he was trying to kill me. He did this to me . . .' She yanked at the collar of her nightgown, revealing the purple bruises. 'He would have killed me if Mickey hadn't turned up when he did. He saved my life.'

'But he killed him.' Even saying it out loud didn't make it seem real.

'He didn't mean it to happen, I swear. It was a terrible accident, just as I told the police.'

Was it? Violet remembered how Mickey had tried to warn her off going to Gloucester Gate. Had he known then what he was going to do?

'Why did you tell them it was you?'

'Why do you think? If I took the blame I could say it was self-defence. But if they thought it was Mickey . . .'

'They'd hang him,' Violet finished for her.

'What else was I supposed to do? I had to protect Mickey. Surely you of all people must understand that?'

She understood it better than anyone. Hadn't she spent most of her life trying to protect her little brother? She looked at Lydia's open, innocent face.

'You really do love him, don't you?' she said.

'With all my heart. And I'd gladly take any punishment for him.' Lydia reached for her hand, grasping it on top of the faded eiderdown. 'We're family,' she said. 'If we stick together we can get through this.'

Violet squeezed her hand gratefully. But at the same time, a doubt prickled at the back of her mind.

'I don't understand,' she said. 'If you love my brother so much, why did you go back to Robert?'

Lydia pulled her hand away, her gaze lowered. 'Please don't ask me that,' she said softly. 'I can't tell you.'

'Why not?'

'Please, Violet. I mean it. I can't tell you. If I did, you'd—'

'What? What is it? I want to know.'

Lydia wrapped her arms around her knees, drawing them closer to her chest. She couldn't meet Violet's eye.

'I had to do it,' she said, so quietly Violet could scarcely hear her. 'Robert swore if we resumed our engagement he wouldn't tell anyone.' She bit her lip.

'Tell them what?'

'That Mickey killed my aunt.'

Chapter 64

'No. No, no, no, no.'

She was on her feet, pacing the room, her hands clenched together to stop them shaking. It was as if she had lost control of her own body.

He couldn't. He wouldn't. She could believe he had lashed out in temper at Robert to protect the woman he loved. But not Elizabeth. Her death had been too deliberate.

He could and he would. And you know it.

Try as she might to protect him, Mickey still had the Malone blood running through his veins. A murderer's blood. Her father and brothers were testament to that.

'But you said Robert—'

'I didn't want anyone to know the truth. Especially not you. I'm so sorry, Violet!' Lydia burst into tears.

'Tell me how it happened. Tell me!' Violet shouted to make herself heard above her stepdaughter's noisy sobbing. It was all she could do not to grab her and shake the truth out of her.

'We – we had to do something,' Lydia whimpered and wiped her face on the sleeve of her nightgown. 'Aunt Elizabeth found out, you see. She suspected I was still seeing Robert behind her back, so she set her bloodhound on us.'

'And he found out it was actually Mickey you were meeting?'

Lydia nodded. 'He told her everything. She said I had to give Mickey up, or she would cut me off without a penny.

She said some awful things, Violet, truly she did. She said that having you in the family was disgrace enough, and I wasn't to repeat the same mistake my father had made . . .'

Violet flinched, but held herself steady. It was nothing she hadn't heard before. 'Go on.'

'I told her I loved him. I said I didn't care about the money, that I'd gladly give up any inheritance for Mickey. But then she said she would have him locked up. She threatened to get her wretched investigator to dig up something on him. The way she talked, I thought she might already have some awful secret that could get him put in prison . . .'

'So you told Mickey?'

'I didn't know what else to do!' Lydia wailed. 'I know I shouldn't have said anything; he was already angry enough about you being cut out of Father's will. He was like a tinderbox.' She lowered her gaze. 'He said he would take care of it.'

Take care of it. The words landed heavily, weighed down with meaning.

'I didn't know what he was going to do!' Lydia said.

'You didn't know?' Violet turned on her. 'Even you can't be that naïve!'

Lydia burst into tears again. 'This is all my fault,' she sobbed. 'But I'm trying to put it right, I swear. I would have even married Robert to protect Mickey.'

Violet stared at her, torn between wanting to slap her and wanting to comfort her.

'What does Robert have to do with any of this?' she asked.

'He saw Mickey that night, after he followed me home.'

Violet stared at her in horror. 'So you were there – when Elizabeth was killed?'

'No!' Lydia shook her head. 'She was already dead by the time I got home.' She closed her eyes, shuddering at the memory. 'I'd had no idea what he was planning to do, I swear.' Her pleading eyes met Violet's. 'But what could I do? We had to go through with it. Mickey brought an old army blanket, and he wrapped up the body and took it away.'

'And Robert saw him?'

Lydia nodded. 'He came to see me after my aunt died,' she said bitterly. 'He pretended to be so concerned. But really he just wanted to use the situation to his own advantage.' Her face was bitter.

'And he promised to stay silent as long as you married him?'

'It was horrible, having to pretend,' Lydia shuddered. 'I couldn't bear to be near him. But I did it for Mickey. I'd do anything to protect him.'

She raised her gaze to meet Violet's. 'Now you know everything,' she said, with a shaky smile. 'I'm sorry, Violet. You don't know how many times I've wanted to tell you. I even hoped Mickey might confide in you himself, as you're so close.'

I wish he had, Violet thought. She wished Mickey had talked to her before any of this sorry mess unfolded.

'So you're going to let Robert take the blame for your aunt's death?' she said.

'Why not? He's dead, so what difference does it make?'

'But he's an innocent man.'

'Robert Dillon is anything but innocent!' Lydia snapped. 'And I don't know why you're defending him. He never had anything but contempt for you. He despised you.'

'But he loved you.'

Lydia laughed harshly. 'He never loved anyone but himself! He was only interested in my money and what I could offer him. He used me when he was alive, so why shouldn't I use him now?'

'Lydia!' Violet stared at her in disbelief.

'Think about it, Violet. What difference does it make now if the police think Robert killed her? As long as it keeps Mickey out of prison. That's the main thing, isn't it?' She reached for her hand. 'Violet?'

Violet did not reply. She was thinking about Robert Dillon.

Lydia was right – what difference did it make? She had no reason to feel any pity for him. As Lydia said, he'd never felt anything but contempt for her.

At the same time, it did not sit well with her that an innocent man should go to the grave tainted by the guilt of a crime he did not commit.

But if it saved her own brother from the gallows . . .

Or would it? What did they say? *The truth will out*. Like scum on a pond, it had a nasty way of rising to the surface. How long would it be before the police worked out who was really to blame for the murder?

No, there was only one way to save her brother, Violet thought.

It was time to come clean.

Chapter 65

The following morning, Inspector Mount and Sergeant Stevens arrived at the hospital to hear Spilsbury's post-mortem report on Robert Dillon.

'There are three sizeable but separate fractures on the back of his skull. Noticeably this one here, which extends right down to the foremen magna . . .' He pointed to the diagram he had drawn. 'This one alone would have been fatal.'

'It must have been quite a fall,' Sergeant Stevens remarked.

Spilsbury glanced at Inspector Mount. At least from his intent expression, it seemed as if he had grasped the significance of what he had just said.

'If he died falling down those stairs then I am Marie Lloyd,' Spilsbury said.

'You think it was foul play?' Mount said.

'I'm certain it was. While it's fairly common to die from such an injury when falling down the stairs, one would have to be extremely unfortunate to hit one's head with such force three times. The position of the injury also gives me cause for concern. It would also be very unlikely, given the angle of the fall, to hit the parietal bones so squarely. One would expect the injury to be on one side or the other, but these fractures are all more central, and all virtually in the same place. Look here – ' He showed them a photograph. 'You see this large contusion, around the sphenoid bone on the right-hand side? This is most probably the injury that was caused by the fall. It would have been enough to knock him out, but it certainly would not have killed him.'

'So someone else finished the job?'

'Very thoroughly, by the look of it. My assessment is that there was a struggle and he fell backwards down the stairs. Then, as he lay stunned, someone most likely seized him by the hair like this' – he mimed the movement on his own head – 'and struck his head repeatedly against the newel post several times, like so – '

Inspector Mount let out a low whistle. 'They really wanted him dead, didn't they?'

'They did seem determined to finish the job.'

'And then there's the question of livor mortis to consider.'

Stevens scratched his brilliantined head. 'Livor mortis?'

'It's the way the blood settles after death,' Spilsbury explained. 'It can be a useful indication of the position of the body at the point of death. And since it doesn't usually doesn't begin to occur until an hour after death, it can tell us a lot about the time of death, too.'

Inspector Mount frowned. 'You're saying Dr Dillon's death happened earlier than Miss Franklin claims?'

'So it appears.'

The policemen looked at each other. 'She's covering up for someone,' Sergeant Stevens said.

'It might well seem that way.' Spilsbury cleared his throat. 'There is one other thing to note though.'

There was a soft knock on the door, and Alf Bennet stuck his head round.

'Pardon me, sir, but there's a telephone call in the office,' he said.

'Tell them to wait,' Spilsbury snapped, irritated.

Alf looked embarrassed. 'It's for the inspector, sir. From Scotland Yard.'

'Oh yes?' Inspector Mount turned to face him.

'They just thought you ought to know, sir,' Alf said. 'Someone has just turned up saying they know who killed Elizabeth Franklin.'

'I understand you've come to confess to murder, Mrs Franklin?'

'That's right.' Violet looked down at her gloved hands. She could never have imagined herself coming willingly to a police station, and yet here she was.

And now she was here, seated in this tiny room facing the two officers, the nerve that had carried her over the bridge to Scotland Yard was starting to fail her.

It was a dangerous strategy she had embarked on, and she was beginning to think she would not pull it off.

'Perhaps you'd better tell us what happened?' Inspector Mount said gently.

Violet took a deep, steadying breath. 'I went to see Elizabeth Franklin on the night she died.'

'You were the mystery visitor?' The smarmy little sergeant spoke up. 'Why didn't you tell us this before?'

'Why should I do your job for you?'

'You're doing it now, aren't you?' the sergeant reminded her with a nasty smirk.

'Why were you there?' Inspector Mount said.

'Elizabeth asked me to come.' She took the letter out of her bag and placed it on the desk between them. They studied it, passing it between them several times.

'It says she wants to discuss a matter of great importance,' Inspector Mount said. 'And what might that be, Mrs Franklin?'

'Was it to do with the will?' Sergeant Stevens butted in.

'I thought it might be. I wasn't going to go, but in the end, curiosity got the better of me.'

'I'll bet it did!' Sergeant Stevens's mouth curled into a sneer. 'I bet you couldn't wait, could you? The thought that you might get your hands on some money at last?'

Violet opened her mouth to answer him but just then the door opened and Dr Spilsbury walked in.

'Gentlemen,' he greeted the police officers with a brief nod. 'And Mrs Franklin, what a surprise. I wasn't expecting to see you.'

'Likewise.' Violet turned to Inspector Mount. 'What's he doing here?'

'I've just received the results of an analysis that was carried out on Dr Dillon, and I thought it imperative that Inspector Mount should see them. Also, I was curious.'

'Curious?'

'To hear what this mysterious new witness had to say.'

He stared at her with that unnerving grey gaze. Violet looked away.

'You were saying, Mrs Franklin?' Inspector Mount prompted.

'The door was ajar when I arrived, so I let myself in. Elizabeth was waiting for me in her study. There was no one else in the house.' Violet carried on with her story, uncomfortably aware that Spilsbury was still watching her closely. 'She had all these papers spread out on the desk in front of her, but I couldn't see what they were. She told me she had been thinking about what had happened with James's will, and she had come to the conclusion that Thomas had been unfairly treated.'

'Thomas? Not you?'

Violet shook her head. 'She said that regardless of her feelings on the matter, Thomas was still her brother's son and he deserved to be treated as a Franklin.'

She remembered her cold, dispassionate voice as she said it, the way she averted her gaze, as if even looking at

Violet was too painful. Any hopes she might have had that Elizabeth had invited her to extend the hand of friendship were quickly gone.

'She had been to the solicitor that morning to draw up a new will,' Inspector Mount said. 'Is that what she told you?'

'And you decided to get rid of her so you could inherit the money?' Sergeant Stevens put in.

Violet turned on him. 'Do you take me for a fool?' Out of the corner of her eye she saw Spilsbury's mouth twitch.

She took another deep breath, calming her temper. 'She didn't say anything about a will,' she said. 'I had no idea what she'd done. She just said she had a proposal for me.'

'What kind of proposal?'

'She wanted to adopt Thomas.'

It wasn't really a proposal, it was an ultimatum. Delivered in Elizabeth's usual peremptory way, as if a refusal was not a possibility. She even had all the papers written up, ready for her to sign.

As if she would ever give away her son, especially to such a cold-hearted bitch.

'Adopt him?' The inspector looked astonished. Even Spilsbury was frowning.

'She said she wanted to ensure he was brought up properly, as a Franklin. She made it clear she didn't trust me to take care of my own son, that if he was left to my care he would end up a hoodlum, or swinging from the end of a rope.'

'Like your brothers,' Sergeant Stevens said.

Violet glared at him. 'Leave my brothers out of this!' she hissed.

'And what did you say to that, Mrs Franklin?' Inspector Mount said.

'I told her I'd see her in hell first.'

'Is that why you killed her?' Inspector Mount asked.

'She said she would prove I was an unfit mother. She told me she had a private investigator who could make a case against me. She said either I gave Thomas up willingly or she would take me to court and force me to hand him over. Either way, I was going to lose my son.'

She felt herself falter and pressed her lips together, willing herself to stay strong. She had to get through this, had to tell her story the way she had decided to tell it.

'Then she dismissed me,' she said. 'She just waved me away, as if I was a servant. Just like she had all those years I'd lived there. But then I thought, not this time. She's not going to turn her back on me and treat me as if I'm nothing.'

'So you poisoned her?' Spilsbury said.

'That's right.'

'With some strychnine which you just happened to have on your person.'

Heat rose in her face. 'She had a bottle of medicine – a nerve tonic.'

'What was it called?'

'What?'

'This nerve tonic. What was the name of it?'

'I don't know, do I?'

'Come now, Mrs Franklin, you must have glimpsed the name on the label, at least?'

'It was Easton's Syrup.'

She saw his eyes flicker and knew she must have guessed the right answer.

'And how did you administer this poison?' Spilsbury asked.

'I put it in her drink.'

'Her tea?'

'That's right.'

'And what did you do then?' Inspector Mount asked.

'I got rid of the body. I wrapped it in an old blanket—'

'Where did you get the blanket?' Spilsbury interrupted.

'I found it in the kitchen, tucked away in a cupboard.'

'You're telling me the maid kept an old army blanket in a cupboard?'

'I'm telling you that's where I found it!'

He sat back in his seat but said nothing.

'I rolled her up in the blanket and dragged it down the stairs to the kitchen, then out through the back door.'

'And you carried her down to the canal?'

She glanced uneasily at Spilsbury as she said it. He was leaning forward in his seat, ready to pounce.

'Over your shoulder, like a sack?' he said. 'How tall are you, Mrs Franklin?'

'Five foot six.'

'Elizabeth Franklin was nearly six feet tall. That must have been quite a struggle for you to manhandle her all that way.'

'I'm surprisingly strong,' Violet said.

'I'm sure you are.' Once again, their eyes met. 'Tell me, Mrs Franklin. Are you left or right-handed?'

The question took her by surprise but she had the presence of mind to answer it. 'Left. Why?'

'Really? You've been playing with your gloves ever since I arrived. I notice your right hand is dominant.' He tilted his head consideringly. 'Perhaps you know the person who really killed Elizabeth Franklin was left-handed?'

Violet thought of Mickey's injured right hand, the fingers clawed and useless.

'You don't think Mrs Franklin killed her?' Inspector Mount said.

'I think Mrs Franklin is acting out of misguided loyalty,' Spilsbury said. 'She came here with a little tale concocted solely to confuse and distract. Isn't that right, Mrs Franklin?'

'I don't know what you're talking about,' Violet said, but she could hear the lack of conviction in her own voice.

'You think she's lying?' Inspector Mount said.

'I have no doubt she paid a visit to Elizabeth Franklin on the night she died, but that is where the truth ends and fantasy begins.' He turned to her. 'She did not murder Elizabeth Franklin, and she is reasonably confident that should she be brought before a court the case against her would not stand. Although I have to say, she is taking a great risk.' His gaze grew severe. 'There was a good chance she might still have ended up in prison. And where would her son have been without her?'

Violet stared down at her hands, unable to meet his eye. He was right, it had been a foolish move. As soon as she stepped into the police station she had realised the risk she was taking, not only with her future but with her son's, too.

'She has deliberately turned the focus on to herself to distract you from discovering the identity of the real killer,' Spilsbury went on. 'However, she has wasted her time as well as your own.'

'How so?' inspector Mount asked.

'Because I already know who the killer is.'

Violet looked up sharply. Spilsbury was staring straight at her.

'So let's go and see what they have to say for themselves, shall we?' he said.

Chapter 66

Matthew Franklin did not look pleased to see them all on the step when he opened the door.

'I thought you'd be here sooner or later.' He looked dishevelled, his clothes rumpled as if he had slept in them. 'My sister has come home from that ghastly hovel of a hotel and is resting in her own bed, where she belongs. The doctor said she's suffering from emotional exhaustion.'

'I don't doubt it.' Spilsbury swept past him into the house. Inspector Mount and Sergeant Stevens followed, with Violet Franklin trailing reluctantly at the rear.

'What's she doing here?' Matthew glared at her.

'Mrs Franklin claims she killed your aunt.' Spilsbury looked around him. All traces of the crime had been scrubbed and polished away, leaving nothing but the strong smell of carbolic.

'Good God!' Matthew turned on Violet, his eyes popping from his skull.

'Calm down, man. She did nothing of the kind.' He looked up the stairs. 'You say your sister is resting?'

'She's just taken another sleeping tablet.'

'What manner of sleeping tablet is she prescribed?'

'How should I—'

'Chloral hydrate,' Violet answered for him.

'Of course.' Spilsbury studied the newel post closely, even though it had been scrubbed clean, like everything else.

'You look as if you could do with some sleep yourself, Mr Franklin?' he said over his shoulder.

'I came down from Scotland on the overnight train, but it was too late for me to book a sleeping car.'

That explained the dishevelled appearance, Spilsbury thought. 'Where have you been?'

'Visiting friends. I felt I needed to get out of London for a while.'

I'm sure you did. Inspector Mount had told him about the suspected blackmail, although they still couldn't uncover what secret Tobias Warriner had discovered about him. Being away no doubt saved Matthew Franklin a great deal of awkward questions.

'It's very touching that you should rush to be at your sister's side,' he said.

'I came as soon as I could. I couldn't leave Lydia to deal with all this on her own. She's not up to it.'

They all treated her like a child, Spilsbury thought as he ran his fingertip along the polished wood of the banister rail. Or a charming little pet, to be cossetted and cared for.

'It must have been rather alarming to learn that a second murder had been committed under your roof?'

Matthew frowned. 'I don't understand.' He glanced from Inspector Mount to Sergeant Stevens and back again. 'I was told it was an accident?'

'Hello?'

A feeble voice from above made them all look up. Lydia stood at the top of the stairs, clinging to the banisters. She looked the picture of fragility, her fair hair loose around her china doll face. She wore a Japanese silk dressing gown, ivory splashed with exotic crimson flowers. From a distance, they looked like splotches of blood.

365

'What are you doing out of bed, my dear?' Matthew called up to her. 'You heard what the doctor said. You need to rest.'

'Don't fuss, I'm perfectly all right.' Lydia gave them all a brave, wan smile. 'Good morning, Inspector. And Dr Spilsbury, too. Goodness, we are honoured!'

Her gaze came to rest on Violet. Her smile did not waver but Spilsbury noticed the look that passed between them.

Lydia ventured down a few steps, still clinging to the banister rail. 'What can we do for you?' she asked.

Inspector Mount cleared his throat and dragged his gaze away from the young woman's slightly alarming state of *dishabille*. 'Some new evidence has come to light that we'd like to discuss with you.'

'What sort of evidence?'

'We now believe that Dr Dillon was murdered.'

'Murdered?' Matthew said. 'But how can that be? I thought – Lyd!'

He swung round and rushed to catch his sister as her legs buckled beneath her. She crumpled into a graceful heap on the stairs.

'Lydia, darling, are you all right? Fetch the smelling salts, someone!'

'I'll get them.' Violet Franklin started up the stairs, but Lydia rallied and her eyes fluttered open.

'I'm all right, honestly,' she said in a faint, breathy voice. 'It just came as a shock, that's all.'

'Did it?' Spilsbury said. 'I can't imagine why, since you were here at the time.'

Matthew swung round to face him, one arm still around his sister's shoulders. 'Are you calling my sister a liar, Dr Spilsbury?'

Spilsbury looked at Lydia Franklin. What little colour she'd had had drained away, leaving her skin the same creamy white as her dressing gown.

'I'm saying the injuries Dr Dillon sustained could not have been caused by a simple fall down the stairs.'

'But it makes no sense.' Matthew frowned. 'Lydia?' He looked at his sister. 'What's going on? For heavens' sake, say something!'

When Lydia spoke, her voice was barely above a whisper. 'Dr Spilsbury is right, Matthew. Robert didn't fall. Someone killed him.'

'Lydia!' There was an imploring note in Violet Franklin's voice. Lydia turned to her, her face wretched.

'I'm sorry, Violet,' she said. 'I tried, I really did. But I can't protect him any longer.'

'Protect who?' Matthew said, looking from one to the other.

Spilsbury glanced at Inspector Mount. He and Sergeant Stevens looked as blank as Matthew Franklin.

Lydia closed her eyes, as if she was mentally gathering herself. 'Violet's brother Mickey was the one who murdered Robert,' she said. 'He also killed our aunt.'

A shocked silence fell.

'I knew it!' Matthew turned on Violet. 'I bet you were in on it together, weren't you?'

'Stop it, Matthew,' Lydia pleaded. 'Violet had nothing to do with it. It was me who brought a murderer into our house, not her. I'm to blame for all of this.' She hunched over, burying her face in her hands, and broke down in tears.

'Would you mind telling me what's going on?' Inspector Mount said to Spilsbury in a low voice. 'Since I'm supposed to be in charge of this investigation?'

'I think Miss Franklin will be able to give a better account than I.'

If she ever stops crying, he added silently. He could not remember the last time he had seen a female with more capacity for tears. They seemed to come out of nowhere.

Finally, her sobbing subsided enough for her to manage a few halting words.

'It all happened exactly as I told you last night,' she said, her voice breaking with emotion. 'I tried to break things off with Robert, and he attacked me. He might have killed me if Mickey hadn't burst in and saved me.' Her hand moved up to touch the necklace of bruises at her throat. 'But then they ended up fighting, and Mickey pushed Robert down the stairs.'

'And he killed him?' Inspector Mount said.

Lydia could only manage the briefest of nods, her eyes closed against the memory. 'He was like an animal. He kept shouting, over and over, that he was going to finish him. I'd never seen that side of him before. He was enraged.'

'No!' Violet moaned softly. 'He wouldn't do that. He couldn't.'

Spilsbury saw her anguished expression and realisation dawned. For once, he had completely misjudged the situation.

'I'm sorry, Violet,' Lydia said. 'We can't go on protecting him forever. I love him as much as you do, but we have to face up to what he is. Mickey is a killer.'

'You say he murdered your aunt, too?' Inspector Mount said.

Lydia nodded. 'Aunt Elizabeth found out we were meeting in secret and told me I had to end it. Mickey got angry and said he would deal with her. I didn't know what he was going to do, I swear,' she said, her words coming out in a rush. 'I thought he was going to talk to her, try to persuade her. But then . . .' Her voice faltered.

'Why didn't you tell us all this at the time?'

'How could I? I still loved him, in spite of everything. I knew he'd done it for me. And – and there was something else.' She looked down at her hands, entwined in her lap.

'Part of me was afraid of him, too. I'd already seen what happened when someone stood in his way. I was terrified of what he might do to me, or to Matthew or—'

'Or Robert Dillon?' Inspector Mount finished for her.

Spilsbury glanced at Violet Franklin. She was staring at Lydia as if she did not recognise her.

'You'll have to excuse me, Miss Franklin,' the inspector spoke. 'I'm finding it difficult to keep up. Yesterday you told us Robert Dillon killed your aunt. Now, this morning, you tell us it's someone else. I have to say I'm finding your story rather hard to believe.'

'I really don't see what's hard to believe about it,' Matthew snapped. 'Anyone can see the poor girl is frightened out of her wits. She's been the victim of not one but two angry, dangerous men. They've both manipulated her in their own way and used her to their own ends. And naïve as she is, she's tried to protect both of them.' He pointed at Violet. 'She's the one you should be questioning. I wouldn't be surprised if she and her brother weren't in on this together the whole time.' He turned on her. 'Where is he? Where's the murdering swine?'

'I don't know.' Violet's voice was surprisingly steady. 'And I wouldn't tell you even if I did.'

'You see? She's as guilty as he is. If anyone incited that brute to kill my aunt, it was her. You should arrest her!'

Spilsbury spoke up. 'On the contrary, Mrs Franklin is the only one out of you who has done nothing wrong,' he said. 'Unless, of course, allowing oneself to be manipulated is a crime. In which case I suspect we've all fallen victim, just as Mr Malone and Dr Dillon did.' He looked at Lydia, still trembling in her brother's arms. 'Isn't that right, Miss Franklin?'

Chapter 67

Another shocked silence followed his words. Spilsbury saw the frown of disbelief on Inspector Mount's face as he looked from him to Lydia Franklin and back again.

Matthew spoke up first. 'You surely can't mean to accuse my sister? Look at her, Inspector. Does she seem capable of killing anyone?'

'No,' Spilsbury answered for him. 'Quite frankly, she doesn't seem capable of anything. But it seems everyone has underestimated her, including your aunt. With fatal consequences, in her case.'

'I don't understand!' Lydia's lips trembled, her grey eyes glittering with unshed tears. 'Why are you saying this? I didn't do anything, I couldn't . . .' She clutched at her brother's arm. 'Tell them, Matthew, please!' she begged. 'Tell them I would never hurt Aunt E!'

'It's true,' Matthew said. 'Lydia was devoted to our aunt. She never left her side.'

'Yes, and that was all part of the role she played,' Spilsbury said. 'She was dutiful, compliant, whatever anyone needed her to be. But underneath it all she was a very different person, one no one was ever allowed to see.'

He turned to Lydia. 'It must have been very difficult for you, Miss Franklin. Your aunt kept you on a very tight rein. She chose what you wore, how you looked, how you spent your time.'

'She cared about me.'

'She had your whole future mapped out for you, including who you would marry when she deemed the time was right. And meanwhile, there was your brother . . .' He glanced at Matthew. 'You had to live under all those restrictions while he was indulged, his mistakes excused and forgiven.'

'This is ridiculous!' Matthew got to his feet. 'You're making Lydia out to be some kind of devious criminal. She's a child, Inspector,' he appealed to Mount.

'She's a young woman,' Spilsbury corrected him. 'And an intelligent one, too. Which everyone might have realised if only you'd stopped treating her like a little pet!'

He looked at Violet Franklin as he said it. She was just as guilty as the rest of them. And she knew it, too. He could see the truth dawning on her face.

He turned back to Lydia. 'Did you ever love Robert Dillon, Miss Franklin? Or was your engagement merely a way of escaping from your aunt's control?'

'Of course I loved him! We were engaged!'

'But then you met Mr Malone.' Once again, he glanced at Violet. 'A man far more dangerous and unsuitable than Robert Dillon. Was that part of the attraction, Miss Franklin? Knowing how much your aunt would disapprove?'

'We fell in love!' Lydia protested tearfully.

'Perhaps you did,' Spilsbury conceded. 'I have no doubt there was genuine affection on Mr Malone's side, at least. Otherwise why would he have done what he did?'

'So you admit he killed my aunt!' Matthew said.

Spilsbury addressed himself to Violet. 'I have no doubt that he was involved in Elizabeth Franklin's murder. But only as an accessory after the fact.'

'No!' Lydia cried. 'No, he did it. He was at the house that night. He murdered Aunt Elizabeth!'

'He was certainly at the house,' Spilsbury conceded. 'That old army blanket was his, no doubt brought with him for the purpose of disposing of her body. But she was already dead when he arrived.'

'No!' Lydia's voice rose hysterically. 'He killed her. He did it!'

'He did your bidding, Miss Franklin. Just as everyone did.'

'This is too awful!' Lydia tore away from her brother's embrace and ran down the stairs to throw herself at her stepmother's feet. 'Help me, Violet, please. I told you what happened, didn't I? You know how violent and unpredictable Mickey can be. Tell them, I beg you!'

Violet looked down at the girl cowering at her feet, her hands clasped together in a pathetically imploring gesture.

'He would have killed her with his bare hands,' she said in a dull voice.

Lydia gasped. 'You see? She admits it. She knows what he's like.' She turned to the policemen. 'You have to listen to her!'

Spilsbury had listened. And he had heard something quite different. Violet was beginning to think for herself at last. The numbness was beginning to subside, and a bright mind was emerging.

'Mrs Franklin is right,' he said. 'Mickey Malone was a boxer, a man of great strength. And also a man with an impulsive temper, as I believe we've established. Would he really have employed something as subtle as poison when he could have snapped your aunt's neck like a twig?'

Inspector Mount winced. 'A trifle unnecessary, Dr Spilsbury,' he muttered.

'And a complete fantasy!' Matthew said. 'Why are you even listening to this, Inspector?' He hurried down the stairs and dragged his sister to her feet. 'Stop it, Lydia, I won't have you grovelling to her. She's a thief and a con artist, just like her brother. Aunt Elizabeth was right – she's ruined this family!'

Spilsbury ignored him, turning to face Lydia Franklin. 'Did you always intend to kill her that night? Or did you snap after your final, bitter argument?'

Lydia stared back at him, dry-eyed for once. Her tears had turned off as easily as they had turned on.

'I suspect the latter,' he said quietly. 'I've no doubt you had it in mind to kill your aunt at some point. But I'm sure you would have preferred to persuade the hapless Mr Malone to do it for you . . .'

'He wouldn't.' Lydia's voice was dull and flat. 'I asked him to help me, but he said no.' She turned her eyes to Violet. 'He was too much of a coward.'

'My brother was no coward!' Violet Franklin spat back, her eyes blazing. 'He didn't want to fight anymore, not after all the death he'd witnessed in France. He just wanted a new start.'

'Lydia?' Matthew sounded hesitant. 'What are you saying? You loved Aunt E!'

'Loved her?' Lydia turned on him. 'I despised her. You don't know what my life was like. This house was like a prison. Dr Spilsbury is right, I wasn't allowed to move without her approval. But I found a way round it.'

'You and Mr Malone communicated in secret, through those advertisements in *The Times*?' asked Spilsbury.

'That was rather clever, wasn't it?' Her mouth twisted. 'She thought I was being so devoted, bringing her a cup of cocoa every night when I came home from Rowton House. She had no idea I was drugging her with sleeping tablets.'

'So you could go out and meet your lover?' Spilsbury said.

'It was the only way I could get out of the house.' Lydia looked almost pleased with herself. 'But then one evening I came home and she was waiting for me. She had found out about Mickey and me, and she told me I had to end it. We argued, and I tried to explain that I was nearly twenty-one and entitled to my own life. But as usual she had to have the last word. She just walked away from me.' Her mouth tightened with resentment.

'So you decided to teach her a lesson?'

'I decided to kill her,' Lydia said flatly.

'Easton's Syrup,' Spilsbury said.

'I knew where she kept it. I wanted to make sure, so I asked Robert how big a dose it would take to kill someone. I pretended I was concerned about her taking it.'

'I'm surprised it worked,' Spilsbury said. 'Easton's is hardly known for its lethal properties.'

'That's what Robert said. So I found some rat poison in the kitchen and used that too.'

They were all staring at her. It was as if a pet poodle had suddenly sprouted fangs and torn someone's throat out.

'And then what happened?' Inspector Mount found his voice at last. 'How did you get rid of the body?'

'My brother.' Violet Franklin spoke up.

'He was very kind,' Lydia said. 'I went to him and told him what I'd done. He told me to get myself an alibi while he disposed of the body.'

'And implicated himself nicely into the bargain,' Spilsbury muttered.

'Robert saw him leaving the house,' Violet said.

'Not just that,' Spilsbury corrected her. 'He also saw you returning home earlier than you'd told the police. Isn't that right, Miss Franklin?'

'But the superintendent at Rowton House gave her an alibi?' Inspector Mount said.

'He was supervising a thousand men,' Spilsbury pointed out. 'He hardly had time to check on the whereabouts of a young girl in the building. If Miss Franklin told him she was there until ten o'clock, why should she lie? I imagine he would believe whatever she told him.'

'Just like everyone else,' Violet muttered. She was staring at Lydia as if she wanted to kill her.

'Robert got too greedy,' Lydia said. 'He was trying to control me, just like everyone else. Everyone always thought they knew what was best for me.'

'No one controlled you, Miss Franklin,' Spilsbury said. 'You did all this entirely by yourself. Your aunt's death might not have been planned, but Dr Dillon's certainly was. Right down to arranging your alibi.' He looked at Violet. 'You arranged for Mrs Franklin to come to the house at six o'clock, knowing that you had invited Robert Dillon an hour earlier. Your intention was that she would arrive in time to see you tragically cradling his body at the foot of those stairs. But it did not work out quite as you'd hoped, did it? First of all, the fall did not kill him so you had to take matters into your own hands – quite literally, in this case. Then Mrs Franklin was an hour late. And despite your efforts to create the crime scene to fit your story, the presence and pattern of livor mortis tells quite another tale. And a rather damning one, at that.'

'My sister was attacked,' Matthew said. Spilsbury had to admire his tenacity, if nothing else. His sister had already confessed to one murder, but he was still trying to absolve her of another. 'You only have to look at her . . .'

'Ah yes, the scratches and bruises. You're quite right, Mr Franklin. I did find traces of skin and traces of face powder under Dr Dillon's fingernails, which I presume came from your sister.'

'There you are, then.'

'But they indicate defensive wounds. The young man was fighting for his life. And I don't doubt he put his hands

375

around Miss Franklin's throat, too, once he realised her intention to kill him. But the bruises are not significant. They're already beginning to fade, I see. They were weak, with very little pressure behind them. Dr Dillon was already too feeble to fight back, thanks to the sleeping tablet you had crushed into his drink earlier.'

He took the piece of paper from his inside pocket.

'This is the toxicology report from my colleague, Dr Willcox. It confirms that traces of chloral hydrate were found in Dr Dillon's system.'

'That proves nothing!' Matthew protested. 'Anyone could have given him sleeping tablets! He could even have prescribed them for himself.'

'Possibly,' Spilsbury said. 'I might not have even thought to test for it if it hadn't been for the missing glasses. You made sure you took them down to the kitchen and washed them up, didn't you, Miss Franklin? It was very clever of you to get rid of the evidence. But not so clever of you to leave the rest of the champagne in the drawing room. A half-empty bottle and no glasses is bound to raise suspicion, don't you think? I went down to the kitchen to look for them, and I found a couple of bloody fingerprints on the tap.' He shook his head. 'Very careless, I would say. I suppose you drugged him and lured him upstairs on some pretext, then staged a fight so you could push him to his death? Is that what happened, Miss Franklin?'

Lydia Franklin turned hate-filled eyes to face him. 'You must think you're very clever, Dr Spilsbury.'

'Certainly cleverer than you, Miss Franklin. Although that really isn't too difficult, is it?'

Chapter 68

April 1920

'I hear you've been given your marching orders, constable Abbott?'

Charlie looked up from the front desk, where he was standing in while the desk sergeant had his tea break. Inspector Jones was beaming at him, his eyes bright above his bristling moustache.

'That's right, sir. Tomorrow's my last day.'

'So you'll be leaving uniform behind, then? Joining the ranks of the detectives?'

'It seems so, sir.'

'It's a pity you're not staying here. We could do with a bright boy like you. Still, I suppose our loss is Scotland Yard's gain.'

'I couldn't have done it if you hadn't put in a good word for me, sir.'

'It was the least I could do, lad. You helped crack the Hodges case, after all.'

'Thank you, sir.' Charlie felt the heat rising in his face at the unexpected praise. 'What's happening about that, sir?'

'They're still blaming each other, of course.' Inspector Jones sighed. 'He says it was all her idea, and she said he made her do it. I reckon they'll be carrying on all the way through the court case.' He jerked his head towards the doors. 'I'm going down to Holloway to have another chat with her now, as a matter of fact. Would you care to join me?'

'I'd like that, sir, if you wouldn't mind?'

'It's the least I can do, son. And you never know, she might decide to talk to you, since you know her.'

Charlie could not imagine what rapport the inspector thought he might have had with Hilda Hodges. But any illusions he had would have been quickly dispelled when they walked into the grim little interview room at Holloway Prison, where she sat waiting for them.

She took one look at him and her face fell. 'Oh, it's you again.' She gave him her usual greeting. Even now, sitting at the table in her drab prison uniform, she still gave the impression that she had better things to do than stop and speak to him.

'Hello, Miss Hodges. How are you getting on?'

'Oh, I'm tickety boo, thanks for asking. This place is a real tonic. Better than a fortnight in Clacton. What are you doing here, anyway?'

'I invited him,' Inspector Jones said. 'You don't mind, do you?'

'The more the merrier, I'm sure.'

She watched them as they seated themselves at the table opposite her. Inspector Jones took his time, opening his notes and uncapping his pen.

'I don't know why you're bothering to make more notes,' she said sourly. 'You must have written all this down a dozen times.'

'Yes, well, it won't hurt to get it all down again, will it? Just in case there's something I missed.'

'Please yourself.' Hilda rolled her eyes.

'Right, so how about you start by reminding me when you and Mr Beckett started this affair?'

'It wasn't an affair. We were in love.'

'But you carried on in secret?'

'Only because we knew my father wouldn't approve.'

'Because Mr Beckett was married?'

Her mouth thinned. 'In name only. They hadn't been husband and wife properly for years, if you know what I mean.'

'I'm sure I can work it out, Miss Hodges. But then your father died and left you the inheritance?'

'He wasn't after my money, if that's what you're implying.'

'I wasn't implying anything, Miss Hodges. Although according to your bank records, you did spend rather a lot of money on him during that time?' He consulted his notes. 'You bought him clothes, expensive meals out, weekends in smart hotels . . .'

'We had to meet in secret,' Hilda Hodges reminded him. 'We had to go somewhere. And what if I wanted to treat him, anyway? It was my money, I could do as I liked with it.'

'Except it wasn't your money, was it? Not all of it.'

Hilda looked so furious, for a moment Charlie thought she was going to lash out. Over in the corner, he saw the female wardress take a step forward. But then Hilda calmed down.

'That was Father's doing,' she hissed. 'I didn't see why Jean should get half of everything when I was the one who'd done all the hard work and looked after him for so many years. All those years fetching and carrying for him, while she was out in the world, swanning about and having a wonderful time.'

'She worked at Selfridges, Miss Hodges,' Charlie pointed out. 'It was hardly the Hippodrome, was it?'

'It was better than being stuck behind a counter selling bacon!' Hilda Hodges snapped back. 'But she was always

Father's favourite. She probably talked him into giving us joint control over the inheritance.'

'Anyone would think he didn't trust you?' Charlie suggested. Hilda flashed him a look of dislike.

'And with good reason, as it turned out.' Inspector Jones fiddled with the cap of his pen. 'Did your sister know about your affair – your romance?' he amended, as Hilda opened her mouth to protest.

'I had to tell her, after Father died. I wanted my share, so Bill and I could set up home together.'

'But the way the estate had been set up, both sisters' permission was needed to withdraw any large sums?'

'I only wanted what I was entitled to,' Hilda said, looking from one to the other. 'It was what I deserved, after looking after Father and this place for all those years.'

'But your sister said no?'

'She had no right.' Charlie could see Hilda's anger building, her muscles twitching beneath her skin. 'She was so self-righteous about it, just because Bill was married. She said I'd end up in trouble.'

'She was right, wasn't she?' Charlie said.

'It was all right for her, she'd had her chance,' Hilda went on, ignoring him. 'At least she'd been engaged. She'd found someone, if only for a few years. Bill was my only chance—'

'And you'd do anything to keep him?' Inspector Jones said.

'Including killing your own sister?' Charlie joined in.

Hilda was stubbornly silent, her thin lips pressed together. 'I'm saying nothing about that,' she said.

'She refused to sign the money over, so you killed her?' Inspector Jones went on. 'Did you plan it, or was it a moment of madness?'

'I told you, I don't know anything about it. Except that he did it,' she added as an afterthought.

'He says the same about you.'

'Yes, well, he would, wouldn't he?'

'If you had nothing to do with it, why did you tell me your sister had run off with a soldier she'd met through the Lonely Hearts column?' Charlie asked.

Hilda stared at him, momentarily lost for words.

'That's what he told me to say,' she said.

'You had us running around on a wild goose chase, looking for a mystery man who didn't exist. And all the time you knew who'd killed your sister.'

'I didn't know anything,' Hilda insisted stubbornly.

'But you've just told us you and Mr Beckett talked about it? You said he told you what to say.'

'And you more or less confessed the day we arrested you,' Charlie reminded her. 'Do you remember what you said, Miss Hodges? "After everything I'd done for him," you said. You were talking about Jean, weren't you? How you'd killed her so you could be together.'

'I didn't mean anything of the kind. I don't even remember saying it. And you've got nothing written down, so it's your word against mine.'

Charlie looked at Inspector Jones. No wonder he was so exasperated.

'What did Mr Beckett do when he found out? Did you tell him what you'd done?' he tried again.

'No comment.'

'What did he say?' Silence. 'I bet you thought he'd be pleased, didn't you? You'd got rid of the problem for him. Now you could be together at last.'

'No comment.'

'But he wasn't, was he? He was horrified. He wanted nothing to do with you. The next thing you knew, he'd gone back to his wife and moved away.'

'That was all her doing,' Hilda blurted out. 'He would never have left me if she hadn't forced him into it.'

'But that's not true though, is it? He left you because he was frightened of what you'd done.'

Hilda glared at him. 'I didn't do anything.' The words came from between clenched teeth. If she'd had a hammer to hand, Charlie felt sure he would have felt it.

'Is that why you decided to kill Mrs Beckett?' Inspector Jones said in his pleasant Welsh sing-song. She said nothing. 'Why did you do it, Hilda? Did you think he'd come back to you if his wife was out of the way?'

'I didn't want him back,' Hilda snapped. 'Not after the way he'd treated me.'

'Leaving you high and dry, do you mean? Is that why you framed him with that note, to punish him?'

'He deserved to be punished,' Hilda muttered.

Charlie pounced. 'So you admit you sent the chocolates, to frame him?'

Hilda looked at him, her mouth an obstinate line. 'I'm saying nothing,' she said. 'Except that he killed my sister and he tried to kill his wife.'

Charlie could hardly control his frustration as he and Inspector Jones left the prison half an hour later.

'I don't know how you do it, sir,' he said. 'Listening to her say the same thing, day after day.'

'Oh, we'll get her in the end,' Inspector Jones said. 'Sooner or later she'll crack and admit to it. Every time I speak to her, I get a bit closer to the truth.' He patted Charlie on the shoulder. 'Patience, lad. That's what you need as a detective. Sometimes it's as much about putting in the hours as it is about getting a lucky break.'

'I certainly put the hours in, trying to find that Lonely Hearts Killer,' Charlie muttered. 'When I think about all those hours I wasted, looking for a man who didn't exist . . .'

'And in the end, it turned out it wasn't a man at all.'

'I never thought about that,' Charlie said. But it was true: Jean Hodges and Elizabeth Franklin had been killed by other women.

'You know what they say about the female of the species, lad. And in my experience, it's turned out to be true.' Inspector Jones shook his head. 'Never underestimate a woman, that's what I say.'

Charlie thought about his wife Annie and his mother Elsie, no doubt battling it out again back in Thrale Street.

'Oh, I don't, sir,' he said. 'Believe me, I wouldn't dare.'

Chapter 69

Mary had outstayed her welcome with her cousin.

Mollie didn't say anything directly, but as the weeks passed she had begun to drop hints about what her future plans might be.

'It's not that I don't like having you here,' she had said, even though her face told a different story. 'But you must have something you want to do?'

Mary wasn't surprised; she and Mollie had never been particularly close. If anything, she was amazed they had lasted as long as they had under the same roof.

'I've got a few plans,' she had replied vaguely, even though the truth was she had no idea what she was going to do. She had fled London in a panic, but now, in the quiet of her spinster cousin's cottage on the Whitstable coast, she found she missed the city.

'Have you thought about going back to Otley?' Mollie had pressed her. 'I'm sure you and George could make another go of it, if you tried?'

'George is courting again.'

A local widow, so Mary had heard through the grapevine. And good luck to her, she thought. Hopefully George had changed his ways, or his new wife could cope better with his gloomy, relentless carping than Mary had. If she was honest with herself, their marriage had been over long before she finally found the courage to walk out on him. She had only stayed with him as long as she had for Terence's sake. With her son gone, there seemed no point in pretending any longer.

In the end, Mary had ended up telling Mollie she would leave by the end of the week, although she had no clue what she was going to do. She had applied for a couple of live-in jobs, but her heart wasn't really in it.

In the meantime, she was doing her best to earn her keep by making herself useful around the house. This particular Monday morning, she was hanging out the washing. It was a particularly fine April day, with spring in the air. As Mary pegged out the sheets, the breeze caught them, making them billow out like sails.

'I thought you'd given up doing other people's house-work?' A voice drawled behind her.

She looked over her shoulder. On the other side of the low wall stood Edgar French – or Tobias Warriner, as everyone called him now – rolling a cigarette.

Her heart jerked at the sight of him, but she made sure her face betrayed nothing.

'Look at you, back from the dead.' She turned back to her washing.

'Did you miss me?'

'Not particularly.'

'Pity. I missed you.'

He was only playing, she told herself. That was typical Eddie, always joking about.

'How did you find me?'

'Mary, please. I can find anyone if I set my mind to it.' There was a reproachful note in his voice. 'I don't suppose you've got a light, have you?'

She took out the matches from her apron pocket and went over to give them to him. Behind his easy smile and casual manner, she could see the past few weeks had not been easy for him. His face was thinner, and there were lines of strain around his piercing blue eyes.

She had meant to step away after she had handed him the matches. But instead she found herself watching as he lit his cigarette and took a long draw. He fascinated her, just as he always had.

'Did you really think I was dead?' he asked.

'I didn't know what to think. The police reckoned you'd been murdered, but Dr Spilsbury said no.'

'Dr Spilsbury is more than a match for me.' He grinned, and offered her his cigarette. It was a casual gesture, but intimate at the same time. After a moment's hesitation, Mary took it.

'But what did you think?' he asked.

Mary thought about it. 'I knew you weren't dead,' she said at last, handing him back the cigarette. 'I could feel it.'

He smiled. 'We understand each other, don't we, Mary? I would have told you I was leaving, but I rather ran out of time. Things were getting a bit hot for me, as you know, and I realised it wouldn't be long before the police were pressing me for those stolen files, so I thought perhaps I should get away for a while. I was just making my preparations when who should turn up but Mickey Malone and that hell hound of his.'

Mary took the cigarette from him without thinking. 'What did he want?'

'Well, me, obviously. Naturally, I thought he must have come to kill me, to stop me telling the police what I knew about him and the Franklin girl. I really thought my time was up, I have to say. There isn't a great deal that scares me, Mary. But I don't mind telling you, being faced with that hulking brute gave me rather a fright.' His hand was shaking as he took the cigarette back from her.

'I'm not surprised.' Mary had seen Mickey Malone lurking outside the house a few times, and she knew how intimidating he was. She was very glad he had never knocked on the door because she wouldn't have fancied trying to turn him away, and in any case, Elizabeth Franklin had made it very clear to Mary that none of Violet Franklin's relatives were to be allowed to enter the house without her permission.

She had thought at the time he was waiting for Violet. But then, when Eddie found out about Mickey and Lydia setting up secret trysts through the newspaper columns, it had all made sense to her.

Looking back on it, perhaps she should have said something to the police. But as far as she was concerned, those advertisements were nothing more than a bit of harmless fun between Miss Lydia and her beau. Why should she get the poor girl in trouble for no reason?

How wrong they had all been. Lydia had pulled the wool right over her eyes, just as she had everyone else's.

'How did you get away from him?' she asked.

'As you can imagine, I was ready to fall on my knees and beg for my life, but it wasn't like that at all. All he wanted was to make sure I wouldn't give him and Lydia up to the police. So I handed over the keys to my safe deposit box and swore I'd get out of town post haste. It was what I intended to do anyway, of course, but he seemed quite satisfied with that. We even shook hands on it, would you believe? Turns out he's rather a gentle giant. I even liked that dog of his!' He looked at her. 'I did feel churlish for not saying goodbye, though. You deserved that, at least.'

'I understood.'

'But I shouldn't have left you to face the music on your own. Did the police question you?'

Mary nodded. 'But there wasn't much I could tell them. They asked me what it was you had over Matthew, and I told them I didn't know.'

'Just as well I never told you,' he said, his smile back in place. 'I didn't want to know.'

'Aren't you ever in the least bit curious?' he asked. 'I would be.'

'Curiosity killed the cat.'

He took another drag on his cigarette. 'All the same, I bet there were times when you wished our paths had never crossed,' he said.

'Never,' she said firmly.

Her answer surprised them both. For a moment they stared at each other.

'You gave me my son back,' she went on quickly. 'I was able to cherish his memory again, thanks to you.'

His friendship had given her more than that, and she knew it. But she would never presume to say. It wasn't her place.

She was pragmatic enough to know that there could never be more to their relationship. Terence's death might have bonded them, just as it had bonded her son and Edgar Warriner. But now it was all over, and for all the talk of things being more egalitarian, they had all slotted back into their rightful places in society.

And even though he rejected it, they both know Tobias Warriner's place would always be further up the ladder than hers.

'I hear the house in Gloucester Gate is up for sale?' he remarked casually. 'I suppose they need the money to pay for Lydia's trial.'

'It must be a shock for her, being in prison.' Although if Mary knew Lydia, she would soon have everyone dancing to her tune.

'And what about Matthew?'

'He's probably still drinking himself to death and blaming everyone else for his downfall,' Mary said bitterly.

'So much for family pride,' Tobias said wryly. 'Elizabeth Franklin will be turning in her grave.'

'She's the cause of all this, the nasty old snob. If she hadn't tried to run everyone's lives, perhaps everyone would have been content.'

'True.' Tobias aimed a smoke ring towards the sky.

'What will you do now?' Mary asked. 'Are you going back to London?'

'Oh no, it's still too soon for that. Besides, I made a promise to Mickey Malone.' He tipped the ash off the tip of his cigarette. 'No, I rather thought I'd try my luck in Scotland. I can make a new start, pick up the business. I'm sure people must be having illicit affairs and getting up to all sorts of trouble up there, just as much as they are down here.' He grinned.

'If there are, I'm sure you'll find them.'

'How about you? Have you made any plans?'

Mary glanced towards the cottage, to make sure Mollie was out of earshot. 'I'll probably go back into service,' she said. 'A nursery maid, perhaps. Somewhere there are children, at any rate. I like children.'

She only wished she had had more herself. Then she might have had a house full of games and laughter, instead of silence and recrimination.

'They have children in Scotland.'

Mary looked at him sharply. 'What are you saying?'

'I wondered if you'd like to come with me?' He studied the tip of his cigarette with an air of nonchalance. 'We rub along quite well together, don't we? And I've missed you.'

His eyes met hers, and suddenly the nonchalance was gone and only true emotion remained.

'I . . .' Mary must have hesitated a fraction too long because the next thing she knew Tobias was stubbing out his cigarette on the brickwork, his brisk indifference back in place.

'My train is leaving from King's Cross tomorrow at three, anyway,' he said, not meeting her eye. 'I've taken the liberty of buying you a ticket, if you want it. And there's also this – ' He reached into his inside jacket pocket and pulled out a letter.

'What's this?'

'It's something I planned to send to the police. The details of what Matthew did.' He held it out to her. 'Take it,' Tobias said. 'It's yours to use as you wish.' He leaned towards her, his voice lowered. 'You can have the revenge you want for your son, Mary. That is, if you still want it?'

Chapter 70

The flat in Queen's Buildings felt empty without Mickey's presence.

Violet knew she should find somewhere else to live, for Thomas's sake. The spring weather had dried out the damp in the walls, but it had brought out the mice and the cockroaches. Violet set traps and every night she would go at the cracks with a lighted candle, but it was a battle she knew she would ultimately lose.

But at the same time, she was reluctant to move because she couldn't give up the hope that one day he brother might come home.

She longed to see him again, just once, even though she veered wildly between wanting to hug him and wanting to strangle him. How could he have been such a fool? Why didn't he tell her the trouble he was in? She would have helped him, if she could.

But then, they had all been fools where Lydia Franklin was concerned. She had taken them all in.

Violet had always thought of herself as a good judge of character, but she shuddered to think how she had believed Lydia's lies. But she wasn't the only one. As Dr Spilsbury said, they had all underestimated her. They had fallen over themselves to protect her, never imagining that she was manipulating them all.

She was still trying to manipulate them now. She had written Violet a long letter from prison, pouring out her love and her sorrow, expressing all kinds of remorse and begging Violet to forgive her and to come and visit her.

Violet had torn up the letter and thrown it on the fire. Her eyes were open now, and she could read the self-pity between the lines. There was no real remorse there. Lydia was going through the motions to get what she wanted, just as she always had.

And no one had been used more than Violet's own brother. Had Lydia really loved him? she wondered. Or had she simply seen whatever everyone else saw, a powerful man with a violent streak whom she could twist to her own ends?

Violet would never forgive Lydia for taking her brother from her. And she hadn't even had the chance to say goodbye to him. It hurt that the last time they had been face to face, it had been in the middle of yet another argument. The last words they had heard from each other had been harsh and unkind.

As the days and weeks went by and Violet did not hear from Mickey, she had started to fear the worst. But then, a couple of days ago, a postcard had arrived from Paris, of all places. There was no writing on it, but the London address was in Mickey's scrawl.

Violet was relieved to know he was still alive, at least. But she also knew there was a good chance she would never see him again. The police were still watching Queen's Buildings, waiting to pounce.

Mickey was an accessory to Elizabeth Franklin's murder. He was also a suspect in the mysterious disappearance of Tobias Warriner.

It was Dr Spilsbury, of all people, who had tipped her off. That day, when Lydia was arrested, he had quietly taken her to one side and told her about the dog hairs they had found in Warriner's room.

'I understand your brother has a dog?' he had said.

'So do a few thousand other people in London!' Violet had snapped back.

'Indeed.' Spilsbury had reached out and plucked something from the shoulder of her coat, then examined it carefully. Violet realised to her dismay that it was a pale fawn dog hair.

'It looks very similar to the ones we found on Mr Warriner's rug,' he commented. Then, to her astonishment, he had rubbed it off his fingers, letting it fall to the ground.

'I really think it would be best if you advised your brother to lay low for a while,' he had said.

'He's already gone,' Violet replied.

But she had not given up on the idea that somehow he would make his way back to them, when the time was right. Which was why she left a lamp burning in the window every night, and why she was so reluctant to find somewhere else to live.

And there was another reason why they could not leave. Nearly two months after Elizabeth's will had been read, her estate had still not been settled.

Which was why she was now putting on her best clothes, preparing to do battle.

'Why do you have to go?' Thomas complained as he watched her adjusting her hat in the mirror over the sink. 'You said we'd go to the zoo!'

'We will, love. As soon as I come home.'

'Where are you going?'

'I have to sort out a bit of business.'

'I don't want you to go!'

'Nor do I, my angel. Believe me,' Violet murmured under her breath.

Matthew had decided to contest his aunt's will. In spite of all the evidence of his sister's guilt, he was convinced that Violet had somehow coerced Elizabeth Franklin into changing her will in her favour.

Violet's own solicitor had told her that she would almost certainly win the case. But it would be costly, and there was every chance that Matthew would appeal against the decision. He could drag her through every court in the land, for months and months.

And until then, Violet would never be free of them.

She had told her solicitor that she would happily give up the inheritance if it meant she could be free of the Franklin family. All she wanted was a small share for her son, just his entitlement as one of James's children.

The front door creaked open. Thinking it was Nan come to watch Thomas, she called out, 'We're in the kitchen.'

She leaned in to peer more closely at her face in the mirror. She had felt as if she was putting on armour when she applied her powder and rouge today. Whatever inner turmoil she was feeling, she was determined that no one else in that office would see it.

Especially not Matthew Franklin.

'I've promised Thomas a trip to ride on the elephants,' she said. 'I'll be back as soon as—'

She looked up and was shocked to see the tall, stern-faced figure standing in the doorway.

'Mary?'

'I'm not stopping.' Mary was instantly defensive. 'I know I'm not welcome.'

'Who said you weren't welcome?' Violet reached for the kettle and put it on the stove. 'You've got time for a cup of tea, surely?'

Mary looked at her warily. The maid had not gone out of her way to make Violet welcome when she first arrived at Gloucester Gate. But Violet didn't blame her for that.

Elizabeth had made it very clear that the maid was to take orders from her and her alone, or suffer the consequences.

Mary had only been trying to survive, like the rest of them.

'I'd best not.' Mary's gaze flicked back to Violet. 'You look like you're going somewhere, anyway?'

'Yes, worse luck.' Violet managed a wry smile. 'I've got to go to the solicitors to do battle with Matthew over the will.'

Mary's mouth tightened. 'They'll never do what's right, will they? Not a scrap of honour among any of them, for all their fine ways.'

Violet looked at her in surprise. She had never heard Mary speak out before. She could only imagine the anger and pain she had kept suppressed all these years.

'I heard about what happened to your son,' she said quietly. 'I'm so sorry, Mary.'

The maid looked astonished, as if she was not expecting such kindness. Then she gave a rare smile.

'He was such a happy little boy. Reminded me of your little one.' She looked at Thomas as she said it. 'Is it true she wanted to take him from you?'

Violet nodded. 'Yes, it's true.'

'Then I'm surprised you didn't kill her yourself,' she said in a low voice. 'I would have throttled her with my bare hands if she'd tried to take my boy.'

A look of understanding passed between them, from one mother to another.

'I take it your brother's not here?' Mary said.

Violet shook her head. 'I ain't seen him.'

'And you wouldn't tell me if you had?'

'Would you?'

The kettle bubbled on the stove, breaking the silence. Violet turned to turn off the gas.

'Are you sure you won't have a cup of tea?' she asked.

'I can't. I've got a train to catch.'

'Where are you going?'

'Scotland.' A faint smile crossed Mary's lips as she said it.

'Then I hope you'll be very happy there,' Violet said.

'Oh, I will.' Mary sounded determined. 'It's about time I put the past behind me and thought about my future, I reckon.'

'That sounds like a good idea.' Violet only wished she could do the same.

'That reminds me . . .' Mary reached into her bag and took out a letter. 'This is for you.'

'What is it?'

'Call it a parting gift. For you and the lad.' Mary smiled fondly down at Thomas. 'It's no use to me now, but with any luck it will be to you. Read it, won't you? I think it might make things a bit easier for you.'

Chapter 71

Matthew poured himself another drink from the decanter, just to steady his nerves. It was not yet noon, and he could almost hear his aunt's disapproving voice in his ear. He heard her a great deal these days. She seemed to haunt the shadows of the house.

He went to the window and looked out across the road. In the gardens, the newly awakened trees were a bright, fresh green in the spring sunshine.

God, how he loathed this place. The house was like a millstone round his neck, weighed down by dark memories.

It was almost a relief to have to sell up. But at the same time, Matthew could hardly bring himself to part with it. Gloucester Gate had been the London home of the Franklins for generations. And now he had been the one to let it slip through his fingers.

Baronet Franklin? You're not fit to have that title.

Once again, he heard his aunt whispering in his ear. He reached for the crystal decanter again. It was almost empty. Damn it, he couldn't even afford a bottle of whisky these days. He was no longer welcome at any of his clubs; he had run up too many debts to show himself at even the lowest of gaming establishments across the river.

And it was all the fault of Violet Malone.

Everything that had gone wrong with this family was down to her. His aunt's death, her disastrous will, the family's disgrace. None of it would have happened if his father had not brought his new bride into the house.

Even his sister being in prison was because of her. If Lydia hadn't been led astray by Violet's thuggish brother, she would never have dreamed of doing what she did. Lydia had told him as much when she wrote to him, and he believed her. His sister had always been very naïve where men were concerned.

One way or another, Violet had been the downfall of his family. But not anymore. Matthew was going to prove he was worthy of his title. He was going to see Violet and her little bastard son off for good.

'Drinking again? Whatever would your aunt say?'

He swung round. There, standing in the doorway, was Violet. Matthew stared into his glass, then back up at her. It was as if he had somehow summoned her.

'Who let you in?'

'I still have a key.'

'You can leave that before you go.' He turned away from her. 'Anyway, I thought we were meeting at the solicitor's office?' He gathered himself enough to sound nonchalant.

'I thought I'd save you the trouble. And the embarrassment.' Violet walked calmly into the room. She had something in her hand – a letter. 'It would be far better if we sorted this out between us.'

'I'd prefer to let the solicitors deal with it.'

'If that's what you want. Although I must say I'm surprised, given what's in here.'

She waved the letter at him. Matthew tried to read the handwriting, but he did not recognise it.

'What's that?'

'Your secrets, Matthew. The reason Tobias Warriner was blackmailing you.' She shook her head. 'You've been a naughty boy, haven't you?'

'I don't know what you're talking about.' He took a steady gulp of his drink. She was bluffing. She had to be.

'I'm talking about embezzlement. Borrowing funds from clients' accounts to pay off your gambling debts.'

'That's nonsense!'

'It's all in here. Mr Warriner found out everything – names, dates, amounts. He caught you red-handed.' She shook her head. 'No wonder he was able to blackmail you. This sort of thing could get you thrown in prison, couldn't it?'

'The money was all paid back,' Matthew muttered.

'Yes, but that wasn't the point, was it? You shouldn't have been helping yourself in the first place. And as for your father's will . . .' She looked up at him. 'That was no surprise to you, was it? What happened to the real one, Matthew?'

'I destroyed it.' He took pleasure in seeing her flinch. It was his brief moment of triumph, and he wanted to enjoy it. 'Old Mr Marchmont had retired, and his son had taken over, and I knew neither of them would be any the wiser, so I took a match to it and watched it burn.'

'Then you wrote a new one and forged your father's signature?'

'Working at that wretched office does have some compensations,' he smirked.

'Except you made the mistake of telling your aunt. I bet you couldn't resist it, could you? You so wanted her approval. Did you think she'd give you a pat on the head and tell you you'd been a clever boy? That was all you ever wanted, wasn't it? That for once she wouldn't see you for the self-serving fool you are.'

She was mocking him. Matthew felt his anger rising slowly like a volcano inside him.

'But I could have told you how she would react,' Violet went on. 'Elizabeth might have been a cruel, heartless old bird but unlike you, she had morals. She knew right from wrong. She wasn't proud of you, was she? She didn't think what you'd done was clever. That's why you argued. She wanted you to own up to what you'd done.' She took a step closer to him. 'What did she do? Threaten to expose you?'

'She wouldn't have dared!'

'No,' Violet said. 'She probably wouldn't. Because you were still her golden boy, weren't you? She was always covering up for you. So she decided to put things right in her own way. She changed the terms of her will, and she told me she wanted to adopt Thomas.' Her lip curled. 'She should have let you face the consequences of your actions for once. Perhaps it might have made a man of you!'

Matthew turned away, unable to stand the pity and contempt on her face. How dare she feel contempt for him! She was a girl from the gutter, not fit to clean his boots.

'You only have Warriner's word for any of this,' he dismissed. 'That letter of yours is worth nothing.'

'And do you really think it will be hard to find proof? No one's looking for it at the moment – but they might if someone tips them off.'

'And is that what you're going to do?'

Violet shook her head. 'No,' she said. 'Not that I wouldn't like to see you behind bars with your sister. But out of respect to your father and your aunt.'

'My aunt!' Matthew spat. 'She despised you!'

'And I didn't think much of her, either. But she was proud of her family name. And your sister has dragged it through the mud enough.'

Matthew eyed the letter in her hand. 'So what do you want?' he said in a low voice.

'Only what's fair. You can keep the house, and the rest of the inheritance can be shared between you, Lydia and Thomas.'

A spark of hope kindled in Matthew's mind. 'And what about you?' he said. 'Surely you want something?'

'Believe me, I want nothing from this family. Just what Thomas is entitled to as James's son.'

'That little bastard will never be equal to us!'

'No,' Violet said. 'He won't ever be like you, thank God. Because I'll bring him up to know what's right and what's wrong.'

'You! What do you and your thug brother know about what's right and wrong?'

'More than you and your murdering sister.'

Her calm, knowing smile boiled his blood. She'd defeated him. This common creature with her gutter accent had got the better of him. She knew it too. He could see the glint of triumph in her dark eyes, and the slight tilt of her lips.

Molten rage overflowed like lava inside him, and suddenly all he wanted was to slash that smile. He felt the heavy crystal tumbler in his hand and lunged forward, thrusting it into her face.

It all happened fast. Violet swerved, then grabbed him, and the next moment he was slammed face down on the table, his face pressed against the polished wood, his arm twisted painfully up behind his back.

'Christ, you're an even bigger fool than I thought!' she hissed. 'I gave you a chance, but you were too greedy and stupid to take it. Now I've changed my mind. I'm sending that letter, and you're going to go to prison for what you did.' She pressed her mouth to his ear. 'You always said I wasn't a Franklin, and you were right. I'm a Malone. And believe me, once you're behind bars you're going to live to regret you ever heard that name!'

Chapter 72

It was not like Dr Bernard Spilsbury to do anything rash. He was careful, considered, some might even say ponderous at times. But when he finally came to a decision, it was always the right one, and he never changed his mind.

So it was a strange feeling for him to be having second thoughts now. Almost unheard of, in fact.

Not that he would have admitted it to anyone, least of all his old friend Willcox. It would create a dangerous precedent, and he would never hear the last of it.

It was bad enough that Willcox was currently taking all the credit for his decision.

'Well, I'm glad to hear you finally saw sense and took my advice,' he said. 'How long have I been saying you need an assistant? He'll make life a great deal easier for you, I'm sure.'

I very much doubt that, Spilsbury thought.

What had possessed him? He always worked alone. He liked working alone, unencumbered by anyone else's thoughts and opinions. He liked to take his time thinking and considering and working things out in his own mind, without having to explain his thought processes to anyone else.

And he could not tolerate stupidity, either. Or inefficiency. Or clumsiness.

Or lateness.

He looked at the clock on the wall of the laboratory. His assistant should have been here at nine, and it was now three minutes past. If this was typical of what he could expect, then he already knew this experiment was not going to work.

'So who is it?' Willcox asked.

'What?' Spilsbury dragged his gaze from the clock, where he had been watching the seconds tick by to yet another minute's lateness.

'Your new assistant. Someone from Barratt's firm, I suppose? He was very keen for you to take on that young man – what's his name? Gordon.'

'I've never heard of Dr Gordon. And no, it isn't anyone Professor Barratt recommended.'

'Not from medical, eh? I doubt if anyone from surgical would have put themselves forward, but I suppose you never know.'

'It's not a surgeon.'

'Then who is it?' Willcox racked his brains. 'I know! It's that new pathology demonstrator, isn't it? Dr Abraham.'

'I wasn't even aware we had a new pathology demonstrator.'

'Good lord, man, don't you take notice of anything that goes on in this hospital?' Willcox said impatiently.

'I don't need to. I have you to tell me.' Spilsbury carefully lined up his microscopic slides in their wooden case, moving them this way and that until they were perfectly square.

'Then who it is, man?' Willcox demanded. 'Come on, tell us the name of this unfortunate young man who will be having to put up with you until his nerve fails him.'

Spilsbury turned to face him. 'I considered the matter very carefully,' he said.

'Most unlike you,' Willcox muttered.

'And in the end I agreed with you—'

'Again, most unlike you.'

'I agreed with you that it would be helpful to have someone to take notes at the scene of a crime, to help with photography and drawing sketches, and to be present at the post-mortem while I am conducting my investigations.'

'Yes?' Willcox narrowed his eyes. 'And what about the rest of it? Preparing the body for post-mortem, cutting it open and weighing the organs, that sort of thing?'

'I have Mr Bennett to prepare the bodies. And as to the rest, I prefer to do it myself. Which is why, rather than having an assistant, I thought it would be better to engage the services of a secretary.'

'A secretary? Are you sure that's a good idea, old boy?'

'I don't see why not. I really don't think I need some over-eager junior doctor, or worse yet, a medical student, looking over my shoulder all the time, making helpful remarks and observations. Far better to have someone unobtrusive to take notes. Someone malleable, who will be there when she's required and disappear tactfully when she is not, and who will not ask foolish questions.'

'And you've found such a paragon?'

'I believe so.'

'So where is she now?'

'She's late.'

He ignored the eloquent look Willcox sent him. He had made the right decision, he told himself firmly. If for no other reason than that he was Dr Spilsbury and he seldom made a wrong one.

He refused to admit the possibility that he had allowed sentiment to cloud his reason. His decision had been based on sound rational thinking. The young woman in question had shown great promise. She had demonstrated perception and good judgement. She was clearly intelligent, if untrained. And she knew when to keep her own counsel. He would have no fear of her gossiping, or chattering away when he was trying to concentrate.

All in all, she had the makings of a perfectly adequate secretary. As long as she learned to fit in with his methods and his way of thinking without being too obtrusive, he believed they could manage very well together . . .

'Good morning.' She breezed in, already shrugging off her coat.

'Mrs Franklin!' Willcox exclaimed.

'I go by my maiden name of Malone now.'

'You're late,' Spilsbury said.

'You're lucky I got here at all. The traffic was awful. I very nearly gave up.'

He watched as she dumped her bag on the chair and proceeded to divest herself of her coat and hat.

'I didn't know you'd changed your name,' he said.

'I didn't know I had to consult you.'

'It seems most irregular.'

'Does it?'

'Very modern.'

She stared back at him blankly. Somewhere to his right, he heard Willcox cough.

'I must say, I'm delighted to see you again, Mrs – Miss Malone,' he said. 'The department hasn't been the same without you.'

'I can tell.' Violet ran her finger along the edge of the desk and inspected it.

'Although I must confess I didn't ever imagine you'd grace us with your presence again. Not after the manner in which you left . . .' Spilsbury busied himself with the files so he wouldn't have to look at his friend's accusing face.

'Neither did I,' Violet said.

'So what changed your mind?'

Violet caught Spilsbury's eye with a knowing smile.

'He begged,' she said.

'I most certainly did not!' Spilsbury said, outraged. 'I approached you with what I regarded as a very sensible and mutually beneficial proposition.'

'It sounded like begging to me.'

'Then I'm afraid you and I are going to have to agree to disagree.'

Willcox sighed. 'I fear you may be doing rather a lot of that in the future,' he said.

Acknowledgements

Writing a crime novel has been an ambition of mine ever since I first sat down at a keyboard, so I'm immensely grateful to all those who helped to make my dream come true. To the wonderful team at Orion for taking a chance on me and Dr Spilsbury – I really hope we didn't let you down. To Editor Extraordinaire Sam Eades for guiding me through the process and sharing her vast expertise in the world of crime (fiction, that is). Also to Joanne Ruffell and Sophie Wilson for reading the book in its early stages. I'm really grateful to you for your perceptive comments, and for bolstering my confidence. And thanks to my copy editor Clare Wallis for making what can be a painful process so easy, and to the design department for bringing Dr Spilsbury so vividly to life.

Many thanks as always to my very patient agent Caroline Sheldon, for championing me and my mad ideas. And to my family and friends, who encouraged me all the way even when I questioned myself.

And finally to Bernard Spilsbury himself. As I soon discovered, it's not easy to write fiction about a real person, especially one as intensely private and infuriatingly difficult to understand as Dr Spilsbury. He has been described as both charming and cold, painfully shy and unbearably arrogant, a genius who changed the face of Forensic Pathology, and a monster who sent innocent men to the gallows. He certainly polarised public opinion during his lifetime, and has continued to do so in the decades since his death.

As you can imagine, I've had to take a few liberties with his life and his character for the sake of my story, but I'm very grateful to the authors who have penned biographies that I could draw from. If you want to find out more about Spilsbury, I suggest you read *Lethal Witness* by Andrew Rose; *The Father of Forensics* by Colin Evans, and *Bernard Spilsbury – His Life and Cases* by Douglas G. Browne and Tom Tullett. Thanks also to Barts Hospital archives, and to the Wellcome Library for allowing me access to his case notes, even if I couldn't decipher most of them.

Credits

D. L. Douglas and Orion Fiction would like to thank everyone at Orion who worked on the publication of *Dr. Spilsbury and the Camden Town Killer* in the UK.

Editorial
Sam Eades
Lucy Brem
Sahil Javed

Copyeditor
Clare Wallis

Proofreader
Marian Reid

Audio
Paul Stark
Jake Alderson

Contracts
Anne Goddard
Humayra Ahmed
Ellie Bowker

Design
Rachael Lancaster
Joanna Ridley
Nick May

Editorial Management
Charlie Panayiotou
Jane Hughes
Bartley Shaw
Tamara Morriss

Finance
Jasdip Nandra
Sue Baker

Marketing
Brittany Sankey